I0831712

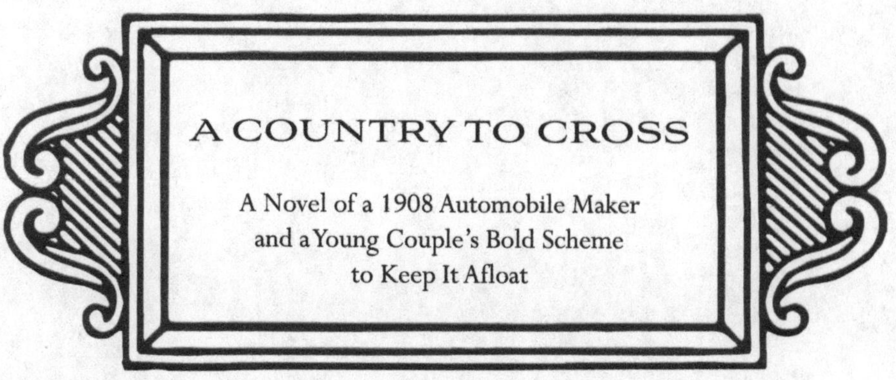

A COUNTRY TO CROSS

A Novel of a 1908 Automobile Maker
and a Young Couple's Bold Scheme
to Keep It Afloat

A COUNTRY TO CROSS

A Novel of a 1908 Automobile Maker and a Young Couple's Bold Scheme to Keep It Afloat

MARK GALLIK

SANTA FE

Sunstone books may be purchased for educational, business, or sales promotional use.
For information please write: Special Markets Department, Sunstone Press,
P.O. Box 2321, Santa Fe, New Mexico 87504-2321.
Printed on acid-free paper

eBook 978-1-61139-713-0

Library of Congress Cataloging-in-Publication Data

Names: Gallik, Mark, 1955- author.
Title: A country to cross : a novel of a 1908 automobile maker and a young couple's bold scheme to keep it afloat / Mark Gallik.
Description: Santa Fe : Sunstone Press, [2023] | Summary: "As part of a promotion, a young couple drives across 1908 America"-- Provided by publisher.
Identifiers: LCCN 2023009613 | ISBN 9781632935397 (paperback) | ISBN 9781611397130 (epub)
Subjects: LCGFT: Novels.
Classification: LCC PS3607.A4166 C68 2023 | DDC 813.6--dc23/eng/20230308

LC record available at https://lccn.loc.gov/2023009613

WWW.SUNSTONEPRESS.COM
SUNSTONE PRESS / POST OFFICE BOX 2321 / SANTA FE, NM 87504-2321 /USA
(505) 988-4418

To Richard Stephen Gallik, my older brother who has guided the way.

CONTENTS

PREFACE

What does it take to keep an engine running? Truly, the possibilities are equal to the number of automobile manufacturers—up to three hundred by last count. From the start, there is curiosity's sake, along with the chance to scamper upon its many, diverging branches. Then again, the weight of ambition is a force all its own, for what person doesn't strive to better his circumstances and those of his loved ones? And when, of course, the tedium of unflexed muscles and unstressed bones becomes too great, the grinds of simple boredom will have their say.

On the other hand, for a few individuals there follow the urges to push boundaries—margins of many sorts and of many widths. And from time to time, there does burn that desire to lead—to be a leader—one who poses in front of others or races ahead when opportunity arises.

Indeed, on and on the list might continue, pushing the limits of imagination, while bolstered by a litany of reasons and excuses. Truth to tell, when concerning an engine there never should occur shortages, that its tank will stay topped and its plugs will keep sparking, forever and ever. So goes the country, as it races to modernize in what remains a fresh, new century. And so venture those people who happen to populate the nation's middle, in a land where the hearts pace faster and enterprise knows no limits.

—Mark Gallik

1
LOBAN MOTOR OF OHIO

"DAMN IT. COME ON, Danny. Keep up, you horse's ass."

An undeniable spring asserts itself upon the calendar, thus erasing the effects of a hard and harsh Ohio winter. And so yet another cycle continues with its changes. The days are lengthening and the air is losing its shiver, with the foliage maturing into various shades of green.

Needless to say, a long winter brings on an enduring measure of restlessness. Already, for more than a month the creatures of the landscape have been scurrying about, altering their routines or disregarding them altogether. And although most fidget and rove in order to reacquaint themselves with seasons' past, there are a few who feel the need to explore. To be sure, the lure of the forbidden and foreboding, and even the dangerous, can be much too powerful for some individuals to resist.

"Horse's ass."

Cautiously, they conceal themselves, two ten year-old boys inching their way through a maze of stumped ashes, prospering white oaks and shrubby vibernum. But as the pair come upon the last bush beneath the shade of the furthermost tree, they halt. There lies before them, after all, a wide stretch of open ground, enough of a gap to betray the boys' furtive plans. Indeed, it's as if the two need to catch their breaths and allow their combined pluck to regain its momentum. And so they rest upon their knickered knees, while their heads lock in backward tilts, their attentions cast upon the high and mighty.

"Didn't I tell you?" boasts Jimmy Swift, local adventurer and notorious truant. "No volcano ever huffed as much fire and smoke. That's for sure."

"Gosh, we sure are close. Close as I could ever imagine," marvels Danny Hatch, Jimmy's latest recruit. "Hmm? Does it always spew out like that?"

"No, not always," replies Jimmy. "Don't you never pay attention?"

From a busy, red-bricked stack, a steady stream of smoke billows into the clear, peaceful sky. Yet black as it may be, in no way does this issue suffer from a dubious reputation. Quite the contrary, for as far as the citizens of Lisbon, Ohio are concerned, these fumes of soot and gas are unfurled standards of honest incomes, prideful innovations and mind-boggling inventions. Then, of course, there are the sparks which summon forth those curious imaginations, this showering upon a particular pair who should be receiving their lessons elsewhere.

"Gosh, Jimmy, just how high up do you think it goes?"

"Well-l-l." Jimmy pauses, as if to calculate an estimate. "Must be a thousand feet. Could be two."

"Yeah," nods Danny, while he gapes upon the wonder. "Even three."

"Possibly," shrugs Jimmy.

"Most likely." But although Danny's appreciation for the smokestack may be unquestionable, in spite of his friend's wealth of information it suffers a wide chasm. "Just what is it for, anyhow?"

"That factory beneath it."

"Factory?"

"Where they make things." Jimmy's patience may be wearing thin.

"Oh." Yet Danny remains puzzled. "What do they make?"

"Automobiles, you horse's ass. Why the fastest and most smartest the country has ever seen."

"Yes." Apparently, Danny's recollections are stirred. "There's one always parked by the courthouse."

"Wouldn't you like to watch how they make them?" offers Jimmy. "Close up?"

"Yeah!" responds Danny's enthusiasm, although it is quick to temper. "How?"

"By following me. Simple as that." Jimmy's reply has no waver. "I know where we can sneak in."

"Uh-h-h. Well-l-l. I don't know. That's a mighty big building. What if we got caught?"

"Come on, Danny. I didn't think you a coward. We won't get caught. Besides, even if we did, there's nothing they could do to us. Not if they found out who my Paps is. Paps has got plenty of pull in this town. People think twice before troubling me."

"Well-l-l. Maybe…"

"Come on. Let's go."

Wasting no time, Jimmy drops to all fours and scrambles upon the ground. And with no possibility to air any further misgivings, Danny trails behind. As luck would have it, the mischievous mites seem to make their way unnoticed toward the midday shadow of the smokestack, itself. Soon, they come upon a corner and then race to another, after which Jimmy locates an unlocked and unguarded basement window. Without any hesitation he slips through, only to be tailed by his reluctant follower, as if both are being swallowed into the bowels of a colossal beast—perhaps to fates unknown.

The sky-high smokestack continues to belch forth. Yet in spite of the perilous imaginations of two ten year-olds, there does persist an undeniable fact: when compared to the industrial giants of the big cities, Loban Motor isn't all that imposing. Box-like in shape, bricked in red and interspersed with tinted windows, the far South Avenue building rises only to a second story, with a boiler and generator room bulging from the rear. Indeed, when square footage comes to mind, Loban Motor shouldn't be mistaken for a major facility.

But if this particular automobile maker isn't all that noteworthy of a company, it certainly has no misgivings when it comes to dressing up like one. With a complete disregard to modesty, four massive, marble columns arise from their plinths to dominate and accentuate the factory's facade. Appearing like stacks of rusticated tires, they pose in support of a projected upper story frieze, which itself is of the same stone, though expertly smoothed and swagged into a more refined creation. Yet there's even more marble, in that the top of the facade not fronted by the frieze is covered with a busy, bracketed cornice. Finally, above the right corner of the upper floor is mounted an imposing proclamation of polished vanadium steel: LOBAN MOTOR OF OHIO.

Striking as the features of Loban Motor may be, however, they are little more than costly embellishments. Within the current atmosphere, where so many small, automobile manufacturers are popping up across the country, every dollar spent needs to own a defined purpose. Indeed, because the competition is fierce, a company with the size and solvency of Loban Motor can sink as quickly as it has been launched.

With this in mind, there arrives an urgency behind the meeting taking place directly beneath that display of vanadium steel. But as it happens, the proceedings are being delayed, with the participants gathering into factions between those who have invested in the company and the man who is Loban Motor, himself.

"Where's Lane?" comes a faint inquiry. "Where is my college boy?"

He's an agitated man, Percy Loban, the whisperer in question. And although his voice may be softened, he does manage to stand as an imposing figure. Not that Mr. Loban carries an impressive physique. In fact, he's fairly round and is nearly short in stature. No, instead Mr. Loban is a man who bears an inner confidence and outward determination, both housed by a crisp, grey shadow check, double coat suit. Regardless, at least for the moment and for good reason, Mr. Loban's usual fortitude is somewhat subdued.

"Just where is college boy?"

"I really can't say, Mr. Loban," replies Freddy Brothers, the company's business manager, he being tall and lanky and not the least bit imposing.

"Didn't you tell him he was needed, Freddy? Wasn't that your task?"

"Was it?"

"Yes." Mr. Loban may be losing some patience. "How am I to carry on, when Lepper is sick in bed? My chief engineer? What I need now is my assistant. I need Lane."

It is an imposing office, paneled by burled walnut and filled with painted porcelains, cut crystals and carved mahogany furnishings, along with commissioned paintings of personal triumphs. But if Mr. Loban's sanctum isn't impressive enough, there does lie another extravagant chamber, this via an open, arched entryway. In what serves as a boardroom of sorts stand additional tasteful embellishments, the most dominant being a Gustav Stickley leather-topped table for twelve and a portrait of President Roosevelt.

They number nine, the people sitting at the Stickley table, while Mr. Loban's talented secretary clears away the aftermath of pastries, coffees and teas. However, not a one is a member of a board, for no such group exists within the framework of Loban Motor. Instead, each person present harbors a more fixed interest, they being the principle investors of the company. To be sure, this assemblage must be consulted, even coddled, through their ongoing misgivings of risking so much money in an industry of far too little history. And beyond doubt, there's only one person up to the task, his moment approaching fast.

"Damn it, Freddy. What in God's name am I to tell them?"

"You'll think of something, Mr. Loban. Talk about the '08 Speed Six, just as Lepper was to do. And when you're done, offer them a tour. You know how impressive is the assembly floor."

"Yes. Of course, Freddy. We'll show the '08 roadster. That'll impress the dickens out of them."

"But Mr. Loban."

"What?"

"The roadster isn't here. Lane has it."

"Lane?" Immediately, the look on Mr. Loban's face alters from the mildly apprehensive to the somewhat perturbed. "Very well, then the touring car."

"Yes, Mr. Loban. Bu-u-t."

"Where is it, Freddy?"

"In the basement. Flugan is repainting it. Remember, Mr. Loban?"

"Never mind that. We'll show it all the same."

"Very good, Mr. Loban."

And so arrives the moment for owner and business manager to return to their guests. As Mr. Loban walks through the entryway, he rediscovers his usual, affable self.

"Friends, I hope you have enjoyed your refreshments. It all seems very delicious." Mr. Loban turns to his secretary. "Thank you, Miss Charnwood. And will you please tell Mr. Flugan to bring up the touring car."

"Yes, Mr. Loban." To which she glides passed her employer to parts known.

"Achem. I believe, my friends, that shortly you may wish to see a finished Speed Six," speaks Mr. Loban, as he walks around the table toward its head, followed by Freddy. "And that you will be as deeply impressed as I am each and every day."

Uncertainties aside, the investors appear willing to accept the spoken attributes of the company. Perhaps the sugary pastries are sweetening their attitudes, or so tell their nodding heads and the agreeable creases upon their lips. Yet one of the investor's bearing rises to the ranks of unbridled enthusiasm, albeit with the heavy dose of a certain bias.

"Percy, my dear boy, that is such a delight to hear," responds Miss Lucilla Antonia Loban.

"Thank you, Aunt Lucie," replies a slightly embarrassed Percy, the nephew.

Yet he shouldn't feel uneasy, for as understood by everyone, his aunt is his most ardent supporter. Decades ago and for reasons which are not likely original, Miss Loban opted for the life of a spinster. Thus, instead of balancing for years and years the money matters of household and family, prudently and skillfully, she's built her stipends and inheritances into a small fortune. Certainly, investing in her nephew's company must be far and away the riskiest venture of her long life.

"Percy, why not tell us the particulars of your new vehicle?"

"Why, Aunt Lucie, such a splendid idea." With the image of the president peering from behind, Mr. Loban is ready to deliver. "My friends, I am bully on Loban Motor, for we have situated ourselves with a bright future of substantial profits. The near future I should say, with the Model '08 Speed Six guiding our path. And how distinct, if only because the Speed Six is an innovative design. No longer will our wooden frames twist with every rut in the road, at the expense of shafts and axles. Now we use strong and unbendable, vanadium steel. And no more will we rely upon the Dodge Brothers for their four-cylinder engines. Instead, we're casting our own sixes en bloc, machining most of the other parts as well. Yes, we're even producing our very own three-speed, sliding-gear transmissions."

The heads of the investors nod in unison, while their eyes keen with interest. Still, a man of caution can never be sure, that behind those bobbing faces, a few doubts may linger.

"But let me say further, my friends, we are diligent in finding ways to cut costs. I realize that the financial panic of the previous year remains a complication to our country's commerce. With this in mind, each phase of the manufacturing process is under close scrutiny. And once again, our Speed Six leads away. As it stands, when full production begins in the coming summer, 80 percent of our new model will be fabricated within these walls. Yes, 80 percent, meaning fewer, unnecessary costs towards the profits of suppliers."

Like a crafty politician, or a nurturing preacher, Mr. Loban pauses, as if to assess the weight of his words, and to catch a breath. And never mind that his figure of 80 percent is somewhat a boast. After all, what's the fault in rounding up a number when aired during the fervor of the moment?

"We control our destiny," continues Mr. Loban. "Why as we live and breathe, the nation's cities are clamoring for quality touring cars and roadsters. If only to clear their atmospheres from the dust of dried horse manure." Mr. Loban looks to the only woman in the room. "Pardon me, Aunt Lucie."

"Oh Percy. For heaven's sake. Never you mind."

The smile on Mr. Loban's face matches that of his aunt's. "As I was saying. To be clear of that unhealthy dust, so that the citizenry may breathe clean air. And at the same time, might I say, they will be able to convey themselves about their towns and cities in a safe, reliable manner. And because of you, my friends, Loban Motor is a part of this: a healthier and more efficient country. And it is happening—rapidly, it cannot be denied—that the congestion found on America's streets will be no more. That the automobile is stamping its cause of order and speediness. Yes, the horse, and its shortcomings, has gone goose."

Mr. Loban pauses to catch a whiff of Lisbon air, which itself must be getting cleaner by the day.

It's during this moment that a hovering Freddy sees fit to interject. "Mr.

Loban. Let's not forget that because of the Speed Six's higher clearance, it can be driven about the countryside."

"Yes. Of course. Our customers at a time of their choosing will be able to flee the crowded cities and refresh themselves upon the country's natural splendors.

"The touring car and the roadster."

"Yes, Freddy. Both the touring car and the roaster will bear what any road might offer. They being of the same frame and engine. Which, of course, lowers the costs of manufacturing and maintenance." Obviously, an anxious Mr. Loban is delivering as much positive information as possible. "Yes, my friends, this is a prime consideration at Loban Motor. But let me reassure that our industry is a clean industry, which uses no child labor nor exploits defenseless woman."

A gap ensues, as the man in charge looks down upon his seated guests. But if Mr. Loban is trying to read the faces of his investors, he may have a problem. Instead of their heads nodding in agreement, now they're turning to one another to exchange murmurs.

To be sure, there's no denying the pressures upon Mr. Loban's shoulders. No longer is he in the lucrative furniture business, this concern having been sold in order to complete his 1904 transition into automobile manufacturing at the previous Washington Street address. And because of the colossal expense to build the current facility, for half of 1907 the founder of Loban Motor was forced to sell shares in his expanding company. More precisely, Mr. Loban's holdings now come down to less than half—a precarious 48 percent—though, so long as Aunt Lucie keeps her health and her six percent, her nephew should retain control.

Of course, there are the other shareholders, some who have put up their own sizeable sums of money and those who have pooled resources into investment groups. There's even a Canadian from Hamilton, Ontario, absent he may be, though represented by his son, Freddy Brothers—that ardent automobile enthusiast and business manager extraordinaire.

Still, the shares and percentages do sum, and Mr. Loban cannot afford to sell any more of his own. Though his status may be safe for the time being, there's nothing to soothe his worries like a solid consensus. As he stands above the murmurs and whispers, Mr. Loban is a man who might settle for something less.

"Well said." Thankfully, the supposed tension is broken. "Well said, Percy Loban," notes Holland Snodgrass, local banker and politician, and investor in Columbiana County's metal, clay and railroad industries, a man from whom others take their cues.

"There's no doubt that 1908 will be a pivotal year for Loban Motor, Percy..."

"Indeed, Loban, we're looking forward to this new automobile..."

Although the praises might blend indecipherably, a beaming Mr. Loban appears to understand every word. Certainly, this is his element, to be the focus of an extolling light.

"Thank you, my friends. Bully for you all," ingratiates Mr. Loban, as he roves about the table to shake open hands and kiss a proud cheek.

Soon, there follows a display of charts and drawings, as held in place by Freddy, who knows by heart where every loose nut within Loban Motor lies, and narrated by Mr. Loban, who doesn't.

"...Do you own the patent on that carburetor, Percy?" asks Mr. Snodgrass.

"Why, yes I do. Freddy?"

"Yes, Mr. Loban. You and Mr. Lepper.

"Achem. As I was saying, it is the most innovative carburetor in the industry. One that is years ahead..."

Before long, Miss Charnwood returns with the news that Hugh Flugan is bringing up the new touring car and its unfinished paint job from the basement to the second floor. And so an entourage forms in order to abandon the office area and seek the rear of the facility and its large service elevator.

As designed, the basement of Loban Motor houses the wood, upholstery and paint shops, as well as an area for storage. Only the assembly of automobiles occurs on the first floor, though it is the busiest and noisiest area with its constant motions of belts and tools. Then there is the second floor, where the casting and machining are done, and where activity will increase once Speed Six production hungers for inventory.

And so, without any instruction, Miss Charnwood leads the way with the rhythmic motions of her pleated skirt and the short, feminine steps of her black oxfords and white stockings.

Meanwhile, Mr. Loban continues his narration of things' Loban Motor, as he assists his aunt. "Let me assure you that we are not a company resting upon its laurels." He raises his voice to above that of the factory hum. "Though our successes may be many, we believe it incumbent to keep at the front of design and innovation. This is why we built this most modern of facilities."

"You've come a long way, Percy Loban," commends Mr. Snodgrass. "In such short time."

"Yes, to think our first model was a mere two-cylinder runabout," agrees Mr. Loban. "Not so long ago."

The walk continues, and the investors take note of the second floor's contents.

"Gentlemen, this is the finest collection of casting and machining tools west of Pittsburgh," points Freddy.

"And in a month or so it will be at full operation," adds Mr. Loban. "Beneath us you can hear the waning assemblage of the '06's. When our contracts are completed for the Fury Fours, the '08 Speed Sixes will be our primary concern. With a greater reliance on more durable, metal parts, of course. Why, as I speak, our wood shop diminishes in size."

The owner of Loban Motor has never been more proud. Indeed, he just might babble on forever, so long as his attentions are not diverted elsewhere.

"Percy?" asks Miss Loban, as she casts her eyes upon a particular worker. "Is that Henry Irish, I see? I thought he worked at the furniture factory."

"No, Aunt Lucie. That would be his grandson, Robert."

"Oh dear." Yet in spite of the minor shock, she manages a smile and even a wave. "Hello, Robert. Nice to see you, young man."

The stroll continues and the group arrives at the rear of the factory, forming a semi-circle in front of an accordion gate and the elevator shaft beyond.

"Flugan shouldn't be long," assures Mr. Loban. And as if to back his words, immediately, the elevator's motor surges with electricity. "There he is, coming up now."

Slowly but surely, the cables stress and an unseen counterweight drops, while the party of investors plus three waits eagerly for the informal unveiling of Loban Motor's pride and possible salvation.

"Yes, any second now," assures an increasingly anxious Mr. Loban.

But before things become too nervous, a large, clean-shaven head rises from the bowels of the factory. Quickly, a brush of walrus-like whiskers emerges, though not thick enough to conceal a stern, disapproving smirk. And what follows are the muscular shoulders and thick, flexed arms belonging to chief mechanic, Hugh Flugan. Yet something is amiss, or to be precise, missing.

"Flugan!" asks a startled Mr. Loban. "Where is my touring car!"

The answer reveals itself in timely fashion, as the service elevator continues its crawling ascent. As it happens, Flugan's call to bring up the touring car is being interrupted by another matter, which, apparently, he considers more pressing. And to this end, the grips of his hands are both sure and strong, his unpriable fingers wrapped around the collars of two, undersized intruders.

The elevator stops and Freddy springs to open the gate.

"What's the meaning of this, Flugan!" is the question from an agitated mouth. "Who are they!"

"Can't say, Mr. Loban."

To be sure, the look of terror fills the face of Jimmy Swift, as he hangs suspended, his toes barely tapping the elevator floor. And the same can be said for Danny Hatch, only more so, as his mastery over his bladder may be crossing a critical juncture.

"Where did you find them! What were they doing!"

"In the basement. Hiding behind the stacks of tires and wheels."

"Did you check their pockets!"

"Mr. Loban, any item small enough for their pockets is under lock and key," answers Flugan.

"He's right, Mr. Loban," concurs Freddy.

"Hmmph!"

Abandoning his aunt to steady her own self, Mr. Loban steps upon the edge of the elevator to loom over the captives. Although his head rages in red at this ill-timed disruption, he appears to be composing himself. Indeed, by pausing for a deep breath, he may be able to conduct a proper interrogation.

Their eyes are bulged open, Jimmy and Danny's, as are their speechless mouths, which also carry distinctive trembles.

Mr. Loban inches closer. "Just what are you two up to? Hmm? You can tell me." Ever so slightly, Mr. Loban eases off, as if he wants the question to sink. "Or better, who was it that sent you? Durant? Did Will Durant send you two to spy on me? You can tell. He'll never know. It'll be our secret."

There's no prompt reply, nor does it appear that any such kernel will push itself passed the curtains of fear.

"Tell me your name." This time, Mr. Loban singles out one of the boys. "Don't be afraid."

A dose of trepidation is gulped, followed by a feeble attempt to break a barrier. "Uh-h-h."

"Come, young man," urges Mr. Loban.

"J-J-J-J..."

"Yes-s-s-s."

"J-J-J-Jimmy, m-m-mister."

"And your last name?"

"S-S-Swift. Jimmy Swift."

"Good. Jimmy Swift. Then tell me, who sent you? Was it Will Durant?"

At last, the inquisition finds a mark, so that the cause behind the outrage may be revealed.

"Hold on, Percy," interrupts Mr. Snodgrass. "I believe I may know something of this young fellow." He redirects his attention toward Jimmy. "Is your father Abner Swift?"

"Yessir."

"Ah, well, there you have it, Percy. He belongs to Abner Swift."

"Abner Swift?"

"One of Lisbon's more notorious drunks. Why, I'd wager he comes before the court on a monthly basis."

"His father is the town drunk?" Mr. Loban appears somewhat confused—or deflated.

"Yes. Nothing to do with a Durant, I would think."

"Yes, of course," agrees a grinning Mr. Loban, who follows with a shrugging confession. "How silly of me to fly off the handle."

"Percy, I think we've all worn those shoes upon occasion." Once again, Mr. Snodgrass looks to Jimmy. "No, I believe this young man and his friend are only up to a little mischief. Hmm?"

"Yessir. That's me, all right," smiles Jimmy, in spite of remaining suspended off the elevator floor.

Thus the tension deflates as fast as it has ballooned.

And it's at this point that Miss Loban chooses to intercede. "Oh Percy, they do seem to be darling boys. Why not give them a few of those pastries, and send them on their way. That is, if they promise to be of no more trouble." She looks at Jimmy and Danny. "You will be good boys, will you not?"

"Yes ma'am."

"Uh, yes ma'am." At last, Danny breaks his silence.

"A splendid idea, Aunt Lucie," agrees Mr. Loban. "Flugan, take these two boys to the boardroom. And Miss Charnwood, offer them some pastries. Yes, Aunt Lucie, they do seem to be nice boys, after all. Just a little mischief is this forgettable incident."

With that, Miss Charnwood leads the way across the length of the second floor, followed by Hugh Flugan, who doesn't see fit to relax his grips of the captives' collars.

"My friends. I am genuinely sorry for this."

"Think nothing of it," assures Mr. Snodgrass. "A mere accident. But since we are here, why not give us a demonstration of your new milling machines? Like this one here? What do you say, my good people?"

The assents are unanimous.

"Why, Holland, I would be delighted. Freddy?"

"Yes, Mr. Loban." Once again, the business manager springs to action. "Robert! We need your help!"

Almost immediately, the demonstration begins in earnest, with the audience captivated by the exacting steps to machine a perfect valve stem. And then there is the 33-tooth gear, which takes even longer to produce—Robert Irish's expertise and proficiency aside.

Meanwhile, downstairs, the captives are set free, with their mouths full of pastry and their hands clutching more for the road.

"See, I told you," mumbles Jimmy Swift, his head held high and proud, as he passes through the front entrance of Loban Motor.

"Told me what?" responds Danny Hatch—his knickers high and dry.

"Told you that if'n we got into trouble, all they'd have to hear is Paps' name. And it would all favor us."

"Oh. That. Hmm?" is the doubtful reply.

Soon, the meeting of the investors returns to the office area. But instead of sitting at the Stickley table, the group opts for the less formal. Only Miss Loban uses a chair, with the others milling about, their empty coffee cups served by Miss Charnwood, with the cordials tended by Mr. Loban's amontillado.

"Let me top your glass, Aunt Lucie."

"Thank you, dear Percy. Oh, this been an exciting afternoon."

Thus continues the gathering and this altered phase of friendly factions and small talk.

"…You're not from Lisbon, Miss Charnwood, are you?"

"Heavens no, Mr. Peppel. I moved from Youngstown, where I attended business school. And where I interviewed for Mr. Loban. He hired me before I had the chance to finish there," shrugs Miss Charnwood. "How lucky was that, can you imagine?"

"Yes. Yes, I can."

While the successful meeting progresses, it can't be denied that the exuberance of the moment is waning. But Mr. Loban is quick to the cause and summons other staff members, thus extending the afternoon.

"Allow me, Holland, to introduce my new designer and draftsman. Willis Clapsaddle."

"Delighted to meet you, Mr. Snodgrass," greets Loban Motor's latest staff employee, his rosy complexion, wavy, blonde hair and red bow tie revealing a happy nature. "Simply delighted."

"Uh-h, pleased to meet you," responds Mr. Snodgrass.

"I discovered Willis in Pittsburgh," explains Mr. Loban. "From the start, I knew his talents were perfect for Loban Motor, and our move away from short-term consultants."

"Hmm? Sounds impressive," nods Mr. Snodgrass. "So Mr. Clapsaddle, you were designing automobiles in Pittsburgh?"

"Oh no, Mr. Snodgrass. I was employed by a glasshouse. Worked there for three years designing bottles."

"I see. Interesting."

In due time, Willis takes his expertise and effervescence elsewhere, thus leaving his employer and the company's most important investor to their own corner.

Bubbly might be an apt description for Mr. Loban, as well. Indeed, the afternoon is going as nicely as can be expected, with the previous trepidations being soothed, if not trounced.

"Percy?" But then there lurks a particular concern, one which continues to badger the company's prospects. "How have you faired with new agents? Or dealers, as you call them?"

"Well, Holland, we are gaining ground. Such as a new dealer in Portsmouth. Quite a coup, I think."

"Hmm?" Mr. Snodgrass' reaction is difficult to read.

"Yes, Portsmouth. And hopefully, into Kentucky," continues Mr. Loban.

"Yes, Kentucky. But do you not think Loban Motor should have grander designs? That the time has arrived to move beyond Ohio, and nearby Pennsylvania and Kentucky? Perhaps Indiana and Illinois, or even broader reaches of the country?"

"Of course, Holland. That is my dream."

"Then should you not be more enterprising with your automobiles? Selling them far and wide? To a country begging for the innovations of Loban Motor? Whether they know it or not?"

Mr. Snodgrass' encouragement might sound like sweet music to the ears of an ambitious automobile manufacturer. But the immediate response from Mr. Loban is a look of frustration, as if he visits the topic of too few dealers on a continuing basis.

"One word, Percy. That being 'publicity'. In a way to capture the public's fascination. Grasping the attentions of the newspapers and magazines, and stirring their weak imaginations with the deeds of your automobiles. Percy, you should be bold, like Durant. Be bully for Loban Motor."

Whereas Mr. Loban's eyes were squinted, now they open widely, absorbing the inspirations as offered.

"What do you think, Percy? Don't you agree?"

"Yes, Holland. Of course. And we will be implementing our publicity plans for the Speed Six. Soon."

"Excellent, Percy. Excellent."

Slowly, but surely, the guests bid their goodbyes. But before Flugan whisks them away in pairs via Mr. Loban's personal '06 Fury Four, they're informed that sometime during the week they will be offered full and complete demonstrations of the new model.

"My assistant engineer will be at your doors with either of our Speed Sixes," reminds Mr. Loban, as he and Freddy stand between the stacks of marble at the front entrance. "No one can explain the workings of our automobiles better than he."

A few more minutes pass and two of the remaining investors, Mr. Peppel and an associate, climb into his Oldsmobile Model R. Meanwhile, Mr. Snodgrass takes the seat of his own, idling vehicle, a Ford Model C.

"Sure would have been convenient if Lane had arrived," mutters Mr. Loban to Freddy, as they both wave.

"Definitely," replies the business manager with a smirk and a smile.

"Don't worry about our assistant engineer," shouts Mr. Loban to his departing investors. "Lane is also our test driver. Very experienced. As safe and cautious a driver to be found. You will be in good hands."

With that, the last three investors sputter away.

"Goodbye! Have a pleasant evening! Goodbye!"

At last, Mr. Loban can let out a sigh. "It went well, Freddy, don't you think? We should be commended."

"Positively."

"Yes." Mr. Loban's turns pensive. "Freddy, I've been thinking. Of the means to publicize our '08. Of capturing the public's fascination by way of the newspapers. We need to be bold. Bullish for Loban Motor."

"Yes. But precisely how?"

'Well-l?" Mr. Loban stares at the products of two competing manufacturers. "We'll find a way, Freddy."

"Yes sir. We'll have them skinned," bolsters Freddy. "If only because our autos are better."

"Of course," agrees Mr. Loban, breaking his trance upon the Ford and Olds. "But damn that Lane, and the mix-up." He shakes his head. "Where can he be? Where is my college boy?"

2
THE LANES OF OHIO

A STEADY PLUME OF DUST tails the Speed Six, its rear tires spinning upon and grinding apart the surface of a Columbiana County lane. Indeed, this completed roadster version of the '08 model is realizing the greatest of its design potentials: touring the countryside, or on this day, flying atop the twisting roads and sharp turns of an informal racing circuit.

In no way, however, is the Speed Six involved in a competition amongst other vehicles. Rather, the roadster is vying against itself, its 44-horsepower engine powering the rear, 31-inch Goodrich tires in order to better its own record upon this three lap course.

Certainly, the open-top, windscreenless roadster is a sight to behold, what with its sleek, mostly metal body emblazed in red, as are the wooden spokes of its busy wheels. In addition, there are its glistening brass parts: the Dietz carbide headlamps, two detachable kerosene side lanterns with a single, stationary rear light, a curvaceous bulb horn, and radiator trim topped by an ornamental cap. And the Speed Six comes with the creature comfort of black leather, twin cushion seats—fine pieces of furniture suitable for any home parlor. Nonetheless, the roadster is a manly machine, as attested by an elongated hood and its muscular engine. Indeed, when all the components are summed, the strapping Speed Six is both a powerful and stylish beast.

Then there is the driver of the '08, who sits crouched and determined behind the right-side steering wheel, he wearing a plaid, touring cap and a pair of goggles. To be sure, there carries an air of urgency, that achieving a personal record is the best way to discover and solve unforeseen problems prior to the critical, but undetermined, date of production.

Axelrod William Lane is his name—after his father Dr. William Axelrod

Lane of Cambridge, Ohio, who in turn is named after his mother, the former Willa Jane Axelrod. And he takes his position as assistant engineer to heart, his unabashed zeal for automobiles knowing no bounds.

Zealotry, however, comes in many forms and degrees. And with the beginning of the third lap drawing near, there awaits a greater love in "college boy's" life, toward whom he races with relentless devotion.

She stands as pretty as any Gibson girl, the former Katherine Marie Kane—after no one in particular—and is dressed much the same in her fluffy white blouse and yellow straw, skimmer hat. And while the young Mrs. Lane watches her husband's approach, she holds above her head a slate upon which is chalked "10:15", this accuracy of timed laps assured by the Elgin silverine watch and chain dangling from her neck. In addition, curiously, she wears a pair of rimmed men's spectacles, though too far upon the tip of her dainty nose to be of any real use.

"Go Axe, go!" encourages Katie, she waving with one hand and steadying the slate with the other.

"Honk!" comes the quick reply from the squeeze of the bulb.

Thus another five-minute separation between husband and wife comes to a close, the Speed Six's resolve bringing about a swift merge.

Wisely, Katie shuffles a few cautious steps away from the road, allowing a little more space for the roadster's approach. And none too soon, for the Speed Six and its driver are in no mood to slow down for what is the start of the final lap.

"A perfect score," he shouts, while passing.

Katie spins upon her button, high ankle shoes and cries out a caution. "Careful, Axe. Careful." Crossing her fingers, she watches her husband and Mr. Loban's automobile disappear beyond a cloak of dust.

As it happens, there's sound reason for Katie's shout and the trepidation so expressed by the digits of her right hand. Undeniably, that first turn does have quite a hairpin to it, meaning that if taken with too much momentum, there could arise a disaster. Still, deep down, Katie knows that Axe is vastly familiar with the circuit, so that even if he pushes the Speed Six more than usual, he should be able to handle this bending stretch. Then again…

"Axe? Axe!"

The confusion and panic from Katie's throat don't emerge so much from the screeching of tires and their struggle to stay upon the road. Nor are they born from an audible crunch and indisputable clang. Rather, the fears quaking within Katie are the result of the sudden cessation of a particular sound, that no longer is the Speed Six's engine revving its way beyond the cloak of dust.

"Axe!"

Dropping her slate, Katie discards all tendencies to freeze and rushes into the earthly cloud. There's no need to breathe, no chance for her lungs to clog, for never have there been fleeter feet. Thus Katie breaks through the dust, where her eyes behold what may be the worst of any stomach-churning outcome.

"Axe! Where are you!"

Confronting Katie is the belly of the Speed Six, the sliding-gear transmission making a stark, rare appearance. Indeed, the roadster has overturned, coming to rest on the driver's flank—although seemingly in one piece. Apparently, on this one particular day the 116-inch wheel base is not quite wide enough.

"Uh-h-h."

Without a doubt, it is a human sound. Not a wheeze spewing from an abused machine, but a familiar moan drawing Katie to the other side of the roadster. Hastening around the corner of the Speed Six, she discovers that the driver's right seat has spilled its contents upon the ground.

"Axe!"

Yet the fright of finding a maimed husband is crushed by her need to come to his aid. Falling upon her knees, gently, Katie cradles his stunned head into her arms, flicking away his cap in the process.

"Axe! Are you all right!"

"Uh-h-h." Axe squints his eyelids apart. "Who is it?"

"Axe! It's me! Are you hurt!"

"Katie?"

"Yes, Axe." She removes his goggles and strokes his brow. "Are you hurt?"

"Huh?" He opens his eyes further, while giving his head a little shake. "Hurt? I don't know."

Without pause, Katie feels and sights her way from the top of Axe's head down to his feet, one of which retains a stubborn contact to a pedal. Then she repeats her examination, this time working her way from the bottom upward. It's when hardly an "ouch" is uttered that Katie breathes a sigh of relief.

"I think you're fine, Axe. Just stunned." Again, she strokes his brow, after which she takes the spectacles from her nose and places them tenderly upon the face of its rightful owner. "There now. How's that, Axe?"

By sure increments, Axe regains his senses, shaking away the results of being slammed to the ground. And with a little help from Katie, he wiggles free from the Speed Six. But the more Axe gathers himself, the greater mounts his frustration, he beginning to comprehend the lost opportunity of achieving a new, personal, three-lap record. Understandably, Axe's temper builds, with there being but one release. First things first, however, and that is to deliver a sufficient warning.

"Katie. Cover your ears."

Quickly, she complies, cupping her hands upon her head like she has on previous occasions.

"#&@$%!"

Truly, the outburst is a curative, Axe feeling a calm, while the expletives scatter to the winds. Wearing a smirk, he nods his head, this being the established signal that all is clear.

Yet as far as Katie is concerned, all is also well, in that her Axe seems to be returning to his normal self. Now, her hands are free to slap away the accumulated dust upon his mechanic's coveralls.

"You had me worried, Axe." Katie delivers a soft admonishment.

"That was quite a spill," he acknowledges, as he feels a bump atop his head. And then Axe opens and shuts his jaw several times, to see if it functions properly. "But you shouldn't be too bothered, Old Girl. It's just an automobile. Who could ever be hurt by an auto?"

"All the same. I think racing for time is becoming a bad idea." With her raised brow, Katie forces a point.

As he sits, Axe touches what may be a loose tooth. "O-o-oh," he moans at the premolar's situation. "Yes. No more racing for the time being. But you have to admit, Old Girl, I had my roadster running smartly." In spite of the tooth, Axe's face broadens.

"If you say so, Old Boy."

The matter is settled. But just as abruptly, Axe's clearer head is jolted by another troubling thought, this being far more consequential than the silly notion of self-preservation.

"My God." Axe turns to his wife with his open and fearful face. "Katie!"

"What? What?"

"Look what I've done to my beautiful roadster! My poor roadster!"

Immediately, Axe jumps to his feet, his first step retaining a slight wobble. Yet this sensation vanishes, as he begins a close scrutiny of the damage done. Certainly, its driver's kerosene lantern is of no further use, bent and broken by its impact to the ground. And the right fenders have become fractured and detached from the body. No doubt the running board, which lies hidden, suffers a similar fate. Still, these are superficial wounds, each being replaceable by a furtive Axe.

"It doesn't seem too terrible, Katie. Not such a bad mishap."

Nevertheless, there remains the other side.

"Axe, what about the frame?" asks Katie, as well she should.

Indeed, this vital component has been a bone of contention for Loban Motor, a source of many complications badgering the previous models. But the '08 with its better design and advanced materials is supposed to put an end to the problem, so that a moment of truth is baring itself. Perhaps running the roadster with reckless abandon does serve a purpose.

To this end, Axe rushes to the bottom portion of the helpless automobile, as displayed so conveniently.

And keeping pace is Katie, she matching his keen interest for the Speed Six.

"It looks fine," notes Axe upon first glance. "So far."

"Seems so to me."

Axe edges closer, with one hand adjusting his spectacles, while the other traces the left side of the frame's rigid metal. Meticulously, he feels his way lengthwise, seeking any minute bend or twist, crack or break. Yet Axe's fingers continue their search unhindered, as do his eyes, they not tripping upon a single defect, let alone any signs of significant damage.

"No flaws in the least," announces Axe, his concentrated scrutiny missing hardly a mark.

Continuing his search along the frame's perimeter, he tracks his way downward. Indeed, it's all to Axe's liking—the rest of the frame's condition and those connected parts. Amazingly, in spite of the stress, each of the four springs has kept its perfect semi-elliptical shape.

"Can you believe it, Katie? Not even the slightest deviation. And look at the drive shaft." Axe gives the elongated part a few admiring pats. "Straight and sure, like the axles."

"Impressive," admires Katie. "Who would believe it could survive this calamity in such good shape?"

In unison, the couple keeps their eyes upon the bottom side of the roadster.

"Thank God, I convinced Mr. Loban to go by way of vanadium," boasts Axe.

"Well then, I should think Mr. Loban will be happy to see this."

"Katie." Responding to the innocent comment, Axe's bearing takes a sharp turn. "For goodness sakes, he mustn't know. God forbid to violate fussy Loban's pristine condition demands."

"Yes, of course."

"He doesn't understand the need to push the roadster." Once again, Axe eyes the frame, the drive shaft, and the rear axle, dirty and unpristine they may be, though strong and straight they are. "No, he should never hear of this little upheaval."

"Axe, it will be our secret."

He grins at Katie's reassurance. Yet at the same time Axe remembers his place, that of being a good husband. His eyes return to hers.

"I know, Katie. It is a mere machine, and not flesh and blood."

Katie's response is but a mere smile, this being as powerful statement as warranted.

"I suppose I've raced the roadster as much as necessary. I know the alterations needed."

Again, the look on Katie's face speaks volumes.

"Hmm? But what next?" Axe gazes upon the quandary of the overturned roadster. "Just how do we right it without further damage?" He thinks deeper, his hands grasped upon his hips. "This could take a while."

"How long, Axe?"

"I can't say. Why?"

"I have a lesson to give. Five o'clock at the Steele's."

"Oh. I forgot. Then we have no time to waste. Hmm? Now let me see. What can we do?"

To be sure, this is a task for an engineer. But overcoming mechanical and physical difficulties is Axelrod Lane's beloved profession, he being inspired and degreed by Ohio State University's engineering school. Before he was lured away to Lisbon, he worked for the Columbus, Delaware and Marion Railway, gaining valuable experience at solving the problems of a problem company. As it happened, living in Delaware had another advantage in that the town is the site of Ohio Wesleyan Female College, where once a winsome Miss Kane studied music—violin, piano and voice in particular. Thus the precisions of engineering and the tempos of musical theory have combined, with the immobilized Speed Six placed in competent hands.

"We'll do it one inch at a time," declares Axe.

"Slow and deliberate," adds Katie. "With no syncopations."

Fortunately, there is stowed a pulley. But just as handy is a sturdy elm tree, which by some skill and more luck Axe had missed during his conflict with the hairpin. It should work out well, meaning that today the two Steele daughters will not miss their piano lessons.

Remarkably, soon, the roadster finds itself tramping on all fours, its driver being as cautious as ever, while its passenger breathes easy. But although the re-oiled engine needs an adjustment, the fuel tank beneath the position of the rumble seat feeds the six-cylinder superbly. And because the metal springs, wooden spokes and rubber tires have survived intact, the roadster is able to spin its way back to town, albeit with a crushed kerosene lantern, busted fenders and unusable running board. As it stands, the most important item now occupying Axe's mind is of how he can steer clear of Mr. Loban for the remainder of the day.

It is neat and tidy, this north side home coated by a tasteful collection of colors: two shades of green, one of blue and another of maroon. A chamfered parlor projects beyond the front porch, while its gable is dominated by a daisy fan and fish scale siding. Even higher, a patterned brick chimney stems from the end of the roofline, while the remainder of the ridge is covered by four wrought-ironed and glass-balled lightning rods. Built twelve years ago by a railroad employee who has since moved on, this single-story cottage is an ideal setting for a happy, young couple.

As for that unhappy crisis which occurred on the prior afternoon? Thankfully, it has passed—mostly—though there are a few loose ends to be addressed, the reason why the Lanes' morning is earlier than usual.

As prepared by Katie, breakfast is full, but as devoured by Axe, out of necessity it is hurried. Yet when he leaves the table, he isn't dressed in his normal office attire of suit, vest and tie, but instead wears work coveralls. Axe may have avoided Mr. Loban on the previous day and thus kept his employer's eyes away from the damaged roadster. And because the young engineer remained artful, he was able to steal away from the factory the required parts and make a late night, surreptitious repair. Yet there remains the engine and its desperate need of a tuning.

"That was delicious, Katie," bids Axe, as he exits through the rear, kitchen door.

"I'll join you in a few minutes," responds Katie, while she clears the table, still dressed in her night robe.

Certainly, it is convenient to have a space behind one's house in order to conceal an automobile. Soon, Axe has the Speed Six started and by kerosene light makes the needed adjustments. And being a man of precision, he's unafraid to use any available resource. Rest assured, Axe has an ideal tool, a flawless instrument to measure an idling engine's sounds.

Having put her kitchen in order, and then doing the same for herself,

Katie emerges upon the outer steps, to greet the dawn and assist her husband.

"What do you think?" inquires Axe, as he turns away from the engine.

Katie listens briefly, tilting her head so that her ears take in several angles. "Sounds like a 'G'. Too high."

"I thought so. But I know what to do."

Armed with wrenches and screwdrivers, Axe returns to his engine, his trust in Katie's perfect pitch being devoid of skepticism. Indeed, by trial and error, he's learned that the Speed Six's engine's greatest efficiency hums the note of "E" at the bottom of the treble clef—the sweetest of tunes. When it comes down to it, that stubborn commutator—the brains to it all—and Lepper's mercurial carburetor stand hardly a chance against the combined talents of the Lanes.

An hour glides by, during which Axe pricks and probes, wrenches and wrests. But the hands of the clock near seven, meaning that Loban Motor will demand the presence of its assistant engineer.

"Still 'E-flat'. I'm sure of it."

"Oh well. It'll have to do for now," shrugs Axe. "I have to get dressed."

"You still should be a little early."

"Yes. But I think it wise to sneak the roadster into the basement and paint the fenders and running board. And keep it down there while it dries."

"Well in that case, you need to hurry," reasons Katie. "Get to the factory before Freddy. And Mr. Loban."

Following a quick wash and transition into suit and fedora, Axe receives a kiss to send him on his way. Normally, he rides his bicycle to work, concealing it in a grove near the factory, a procedure humoring Mr. Loban's disdain for two-wheelers. Yet on this morning Axe has the roadster, this counter to a Loban Motor rule proscribing the private use of company automobiles. Indeed, the Speed Six should have spent the night within the factory and not behind the Lane home. Thus the trepidation felt by Axe, as he drives through the streets of Lisbon. Should he encounter Mr. Loban, or for that matter, Freddy Brothers, then an explanation will have to be concocted, this complicated by the unpainted fenders and running board.

"Mr. Loban, I sure hope you're enjoying a large breakfast," mumbles Axe, as he drives a circuitous route around his boss's neighborhood.

As luck would have it, his tour of Lisbon comes replete with the faces of strangers. Even Axe's entry through Loban Motor's rear service door draws no real interest, the workers being anxious to begin another day assembling Fury Fours.

"You're early," notes Wilbur Berry, chief electrician, who hitches a ride down the elevator with Axe and the roadster. "Suppose you're putting in all hours to get the Speed Six ready."

"You have no idea, Wilbur," replies Axe.

Soon, his clandestine paint job is completed in the proper shade of red, and should be indistinguishable. Followed by a thorough cleanup, at last Axe can step back and calm himself. As far as he's concerned, except for the lessons learned and a promise made, yesterday's accident is a forgotten matter.

And so Axe is able to ascend to the second story and nestle to his slant top desk, situated within a shared, nondescript office of other staff employees. As it happens, no one is present. Yet Axe isn't surprised to find upon his library table one of Willis Clapsaddle's fresh drafts. From a drawer, he pulls out a notebook of his own figures, to match and compare, and to calculate the ultimate efficiencies and costs. Immediately, Axe raises his brow and nods his head.

He isn't alone for long, however, as two of the four occupants make their appearances.

"Willis. This is perfectly meticulous."

"My pleasure, Axe."

Accompanying the draftsman/designer is the business manager, whose desk sits just beyond Axe's table.

"Good morning, Axelrod."

"Morning, Freddy. Sleep well?"

"Not as well as you, I suppose. Weren't you a little tardy this morning?" he poses, while clutching a couple of ledgers.

"Late to the office, but not the building. Working like a beaver for Mr. Loban takes me to all corners of the factory. Much like you, Freddy."

"Of course."

"By the way. Now that you're here." Axe wears a serious look. "Can you tell me where I might find the five-sixteenths iron washers?"

Freddy's response is quick. "Cabinet 'AAA', in the basement."

"And the file cleaners?"

"In the machine shop. The blue shelf."

"Oh, I see. What about the three-sixteenth flathead bolts?"

"Two inch or three inch?"

"Three, of course," stresses Axe.

"They're on order. But there should be some loose ones in assembly. Ask there."

"Of course, Freddy. I should have known."

"Is there anything else, Axelrod?"

"No. That should do it. Your assistance is appreciated, Freddy. Like always."

Freddy places his ledgers upon his desk, exchanging them for several others. "By the way, Mr. Loban probably needs to speak with you," he reveals.

"Is he in his office?" Suddenly, Axe becomes a bit anxious.

"Not as yet. But when he does, you should see him. Questions concerning the roadster."

Abruptly, Freddy leaves Axe to speculate on his own, or perhaps ponder his fate. Yet should there be any cause for alarm, the assistant engineer thinks? After all, impromptu meetings are a matter of routine with Mr. Loban, although usually these are held with Kimble Lepper in attendance. Still, there shouldn't be any undue concerns, especially since Axe understands fully that mulling over the near future is a far sight worse than experiencing the moment itself.

With this in mind, he's able to busy himself into one of his assignments: calculating cost-cutting measures. Then again, if this work proves to be tedious, Axe can enliven it by mixing in one or two of his favorite cost-adding schemes. Anything to pass the time while the paint dries.

Eventually, Mr. Loban does arrive, his bellowing voice announcing the fact throughout the office area.

Meanwhile, Axe waits a few discreet minutes before leaving his desk, confident that his improvised responses should satisfy all ticklish questions.

"Mr. Loban." Axe knocks on the open doorway. "Freddy said you wished to speak to me."

"Lane. Come and have a seat," invites the owner, who sits at his expansive, kneehole desk.

"Thank you, Mr. Loban. Good morning."

"Good morning to you, Lane."

"Have you heard from Kimble, Mr. Loban?" While he sits, Axe offers some small talk. "How is he?"

"Oh, his doctor said he should be well enough for tomorrow. Though I could have used him, yesterday. Or you, for that matter. To help with the investors."

"I'm sorry about that, Mr. Loban. Willis told me earlier. I wish I had known."

"You're not to blame."

"Did the meeting go well?"

"It did. But we did miss our demonstration. By the way." Mr. Loban changes direction. "How is the roadster handling?"

"Oh, it rides soundly, Mr. Loban. Rest assured." Axe's tone becomes enthused. "In fact, it's a frolicking pleasure to drive. Though I do wish its wheel base could be wider."

"We'll reconsider wheel bases with future models. But I am glad to hear of the Speed Six's progress. We should set that production date. Perhaps have a staff meeting in a couple of days for that reason."

"I'll look forward to it." Axe leans ahead. "I can't tell you how much, Mr. Loban."

"I feel the same." Mr. Loban nods to show his appreciation for Axe's fervor. "As for the investors? I need you to take them for those demonstrations in the touring car. Miss Charnwood has a schedule."

"I'd like that, Mr. Loban." Truly, there's nothing false in Axe's words.

"Excellent. But Lane, I am trusting you." Mr. Loban's demeanor turns more seriously. "Give them pleasant drives. Show them the Speed Six's virtues. Be patient with their questions. And if they wish to give the roadster a try, oblige them. Any time, any day."

"I will, Mr. Loban. You can count on me."

"Yes, I can, Lane. I see how you work with people. You can sell our '08, as well as any at Loban Motor."

"Thank you, Mr. Loban."

"Very well. I'll leave you to it."

As Axe exits his boss's office, he's a bit astonished by the wave of genuine flattery and undeniable confidence. Indeed, Mr. Loban's practice has been to offer such accolades on a grudging basis, and do so with no uncertain conditions.

"Here you are, Mr. Lane." Ever efficient, Miss Charnwood hands Axe a schedule, as he passes her desk.

"Thank you, Miss Charnwood," he acknowledges with a smile.

Something may be afoot, but as to what, Axe cannot say. For that matter, he's not even sure if he could pose the appropriate question, so sudden is the feeling.

The day continues into the afternoon, upon which Axe abandons his desk of facts and figures in order to make some precision measurements, as assisted by Clapsaddle. And so it's off to the machine shop, to erode the clock in a world of cylinders and calipers, pistons and .001-inch tolerances. That is until…

"Willis. It's nearly four o'clock. I have to be off."

Parked outside, the touring car awaits, it requiring only a spark-control adjustment and three turns at the starting crank. Concerning his destination,

Axe's scheduled demonstration for the day is to take the family of Holland Snodgrass on a spin around town or, if need be, into the countryside. And so it's off to the West Walnut Street address of one of Columbiana County's most influential men.

Coming to a stop in front of the Snodgrass home, Axe can ponder: of the beauty of its Italian inspiration and its relatively modest structure. Indeed, it reminds him of the many brick houses in Katie's Delaware, these belonging to mere professionals and not movers and shakers. Perhaps modesty is the truer nature of Holland Snodgrass, a prominent man who impresses with his inner substance and not an outer luster.

The hand brake is set and the engine left to idle, allowing Axe's feet to caper for the front door. Immediately, his knock is answered by a beaming twelve year-old, clad in a one-piece sailor dress, her parted, dangling hair banded by two, bright blue ribbons.

"Mr. Lane! You're here!"

Quickly, the other two Snodgrass daughters join their sister, they being slightly older and dressed in lengthier versions of similar nautical themes, though with rosette, Panama braid hats topping their crowns.

"Mother!" Together, they turn around and chorus the announcement. "Mr. Lane is here!"

Apparently, the girls' attentive trait is inherited from their mother, who herself must have been hovering somewhere near the front hall.

"I hope I'm not too early, Mrs. Snodgrass."

"Heavens no, Axelrod. Your timing is perfect."

Axe is struck by Mrs. Snodgrass's choice in headwear: a wide-brimmed, Milan straw affair, festooned in fussy feathery and a green satin bow. Indeed, how fortunate that this enormous pediment will be protected by the touring car's canvas top and glass windscreen—and not the roadster's vulnerable airiness.

"Axelrod Lane." Joining the crowd is the man of the house. "So kind of you to offer a drive."

"Believe me, sir, it is my pleasure."

"Wonderful." But then Mr. Snodgrass's eyes glance upon the touring car. "My it is a sight to behold. Don't you think, dear?"

"Oh yes," concurs Mrs. Snodgrass. "Oh, what a lovely shade of green."

"Then shall we? Girls, are you ready?"

The Snodgrass daughters bounce upon their toes. "Yes, Father. Yes."

"Axelrod. Please show the way."

"Gladly, sir."

With a little help, Mrs. Snodgrass and the girls find their snug seats to the rear, while Mr. Snodgrass and Axe hop into the front.

"Is everyone ready?" asks the driver. "Here we go." After honking the horn, Axe engages first gear.

The jaunt begins in earnest, as if every artery in Lisbon is to be given its due. Soon, Walnut Street is traded for Chestnut via Pritchard Avenue, and Pine is reached by way of the Thomas Road. Meanwhile, Axe regales his gleeful passengers with the attributes of the touring car.

"…If need be, I can fold the top in ten minutes."

"Gracious." Mrs. Snodgrass leans forward just a bit. "How convenient."

"Mrs. Snodgrass, I can stop if you like."

"Oh dear no, Axelrod. Please continue. There'll be other occasions to fold back the top." She edges closer to Axe's ear. "Might you can take me for a drive in the roadster."

With their happy, open palms, the girls wave at every schoolmate they spy, while Mr. Snodgrass tips his hat toward constituents—past, present and potential. But eventually, the streets of Lisbon begin to repeat themselves, making a change of venue all the more enticing.

"So you were saying, Axelrod, the touring car can almost match the speed of the roadster?"

"Yes sir. They have the same engine, after all."

"Then why don't we leave town for the countryside?" proposes Mr. Snodgrass, who then looks to his family. "What do you say, Lydia? Girls? Should we ask Mr. Lane to drive his car as fast as he would like?"

"Yes! Yes!" The response from the rear seat is quick and unanimous.

"There you have it, Axelrod. A request from the ladies. Shall we?"

While his careful eyes stay upon the street, Axe offers a devilish grin. "Whatever you say, Mr. Snodgrass." He raises his voice further. "Ladies, hold on to your hats."

To be sure, the road to distant Salem has its dangerous contours and curves, along with an infinite number of spoke-splintering ruts and spring-splitting protrusions. Yet Axe knows by experience that this country lane has a couple of mile-long stretches of the relatively smooth and unwinding. There's little doubt, that such a setting begs to be plied upon by four capable tires, these inflated properly and powered by 44 horses.

The throttle responds without protest, and the three-speed transmission slides smoothly. As for the touring car's occupants, they hang on for dear life and enjoy every minute. Meanwhile, Axe pushes the Speed Six, coaxing every bit of energy and velocity the road allows. Unfortunately, too soon the touring car races through the favorable section and into what is perhaps the roughest. Thus, with the protocols of safety foremost on his mind, Axe slows accordingly.

"Can we scorch it again, Mr. Lane!" is an eager request from the rear seat.

"Yes, yes! Can we!"

"Why, sure girls," replies Axe, as he looks to an approving Mr. Snodgrass. "I'll turn around."

So continues the demonstration drive of no particular destination, miles filled with agile turns, responsive pedals and, of course, flat out speed.

"How fast have we've taken it?" asks Mr. Snodgrass during a lull.

"Can't say precisely, sir. I've only put a speedometer on the roadster. But we surely surpassed forty today. Possibly forty-five."

"Impressive," judges Mr. Snodgrass. "Betters the Fords by a long shot."

By any measure, the drive is a monumental success. So much so, that its eventual end, at the exact spot where it began, comes with a profound reluctance. Nevertheless, Mrs. Snodgrass and her daughters do have enough resolve to pry themselves apart from the Speed Six.

"I so enjoyed myself, Axelrod," she thanks. "And I'm looking forward to our next drive."

"Thank you, Mr. Lane," adds her eldest daughter. "Father, I hope you get one just like it?"

"Oh, will you, Father?" agrees the middle. "A green one?"

"Goodbye, Mr. Lane," bids the twelve year-old. "Thank you, so much."

While his family waltzes into their home, Mr. Snodgrass lingers curbside with Axe. "It appears that Loban Motor has produced a superlative machine. You should be proud, Axelrod."

"I am, sir. We're all very proud."

Regardless, Mr. Snodgrass interjects a smirk. "I suspect you find Percy Loban's character as somewhat bumptious. But one must understand that running a business within the climate of a maiden industry is a complicated matter. Percy should be allowed his faults and stumbles."

Axe acknowledges with a few nods.

"I'll give him this," continues Mr. Snodgrass. "He knows to keep his transactions simple, to steer clear of pettifoggers. Certainly, no species of humanity can kill a company better than they."

"I understand precisely, Mr. Snodgrass."

"Still, I must say, Axelrod, I have some misgivings. The business of selling the Speed Six to the public."

"Yes, Mr. Snodgrass. A touchy subject."

"But Percy and I have been discussing the matter. And I believe we will find a solution. In fact, it may come to pass, Axelrod, that you, yourself, will play a part in publicizing the Speed Six."

"Really?" This is news to Axe.

"I shouldn't say more. Except that I believe you can help sell this automobile to the public. Your abilities behind the wheel and knowledge of the '08 have certainly sold me."

"Thank you, sir." Axe's words are brief, the almost cryptic disclosure and accompanying flattery being a bit overwhelming.

"Thank you, Axelrod." Mr. Snodgrass offers his hand. "Have a pleasant evening, and tell Katie 'hello' from all of us."

"I will, sir."

Still a little stunned as he reclaims the driver's seat, Axe tries to interpret Mr. Snodgrass's parting words. While the engine drones, it takes him a couple of blocks to stumble upon a reasonable slant. But of course, Lisbon's most estimable citizen must be alluding to that avenue of promotion used by other manufacturers. Indeed, it's the same idea Axe has pushed, albeit with lukewarm responses from Mr. Loban.

"Racing!" Axe's foot stomps upon the transmission brake, while he eases the throttle and steps off the gear pedal. "He wants to race the Speed Six!"

Eventually, Axe calms himself, and is able to continue his return to Loban Motor. Needless to say, his mind is flooded by what little was heard, and what can be expounded. Indeed, entering the burgeoning world of automobile racing would lead the company into a rush of development. Hunkering behind the wheel, Axe pushes the throttle and takes a racing curve onto Beaver Street

Yet before he's able to gun the engine further, another thought enters his head and thus deflates his surge upon the straightaway.

"Katie."

Perhaps Axe's head should stay out of the racing car and its known perils. However, there's no reason to believe that he isn't the best candidate to run a team. After all, a driver can be hired, but who knows more than he about the Speed Six, to make it competitive? Come what may, for Axe, the future looks brighter.

Before long, he drives to the rear of Loban Motor and secures the touring car on the assembly room floor. No staff members are present, and by the time Axe departs only a few workers remain. Setting a brisk pace, his amble home shouldn't last long, while his anxious news for Katie will have little time to wait.

Upon crossing the Little Beaver Creek bridge, Axe approaches the adjacent railroad tracks. It's here that he makes out a figure, who gathers into an oversized pail stray lumps of P.I. & W.R.R. coal.

"Hey, Jimmy Swift! What's this I hear about you at the factory!"

As for Jimmy, he ceases collecting coal, although he doesn't give ground. "What's it to you, Axe?"

"Everything. Why I ought to take you across my knee and spank some sense into you.'

"Oh yeah. You and who else?"

"Me and this right hand of mine." Axe comes to a halt. "With the other tied behind my back."

Yet it's all for show—Axe's anger. After all, he was once Jimmy's age, sticking his curious nose into settings where it didn't belong. Coupled with a crooked smile, Axe offers the boy an approving nod. And ever so slightly, he protrudes his tongue, upon which rests a penny-sized bubble. Giving a gentle blow, Axe frees the dome of saliva to float to the ground.

"How did you do that?" marvels Jimmy.

"By using my knowledge of engineering and physical properties," muses Axe.

"Huh?"

"Oh, never mind, Jimmy. Hmm? I bet you snuck through a basement window, didn't you?"

"Sure did. Me and my friend, Danny."

"Danny?" Spotting a sizeable chunk of coal, Axe reaches down and tosses it into the pail.

"He's in my class," explains Jimmy. "Not a bad fellow, when he's not a horse's ass."

"Horse's ass? Sounds typical. But tell me. Seriously. How riled did Mr. Loban get?"

"Fairly riled, you can bet."

"Did that vein bulge out of the side of his forehead?"

"Sure did, Axe. And there was another one next to it."

"Oh, then he was riled, for certain," chuckles Axe. "Wish I could have seen it.

Together, they continue to gather more coal, and, soon, the pail becomes full.

"Can you carry that home, Jimmy? By yourself?"

"I do it all the time."

"Then I'll see you some other time." And so Axe resumes his walk home, while he offers a parting thought. "Jimmy. The next time you and your friend want to see the factory, ask me first. I'll give you a tour. Whenever Mr. Loban isn't around."

"Will you, Axe?"

"Of course. And I might just take you for a drive someday. We do make the best automobiles, after all. And every person in the country is going to know. You can bet."

3
A SCHEME UNFOLDS

After a busy, talkative dinner, followed by a kitchen clean-up, Katie and Axe are unable to calm themselves. Later, as they take to their bed, the night proves restless.

Certainly, Axe's thoughts rev through the sundry modifications of a Speed Six racer.

As for Katie, though excited that her husband's company could be taking another leap forward, she has her doubts and dreads. While Axe prattles of metallic spokes and larger tires, and of a more efficient carburetor, her thoughts fix upon the reckless tactics of race competitors. More importantly, Katie knows of the ease to lure Axe into the driver's seat or, just as fearful, the riding mechanic's. Sensing the need to reaffirm her feelings, she takes a deep breath and cozies her head upon his shoulder, readying herself for what could be the first in a series of firm stands.

"Axe, tell me again what Mr. Snodgrass told you? Exactly his words?"

"Exactly?"

"Did he use the word 'racing' when he complimented you? Of your engineering abilities?"

"Engineering?"

"Axe?" Katie props up her head and looks into his eyes. "What else would he compliment?"

"Well-l-l?"

"Axe, you're one of the finest auto engineers out there. And this isn't from just myself."

"Who then?"

"The wives of the men at L.M., of course."

"Oh, yes. Them." He pauses, to let sink this unexpected wave of accolades. "Really?"

"They talk about you all the time." Now it's Katie's turn to take pause. "You have no idea, do you, Axe?"

"Idea about what?"

"Of how well-regarded you are at L.M."

"Oh?"

"Axe, you mean to say Mr. Loban never compliments your work?"

"When it suits him, Mr. Loban compliments everyone," smirks Axe. "It carries little weight with me."

"Well, maybe it should. Mr. Loban really does hold you in high regard."

"Did Mrs. Loban tell you that?" There's a touch of sarcasm in Axe's tone.

"Perhaps." Softly, Katie returns to her cuddle. "No, Mr. Loban would be a fool to let his engineer drive a race car. You're much too valuable to him. Just as you are to me." With her point made, Katie ceases talking and puts her lips to a different use.

"Mmm. If you say so." Rest assured, Axe enjoys the moment, while he puts aside Katie's revelation.

In the end, the Lanes find a night's sleep, and so aren't too resentful of Lisbon's roosters pre-dawn activities. Slowly but surely, Axe and Katie rouse themselves, washing their faces and seeing to their personal functions before migrating toward the center of their tidy universe.

The kitchen is dominated by an Acme refrigerator/sideboard and a coal-burning Sunshine range—the former acquired in payment of violin lessons for the Stanford twins and the latter in exchange for installing electrical wiring into said family's home. From a boiler atop the stove, Axe pours a cup of coffee. Meanwhile, he admires Katie's domestic adroitness, she wielding simultaneous utensils for bacon and eggs and for pancakes, this rhythm keeping time for her sweet hums of Dvorak.

"Is that one of his American tunes?" inquires Axe, as he sits at the table.

"Yes it is," smiles Katie. "Of a songbird."

"I love it. I think it may become a favorite."

"Umm. Me too, Axe."

Before long, Katie dishes out the breakfast fare and, upon pouring herself a cup of coffee, finds her seat.

"Katie, are you giving any lessons today?"

"Yes. It's Thursday. This afternoon at the Snodgrass's. Piano, violin and viola. I may be late."

"Then perhaps I'll dawdle at L.M. No sense coming home to an empty house."

Because breakfast proceeds along its normal course, in little time Axe is ready to part, a kiss at the rear kitchen door providing a spark of additional energy.

Katie hands over a paper sack. "Two sandwiches and two pickles."

Axe grasps his lunch and allows his nose a quick scrutiny. "Mmm. Hogshead cheese and cheddar. Liverwurst and Swiss. My favorites."

"Don't let Mr. Loban forget how important you are at L.M." reminds Katie, while Axe walks toward the tool shed. "Too important to drive a race car."

Axe emerges from the shed with his Schwinn safety bicycle. "Fear not, Old Girl," he announces as he mounts his bike. "If need be, I'll take a firm stand."

"That suits me wonderfully." Katie blows an additional kiss. "Have a nice day, Axe."

"Yes, a firm stand," he assures, as he pedals away. "The likes of which L.M. has never seen."

As Axe takes to the street upon his Schwinn, however, a forgotten thought surfaces, of how the refrigerator's cool is losing strength. Nonetheless, before he reverses course, his eyes catch sight of the "ICE" sign displayed from within the parlor window. Yet again, he's reminded of Katie's constant efficiency.

With that, Axe is able to speed away, toward the direction of Loban Motor and an impending workday. Yet sure to form, after pedaling a few blocks, he comes in contact with that minor subject in question. In Lisbon, Tice & Hardy is the business tending to domestic ice needs, and one of its horse-drawn delivery wagons is parked in front of the Davidson home. Needless to say, it is an irresistible pause for consideration.

The brown mare gives no regard to Axe's approach, as he sizes up the load space situated behind the wagon's driver's seat. How primitive it seems in these modern times, yet how simple, he thinks, to take the box-like, wooden structure and install it onto the chassis of a Speed Six. Using his forearm as a rule, Axe makes an estimate of the load space's dimensions, coming up with a 44.25" x 54" x 72.50" measurement.

"Hmm?" relishes Axe of yet another burgeoning project.

Indeed, not only would it be an easy fit for the Speed Six, but it could be squeezed upon a Fury Four, an important concern should there arise a surplus of '06s. Whatever the case may be, Willis Clapsaddle should appreciate the idea, and perhaps Mr. Loban will show some interest. Even the men of the wood shop will understand the significance of the extra work. But especially, there is Katie, to whom Axe can't wait to tell of his latest scheme, and then listen for her own angles concerning the stimulating topic of load spaces.

Before the iceman returns, Axe resumes his trek southward. Soon, he crosses Little Beaver Creek and arrives at the grove of trees, to deposit his bicycle with the others owned by Loban Motor workers.

With the promise that his day is to be filled by propositions and new projects, Axe's walk to the factory contains a noticeable skip. Yet, when he reminds himself of Katie and her valid concerns, his final steps become more determined.

"Don't worry, Old Girl," mutters Axe. "Mr. Loban won't oblige me into a race car. I'll steer him away."

Unfortunately for Axe, this particular Thursday unwinds like most of the others at Loban Motor. Conspicuous by their absences are Mr. Loban and Freddy—Miss Charnwood's lack of an explanation withstanding—and inconspicuous by his late arrival is a sniffling Kimble Lepper. Still, Axe does bury himself in his work and also manages to toss around his delivery truck scheme, receiving favorable reactions from both the chief engineer and Willis Clapsaddle.

To be sure, something must be up, or so tell the agitated hairs on the nape of Axe's neck. More's the pity, for part of the night and all of the morning he's rehearsed his responses to what he imagines will be a resounding proposal. But now comes a frustrating wait, compelling Axe to bide his morning with load body dimensions, types of wood, weight allowances, costs, etc.

Soon, however, his concerns press toward another direction. Thankfully, there awaits a demonstration drive for an investor. To be exact, Axe has a noon appointment with Miss Lucilla Loban. Thus an early lunch is in order, a tasty diversion centered around the assemblage of Katie's loving hands. Indeed, what better way to deplete his anxiousness than to follow a filling meal with a drive upon Lisbon's streets, or wherever Mr. Loban's aunt chooses to go? For Axe, already the clock is picking up its pace.

The touring car has never performed so magnificently, nor has it ever conveyed a primmer entourage. As things are playing out, Axe's demonstration drive isn't for Miss Loban's benefit alone. Throughout the noon hour and probably into the next, the touring car becomes a taxi for Mr. Loban's aunt and her friends, its driver serving as an errand boy of sorts.

And around and around they go: Axe, Miss Loban and what is proving to be a confusing succession of passengers and their destinations. First, there's Mrs. Kember, who is taken directly to the Methodist Episcopal Church. And then it's on to the addresses of Mrs. Dodson and Mrs. Wickham, both of whom have dire shopping needs at the various hardware, grocery and drug stores, and at the florist's. Eventually, these two ladies are swapped for Mrs. Brown and her visit with the dentist and for Mrs. McKay's latest appointment at Dr. Steele's. Meanwhile, there's time to return Mrs. Kember to her home, after she has her diversion to the carpet store. And when the patients are released and delivered to their Walnut Street addresses, it's on to the domiciles of Mrs. Pritchard, Miss Coles and Mrs. Stipes, the reason behind their invitations becoming apparent after Axe ushers the last passenger.

"Won't Celia be joining us, Lucie?" asks Mrs. Pritchard, as she settles herself.

"I'm afraid not, Eva," replies Miss Loban from her front seat. "She's feeling rather poorly."

"No doubt due to that son of hers," joins Miss Coles. "Why, the things I've heard. It would stir the dead."

"Do tell, Anna," insists Mrs. Stipes. "Do tell."

"Where shall I start?"

So begins the flood, the likes of which Axe's captive ears have never endured.

"...And why do you suppose he spends so much time in East Liverpool? Such a town. Tsk. Tsk."

"But he's not the only one, don't you know, Anna," adds Mrs. Pritchard with her worth. "I could tell you stories that no other person but..."

The banter continues, with the noise of six cylinders posing no barrier in the least.

Yet as stupefied as Axe may be, he remains a patient and attentive chauffeur. This in spite of the fact that his occasional blurts of Speed Six attributes fall upon deaf ears. Lacking the ability to get a word in edgewise, Axe has no choice but to resign himself to his defenseless position behind the driver's wheel.

"And have you heard about that young woman from Youngstown?"

"Oh, dear. Tell us more.

"Anna, please," reminds Mrs. Stipes, as if delving further may be inappropriate. "Sh-h-h."

Ever adroitly, the ladies shift their cackle to other scandalous directions, as their tour of Lisbon continues.

"…Just how do you suppose Mr. Kerry found the money to start his insurance company? Why, it was…."

Mercifully, wagging tongues have limitations, and in due time their weary masters ask to be taken homeward. None too soon, the "demonstration" drive comes to its expected conclusion when its hostess is accompanied to her doorstep.

"So kind of you, Axelrod, for this afternoon. We should do this again. Soon."

"Yes, Miss Loban. It's been my pleasure."

"You're such a sweet and able young man, Axelrod."

"Thank you, Miss Loban."

"And I know that you're much too thoughtful to be bothered by my nephew. Such as when he refers to you as 'college boy'. Don't feel resentful. That's just his way. Why Percy is a 'college boy' himself. Expelled from five of the best!"

"Really? You don't say?"

Never at one sitting has Axe learned so much of his adopted town. And never before today could he have imagined the intricate webs and potential storms lurking beneath the surface of Lisbon's otherwise calm streets. Better to leave those levels where they lie, thinks Axe, or keep them in the hands of such experts as Miss Loban and her friends. Still, that one tidbit concerning his employer's past just might prove to be useful—five colleges?

By kind providence, Axe returns to Loban Motor in one piece. Yet it's no great shock that the moment Axe settles into his desk, he finds himself being summoned to Mr. Loban's office. At last, the time may have arrived for Axe to stand his ground.

He enters the room to see his boss sitting at his desk, with Freddy Brothers by his side. But as well, Hugh Flugan is present, though dressed in a shirt and tie and not his usual work clothes.

"Where have you been, Lane?" asks Mr. Loban, whose mood doesn't appear to be patient.

"With your Aunt Lucie, Mr. Loban. Remember? Her demonstration drive?"

"Oh? You mean to say, it took you this long?"

It's frustrating that Axe has to explain himself. "Yes, Mr. Loban. Aunt Lucie has an endless number of friends." Axe shrugs his shoulders. "Should I have turned them away?"

"Well. Of course not."

Now, Mr. Loban seems embarrassed—a proud accomplishment on Axe's part.

"But they were impressed with the Speed Six, Mr. Loban. All of Aunt Lucie's friends. And believe me, they know how to spread the word. In a matter of days their network will range beyond Ohio."

"Very well, Lane. Then it was a sound decision to entertain my aunt's friends."

"I thought you would agree, Mr. Loban."

"But in regards to this, that you can sell the Speed Six remains incontestable."

Such a compliment arrives often as a precursor to an unusual demand. With Katie's concerns in mind, Axe girds himself and folds his arms across his chest.

"Thank you, Mr. Loban. I am keen on our Speed Six, after all."

"Excellent. But then again, aren't we all are. Freddy? Flugan? Keen on the Speed Six?"

"Keen to the extreme," agrees Freddy with his immediate enthusiasm. "From the start."

Somewhat less than loquacious, Flugan nods his reply.

"Suffice to say, every man in this building carries a perfervid zeal for the Speed Six," continues Mr. Loban. "But you, Lane, seem the best suited for the task ahead."

"Oh?" Axe takes a deep breath, so that his words of refusal might spurt forth in full force.

"Yes. And I've been discussing the matter with the staff, and others, and have come to the conclusion that the best way to promote the '08 is to..."

The moment stops for Axe, its split second stretching so that he's forced to anticipate "racing car" flying out of Mr. Loban's mouth.

"...send it on a tour, so that the public might view Loban Motor's latest."

"I beg your pardon? A tour?" Needless to say, Axe's angst feels a serious collapse.

"Yes, Lane. A tour, to show off the Speed Six. Especially to the cities where we lack representation."

"Mr. Loban, you're not referring to the Glidden Tour? I thought you were sour on their rules."

"Glidden Tour? Posh. No, our plan has you and Flugan taking the Speed Six into northern Ohio. And a bit beyond."

"Oh, I see. Where exactly do you have in mind?" inquires Axe.

"Well-l-l."

It's at this point that Freddy intercedes. "On a circular route. A wide loop beyond Youngstown, to Erie and Cleveland. Then Toledo and returning through Akron."

"You need Hugh and me for this?" Axe is a bit perplexed.

"Our Cleveland dealer may not renew his association, and Toledo is wavering." Freddy is quick to explain. "And we have no one in Erie, nor at so many points in between. Ashtabula, Sandusky, Fremont, Tiffin, Willard, Worster, Ashland..."

"Freddy, enough." Mr. Loban raises his voice, only to lower it. "Achem. So you can see, Axelrod, that your task, and Flugan's, is to not only keep Cleveland and Toledo, but to find for us new, reliable dealers."

"I understand, Mr. Loban. But how many miles would that come to? And what of the roads? Are some of these cities actually connected to one another?"

"Axelrod, it may sound like a difficult journey. Which is why we're sending the two of you. You should be able to see to any mechanical problems, certainly. As for the number of miles, and the time spent away from Lisbon? We're calculating the figures."

Suddenly, the phrase "time spent away" brings a sure trepidation to Axe, the truer meaning being time spent away from Katie.

"It shouldn't be for too long," notes Freddy. "A few days at most."

"So there you have it, Axelrod. The two of you will have a grand little adventure." Mr. Loban stands up from his chair and then steps around his desk.

"It can be done." To his credit, Axe nestles up to the scheme. He looks toward Flugan. "Hugh and I always work well together."

Indeed, during the previous spring, when a production run of Fury Four commutators proved faulty, Mr. Loban dispatched by rail the tandem of Axe and Flugan, to where there were concentrations of those '06s: Pittsburg, Columbus and Wheeling

"Yes. The two of you did a splendid job with those commutators," notes Mr. Loban. "Averted a disaster."

"Thank you, Mr. Loban."

"Thanks, sir."

With a wide reach, Mr. Loban is able to pat two backs simultaneously. "So Hugh. Axelrod. I'm sure you're both anxious to ready the Speed Six for the journey ahead. We'll talk more of the details and destinations. But I'm certain that in a week's time, all will be prepared."

Although he's had no time to ponder, as far as Axe is concerned, there's little reason to worry over the Speed Six. Yet there does come to mind an important item, one which needs to be settled immediately.

"Mr. Loban, which will it be?"

"What?"

"The roadster or the touring car?"

"Oh?" Mr. Loban looks to Freddy, and with a shrug makes his decision. "The touring car, I should think. Yes, ready the touring car."

Although he would have preferred his beloved roadster for the long, open trek, nonetheless, Axe is enthused. "The touring car it is."

Suffice to say, the thoughts of 44.25" x 54" x 72.50" load spaces and Tice & Hardy are all but forgotten. The remainder of the afternoon hastens, as Axe and Flugan leap into the task. Indeed, the touring car becomes the victim of a thorough inspection. Every inch of its frame is given a minute scrutiny and each wheel spoke caressed by careful hands in search of chips or hairlines. And after the Speed Six is taken for a drive into the countryside, its engine receives an exhaustive search for signs of trouble, as is its transmission, as are the brakes, as are the steering gear and linkage. Slowly but surely, they're drawn to a single conclusion, that in spite of a few inherent weaknesses the '08 Speed Six touring car is a sound automobile.

"We could leave tomorrow, if need be." Flugan scratches his head.

"But I don't think Mr. Loban and Freddy are ready as yet."

"You're right, Axe. Those two will need at least a week."

Axe smiles in response as he stares at the touring car. "All the same, we should carry some spare parts. Especially tires, and for sure a carburetor."

"Maybe two carburetors," furthers Flugan.

With their day nearly over, as is almost the week, there's not much more to be done to the touring car, except to give it a good washing, waxing and furniture polishing, which can wait for Friday morning.

So late is the day that Axe's Schwinn is the last bicycle reclaimed at the hideaway grove. But whereas his worries were hovering over the Speed Six, now, they light upon Katie. Indeed, the two of them are to be apart for an unspecified number of days, or perhaps weeks. Busy as he should be, Axe understands that his portion of the separation might be bearable, with exhausting days on the road becoming sure remedies for restful nights. No, his concerns are for Katie, who will have to bide her time on her own, and in a town where she has no family.

Darkness approaches when Axe returns home, he entering through the rear kitchen door. What first greets him is the delectable aroma of steak, followed by a more pleasant sensation.

"You're home!" Katie's arms grasp Axe, while her cushy lips reach up to render an aggressive smooch.

"Hold on, Old Girl. Why the excitement?" To say the least, Axe is taken aback.

"You're going to Cleveland, of course."

Although Axe is aware that news can travel with a fury in Lisbon, that likely the town harbors few secrets, he's shocked of how Katie knows of his impending trip. After all, it was only a few hours ago he learned of the promotional tour himself. Yet even more surprising is that Katie is overjoyed with the news and exudes no apprehensions. Thus the sense of relief compels Axe to plant his pucker upon her cheeks and forehead.

"I'm so proud it's my husband who's going to promote the Speed Six. My Axe."

Katie's wrap becomes even tighter, while her receptive face suffers an additional onslaught of moisture.

And so the mood for the dinner conversation is set, with the steak and its beans, carrots and potatoes being the centerpiece.

"...Mrs. Snodgrass told me," replies Katie to a casual question. "Mr. Snodgrass too."

"That makes sense," speaks Axe through a mouthful.

"We had a little time after the girls' lessons. They really are talented."

"What else did Mrs. Snodgrass say?"

"Well, she's hopeful for Cleveland. That the dealer can be brought back into the fold, and with that, Toledo. But she hasn't much faith in Erie. Too close to Buffalo, and Pierce-Arrow and the Thomas Motor Company. Thomas has entered that race around the world, don't you know. With their Flyer."

"Yes. The Flyer and its powerful six. Hmm? So Mrs. Snodgrass likes our chances in Cleveland?"

"And several places where L.M. has no dealers. Like Tiffin, Worster. But mostly, Mrs. Snodgrass spoke of Cleveland. Mr. Snodgrass too. Of how important that city is to L.M."

"Yes," agrees a frowning Axe. "We need Cleveland."

"But I think Mr. Chagrin is the problem there. L.M. could do with a better dealer, though that has its complications. Mrs. Snodgrass doesn't think too well of him. Nor does Mr. Snodgrass. Stubborn and wishy-washy, she spoke of him. Among other things."

"She knows Chagrin?"

"No, but she has a cousin in Cleveland, whose best friend's husband has done business with Mr. Chagrin."

"Really." There's a bit of dread written on Axe's face.

"Yes." Katie pauses. But then an inner thought surfaces, a swift conclusion punctuated by a smirk. "This Mr. Chagrin seems to have a lot in common with our Mr. Loban."

"Well, if that be the case, then I can manage Chagrin. That sort is always defenseless to shameless flattery. I just need to polish my skills." Axe's look turns sly. "Polish my skills and I'll have Chagrin thinking himself the industry's genius. Pulling a fast one over the competitors. Hmm? That's a good thought."

"O-o-oh," responds a beaming Katie. "I'm going to help."

"Yes, you will, Old Girl. We'll put our heads together and come up with a perfect persuasion. And if need be, a devilish one. By God, downright devilish."

Soon, the filling portion of dinner is done, of which Katie clears away in trade for two dessert plates and their wedges of yesterday's chocolate cake.

"Mmm."

Hence, the mood is altered, mellowed by sugary yearnings, as opposed to the boisterous demands of empty stomachs.

"But you are fine with this?"

"We being apart?" Katie has no problem recognizing the crux of the question. "It's not as if this is the first time. Remember the commutator episode?"

"Yes, Katie. But I'll be away much longer than that. Not just two or three days at a time."

"But Mrs. Snodgrass and I figured you shouldn't be away much more than two weeks."

"That's a long time, Katie."

"But Axe, we've been apart longer than that. Remember, before we were married. When you took your job, here. That was five months before you returned to Delaware and our wedding."

"Five months and six days," recalls Axe of that particular misery.

"But we did manage."

"Certainly."

"And if I remember correctly, Axe, that five months and six days of separation did much to make our wedding all the more exciting." Gracefully, Katie twirls her fork and piece of cake.

"It sure did, Old Girl."

"Our wedding night too, Old Boy." In tantalizing increments, Katie guides the morsel into her mouth, only to extract her fork in a slow slip. "Mmm."

Eventually, the evening finds its way into the parlor, or to be exact the Lane's sparse music salon. Although the couple's accounts have yet to afford them the command of 88 keys, this in no way prevents the room from being filled with the melodious offerings of a lilting talent. After all, Katie does have her voice, as well as her viola and the recent birthday gift that is her mandolin. But especially, there is her violin, she wielding its bow with little provocation.

Upon the end of the parlor sofa Katie has situated herself, while in hand and under chin she coaxes from her instrument a portion of a sweetly suite of Norwegian origin. As for her lap, it serves as the most sublime of pillows for the most appreciative of patrons, one who in spite of having his eyes closed, is able to envision and anticipate each swing of his wife's arm.

"Someday soon, I'll get that piano, Katie. This will be my next goal in life. A piano for the parlor, and all of Lisbon will send their children here for their lessons."

Katie smiles as she continues to play.

"You won't be lonely without me, will you, Katie?"

"I'll make do."

"Are you sure?" Axe opens his eyes.

Katie stops her violin and lays it aside. And then gently, she removes Axe's spectacles and proceeds to wipe them with her handkerchief.

"I'll stay busy, Axe. I have my lessons, and there is choir practice. And it would be a fine idea to become more familiar with the church organ. Oh, and Mrs. Snodgrass has invited me to dinner. Hmm? Perhaps I might borrow one of the girls to stay with me for a night or two."

"A find idea. You should ask, tomorrow."

"I think I will, Axe." Katie gives the spectacles a few more wipes and then returns them to their place. "Yes, I think I may have a wonderfully nice time while you're away."

"Not too nice, I hope. You could feel a little misery. For my sake."

"Very well, Axe. If you like, when I feel too much happiness, I'll think of you and become sadden."

"You and your happiness. Your gay frivolity in my absence. Mark my words, consorting with the Snodgrasses and the church choir will only get you into trouble, Old Girl. And exposing your innocence to the conspiracies of the church organ? Whew. A path to depredation."

"Axe, you devil, you." Katie renders a frisky slap upon his chest. "Why, I've of a good mind to bend you across my knee and set you straight."

"Me? Set straight?" counters Axe. "Impossible. By God, I'm beyond redemption, and proud of it."

"Old Boy," responds Katie with a false tone of admonishment. Bending down, she presses her nose against her husband's. "I should go with you. Sit in the rear seat and make sure you don't get lost. And keep you out of trouble."

Katie delivers a series of lip to lip pecks, followed by a giggle.

"Mmm. That would be fine by me," agrees Axe. "Though I can't speak for Hugh and Mr. Loban."

"Mr. Loban? Spuh."Yet once again, Katie applies her kisses, doing so with more resolve.

"Now what were you saying at dinner?" asks Axe, after given a chance to breathe. "Our wedding night?"

Again the giggle, with noses remaining bunched. "Only that it begs repeating," replies Katie, pushing aside any vestiges of ambiguity.

As far as Axe is concerned, Hugh Flugan can stay in Lisbon, so that Katie can take the front seat of the Speed Six for herself.

As for Mrs. Lane, giggles aside, she means what she says—every last word of it—so that the agenda for the rest of the evening and its ultimate goal are set inalterably. No doubt, of course, only to be repeated.

4
INTRODUCING THE SPEED SIX

THE BEGINNING OF THE WEEK proves hectic at Loban Motor. There are staff conferences, discussions with workers and a meeting for investors, as well as assemblies including members from all three circles. Of course, hovering over these sundry bubble groups is Percy Loban, the progenitor of Loban Motor, who encourages, admonishes and foments disputes, all while deferring important decisions.

In spite of this, however, there does emerge a measurable amount of progress. An itinerary is outlined. Even more astonishing, vital letters are composed and posted, as well as a few telegrams readied for the wires—proclamations of impending arrival. Understandably so, with Speed Six domination looming, the times are exciting at Loban Motor.

As for Axelrod Lane, he sees fit to take advantage of the confusion by working on his beloved roadster. Needless to say, for some time he's harbored a few pet modifications, some of which are coming to fruition. The roadster's wheels are now 34" in diameter instead of 31", and are mounted with the more appropriate tires, all discovered in Loban Motor's basement inventory. In addition, there is Axe's own sparking device, this allowing the driver to ignite the carbide headlamps without leaving his seat. Yet the most prideful of his modifications is applied to the troublesome carburetor, a concerted tinkering and toying which by his best calculations has gained an extra horse. Finally, after a few other engineering triumphs, Axe sees fit to pander to his artistic urges. Now, the roadster's crimson body is highlighted by linear and curved, yellow outlines, thus giving its sound foundations a further, undeniable allure.

Under Axe's care the roadster is becoming a beauty beyond workability, this achieved because Mr. Loban and Freddy are too involved with other matters. Truly there is but one who should share the glory, a significant other whose appreciations are both genuine and unwavering.

It's a familiar country lane, part of a recent racing circuit no longer being put to that specific use. The roadster glides along gracefully, avoiding the potholes with ease and gleaming proudly in its spit and polish. Indeed, a person would be hard-pressed to find any signs of the Speed Six's mishap only a few days prior. And oh, how the automobile responds with its larger wheels and carburetor modifications, these manifest changes bringing much joy to its driver.

But then there are the conclusions of the roadster's passenger, whose sensitivities are just as aware. On this occasion, however, the drive is a leisurely one.

"A pleasing sound and a smoother ride," Katie notes, her eyes closed blissfully and her head tilted back.

"Interesting." With that Axe brings the roadster to a gentle stop within a handy, secluded glade, leaving the engine to idle. "What do you hear, now, Katie?" His suspicions are that "E" at the bottom of the treble clef is an out-of-date gauge.

"Hmm?" Her eyes remain closed. "Definitely a 'G'."

Axe nods in agreement. "Then my carburetor doctorage has changed our tune. From here on out, Old Girl, we'll sing a song of 'G'."

"I'll remember that."

To say the least, it is a sublime moment. Looking about, to make sure of no lurking witnesses, Axe plays upon a pent urge—or a devilish notion—nudging closer to his wife, who still leans back. Make no doubt, it's Katie's soft, exposed neck that is the initial target of his ambitions.

"Mmm," she groans in a defenseless response to his seductive pecks.

Certainly, Axe knows his wife's weaknesses, as he continues to explore her tender neck and cheek. "Katie?" he mutters, as he clasps his right hand.

"What?" she purrs.

"Let's do it. Now."

"Oh, Axe." But her protest is mild. "For shame."

"I don't care," he continues with his soft voice. "No one will notice."

"Ah-h-h. If you say so, Axe. Ah-h-h." Thus Katie's surrender is complete.

"Good," he replies. Yet abruptly, Axe pulls away, his change in tone indicating a move toward a different sort of passion. "Katie. Let's switch seats."

"Pardon?" She pops open her confused eyes, focusing them upon her husband's open and fervent face.

“I’m saying, let’s trade seats. I want to see if you can drive the roadster.”

“What? Me drive?” Admirably, Katie does her best to gather herself. “Axe, that’s foolishness.”

With good reason she issues her protest, for never could a dainty woman be expected to handle the steering wheel, pedals and hand devices of a rampaging, six-cylinder automobile.

Then again, it cannot be denied that certain urges within Katie have been alerted, which, of course, must be allowed to find their release. Perhaps a few jerks and jolts upon an extremely short stretch of road will help her find a sufficient amount of gratification.

“Do you really think, Axe?”

“Absolutely,” he answers. Expediently, Axe leaps from his seat and races around the roadster.

“Axe!”

Quickly, he stands at her side and with a firm nudge begins to lay claim to the passenger seat.

“Are you sure, Axe?” Tilted toward the right side of the roadster, it seems Katie has no choice in the matter. “All right, Axe. You don’t have to push any further.”

Although the driver’s seat is identical to the passenger’s, it is encompassed by an array of gadgets and mechanisms, meaning that it takes a moment for Katie to settle herself. Ever so slightly, she hikes up her skirt and tucks under the excess folds, thus assuring that the foot pedals are within view. Giving a swift brush to her hair and adjusting her coat and hat, Katie even straightens her collar along with her red bow tie.

“Are you comfortable?” inquires Axe in a far too calmly manner.

Such a complicated question being posed at a complicated moment. At least this is how Katie feels, overwhelmed at being shoved behind the controls of an ultra-modern beast of a machine. She nestles further into her seat, while staring at far too many command devices and confusing gauges.

Before Katie reaches the point of becoming entranced, however, a genuine sense of familiarity takes hold. With the Speed Six’s engine vibrating throughout, she takes a reassuring breath, looking to the floorboard where her feet rest adjacent to three pedals. Indeed, it is much like a piano. And although there are no black and white keys above, there is the steering wheel, which Katie grasps in anticipation of a forthcoming melody of sharp twists, flat turns and natural straights. As far as the throttle and spark-control on the steering column and the handbrake and gearshift at her right side are concerned, the Lisbon’s

Methodist Episcopal's organ stops come to mind. Perhaps the Speed Six isn't such a complicated matter, reasons Katie. Sure, it may be sizeable and requires some muscle, but the roadster could be played with the same dexterity as with a musical instrument, perhaps capable of producing a similar harmonious air.

"Katie? If you don't want to drive, I understand. We can trade seats again."

"What?" Katie's concentration is broken. "Oh no, Axe. I want to drive." She returns her eager head forward and readjusts her grip at the wheel. "Yes. Tell me what to do."

Thus, while the mindful engine hums its "G", the lesson begins in earnest.

"Hmm? Now let me see?" As to how to teach the singular ways of the Speed Six, Axe's confusion may be just as ringing as his wife's. "Yes. The pedals. We should begin with the pedals."

"That sounds fine to me," agrees Katie, as she redirects her attention to the floorboard.

"You've watched me drive enough times. So you know what the pedals do."

"Somewhat," confirms Katie. "I think."

"Good. So. Firstly. Never push the middle pedal, unless we are at a complete stop. That moves the reverse gear. Step on it at a good speed and the transmission will strip."

"Oh dear." There's a trepidation in Katie's voice.

"You'll not stumble into that. You're too sure-footed, Katie. Though I can't say the same for Freddy." Axe shakes his head, as he muses aloud. "Kimble has yet to get over that episode."

"I'll be careful with the middle pedal. I promise."

"Then we can look at the left pedal, the gear pedal. L.M.'s idea of a clutch. Katie, you've seen how I push it slowly to the floor? And the roadster moves forward?"

"Yes."

"That way the gear engages without a jolt. If you push it too fast, you'll jolt the roadster."

"I'll be careful. For certain, Axe."

"Excellent. Now, see the right pedal, the transmission brake? When we need to stop, lift your left foot off the gear pedal to put the roadster into neutral. Then stomp your right foot upon the brake pedal."

"I see. Yes."

"There's the handbrake, which is set. See how it's pulled rearward?"

"Yes."

"And next to it is the gearshift, which I pushed forward to first gear."

"Yes."

"When you release the handbrake and gently push the left gear pedal, the roadster will move." Now, Axe reaches through the steering wheel and touches the throttle lever. "Nudge this forward and the roadster will gain speed. Then you take your left foot off the pedal and bring the gearshift to the middle, and step on the pedal again, and nudge the throttle more. The roadster will go a little faster."

"How fast?"

"Not too fast, Katie. Twenty miles. Even more. But if you then step off the pedal, move the gearshift all the way to the rear, step again and throttle up. Well, we can go above forty. Even fifty."

"Gracious."

"Don't worry. I'll make sure you stay in second gear." Axe's grin turns sly. "For now."

"Mercy."

Abruptly, Axe returns to the lesson. "Don't bother with the gauges. I'll watch them."

"Fine with me."

"Then we'll go over this once more?"

"Please do, Axe."

"We're on level ground, so you can release the brake. Pinch the handle firmly to let it spring forward."

Katie follows the directions—hesitantly at first, but successfully in the end.

Again, Axe goes over the procedures and protocols.

"…Are ready, Katie? Ready to push the left pedal?"

"I think so."

It's a moment of truth for Katie, to be in actual command of the Speed Six, as opposed to an interested spectator. Her heart surges, for it needs to beat a little faster if it's to pump enough blood and oxygen into her left foot. Cautiously, Katie guides the sole of her button shoe upon the pedal, and with a sure measure of might engages the first gear. The resulting force sends a tingle up her leg, continuing onward to parts better left unsaid. Yet it also powers the drive shaft, as well as the differential and rear wheels. The result is an undeniable forward lunge—slow and steady, yet powerful and responsive.

"Axe! We're moving!"

"All the way to the floor, Old Girl," responds his tutelage. "Easy does it, Katie. Make your way to the road and keep your eyes upon it."

Like a statue, she stiffens her resolve, with her eyes focused as directed and her grasp upon the wheel becoming even firmer.

Yet there comes a sort of relaxation by the whisking effects of ten miles per hour, the sensation of which cannot be felt from the passenger's seat. Indeed, driving the roadster becomes enjoyable, if not invigorating.

"Mind that turn," warns Axe of an approaching complication. "Move toward the right."

Suddenly, Katie's stomach churns, as her interval of joy takes an unexpected turn. And much to her chagrin, it arrives all too soon—this unforeseeable snag to her moment's triumph.

"You're doing fine," are the encouraging words.

As it happens, it isn't the sharpest bend in the road. In fact, it's quite minor. Nevertheless, Kate tackles the turn with every bit of determination, putting not only the strength of her hands and arms into the task, but the weight of her shoulders, as well.

"Magnificent, Old Girl. My goodness, you are a natural," notes her instructor, who, upon recognizing a straight stretch of the road ahead, offers a suggestion. "Let's shift to second."

She responds with a few acknowledging nods, her eyes not veering from the road.

And so the lesson continues upon the straights and curves of Columbiana County's dusty roads—at breakneck speeds of 25 m.p.h. Not unexpectedly, a smattering of bystanders is encountered, evenly divided between gawkers, shruggers and hat-tippers. Regardless, it's up to Axe to acknowledge the citizens, and to fret over what they may think and what their tongues might wag. As it happens, Katie is much too busy for any of that, she commanding under foot and within hand what to her is the finest roadster in America.

"Do you think you've driven enough?"

"Pardon? What did you say, Axe?"

"Are you getting tired, Katie?"

"Heavens no."

A number of uneventful miles are accumulated, the beautiful Ohio scenery appreciated by one and ignored by another. To be sure, the Speed Six, along with its driver and passenger, may be content to continue the pace for hours on end. Unfortunately, Axe takes a casual glance at his watch, and becomes alerted to the quick reckoning of elapsed time.

"Katie. We need to slow down," he announces, reaching to tap back the throttle. "Step off the pedal and let it roll to a stop."

"Why, Axe? What is the problem?"

"We need to switch seats and return to Lisbon. I have a meeting with Mr. Loban and you have to play piano at Mr. Brown's shop. Remember?"

"Oh," replies Katie, as she lifts her left foot. "For his customers. I forgot."

"Though who's to say we can't repeat this process later today? And tomorrow?"

"Wonderful, Axe. Wonderful."

Before the roadster completes its stop, Axe races around to occupy the driver's seat, which just as briskly is abandoned by Katie. Immediately, his right foot pushes the middle, reverse pedal, thus beginning the return to Lisbon. In no time, the succession of gears shifts to third and Axe has the roadster accelerating above 40 m.p.h.—without the benefit of a windscreen.

Yet beyond pressing appointments, the urge to rush does have a greater significance. Too soon, the moment to depart Lisbon will arrive, meaning that too soon the days of preparation will come to an end.

The sun lights the eastern horizon, signaling an end to a week's worth of preparations. Carefully, the touring car has been loaded with the essentials of the road, but in a manner not cluttering the Speed Six's tasteful lines and inspiring curves, nor spoiling the emerald green paintwork. And although personal effects and spare parts take up the lion's share, it is a large satchel which houses the salesman's most vital elements: portfolios of Willis Clapsaddle's drafts and drawings, and tinted photographs from Mr. Gorsuch's studio.

There's not much point for fanfare, the need being to get an early, uncomplicated start for the journey ahead. Parked in front of Loban Motor, the idling touring car has Flugan making minor adjustments to its engine. Meanwhile, Axe stands at the ready, listening to the farewell wisdoms of Mr. Loban, absorbing a few of his boss's words, though deflecting most.

"Don't forget the importance of Cleveland," reminds Mr. Loban. "I don't care what must be done to bring Foster Chagrin back into the fold. Flattery, blackmail, physical threats. Damn it, Lane, use simple logic if all else fails. Put your college testimonial to use."

"Simple logic," echoes Freddy. "Be bully for Loban Motor."

"Thank you, Freddy," reacts his annoyed captain. "Lane. Retaining Chagrin's established dealership is preferable. But failing that, find me the next best thing. We must be represented in Cleveland."

"I understand fully, Mr. Loban. It's win Cleveland or fall on my sword."

"Well, I wouldn't take that road. Just be successful." Mr. Loban looks toward Axe's partner, who is securing the engine hood. "See after my college boy. And don't park my touring car by those seedy neighborhoods. And their saloons."

"We won't, Mr. Loban," assures a forthright Flugan, while hopping into the passenger seat.

"We'll guard the Speed Six's virtue with our lives," assures Axe, he taking the wheel.

"Very good." Mr. Loban leans closer. "Don't forget to wire me. I want to know of your daily progress."

"We need to set the production date," adds Freddy to the urgency.

Axe releases the handbrake and presses the gear pedal. "Tomorrow, Mr. Loban. Freddy. By God, I would set that production date for tomorrow," he assures. "Damn it. Begin today."

Without so much as a wave or a nod, Axe taps the throttle and steers the touring car toward Lisbon itself.

Thus the tour for business and promotion begins, the hopes and sakes of owner, investors and employees strapped upon the shoulders of an assistant engineer and a chief mechanic. But as the Speed Six glides upon the streets of Lisbon proper—before the initial leg of northern Ohio and those slivers of Pennsylvania—Axe has in mind a tiny diversion. Since, for the moment, he's the driver, Hugh Flugan has little say.

As Axe comes to an imminent stop, he toots the horn. And before he's able to jump out of the Speed Six, Katie rushes out of the front door of their house. What ensues is a farewell embrace, this being an identical repeat of the early morning's goodbye.

"I should be back in less than two weeks."

"I know, Axe."

"And there will be a message for you in our telegrams. Daily."

"I know."

"And…"

Eventually, the Lanes pry themselves apart, so that Axe rediscovers the wheel and creeps away the touring car. And because his kind offer to Flugan for a fond farewell to his wife of twenty years is declined, the two are irrevocably on their way northward. That is, until Axe spots a familiar figure at the edge of Lisbon.

"Hey, horse's ass," he shouts, as he slows and then matches the pace the

Speed Six to the amble of one Jimmy Swift. "Where are you going?"

"School, if it's any of your business."

"Really? Hmm?' The Speed Six sputters and Axe leans from his seat. "How would you like to earn a dollar, Jimmy?"

"A dollar? What do I have to do, Axe?" is the immediate reply.

"Just look in on Mrs. Lane, while I'm gone. For a week or so. Do some chores, if she asks."

"Is that all?"

"Sure, Jimmy. When I return and Mrs. Lane has good things to say about you, then I'll give you a dollar. Two, if you really work hard for her."

"Wow."

"Then, what do you say?"

"It's a deal, Axe. You betcha."

"Good. Then I'll see you, Jimmy." But before Axe trips the throttle, he sees fit to add a few final words. "One more thing."

"What is it, Axe?"

"If you're going to school, you're walking the wrong way. It's that direction. Turn around."

To which Jimmy shrugs and smirks, as he's left behind in the dust.

There is no greater truth than a sweet sorrow's parting, especially when the party in question is Axelrod and Katherine Lane. Yet as the assistant engineer shifts gears in order to put some distance between himself and his loving bride, he knows that in a few days' time the now widening gap will find itself being shortened. Only Axe's patience and endurance should be tested.

Nevertheless, as he and Flugan leave behind Lisbon, another separation comes into play. Certainly, when Axe returns to Katie, she will be the same as when he left. But can the same be said of the roadster, which waits under canvas on the factory's basement floor? Indeed, will his brilliant and furtive modifications be left unmolested during his absence? Perhaps Axe should have explained his actions before leaving Lisbon? Then again, he reasons, there are plenty of other worries looming ahead. Better to take on those and forget the concerns lying within the bowels of Loban Motor, to be fixed or restored at some future date, if need be.

Unquestionably, the frets and fears of an individual matter little in the grand scheme of things. More so than the others, Ohio is the middle state—of industry and transportation—thus the need for an automobile manufacturer to conquer it all. Throughout its lands there are concentrations of gas, oil and coal, and of rich agriculture. Yet just as important, Ohio is bounded and traversed by an overwhelming combination of great lakes, great railroads, canals and navigable rivers, not to mention a slowly expanding web of semi-serviceable roads. Meanwhile, thanks to the late Senator John Sherman and his trust-busting ways, the competition of industry is fierce and fair, if not confusing or chaotic. What a fray into which Loban Motor is re-entering, and what a fray into which it is flexing its muscles.

"Which road do we take?" queries Axe, concerning a countryside fork.

"Don't remember, for sure," replies a shrugging Flugan. "Take that one and we'll see soon enough."

What Axe and Flugan have known all along, is that unlike the railroads, there is no workable system of highways connecting the cities. Quite the contrary, in that any automobile seeking a far-reaching and specific destination is left to its own devices. Yet the Speed Six's masters are resourceful, if not prepared. From a borrowed map, Axe has devised a feasible route, which for all practical purposes is a list of the small towns, tiny communities and forgettable place names linking the significant centers of population. Although many of the roads promise to be poor and deplorable, with the aid of a compass and local advice, they can be defeated. Thus it's on to Youngstown, to reconfirm and bolster commitments amidst the blast furnaces and Bessemer converters and that city's agitated sky.

Shockingly, the two emissaries of Loban Motor reach the industrial center of the Mahoning River Valley within the span of three hours. Yet there comes no surprise from the welcome of Arthur Grimble, the Youngstown dealer and unwavering enthusiast of the Fury Four. Now, with his re-acquaintanceship to Axe and Flugan, and an on-hand confirmation of Loban Motor's latest creation, he'll have a six-cylinder automobile to peddle, giving him a certain edge over the competition.

And so, because of Youngstown's friendly and uncomplicated welcome, Axe and Flugan return to that filigree confusion of country roads.

The journey proceeds as planned, with a few flat tires and needed adjustments to the carburetor providing further obstacles. Between Youngstown and Sharon, Pennsylvania, Axe and Flugan become lost only on four occasions and are able each time to rediscover their itinerary. In addition, the pair need only once to bathe the fouled spark plugs in kerosene. So far, so good for the touring car, and so far, so good for its occupants, especially since Axe's ears are given a hotel room of their own for the night—away from Hugh Flugan's notoriously uproarious snoring.

Thus refreshed and restored, Axe, Flugan and the Speed Six make an early morning return to the road. As it happens, they're entering virgin territory for Loban Motors—the upper valley of Pennsylvania's Allegheny River. Yet how appropriate it seems and how opportunistic it begs to make an inroad into Franklin—this city at the heart of the oil industry—where the combustible blood is refined and from where it flows.

Unfortunately, for two strangers from Ohio, Franklin is a hectic and confusing place, with the booming influxes of commerce vying to establish themselves in this established town. Still, Axe and Flugan are up to the task, to make a thorough search of Franklin.

"…That it is Mr. Swan," leads Axe through the demonstration. "The springs are configured precisely to offer a steadier ride. Very astute of you. But of course, you are a fellow Ohioan."

Indeed, a dealer impressed is a dealer gained, never mind that the man in question is something of an upstart when it comes to automobiles. With an exchange of handshakes, as well as promotional documents and company guidelines for Mr. Swan's assurances, the deal is struck. Thus a frontier market is penetrated, and Axe and Flugan are free to race toward Meadville and those important cities beyond.

The roads between Franklin and Meadville are sound enough, but as the Loban pair discover, the bridge over Sugar Creek isn't. Thus an alternate route must be divined, and yet another when the Warden Run span appears to be an even more doubtful proposition. And then there's Woodcock Creek and its crossing of weak timbers and rusting nails, which at first glance and by further scrutiny appears to be the riskiest of all…

Ultimately, the route to Erie brings lesser perils, though this Great Lake city is proving to be all the more frustrating. What pans out almost immediately is that Erie, Pennsylvania is a city held under the sway of Buffalo, New York. Yet just as bitter to Axe, is that the citizens' automotive tastes are equally enthralled with Detroit—along with cravings toward Cleveland. What awful tastes they must have, he concludes, incapable of appreciating the toothsome fare of Lisbon, Ohio.

"Damn them. Damn that hoakum town and their willy-nilly dealers," notes Axe from the passenger seat. He takes a final, over-the-shoulder look at Erie, now well to the rear. "A waste of time, that contagion town. Damn me, if I ever return."

To which Flugan agrees with his silent nods, while he drives the Speed Six "I sure hope they don't have the same damnable people in Ashtabula," remarks Axe, as he looks forward. "Let's get the hell out of here, Hugh. Back to Ohio, where we belong."

As luck would have it, the roads paralleling Lake Erie are sure ones, and the return of assistant engineer and chief mechanic to their home state occurs without mishap.

The end of day four finds them in Ashtabula, affording the pair just enough time to rush through their appointment. But as to what sort of impression the Speed Six makes upon Mr. Johns, Axe cannot say? Not once does the Ashtabula dealer's mouth smile or frown, nor does his head offer a shake or a nod.

"You just think about it, Mr. Johns," bids Axe, he being lost of patience and eager to locate a dinner. "We'll be at the Hotel Ashtabula. But at any rate, Loban Motor will keep in touch."

As for Mr. Johns' side of the farewell, he contributes nothing but a handshake.

"Did you see him blink?" inquires Axe, when he retakes his driver's seat and waits for Flugan to crank the Speed Six's engine.

"Once or twice, I believe."

"Then Johns isn't a statue. Though he had me fooled.

The engine turns over and Flugan finds the passenger's seat. "Well, you won't say the same of Foster Chagrin. That's for certain."

"I, for one, am looking forward to that encounter." Axe puts his foot on the gear pedal and nudges the throttle. "We'll make him see the light. Cleveland is too important, so we'll not take 'no' for an answer. I really don't want to explain to Mr. Loban our failure in Cleveland." Axe shifts to second. "What do you say, Hugh, that we conquer that town? Show no mercy?"

"If you say so, Axe."

"And when we're done with Cleveland, I'll buy you a pint of rye to celebrate. You can drink it down, while I do the driving."

"I'll hold you to it, Axe," grins Flugan. "By God, I'll ring Chagrin's neck if he keeps me from that bottle."

"Good man, Hugh Flugan," affirms Axe. "We'll win Cleveland and have a grand time."

It's a drizzly, early morning when the duo begins their fifty-mile drive to

Cleveland. Yet by the time they reach the outskirts of the city, the clouds part their way in lieu of a blue sky. Unfortunately, three hours of muddy roads have made a mess of the touring car, the only solution being a sound and thorough scrubbing.

"It'll be ready in an hour," responds the owner of a garage to an urgent request. "Six bits will do it."

"Excellent," replies Axe, who turns to his cohort. "We'll have the time to make ourselves presentable."

Flugan nods in agreement.

"Do you mind if we use your back room, Mr. Vincenti?"

"Not at all, sir. But it might not suit you two. Crammed and greasy. But feel free to use the alleyway."

Axe looks to Flugan, and then shrugs his shoulders. "Okay."

Soon, a spotless Speed Six returns to the streets of Cleveland, heading for the Huron Road address of Foster Chagrin's Automotive Sales.

"We're going to be early," notes Flugan, as he glances at his watch.

"We'll go at any rate," replies Axe from behind the wheel. "And if Chagrin is there, then we'll feel free to impose ourselves. If he isn't, then we'll wait and fume, and gather our resolve."

As it plays, Chagrin isn't at home, that is to say his place of business. And so the wait for the Loban pair, the duration being unknown. But at least Foster Chagrin's dealership does come with a view, the lobby being enveloped with promotional material: posters, photographs and framed paintings.

"Chagrin seems to be interested in every automobile known to man," observes Axe with touches of both sarcasm and uneasiness. "I hope he still has room for us."

As he gazes at the wall's artwork, Flugan expresses his doubts with a few head shakes.

"Exactly," agrees Axe.

Too soon, however, does their wait become prolonged, with the lobby's adornments losing the power to fascinate. Thus the inclination for the pair to leave the comforts of their chairs and sidle their way through and throughout Chagin's busy enterprise.

"If anyone asks, tell them their boss encouraged us to look around," whispers Axe.

Indeed, they do have a look—nonchalantly at first, but soon with some purpose. And the more Axe and Flugan snoop, the more they realize that Foster

Chagrin is the proprietor of a first-rate facility: from its exterior of intricately patterned brickwork, to its interiors of plush furniture and ornate lighting, and to Chagrin's capacious, extravagant and unoccupied office.

"Look there, Hugh," notes Axe of a wall adorned with framed photographs. "The grand mansions of Cleveland. Euclid Avenue, I do believe."

"Our Chagrin must have some grand designs for himself."

"Indeed, he does, Hugh. Hmm?"

As Axe thinks further, he's coming to the conclusion that Chagrin's motivations may not be as advertised. In fact, he may own little in common with the confused progressive that is Percy Loban, carrying instead the ambitions of a Rockefeller Baptist or even a Social Darwinist—two faiths which follow different paths toward the same results.

"I hope he's vulnerable to persuasion."

Before long, the pair migrate elsewhere, exiting the office toward the all-important car park itself. And there they await, automobiles of sundry manufacture posing in neat rows beneath three-sided garages, the protective structures, themselves, appearing sound enough to withstand the worst of Lake Erie's wintry gales.

"Must be four dozen of them," observes Axe.

"Umm."

Like two eager buyers striving to cloak their appetites, they step forward for a closer scrutiny.

"Oldsmobiles, Hugh. I wonder of the rumor they're going to six cylinders?"

Almost casually, Flugan opens a hood. "No. Still four."

"Disappointing," mocks Axe's disdain, before continuing the car park rummage.

"What do you make of that, Axe? I'll wager it's French. Look at the doodads."

Axe leans ahead and reads the signature upon the vehicle's radiator grill. "Lion Peugeot. French, all right. And by the looks of it, this auto has the immodest and impractical design that comes with that nationality. Hugh, gander at the luxuries. The seating alone must require ninety man-hours."

"At least," agrees Flugan. "And this sizeable auto is powered by a pitiful one-cylinder."

"Really?"

"Look for yourself."

Upon confirming Flugan's shocking allegation, Axe scratches his head. "I would be pressed to coax twenty miles out of this tortoise. My God, the French.

But I wonder? When we meet Chagrin, will he be wearing spats and wanting to kiss our cheeks?"

The pair moves on, and after spending a few minutes with the British Napiers, the Dutch Minervas and a Belgian F.N., there can be but a simple conclusion.

"Mr. and Mrs. Chagrin must have done the grand tour of the fads of Europe," smirks Axe. "And by the looks, returned hoping that one of these pompous manure wagons will catch the public's fascination."

"Good luck with that notion," furthers Flugan.

The diversion of the foreign makes comes to a quick end, however, when Ramblers and Franklins are encountered, more vehicles to captivate Axe's low opinions. Yet even these familiar competitors have less of a hold for the curious, if only because the machines are parked next to a couple of stark reminders of home.

"Look there, Hugh. At the far end.

Quickly, Axe and Flugan bee a line toward twin Fury Fours.

Although the '06s are nearly a part of Loban innovation history, as far as Axe is concerned, they're sound automobiles, enough to guarantee their assembly for a bit—in spite of the Speed Sixes' coming.

"God, I love this crimson red," he reaffirms. "I hope we keep it."

As for Flugan, he scrutinizes even closer, as if he's trying to single out a particular example from a two-year production run of about 800 Fury Fours.

"I remember this one," he announces with pride, his fingers stroking the dashboard composed of beech. "See the dents. The wood shop wasn't too exact with this one. Had to pry and hammer it into place."

"Hmm? Then that might explain the dents in that door of our Speed Six," deduces Axe. "I say the sooner those doors go metal, the better they will slam shut."

"More metal, less creaking and groaning," adds Flugan.

The two might mingle with the Fury Fours for hours on end. But time and timeliness mean everything, and to have Foster Chagrin return from his affairs to a lobby empty of his Loban appointment will not do.

"Maybe we should return inside," suggests Axe. "How awkward if Chagrin caught us prying about."

As luck would have it, no sooner that the Loban pair reacquaint themselves to the comforts of the lobby, then the front entry door whisks open, followed by brisk and confident footsteps. For Axe, there can be no mistake as to whom wears the spat-less shoes in question.

"Mr. Chagrin?" he greets, as he rises with an outstretched hand. "Axelrod Lane of Loban Motor. Pleased to make your acquaintance, sir."

"I'm honored, as well," returns Chagrin from his cigar-stoked, mustachioed grin. He shakes Axe's hand. "Loban has spoken of you." And then Chagrin turns to Flugan. "You must be his chief mechanic? Flugan?"

"Yessir."

"Gentlemen, I hope you haven't been waiting long."

"Not in the least," replies Axe. "We were only beginning to enjoy the surroundings. Yes, a proud establishment, Mr. Chagrin."

"Why, thank you, Mr. Lane," beams Chagrin. "Perhaps you two would like a tour. See what we offer?"

"Splendid, Mr. Chagrin," feigns Axe.

As Chagrin takes a step, he reveals that his substantial frame has concealed immediately behind a much slighter person. "Gentlemen, this is Horton Short," comes the brief introduction. "Very well. This way."

Thus it's another meander through Chagrin's Automotive Sales, disagreeably repetitive as far as Axe is concerned, albeit vital as an aid to persuasion and negotiation.

First, the office area is given its due, and then comes the fully-equipped mechanic's garage, this followed by a ponderous walk through the car park. All the while, Chagrin serves as a convivial host, while reigning as the unswayable man in charge.

"...We at Chagrin's Automotive are proud of our European associations," he crows. "So far, they appear to be promising."

"Very promising," echoes Short.

"Though the Ramblers remain our best sellers."

"That seems interesting, Mr. Chagrin. But say, are those the last of your Fury Fours?" inquires Axe, his way of diverting attention back to Loban Motor.

"Hmm?"

"These are the only two in inventory," interrupts Short. "But we expect delivery of eight on Tuesday, to complete our contract with Loban Motor. Mr. Chagrin?"

"Uh, yes, Horton. You are correct."

Perhaps Short's assertion should be taken as a slap. Yet Axe is much too quick to accept such a blow.

"Well, of course. Chagrin's Automotive doesn't distribute commercial vehicles," he expounds, while ignoring a perplexed Flugan. "Which is the future of the Fury Four. Delivery vans, open-bed trucks, dual-usage vehicles, funeral hearses, military service and the like. Loban Motor from this day on is concerting its efforts for the public by way of our innovative and powerful Speed Sixes."

"Really? So the new automobile is into production?"

"Yes." Again, Axe ignores Flugan's face. "Would you like to see one? We're parked on the side street."

Although the tour is brought to an abrupt end by Axe's adept hand, Chagrin doesn't appear to be bothered. "By all means, show the way."

Soon, the group approaches Loban Motor's latest, it being Axe's turn to master the ceremony.

"Mr. Chagrin," announces the calm and confident assistant engineer. "This is a touring car version of our Speed Six. My apologies for not bringing a roadster."

Without any urging, Flugan rushes to open the hood, thus revealing the six-cylinder engine.

"Hmm? I must say, this is a cut above the Fury Four. En bloc." It seems that Chagrin's initial reaction is favorable. "More impressive than the drawings sent to me."

The response from Axe is to explain the features of the Speed Six, and to gauge the facial expressions of Chagrin—and even those of Short.

"...And yes, Mr. Chagrin, we have made liberal use of vanadium steel. For the sake of strength without the compromise of added weight. Only a few token parts are of wood."

"Such as?" asks Short.

"Well, of course, the dash, fenders, spokes. And there are the doors." As he speaks, Axe's hopes are that Chagrin and his assistant don't run across any dents. "Little else."

"Hmm?" replies Chagrin, as he scrutinizes the touring car with a careful eye.

This may be a crucial moment, figures Axe, one requiring immediate action. "Mr. Chagrin. Would you care for a drive? Ply the streets of this great city?" As it happens, Axe is positioned to offer the door-less, front passenger seat. "Make yourself comfortable, Mr. Chagrin."

The engine purrs when it's cranked over.

"Here that?" notes Axe, when the passengers shut the rear doors. "A perfect and careful fit."

Before long, the Speed Six is on its way—with Axe at the wheel and Chagrin by his side, and with Flugan and Short upon the rear seats. Already, much has been spoken concerning the virtues of the '08, including information regarding costs and profit margins, along with a promise of reducing the former and widening the latter. Could it be, thinks Axe with his eyes upon the street, that the moment begs for a more aggressive approach? After all, Cleveland is swarming with wildly-misguided and poorly-applied automotive designs. Why not take a full share of pot-shots at such engineering ineptitude?

"Will you look at that, Hugh Flugan." Excitedly, Axe glances back at the rear seat. "Parked there, the three P's. A Pierce, a Peerless and a Packard. Some coincidence."

Regardless, Axe knows better. That because the Pierces are produced in not-too-distant Buffalo, the Peerlesses being home-grown and the Packards hailing from Detroit, though formerly of Warren, Ohio, seeing these vehicles within the same city block is not at all noteworthy.

"And fine automobiles they are, Mr. Chagrin," continues Axe. "Premium autos for certain. Though it will be a cinch for our own quality Speed Sixes to underbid them. Give them a run for their money." Axe steers and boasts without batting an eye.

"Hmm?" considers Mr. Chagrin.

The blocks accumulate more fodder for Axe's attacks, especially those makes of Cleveland manufacture. "A brand new Winton, I see. Not even up to par with our '06s." This followed quickly by a sighting of the bizarre. "Can you believe it? A White? Steam-powered? That contraption belongs on the rails, and not the fair streets of Cleveland. Don't you agree, Mr. Chagrin?"

"Oh, I do, Mr. Lane. I'll never deal in the non-gasoline."

"Good man, sir," encourages Axe. "A vision of my own sentiments."

But even as these words spill off of his lips, another Cleveland product comes into view. This time, however, Axe counts on a little support, that the moment is ripe to unleash a bitter former employee.

"Is that a Baker, I see?" Axe raises his voice for all to hear. "Electric automobiles? How interesting."

"Interesting?" interrupts a timely Flugan. "Interesting to a child looking for a Christmas toy. Or a gelded man with no pride. Why, I'm of a mind to leap from my seat and slash that Baker's tires."

"Easy now, Hugh Flugan." Axe wears a look of embarrassment. "But our Mr. Flugan may have a point, Mr. Chagrin. That we not of the castrata nature should avoid machinery of no true vision. Like the Bakers, and like far too many other makes."

"I agree, Mr. Lane. As I mentioned before, nothing but gasoline for me," nods Mr. Chagrin, after which he glances rearward. "You have every right to be outraged, Mr. Flugan."

"Exactly, Mr. Chagrin," adds Short.

A sly grin creases Axe's face, its construction rising from a sound foundation. But he realizes that a new diversion should be taken, that too soon the subject of downtown automotive infestations is sure to repeat.

"Is this the way to Euclid Avenue?" inquires Axe, as he makes the turn toward a suspected weakness.

"Why yes," replies Cleveland's most exuberant citizen.

"Good. I've heard so much about that neighborhood, and I'm dying to see it."

"Wonderful, Mr. Lane. And you will not be disappointed, let me assure."

Indeed, Axe isn't displeased when he and the Speed Six's passengers enter into Cleveland's most esteemed neighborhood: an unrestrained pageantry of thick, granite turrets and their conical roofs, of multiple, skyward chimneys and of extravagant Greek columns and massive Roman arches. To be sure, a millionaire's row of mansions they are, though palaces they could be were it not for the absence of nobility. Nevertheless, these are the environs of Cleveland's ruling elite, where ways are concocted to enrich riches, skirt regulations and secure positions of power for untalented offspring—in other words, aping the behavior of noble bloods.

Fortunately, and in spite of the confused senses coming with Euclid's grandeur, Axe is able to keep to the subject of automobiles, if only because his view becomes interrupted by one particular object.

"A Silver Ghost?" he mutters to himself, whereupon he takes his astounded, left foot off the pedal and allows the Speed Six to coast. "A Rolls Royce?" marvels Axe at the spectral vision.

"Pardon me, Mr. Lane. Did you say something?" asks Chagrin.

"Oh. Mr. Chagrin. I'm admiring that Silver Ghost. What a magnificent brute."

"Yes, indeed," replies Chagrin. "It belongs to Ambrose Swasey."

"And a determined man he must be. That Silver Ghost may be the only such sample in the entire country."

"Quite probable." Likely, Chagrin's nonchalant reply is owed to frequent encounters.

"Why, Mr. Chagrin, I believe my wife and I could take up residence in such a monstrosity. That is were it not for the awful difficulty in ordering spare parts. Yes. This is why we use standard bolts, nuts, studs, etc. To make repairs with few complications."

The tour of Cleveland's grandest neighborhood continues, with Chagrin spouting out a notable name for each passing address, while a disciplined Axe maintains a keen look. But suddenly, a careless squirrel scampers across and the driver reacts instinctively. The resulting jolt pauses the Cleveland native's babble and re-invokes Axe's design.

"You know, Mr. Chagrin. I believe you would be a perfect fit for Euclid. And if not already, a frequent guest to its functions. Dare I say-y-y." Axe's flattery fades a bit.

"You were saying?" Apparently, a vulnerable Chagrin lacks a certain immunity.

"Well, Mr. Chagrin. My hunch is that because of your devotion to industry and your innate abilities for business, you and Mrs. Chagrin will someday become a member of this remarkable community."

The response is an immediate ear-to-ear smile and a bobbing head. "Thank you, Mr. Lane."

"You're welcome, sir. And might I say, Mrs. Lane and I look forward to an invitation for your first Euclid gala. Whenever the season and for whatever the excuse."

There can be little doubt that Axe's effort to recapture Chagrin into the Loban fold is having some success. Yet also, he grasps that no agreement has been made, let alone a contract signed.

"Once again, my apologies, Mr. Chagrin, that we didn't bring the Speed Six roadster. Especially since our ambitions for it are even greater than this touring car."

"Really? Mr. Lane, you make it sound as if the two versions are entirely different models," notes Chagrin.

"Different bodies. Two seats with a rear rumble, and, of course, no doors. But they do have the same frame and engine. Though the roadster does have a modified carburetor, with a different needle valve and adjuster, and throttle valve, and chamber float, and air inlet. Oh, and larger wheels, allowing for more speed. Fifty-five miles." Yet another occasion for Axe to ignore an uninformed Flugan.

"Fifty-five, you say?"

"Yes, Mr. Chagrin. And we should get more horses once we a-fix another one of my patents to the carburetor. That is a patent pending." This boast comes in spite of Axe having yet to begin the paperwork.

"Sounds impressive."

"Impressive, indeed, Mr. Chagrin." Apparently, Short is gaining the same interest.

"I'll tell you, Mr. Chagrin," continues Axe in an almost dreamy-eyed fashion. "There's nothing like tearing the countryside in a roadster responding to command." And then he offers a sly grin. "Or on a Euclid Avenue, for that matter."

The touring car's occupants chuckle in unison, even Flugan, who shakes his head all the same.

"Yes, Mr. Chagrin. I can't wait to get you down to Lisbon and demonstrate first hand. What a time we will have. Why, I've established my own circuit of county roads, which I use regularly to race against myself. Pushing the roadster is my passion."

To be sure, Axe's zeal for the sleeker version of the Speed Six is undeniable, if not downright infectious to those who are otherwise perfectly sound of health.

"It is a pity you couldn't bring your roadster," nods Chagrin.

"Ah. One moment, Mr. Chagrin." Quickly, Axe reacts. "Mr. Flugan. Could you hand us a portfolio?"

"Certainly."

Before he can realize, the Cleveland dealer has a portfolio placed upon his lap.

"These are more design drawings of the roadster and the touring car. And there are some photographs." Axe keeps one eye on the road and the other on Chagrin, who thumbs his way through the portfolio. "The latest of the roadster is the tinted photograph. That one in red."

The photograph in question is of the roadster with a smiling and confident Katie behind its wheel.

"I must say, this is a captivating, uh-h-h, automobile."

"Why, thank you, Mr. Chagrin," replies Axe.

"I see you employed the talents of a local beauty. Very nice."

"Oh, no, Mr. Chagrin. We hired no one. The lady in question is Mrs. Lane. My wife."

"Oh? You have to pardon me, Mr. Lane," offers a slightly ruffled Chagrin. "Please, take no offense."

"Offense, Mr. Chagrin? Hardly. But you may find it interesting that Mrs. Lane is not merely posing. That she does, in fact, drive the roadster." By now, Axe's immunity to Flugan's bewildered looks is utter.

"Drive, you say?"

"Yes, upon the roads of Columbiana County."

"Remarkable, Mr. Lane. Although not unlike Alice Roosevelt, some would say."

"Alice Roosevelt, for certain, Mr. Chagrin," repeats Short of the President's daughter's name.

"Alice Roosevelt? Hmm?" mulls Axe. "Why, in some circles, Mr. Chagrin, that might be taken as a brilliant observation. Alice Roosevelt? Yes."

Indeed, as Axe thinks further, he concludes that Chagrin has nothing to do with Social Darwinism or the Rockefeller Baptists, and is but a simple Republican progressive. If this is the case, then the ease at which he can be manipulated is no mistake, that Chagrin's faith is his weakness—like Percy Loban.

"It is?" considers Brother Chagrin. "I suppose it is."

"Yes. The new Loban roadster's weight and power can be manipulated by a woman," advances Axe. "For those households where the wife has any say, this is a sellable point. A distinct advantage over those other manufacturers. Though Alice Roosevelt may not have many admirers in Cleveland, there still must be..."

"Oh no, Mr. Lane," interrupts Chagrin. "The lady in question does have her share of admirers."

"Does she? How interesting. That from an engineer's view, Loban Motor's efforts have been spot on."

As far as Axe is concerned, the deal is done, that Chagrin's Automotive Sales is returning to its prominent position beneath the Loban Motor umbrella. Only the particular numbers and figures remain in the air.

The drive continues, the route reversed toward the direction of Huron Road. Yet in spite of the triumphs in hand, and while Chagrin's nose is buried in the Loban Motor portfolio, Axe can't help himself when his appalled eyes encounter more examples of automotive incompetency.

"...A Stearn, can you believe? Very costly. But with a double chain drive. Primitive. Tsk, tsk....And a Schadt? From Cincinnati? Hardly more than a lily-frail horse buggy....Take a look at that Thomas Flyer. Another double chain. Sixty miles per hour?"

Eventually, the entourage returns to Chagrin's Automotive, with its dealer remaining engrossed by the contents of the satchel. A decision is pending, it being obvious that a spur-of-the-moment tussle with hard facts and matters of money is flooding Chagrin's head.

As he kills the engine, Axe knows better than to push the process, that perhaps Chagrin may need all the time in the world. But then suddenly—and just as quickly—a slight bobbing of the head reveals that the decision is made, one leaning toward Loban Motor's favor.

"May I keep this?" asks Chagrin of the portfolio.

"Of course, Mr. Chagrin," insists Axe.

"Excellent."

A pause ensues—slight, although lengthy if only because of the anticipation. "Mr. Lane. Tell Percy Loban, I'll visit Lisbon next week. Wednesday or Thursday. Tell him we'll continue our association." Chagrin takes a breath. "I want to sell the Speed Six. Immediately." And then his eyes leave the portfolio and look toward Axe. "Assemble me a hundred. Thirty of the touring car and seventy of the roadster. Make sure Percy grasps my commitment, and that he moves aside all other orders."

"I will, Mr. Chagrin. Of course." Axe's enthusiasm bursts at its seams, although he does manage enough calm to reach out and shake hands. "Congratulations, Mr. Chagrin. And might I say, Mrs. Lane and I look forward to your first Euclid Avenue affair."

Thus ends the culmination of the Speed Six's grand tour of northwestern Pennsylvania and northern Ohio, for nothing can better Foster Chagrin's decision to favor Loban Motor. Soon, the representatives of one business and the proprietor of another are able to part company, there being much work ahead. The first item on Axe and Flugan's revised agenda is to locate a telegraph office and send a message to Lisbon of the momentous news. Unfortunately, the wait for the return wire proves to be an intolerable hour. Yet when it does arrive, the response from Loban Motor is unequivocal: Axe and Flugan's presence in Lisbon is required, forthwith, that their appointments to those other dealers are being cancelled. At last, the production of the Speed Six is beginning without delay.

Although the day is waning, the two men in question waste no time to point the Speed Six southward. First things are first, however, and that is for Axe to make good on a promise by purchasing a pint of celebration. As for his fortified companion, before the pair leave the wondrous environs of Cleveland, he, too, in his special way keeps a vow made a few hours prior.

"I can't believe you slashed the tires of that Baker. All four of them?" questions Axe, who remains incredulous at the vandalistic act. Yet in spite of the lingering shock, he retains enough good sense that compels him to flee Cuyahoga County. "Damn it, Hugh. What the hell were you thinking?" Nevertheless, because he does own a grudging admiration for bold action, Axe manages an inner grin.

Flugan is a bibulous drinker, this Axe knows, so that there's not much to fear—aside from an overtaxed stomach and, of course, further encounters with Baker Electric. And so when the boundary of Summit County is breeched, he's able to relax both the throttle and himself.

Certainly, there's plenty of justification for congratulating himself, that his encyclopedic knowledge of automobiles and the concerted ease of its application were able to return Foster Chagrin into the light. Indeed, the future of Loban Motor, itself, is looking brighter.

"We surely had that Chagrin dangling from our fingers. Didn't we, Hugh?" boasts Axe, whose streaks of modesty compels him to share the glory.

"I'll say," responds Flugan, who celebrates with yet another nip of his rye. "But it was purely genius to have those photographs made. Especially of your Katie. Yes, indeedy. Loban Motor owes a substantial debt to that little lady of yours. Heh, heh."

An honest assessment coming from the many truths within a bottle. As Axe stares at the road ahead, he thinks further, of how the culmination of his stage-managed efforts toward Chagrin was crowned by Katie's sudden appearance.

"You're right, Hugh. We do owe her. Me especially." Smiling, Axe mumbles to himself. "Old Girl."

Although his head may be inflated, his heart begins to sink with those rekindled feelings of separation. Axe leans closer to the wheel and nudges the throttle, determined to narrow the distance as much as he dares.

And so presses the evening, with the ensuing loss of light forcing the pair to spark the headlamps and ignite the lanterns. It seems that the want to find safe accommodations for the night is losing its impetus. But as well it should, what with Hugh happy with his rye and Axe determined to accumulate the miles. To be sure, the darkened roads to Akron are proving to be fair, and because Axe is familiar with the route between Canton and Lisbon means that home may be achieved before the following noon.

"Hugh. We should pull to the side and make a fire for my coffee pot. Hugh?"

Axe sees that his cohort is fast asleep. He shakes his head in amusement, although understanding of how vital that pot of coffee just might be. Yet before Axe can slow the Speed Six, an unexpected jolt and a crunching sound give way to a sudden loss of power. His stomach sickens at this complication, for instantly he realizes the problem and of the implication that the return to Lisbon will have to wait for another day.

"What?" asks Flugan, his unperturbed sleep disrupted by the loss of the road's rhythm. "Where are we?"

"God knows," answers Axe. "God knows where, with a broken drive shaft. Uh-h-h-h."

5
OPPORTUNITY AND PRACTICALITY

Life continues elsewhere, as it has been all along. Word has reached Lisbon of the Speed Six's predicament, that its triumphant reappearance is to be delayed. And although this may not be much of a complication to Loban Motor, for a wife whose anticipations have been piqued with the promise of her husband's early return, a certain frustration must be given its due.

The Saturday morning finds Katie walking home after spending a pre-noon hour shopping for essentials. And although one arm carries a package from the butcher, the other is allowed to dangle free, for the young Mrs. Lane is accompanied by a dutiful escort.

"When's Axe coming home?" asks Jimmy Swift, who totes a bundle of groceries.

"Oh, that's hard to say. They broke down near Akron, so I've been told," answers Katie. "Ugh."

"Gosh, Mrs. Lane. That's too bad," continues Jimmy. "But I bet Axe will fix the problem soon enough. For sure, there's no one with a keener head as his."

"Positively, Jimmy. Axe and Mr. Flugan may have the touring car back on the road as we speak."

"I sure hope so, Mrs. Lane. Axe has been gone too long." But then Jimmy pauses, as if pondering over his next question. "Say, Mrs. Lane? Do you miss Axe much?"

"Of course, Jimmy. From the moment he left."

"That's funny. Because you're sure not like my mother."

"Oh?"

"When Paps leaves home, Mother is her most happiest. And the longer he's away, the happier she gets."

"Really? Well, I suppose that happens sometimes."

"Not with you and Axe, Mrs. Lane. You two could never be like that."

"Thank you, Jimmy," responds Katie, to what can be taken only as an honest assessment. "You know, I baked a pound cake this morning. How would you like a piece?"

"Would I ever, Mrs. Lane. And I wouldn't be surprised if my stomach has enough room for two."

"Goodness, you sound like Axe." Katie smiles at Jimmy's natural audacity. "Very well. Two pieces it is."

All too soon, Jimmy finishes his cake and excuses himself, bounding for parts unknown. And as if by some pre-arranged progression, when Katie is left alone, the clock begins to unwind more slowly. The tedium of household chores offers no immediate remedy, however, instead serving to concentrate and lengthen her worries over Axe. Indeed, mopping the kitchen floor and beating the rugs afford a perfect match to her forlorn thoughts of separation.

"If only I could be certain to cook a dinner for two," whispers Katie, as her hands clasp her pouting face.

Nevertheless, it should be noted that Katherine Marie Lane is not a woman who pines for long. Certainly, there are alternatives to these mind-numbing, hour-stretching duties of the household. Unfortunately, Katie has satisfied her shopping needs for the foreseeable future, and for some inexplicable reason her usually reliable violin offers no temptation. She could amuse herself at the nickelodeon, but to do so without her husband seems a tad improper. Or perhaps Katie might take a stroll about the neighborhoods to drop in on friends and acquaintances, although to spread her present gloom may be something of a thoughtless act. Meanwhile, the amusing antics of Jimmy Swift are nowhere to be found.

Ah, but then there is that last and lasting resort, a patient pillar of faith which happens to be Katie's very own Methodist Episcopal Church.

"The organ," she exclaims.

Without her hat, Katie plunges through her front entry. And beyond the margins of her home, the five block march southward is taken at a blur, with none of the usual noteworthy structures of Lisbon receiving much notice. That is until a hasty Katie nears the corner of Washington and Market Streets.

Perhaps it is the grandest building in Lisbon, the Methodist Episcopal, outrivaling the other churches and even Columbiana County's proud courthouse. With its high, pointed tower, thick walls and arched windows, the Lanes' house of worship pays reverence to ancient times, while its red brick construction tells of the region's wondrous clay and its associated industry.

The sanctuary is empty and silent as Katie walks through the side entrance. And because enough natural light filters through the windows, she doesn't bother to locate the electrical switch. Truth to tell, the church's enduring interior exudes a sure comfort, while the beams of sunlight form a perfect guide toward the organ.

Katie accepts the directions, and in little more than an instant nestles into place. She pauses, to catch her breath and gather in the divine invention of musicality above and about her lap. Technically, it is a choir organ, one of the Barckhoff Company's more modest creations, meant to accompany rather than solo. But its voice comes via pipes instead of reeds, which themselves are governed by an impressive double row of keys.

"Hmm, where shall I begin?" mutters Katie, as she revs up the recently installed electric blower.

First things first, and that is to pull her favorite stop, the woodwind. This done, instinctively, Katie's gentle feet touch the bass pedals, the initial feeling being similar to those incremental demands of engaging the gears—and the opposite of a cautious reverse or an urgent transmission brake.

Instinctively, Katie ignores a convenient, Wesley hymnal, instead relying upon her own recollections, whatever this may be. To her surprise, when the fingers of her right hand peck at the keys, a genuine tune emerges, it having the tones of something Mendelssohn. But just as quickly, Katie's heart recalls a title, the "Wedding March", this being the very same piece performed on violin at her own nuptials.

"Mmm."

Katie's left hand joins in with some accompanying chords, while her voice delivers a trill. With a misplaced note, the "Wedding March" proves to be a superb aid for a marital reminiscence verses the void for a stranded husband.

Deservedly so, Katie loses herself into her musical gifts and wants, giving Mendelssohn and her memories a round. Yet before she edges toward a different challenge—musically, or otherwise—her senses detect the rush of a door, thus bringing her effort upon the organ to a halt.

Certainly, there can be little doubt that into the sanctuary enters an interloper of sorts, though this one comes with good cause.

"There you are, Katie. I've found you."

"Axe!" To which Katie pivots upon her seat and faces her interruption.

In mere seconds Axe shortens the distance and lifts Katie into a tight embrace.

"You're home, Axe," she moans, as much as her smothered face allows. "You're home."

No longer does the Barckhoff organ hold any interest, and as soon as the Lanes are able to gather themselves, the blower is switched off.

"I still have the car," announces Axe. "Let's take it home."

To which, arm in arm, the couple march down the aisle toward the front entry of the church.

The light of day reveals to Katie that her husband is a little worse for wear, the time spent on the road and repairing the touring car being the blame. Yet as far as she's concerned, never has he seemed so handsome.

Like a true gentleman, Axe escorts his lady to the passenger side, after which he rushes around the idling Speed Six to reclaim the driver's seat.

"Home, sweet home."

Axe keeps his eyes upon Katie while he releases the handbrake and engages the gear pedal. Within the matter of a minute, he knows he'll be parking the Speed Six at a certain Pine Street address and, immediately thereafter, will carry his bride across the threshold.

As for Katie, she resumes her hold of Axe's left elbow and brushes her cheek into his shoulder. And although her heart races with expectation, the overall feeling within is a sure calm, a genuine comfort coming from a separation's downfall.

"Home, sweet home, Axe."

It's into early evening, and the cellar plays host to the household's bathtub of hot, soapy water. At last, Axe's accumulated grime from both automobile and road is being removed. But the tub is crowded with an additional participant, so that each Lane has a devoted, face to face, wash attendant.

"…Cleveland was a dandy city, Katie."

"So I've heard."

"We'll have to make that journey together. In fact, I've put the wheels in motion for future invitations. Parties, social affairs and such." Axe speaks almost matter-of-factly.

"Really? From whom?" asks Katie.

"Well, for a start, Foster Chagrin. He really was taken by the roadster, especially when I showed him that photograph of you behind the wheel."

"So the two of you became fast friends?"

"In time," replies Axe. "Once I reasoned Chagrin was a Loban Republican, I knew I had him."

"That was very astute of you," commends Katie—though with flakes of sarcasm. "By the way, Axe, to what political party are you, yourself, registered?"

"Uh? Oh, my political affiliation is somewhat casual, don't you know."

"The party, Old Boy?" Playfully, Katie presses for an answer.

"Uh-h-h, Republican?"

"Of course," continues Katie, as she shakes her head. "And do you remember why you made the choice?"

"Yes." Within Axe's recesses a bell rings. "To make Mr. Loban happy. Right?"

"It was Father, Axe."

He shrugs his shoulders at what to him is an insignificant matter. But then Axe's eyes are captured by a specific portion of Katie's exposed skin.

"Oops. I missed a spot," he notes, as he applies the wash cloth.

"Now how did that get there?" remarks Katie, who accepts the attention all the same.

Somewhere during mid-wash, Axe's impoverished stomach growls for consideration. As best he can, he ignores the needs and favors his wants, savoring his sublime situation and the titillating vision it beholds. But the alimentary commotion persists, so much so that soon it draws the concerns of another.

"Axe, you must be starving. Poor thing. Let me find something."

By sure increments, the Lanes rinse and towel themselves, and even manage a certain degree of modesty by the use of their night robes. This done, Katie sees fit to prepare a dinner of ham and cabbage, et. al., her furious pace set by the lovely lilt of her singing voice.

"Oh, how I missed your cooking," observes Axe, while he sits at the table, his senses becoming overwhelmed. "Among other things, of course."

Soon, that one remaining hunger will be squelched—or stuffed—and the Lanes should be able to settle into a deep repose. Thankfully, no longer will either Katie or Axe have to suffer a night in a half-empty bed, nor awaken to a lonely dawn.

To say the least, that morning is proving to be a late one. More precisely, the burgeoning light isn't being given a proper due by two of its progeny. Still, the Lanes have earned the right to a lazy sunrise, and so are pardonable if they choose to stay in bed.

"When is Mr. Loban expecting you?" moans a drowsy Katie.

"Don't know," is the even drowsier reply.

"Does he even realize you've returned to Lisbon?"

"Sh-h-h."

Another ante meridiem hour elapses before the Lanes budge more than a few inches. Even then, it takes a few choice words from Katie to coax her husband out of their bower altogether.

"Axe, do you think that L.M. has started Speed Six production without you?"

Thus inspired, he's out of the house within twenty minutes, fully dressed and cranking the touring car's engine.

"Good luck with Mr. Loban!" bids Katie from the front porch.

"Thanks, Old Girl!" replies Axe, who frowns all the same.

Soon, after finding South Avenue, he has the factory within view. But as to which of its doors Axe should enter, he isn't quite certain, that is until the words "Speed Six production" return to mind. Upon entering the grounds of Loban Motor, Axe steers the touring car toward the assembly floor side entry. As far as he's concerned, unpacking the load of spare parts and tires can wait, as will his meeting with Percy Loban.

It's a different sort of clamor greeting Axe's ears as he enters the building. To the uninitiated, noise may very well be nothing but. Yet to Loban Motor's assistant engineer, the music of Fury Four assemblage is not being played at this moment. At first, Axe's eyes meet the face of a stranger, no doubt an employee hired only days prior. But then his heart skips a beat when he spots a propped up steel frame, the first step in assembling an automobile. Quickly, he sees another, as well as a few bodies and six-cylinder engines.

"Welcome back, Axe," greets Robert Irish, while he readies a hoist.

"So Mr. Loban has begun production?" responds Axe, keeping his dazzled scour upon the room.

"I'll say. He and Brothers are both in a tizzy."

In reality, Axe had expected such. But to bear witness to the actual event is a different matter, the rising sense of excitement being undeniable.

Yet the feeling within may not be containable when Axe scans the room to its far end. And there it awaits—an almost completely assembled Speed Six roadster—its frame propped up not on carpenter horses, but by its very own wheels. Axe wastes no time and breezes a path through the first floor. And although well short of his target, his eyes are able to discern that, indeed, the wheels are not to the prescribed diameter, but are of his own preference—34 inches!

"I don't believe it," mutters Axe of the pleasant surprise.

Still, what has become of his other surreptitious modifications, he mulls? And so begins a frantic search of the roadster for those additional ingenious innovations, the foremost being his alterations to the carburetor.

"They kept my changes," marvels Axe of a discovery, as he looks toward a bolt-tightening George Hiscox. "How do you like that, G.H.? Mr. Loban favors my changes."

"If you say so, Axe," shrugs Hiscox. "But he was sure in a lather the day you and Flugan left town. After Freddy found the finished roadster and what you had done to it."

Axe's response is a shrug of his own. "That's hardly a worry. Wouldn't you say, G.H.?"

In truth, Axe may have a point. For although clandestine invention is difficult to keep at Loban Motor, he's discovering that the need to conceal may be losing its motives. Indeed, that Mr. Loban, along with his underlings, has chosen to retain the unauthorized modifications is the greatest of compliments for "college boy"—a landside vote of confidence. And because this sort of notion can prosper, shortly Axe may burst his way into his employer's office and make known more demands.

On the other hand, the few steps it takes to exit the assembly room can offer enough space to give pause. And the exertion required to ascend the stairway will sap away portions of determination. As Axe enters the office area, his heart feels an ever-so-slight change.

"Good morning, Mr. Loban. My apologies for being late," offers Axe, as he walks into his employer's office. "And I hope you're not displeased with my improvements to the roadster."

A stern Mr. Loban sits behind his desk, with his devoted Freddy attending. But also present are Kimble Lepper and Willis Clapsaddle, and of course, Miss Charnwood. Instantly, Axe takes note of Hugh Flugan's absence, who, undoubtedly, is helping to strengthen the inventory of engines in the machine shop. But more so, the assistant engineer realizes that he's outnumbered, as all eyes are directed upon him.

Surprisingly, the look on Mr. Loban's face alters to one of perplexity.

"Improvements?" asks Mr. Loban through a pinched face. "Why should I be bothered by improvements? That's why I hired you. You and your sheepskin."

"Oh?" Axe gathers a breath. "So then, Mr. Loban, you like my modifications?"

"Of course. And quite possibly for the touring car. Especially the carburetor improvements. Kimble, here, is particularly impressed."

"Yes, I am, Axe," concurs Lepper.

Before Axe's eyes and ears, the good news divined by himself on the assembly room floor is confirmed. Or at least this is what he would like to believe, were it not for a tincture of disapproval in Mr. Loban's voice.

"Indeed." Not to mention the expression etched upon his face.

"I almost forgot," continues Axe. "By my calculations, the touring car made 81.3 miles per pint of oil."

"Is that so?" In spite of what should be taken as a positive, Mr. Loban offers a sure lack of enthusiasm.

This, in turn, compels Axe to prattle even more. "Mr. Loban, we did as you suggested, and gave demonstration rides to persons likely interested. Dozens upon dozens. Even to a few gentlemen who were waiting for street cars. Oh, and we spoke to a number of newspapers."

Not only is Freddy mimicking his employer's response, but as Axe is beginning to notice, so too are the others in the room.

"We had quite a few punctures, of course. But the engine performed admirably. Hugh and I had to fiddle with it only occasionally."

The less than positive response persists, which itself seems to edge toward the downright negative. Thus cornered, Axe gathers himself.

"Mr. Loban. This is all good news, I would think. But something seems wrong." Axe pauses, only to follow with an irrevocable step forward. "What is it?"

Rest assured, this could be taken as a provocation, which is Axe's intent—somewhat.

And it seems that Mr. Loban is accepting it as such, his readable mood loosening ever so slightly. "Lane, I appreciate the wonderful news. That you and Flugan performed your task is what I've come to expect. Bu-u-t?" Mr. Loban creases his brow.

"Yes-s-s."

"There is this concern, Lane, which I find distracting." Perhaps Mr. Loban is being diplomatic.

"I don't understand, sir."

"Then I'll make it plain. We've been in contact with Foster Chagrin, as you may surmise."

"Of course, Mr. Loban."

"And he was flowing with compliments of your character," continues Mr. Loban.

"Yes, he was," agrees Freddy.

"Achem," reacts Mr. Loban. "But he did, Lane, inform us of a matter. A matter concerning your wife."

"Katie?"

"Yes. Katie," answers Mr. Loban, who extends his open palms in ready for a question. "Have you been allowing Katie to drive my roadster? Behind my back?"

"Well-l-l." Although Axe hesitates, the guilt upon his face is tantamount to a confession. "Mr. Loban, 'behind my back' is an awfully strong way to put it. It's not that I've been sneaking around with my wife."

Though unintentional, Axe's odd phrasing brings a slight pause to Mr. Loban's admonishment.

"You should have sought my permission."

"But Mr. Loban. You are a busy man. Besides, I am the test driver, and teaching Katie is part of the test."

"What test is this?" asks Freddy. "I've seen nothing."

"Nothing sanctioned, of course. All part of my devise, Freddy. But I have been taking care of the roadster, Mr. Loban," insists Axe.

"Yes, so I've seen," responds his smirking employer. "Nevertheless, the matter before us is Katie and my Speed Six. An action I find somewhat disturbing."

Yet another strong word, "disturbing", coming from Mr. Loban. If Axe wants to keep his employer mollified, then he had better tread cagily.

"'Disturbing', Mr. Loban? Do you really mean that? After what Foster Chagrin should have told you? Or what he certainly told Hugh and myself."

"Chagrin informed me of everything related to our association," declares Mr. Loban. But then a look of doubt wears upon his face. "What did he tell you, Lane?"

"The reasons behind his change of heart. For Loban Motor and especially the roadster."

"Yes. That." Now Mr. Loban seems a little confused. "Which was?"

"That he plans to promote the roadster to female drivers as well as male." As if to accent his assertion, Axe whirls his hands. "Mr. Loban." And then he rests his arms. "Mr. Chagrin wasn't terribly eager. It was a complicated sell. That is up to the point when-n-n."

"When what?"

"Yes. When what?" comes the echo.

"When he saw the photograph of Katie behind the wheel of the roadster."

"Photograph? Do you know of a photograph, Freddy?"

"No, Mr. Loban."

"Mr. Loban," continues Axe. "I had the photograph made. And Chagrin was quite taken by it. Which led to his idea of promoting the Speed Six with women in mind."

"Women? Drive? Balderdash."

"Mr. Loban, I witnessed quite a few female drivers in Cleveland," recalls Axe with a nod to exaggeration. "And their numbers are sure to grow."

"That may be, Lane. But I would hardly call grasping a tiller while sitting atop a one-cylinder buggy driving. Does Chagrin really expect women to control a powerful and complicated Speed Six?"

"But Mr. Loban. One such woman does just that. Remember?"

"Remember? Achem. Yes."

Axe pauses in order to allow Mr. Loban to recall the point of contention—from only a few seconds prior.

"Mr. Loban. I thought we established the fact that Katie drives the roadster?"

"Have we now? Well? It is, after all, quite a handful of automobile." Incredibly, Mr. Loban's mood has altered from the objectionable to the doubtful.

To be sure, this brings no small measure of confusion upon Axe. It seems that instead of defending Katie's abilities behind the wheel, now he must prove them.

"Very well, Mr. Loban. Then I suppose a demonstration is in order. And the sooner you're convinced, the sooner we can build Mr. Chagrin his roadsters."

"Just what do you have in mind, Lane?"

"Meet me down at the front entry, sir. If you don't mind."

Abruptly, Axe steps away, thus making further objections from his employer less of an option. Still, there does arise one minor complication to a hasty withdrawal.

"Freddy?" Axe stops in mid-stride and poses a question. "Where can I find the roadster?"

"It's parked in the washing shed. Why?"

"Fine, Freddy. Then I'll see you, Mr. Loban, in a minute or two."

Soon, Axe locates the roadster and cranks the engine. Yet the brief time it takes to drive to the front of Loban Motor does nothing to wither his resolve. To the contrary, for as far as Axe is concerned, Katie's honor and abilities are being impugned, this slight being the same as if applied against himself—or worse. Indeed, Mr. Loban needs to be set straight, and if his "college boy" has to be rude and insistent, then so be it.

Yet while the engine idles, Axe discovers he's being forced to sit and wait—no doubt a Percy Loban ploy. It's all the assistant engineer can do to maintain his composure and keep cool his temper.

"Calm yourself, Old Boy. Stay calm." It's almost as if Katie is the whisperer, herself.

In a nick of time, the subject in question emerges, ably accompanied by Freddy.

"Mr. Loban, I hope you're not cross with my brusque behavior." Admirably, Axe eases toward the conciliatory.

"Nonsense, Lane. You are, what you are. Just as I am, what I am," notes Mr. Loban, as he slips into the passenger seat. "Still, I am curious. Though this better be worth my time."

Meanwhile, Freddy climbs into the rumble seat.

"Then, sir," informs Axe. "We'll just have to see." He pushes the gear pedal and taps the throttle. "Hold on to your hats."

Quickly, Axe guides the roadster toward Pine Street, with only a couple of rolling stops to hinder the way. And before he can realize—or for that matter, his bewildered captives—he's setting the handbrake in front of his house. With hardly a hint of explanation, Axe leaps from his seat and rushes through the front door.

"Katie! Where are you!" Axe cannot contain his excitement, thus giving aid to a moment of confusion.

Fortunately, Mrs. Lane is a beacon of calm, her aproned-self ready to steady the situation. "Axe! Axe! What's happening! Why are you home!"

But upon seeing that his agitated state is spreading needlessly, wisely, Axe takes a deep breath, followed by a calming smile. "How would you like to take the roadster for a spin, Old Girl?"

"What? Now? Axe, I'm busy with housework." To say the least, Katie is roundly confused.

"Katie, this is important," pleads an open Axe. "I really need you. Please, put it aside?"

Instantly, Katie understands the gravity of his request—whatever the impetus. "Of course."

"That's my girl." Axe wastes no time. "Come. Let's go. Gather your hat and gloves."

"Okay, Axe." Quickly, Katie unties her apron.

In the meant time, he looks around. "Where are the goggles? We'll need the goggles."

When they exit their house and walk toward the roadster, Axe has Katie by the hand.

"Axe, are you up to what I think you are?" she asks, upon spying Mr. Loban and Freddy.

"Yes."

"Oh, my stars."

But when Mr. Loban sees both Katie and Axe approaching the roadster, he, too, airs his complaint. "Lane, you're not about to do what I think you are?"

Axe has no choice but to ignore the protest and surrender one pair of goggles. "Here you are, Mr. Loban." As for the other pair, they're given to Katie while she's helped into the driver's seat.

"See here, Lane."

Yet leave it to Katie to squelch this objection, she being quick to her seat. "Good morning, Mr. Loban," she greets with a captivating smile. "Such a delight to see you."

"Achem. Yes. Thank you, my dear."

"And in such a wonderful automobile."

Meanwhile, another matter needs to be addressed.

"Freddy." Axe squanders not a second. "Did the rear axle seem out of sorts to you?"

Eager to lend his expertise, the business manager leaps from the rumble seat to take a peek beneath the roadster's body. "Hmm? It looks fine enough to me."

"If you say so, Freddy," agrees Axe, who helps himself to the vacated seat. "Sorry, but I need to tag along." And then he leans forward to catch Katie's ear. "What do you say, Old Girl? That we try our old circuit? See if we can push passed fifty."

With her husband's plan of action thus delineated, Katie's eyes draw wide and her stomach churns. Yet like a counterbalance, her heart races—not so much from fear, but for the cause of exhilaration. While Katie grasps the steering wheel, stoically and be-goggled, she gazes ahead.

"Mr. Loban," notes Axe of the obvious. "You are in for a ride." And then he boasts. "There are few as skilled at operating the Speed Six as my Katie."

With his hands upon his wife's shoulders, Axe squeezes forth a little encouragement.

As for Mr. Loban, he would do wise to hold on tightly. And then there's Freddy, who is about to receive two lungs' worth of tire-induced dust.

Honk! Honk! Axe can't resist squeezing the bag.

To be sure, the moment is a truthful one, that it's vital for Katie to apply the pedals, gears and throttle as smoothly and effortlessly as possible. But as for steering the roadster, there's no denying that the use of brute muscle is in order. To the rhythm of an Irish polka trapped in her head, Katie proceeds, ignoring as best she can her passenger's folded arms and disapproving head.

"We'll return in a few minutes, Freddy!" assures an apologetic Axe.

As nervous as Katie may be, the streets are a sublime venue—straight and fairly empty of potential hazards. Thus she's able to concentrate on the matter at hand, of impressing Mr. Loban.

"How about a little more speed, Katie?" suggests Axe.

With that, she lets off the left pedal in order to shift to another gear, tapping the throttle. Soon, Katie finds herself steering the roadster across the Little Beaver bridge. And when Loban Motor, itself, looms, the fact that the countryside of Columbiana County lies just beyond is not lost. Deftly, Katie shifts to third.

Honk! Honk! Once again, Axe cannot help himself.

Thus continues the grand tour of parts south of Lisbon, a land familiar in every detail to either of the Lanes. The polka plays on, as does the Speed Six.

"Mr. Loban, I believe this is the smartest auto in all of Ohio! America, for that matter!" Axe's exuberance knows no bounds, as the drive begins to lengthen. "More throttle, Old Girl!"

Without hesitation, Katie and her expanding confidence comply. Indeed, she might run dry the roadster's fuel tank, especially after her leftward glances tell her that Mr. Loban is loosening his grip and, possibly, is losing his doubts. Thus the miles accumulate.

But, oh, how there looms an ideal hazard to rural navigation. To be sure, Katie's familiarity churns when she spies the bright green barn marking the approach of an unyielding bend. Yet she's quick to adjust, easing the throttle and reaffirming her grasp of the wheel.

But then there's Axe, who seems to have forgotten the incident of only a few weeks prior, and the ensuing pledge to end his reckless ways. "Don't slow down, Katie! Give it more gas!" Yet suddenly, Axe spots his nemesis. "Oh, my God!" Quite correctly, he leans into the severe bend.

Indeed, it may the sharpest of all road curves, so that Katie's belated caution may not be enough. Yet although her esophagus may be trying to strangle her rapid heart, at this instant, her resolve takes command. With gritted teeth, Katie employs her all and guides the Speed Six along the widest arc of the crude, narrow road. To be sure, this is a moment of truth, a partitioned second not allowing for even a smidgeon of error.

But timing and dexterity are everyday events in Katie's world, like playing Mendelssohn on a Barckhoff organ. And so it comes as no surprise when all four tires of the roadster remain within the confines of this devilish stretch—to the outer edge of the very last inch. Quickly, the road begins to straighten and Katie is able to catch her breath, thus giving her internal organs a chance to realign themselves. Be that as it may, an ensuing calm will have to wait, for her ears capture a loud disruption from her immediate rear.

"Katie! Stop!"

In reality, the command from on high comes as an added relief. Katie eases off the gear pedal and throttle, and applies the handbrake, thus slowing the Speed Six. Still, before she can ask for an explanation, her husband leaps from the rumble seat of the rolling roadster and jogs along the passenger's side.

"Axe!"

But "college boy's" wild-eyed head is impervious to his wife's protest. Instead, its focus centers upon Mr. Loban, the owner of the Speed Six roadster, whose normal ruddy complexion has turned somewhat pallid.

"Did you see that, Mr. Loban! Did you see how Katie conquered that impossible swerve! Why, I'd wager no professional racer could make such a skillful turn!"The Speed Six comes to a complete stop, and Axe gestures toward that part of the road already traveled. "Just look at the tire marks, Mr. Loban! Look how they took that swerve! A fierce work of art upon the road!"

Perhaps because he's catching his breath, Mr. Loban is able to look rearward. But then he touches the top of his uncovered head.

"My hat? Where's my hat?" exclaims Mr. Loban.

The engine chugs in neutral, as Katie awaits the next command,

Meanwhile, her husband congers his next words. "Mr. Loban, we'll find your hat. What is more important is that my Katie has just proved a point. Mine and Foster Chagrin's."

Incredibly, Mr. Loban seems unimpressed, as if an expendable Fedora holds a greater significance than the possible failure of a promising and expanding company. Could it be that more drastic action from Axe is in order, so that a vital point might be registered—something like a confession of sorts?

"Katie. Kill the engine." She complies, after which Axe steps toward the front of the silent roadster. "Listen to that, Mr. Loban," he speaks, as he raps the fender with his knuckles.

Apparently, his boss' attention is captured, for Mr. Loban replies with a confused shrug.

"Ash, Mr. Loban," details Axe. "Like on all the Fury Fours." But suddenly, he ceases his rapping and rushes around to the driver's side fender. "Hear the difference, Mr. Loban?" Again, Axe brings his knuckles into play. "We're using beech now. Not ash." He lets out a sigh. "Mr. Loban, I had to replace this fender, myself. After I had damaged it."

"Damage?" Mr. Loban loses his puzzled look.

Now, it's Katie's cue to turn pallid.

"Yes, Mr. Loban. When I had my mishap with this same curve. When I rolled the roadster on its side."

"You did what!" The vein on the side of Axe's employer's head begins to show.

"Mr. Loban. Let me assure you, it's not as severe as it sounds. The roadster took the punishment, and after a little repair, is as flawless as ever. Better, in fact, when it was first assembled." In no way, does Axe plead, although he keeps well short of the forceful.

Yet the manner of his approach must be having some effect on Mr. Loban, his shock from the revelation of his roadster's past abuse altering into a readable smirk.

"Mr. Loban, you are a witness—or better, a participant—of the Speed Six's special design allowing it to be guided by diverse drivers. Potential customers all."

Ever so slightly, Mr. Loban tilts his head.

"It is a simple fact that cannot be denied. My Katie, my female driver, took that lethal turn at the approximate speed where I had failed." Axe blinks for a second, blithe to omit his wife's prudent five mile-per-hour speed reduction. "Suffice to say, it requires an extraordinary female driver to handle the Speed Six. But the same could be said for the male drivers, Mr. Loban. I know of many who I would not trust behind this wheel. And I'd wager, you do too."

"Perhaps." That Mr. Loban doesn't hesitate with his reply is a good sign.

"Frankly, those people are not deserving of the Speed Six, and will have to be satisfied with Olds and Ford and Pierce, or those pell-mell European contrivances."

Her hands remaining at the steering wheel, Katie's heart is all a-flutter with Axe's persuasive words, these being not that far-removed from the sweet talk of their courtship. And it's no surprise when her husband places his hands upon hers.

"Yes, indeed," continues Axe, as he looks into his wife's goggled, but sedated, eyes. "There are quite a number of Katie Lanes about, waiting for a Speed Six. And there are plenty of Axelrod Lanes and Percy Lobans, who appreciate a quality machine and its fair price."

An undeniable nod rolls off Mr. Loban's head, followed by more in a slight, rocking motion.

"Well, Mr. Loban? Have you seen enough? Should we not return to Lisbon and prepare for Foster Chagrin's visit? And more of his kind, I should think?"

"Yes, Lane. There's much work to be done."

Thus with this grudging approval, Axe lets out a sigh of relief. To be sure, it is a triumph, one undertaken with some risk—a familiar pattern for Axe. He refills his lungs with a blast of fresh air, and then releases himself from Katie to grasp the starter crank.

"Home, Old Girl. Take us home, if you please."

In due time, the three reach "home", that is to say Loban Motor's front entrance.

"A most enlightening drive, Katie. In spite of your husband's antics. Thank you, my dear."

But while Axe is quick to leap out of his seat, with Mr. Loban following suit, Katie is at a loss as she sits behind the wheel. After all, there remains that fourth member of the party.

"What should I do? Axe? Mr. Loban? What about Freddy?"

The two gentlemen look at one another. It seems that during the excitement, Freddy Brothers' stranding has become a forgotten matter.

"If you don't mind," suggests Mr. Loban. "We should ask our female driver to take the roadster to Freddy? It's not a bother, is it, Katie?"

"Of course not, Mr. Loban," she replies with some surprise. "I'll take it to him, immediately."

And so another endorsement is heaped upon the Lanes' roster of successes.

"I'll see you this evening, Katie," imparts Axe with a wave, as he and Mr. Loban step away.

As it happens, almost capriciously, a heady responsibility is forced upon Katie, she feeling the weight's impact. That she would be allowed to drive alone Mr. Loban's roadster is an utterly unforeseen turn. As far as Katie is concerned, all eyes are upon her, with no choice to ponder and no chance to protest. Thankfully, the urge for her left foot to ease upon its pedal arrives, while her right hand returns a wave goodbye.

"Have a nice day," bids Katie, thus showing the backside of the roadster to its caretaker and its patron.

But before the two former passengers move to enter the building, they stand and watch their remarkable vehicle and its precious driver.

"She really has no problem with the Speed Six," observes Mr. Loban. "Remarkable."

"Yes sir. Although, I do admit Katie's musical abilities have simplified her adjustments to the Speed Six. But I believe, Mr. Loban, a tone deaf woman with no rhythm in the least could be taught to operate that auto. Why, I'd wager that I could teach your Aunt Lucie. That's how well-designed is our Speed Six."

Perhaps Axe is reaching too far, for the immediate reply from Mr. Loban is a stern look.

"See here, college boy. You're not to sneak behind my back with my Aunt Lucie. Understand? She's to remain a passenger. Though I do grasp your point

"Yes, Mr. Loban. But I really do see the Speed Six as a practicality for our customers. And an opportunity for Loban Motor."

"Hmm? Opportunity and practicality? I like the sound. Write that down. We may use it."

"Yes, sir. I will."

6
EAST LEADS WEST

Needless to say, work at Loban Motor is moving briskly, the increased production coming from both new machinery and recent employees, and those established counterparts. But then there occurs the appearance of Foster Chagrin, coincided by a prolonged visit of the like-minded dealer from Columbus, and all the hoopla these combined events involve.

Thus the long, exhausting hours expended by Loban Motor's assistant engineer—the fixer of too many pickles. And thus the patience being forced upon said employee's wife, whose late night meals and time spent alone are becoming matters of routine.

"Ugh, I thought Peck Williams would never leave Lisbon. That he was abandoning Columbus to set up shop here," remarks Axe, as he settles himself into bed directly from the dinner table.

"Are all the agents so peculiar?" joins Katie, she having finished in the kitchen.

"Absolutely. Without fail," affirms Axe. "They are middlemen. Wanting to be part of industry, but lacking the talent to screw nut to bolt." He offers a smirk. "So instead, they sell."

"I suppose that's how commerce works. Finding ways to raise the costs the public must bear." Katie delivers her own version of a smirk. "There must be a better way."

"Careful now, or you'll sound like a radical," amuses Axe, as he spreads apart the covers.

"I'll remember that," returns Katie, as she joins her husband's side. "Comrade."

The following dawn finds Axe pedaling his way to Loban Motor and its undesignated bicycle hideaway. But on this day, he's earlier than usual, meaning that the night watchman is the only employee present.

"Morning, Mr. Lane. My, you done beat everybody here."

"Morning, Clarence. How was your night?"

"Oh, pretty much like the others. How 'bout you?"

"Uneventful, I suppose. Say, is the steam up?"

"Oh, I got the boiler stoked good. Generator's ready, iffin' you want to start the machinery."

"Thank you, Clarence. I just might take you up on that."

There is that new machine, acquired for the purpose of making Speed Six valve stems and other, less specific parts. That Axe isn't an expert doesn't disturb him all that much. But that he is a rank amateur does. And so the want to find the middle ground, this requiring a little practice. Indeed, Axe could lose himself for hours on end, that is if he could afford the time.

Eventually, he makes that valve stem, one which might pass inspection. But the temptation to give it another try is thwarted by a call to duty. Yet another staff meeting is scheduled for the early morning, with Axe's pocket watch telling him that he has but ten minutes to prepare himself.

"Good morning, Mr. Loban."

There's a mild surprise when Axe enters the office and finds only his employer and Freddy present.

"There he is. Our superb engineer." Mr. Loban's arm stretches his invitation. "Come, Axelrod. Have a seat. Freddy, pour our man a cup of coffee and offer him a wedge of Aunt Lucie's mincemeat pie."

"Beg your pardon, Mr. Loban?" For Axe, what may be fairly astonishing is his employer's initial approach, that his tone contains no hints of the usual self-assured or supercilious.

In response, Mr. Loban's relaxes even more. "Heh, heh. Let's sit, Axelrod. We need to discuss a few things." Apparently, Axe's puzzled face is readable.

"Several things," repeats Freddy with coffee pot in hand.

"I see," replies a cautious Axe, as he takes the chair in front of Mr. Loban's desk. "To what do I owe the pleasure?" Indeed, the smell of conspiracy taints the air. "No sugar or cream, Freddy. I'll have it black."

"Very good, Axelrod," resumes Mr. Loban. "So have you and Kimble finished with the carburetor?"

"Mr. Loban, they've been tested and are in production. And we switched out the older ones."

Axe knows full well that this is common knowledge, that Mr. Loban has been apprised. To be sure, the reason behind such a meaningless question is to create an opening for what owns a greater relevance.

"Yes. Of course. Kimble had mentioned this the other day."

Calmly, Axe focuses upon Mr. Loban's twiddling eyes.

"So Axelrod, how is your wonderful Katie?"

"Katie remains wonderful, sir. Thank you." Although she may be Axe's favorite topic, he's becoming weary of Mr. Loban's sidled approach. "How did you find Foster Chagrin's visit? And Peck Williams'?"

"Ah, yes. Foster Chagrin," beams Mr. Loban. "Suffice to say, his visit was a resounding success. As was Peck's. No small thanks to you and that wonderful Katie."

"That is wonderful, Mr. Loban." Instead of yawning, Axe takes a sip of black coffee.

"Yes, it is, Axelrod."

"Exactly, Mr. Loban," joins Freddy, as he stirs the cream and sugar of his own cup.

"Yes, gentlemen. And for surely, the opportunities being vested upon Loban Motor are golden. All because of the practicalities of our innovations. Yet there remains that question of promotion." At last, Mr. Loban may be getting to the crux of the matter. "And it's of this subject I have been discussing with Mr. Snodgrass, among others, the consensus being that we should have a firm handle publicity and promotion."

"We already have narrowed it down to two," notes Freddy. "Both have contacts with Horseless Age and the Saturday Evening Post, and others.

"What this means, Axelrod, is that no longer will you and Flugan tour the cities of established and potential dealers."

This is good news for Axe, that no more will he endure separations from Katie. Nevertheless, he realizes that such information can be delivered without the ceremony of coffee and mincemeat pie. Certainly, there must be something more consequential on the agenda.

"And likely you understand," continues Mr. Loban. "Competitive racing is far too costly for Loban Motor. We won't involve ourselves with that enterprise."

As if on cue, Freddy nods several times.

And because he's polite, Axe does the same.

"Of course, the impetus behind competitive racing is for a manufacturer to demonstrate his creations," furthers Mr. Loban. "It all comes down to news. We need to be the news on the minds of the public. Or to be precise, Loban

Motor needs to be in the newspapers, written about in as many as possible."

"I see." Axe's nods become more genuine. "And I believe you have a plan, Mr. Loban."

"Yes, I do, Axelrod." Mr. Loban tilts his head and raises his brow. "Suffice to say, news can be manipulated. Damn it, the newspapers do it for the sake of circulation. Who's to say that Loban Motor cannot the same? Manipulate the news and increase circulation?"

Axe stills his head and begins to salivate. He knows a grand design when he smells one. Indeed, Mr. Loban's point concerning newspapers is almost verbatim of what Axe had remarked to Freddy a month prior.

"You've seen the attention that New York to Paris race is drawing, Axelrod?"

"Yes, Mr. Loban. But as far as I'm concerned, it's all a farce. None of those autos can hold a candle to our Speed Six. Not even the Thomas Flyer."

"Interesting that you would call it a 'farce'," acknowledges Mr. Loban. "This particular 'farce' being a manipulation of the news by a particular newspaper—the sponsor of the race."

"Hmm?" considers Axe."

"But I see no purpose to judge the Times. Or any of their sort. Business is business, after all." Mr. Loban offers a shrug. "Loban Motor, too, is a business. Nothing more."

"Mr. Loban. I disagree." Axe shakes his head. "Newspapers come and go, and are at the mercy of their weak-minded, unscrupulous proprietors, and their fickle readers. But we are the vanguard of a new industry. Capable of moving a country."

"Precisely, Axelrod!" Apparently, the feeling is catching, and Mr. Loban cannot contain his enthusiasm. "A country to be crossed by Axelrod Lane! Crossed in the Speed Six with those newspapers at your heels!"

"Pardon?" Much like negotiating the backroads of Ohio, Axe is baffled by this unexpected disclosure.

"I want you to drive across the country in the roadster," repeats Mr. Loban.

"Coast to coast," affirms Freddy.

This is stunning news to Axe, there being no previous hint of its arrival. And that it comes from mutual sources, each using different phrases, means that there's no ambiguity. Indeed, there seems to be a plot of sorts, it sending Loban Motor's assistant engineer on a lasting journey and an intolerable separation from Katie. No wonder Mr. Loban and Freddy are behaving strangely, realizes Axe.

"Drive from coast to coast?" arises the question from his wide-open, doubtful face. "That's a very tall order, if not overly impossible."

Certainly, Axe isn't understating the facts, that for all practical purposes only the railroads can navigate across the country from coast to coast. But Mr. Loban's determined look, ably backed by Freddy's, tells him that no wishful thought is being aired nor a tasteless joke played.

"Mr. Loban, you can't be serious."

"Of course, I'm serious, Axelrod. And the feat has been achieved by a number of intrepid autoists. With the fanfare that could prove a wonderful opportunity to Loban Motor. Opportunity and practicality."

Axe's own words are being thrown at him, a sure sign that a coast to coast scheme is genuine, with Mr. Loban allowing little wiggle room for his assistant engineer. To be sure, a forced separation from Katie may be impending, its duration dwarfing the likes of promotional jaunts through Ohio and Pennsylvania.

"Opportunity and practicality," repeats Mr. Loban of those dreadful words.

Yet while Axe's face becomes pale at the thought, he does feel a deep, growing stubbornness. He draws a deep breath and puts forward his right foot. As far as he's concerned, it'll be the end of his association with Loban Motor before he parts from Katie for what could be weeks if not months.

But before he can rise and deliver a resounding opinion, Mr. Loban interrupts—likely with a few details.

"Axelrod. As you know, we've become impressed with Katie's abilities behind the wheel. As have others. The majority opinion favors that wonderful Katie of yours."

Again, Axe is caught in mid-stride. Truly, he's left with little choice but to be brusque.

"Mr. Loban? Why don't you come out with it? What in the hell are you talking about?"

"Well-l-l, Axelrod. Achem. Do you suppose that it is possible? That is to say? Do you think you might convince Katie to accompany you on this trek of opportunity and practicality?" Although Mr. Loban may seem reluctant, instantly, his mood alters. "Imagine, the pair of you."

"From coast to coast," reminds Freddy.

"Yes. A splendid couple taking the Loban Motor Speed Six roadster on a trek to captivate the country!"

Now, there's no space whatsoever to wiggle. Indeed, Axe's large, comfortable chair is all too confining.

"What do you say, Axelrod?" continues Mr. Loban. "Are you not eager for such an adventure? To show off your roadster with that wonderful lady as your co-autoist?"

No doubt, the question is posed. But as stunning as the proposal may be, some sort of immediate reply is expected. If only Axe had all the time in the world to consider, let alone an hour or two.

"Hmm?" answers Axe. "Katie crossing the country in the Speed Six would put some ginger into its promotion. I'll give you that, Mr. Loban. Bu-u-t?"

A whirlwind of thoughts tours within Axe's head. Beyond doubt, it is a tempest of sorts. Yet to Axe's surprise, he finds the turbulence not so disagreeable, that most of Mr. Loban's proposition is settling into a calm. Imagine, he ponders further, to spend all of his hours with the one he cherishes the most, and all the while guiding and tending that object to which he's become devoted.

Placing his cup and saucer upon the desk, Axe stands and extends his open, right hand. "By God, I'll do it. I'll take the roadster across this country of ours. And damned if I won't be successful."

With equal enthusiasm, Mr. Loban shakes his hand. "Wonderful, Axelrod. Congratulations. Congratulations on your eventful decision."

As much as the barrier of the desk allows, the two continue to exchange their shakes, along with off-hand pats and other congenialities. Yet leave it to that other present person to bring up an all-important question.

"What of Katie?" asks Freddy. "Will she agree? And is she up to the journey?"

"Oh?" Axe releases his handshake and looks to Freddy. "I believe she will." And then Axe returns to his employer. "Don't worry, Mr. Loban. It may take some time, but my girl will itch for the chance."

"Excellent, Axelrod. Then go to her. Take the roadster. Bring her to us."

"I will, Mr. Loban," consents Axe, pushing aside any chance for second thoughts.

In no time, Axe has the Speed Six racing upon South Avenue. Yet when he reaches home, he opens the front door with some apprehension. Within the same instant, however, Axe discovers Katie applying a feather duster to the parlor entry transom, with one foot teetering upon the arm of a chair and her other atop the backrest—a precarious pose.

"Axe, is that you?"

"Katie. For goodness sake."

Quickly, Axe rushes to her aid, resting her bottom upon one shoulder and wrapping his arms around her pleated legs.

"Is this how you carry on in my absence?"

“Absolutely.” Almost nonchalantly, Katie continues her dusting.

Yet within the span of a few seconds, she finishes her chore so that Axe can release his captive.

“Why are you home?” asks Katie, as her feet settle. “Has something happened, Axe?”

“Nothing,” assures Axe, though with a measurable lack of punch.

As she faces her husband, Katie plies a feathery tickle to his nose. “Then to what do I owe the pleasure?”

To say the least, Axe is hesitant, his manner being readable.

The response from Katie is a doubtful frown. “Something has happened, hasn’t it?”

“Perhaps.”

“Well, so long as there’s no great upheaval to our cheerful routines. I do love our routines.”

Axe raises his brow and takes a deep breath, releasing the air in slow increments.

“Axe? You’re not going away, are you? You’re not leaving me behind, again?”

“Well, no. Uh-h, yes.”

“Axe. Tell me.”

“Don’t worry, Katie.” His hands clutch her shoulders. “I won’t leave you behind in any way, if only because I want you to come with me.”

“What?” Confused, Katie’s face widens. “With you to where?”

“Well.” Axe’s grasp alters into a coercive rub. “It’s Mr. Loban’s idea.”

“Idea?” With the revelation that there is to be no impending separation, Katie becomes stirred.

“To cross the country.” At last, Axe discloses the design. “Mr. Loban wants the two of us to take the roadster across the country.”

“I beg your pardon?”

“He wants us to drive across the country. Coast to coast. To promote the Speed Six.”

“Drive from coast to coast?” Though Katie may be stunned, her inner recesses begin to make a connection. “Coast to coast? No wonder Mrs. Snodgrass was behaving so strangely when we last spoke. Mr. Snodgrass too. But also Mr. Chagrin and Mr. Williams. Hmm? Perhaps I saw this coming.”

“Are you saying you had your suspicions? Katie, this is all news to me?”

“I’m sorry, Axe. But I wasn’t sure, myself. I thought it was just a silly hunch on my part.”

"So then you've been able to mull over the idea?" asks Axe.

"No. Not with any regard, I suppose."

"But you seem to be fine with the idea, Katie."

"Perhaps. The two of us touring the country." Still, the beam on Katie's face contains a twitch of apprehension. "But from coast to coast?"

"It does sound like a tall order."

"Can we do it, Axe?"

"Of course. The two of us and the roadster, with L.M. to back us."

Certainly, to conquer the length of America is a dreamy vision, one adoptable by a young, enterprising couple. And because such a journey has been accomplished on still only a few occasions means that it remains some sort of feat. Indeed, what an ideal situation to introduce an automobile to a captivated country of burgeoning enthusiasts.

"Our roadster has my full confidence. That its power and stability can take on any road in the land," continues Axe. "Better than the horse and wagons."

Regardless, there remains that matter of simple logistics: untold miles of complications and potential adversities. Modern machinery and innovations aside, the country remains very wide.

"Are you certain, Axe?" Although Katie may be an easy convert, she has the right to know more. "How long will we be away?"

"I haven't been able to make the calculations. But I think hardly more than a few weeks."

"That doesn't sound too terrible. Not at all."

"Then you are agreeable, Katie? We can accept the offer?"

"Yes, I think I am." She smiles and nods her head in quick successions. "And yes, we can."

"Wonderful." Overjoyed, Axe wraps his arms around Katie and plants a full kiss. Yet his fervor rises to the point where he cannot squander a second. "Get your hat and coat, and we'll see Mr. Loban at once."

"But Axe, there's more dusting to be done."

"Katie, it can wait. We need to hurry. Mr. Loban's coffee is getting cold."

Once again, for more times than she would dare count, Katie is whisked away by Axe. In short order, he delivers her to Loban Motor's doorsteps.

"Welcome, my dear." As the Lanes enter his office, Mr. Loban leaves the security of his desk. "Have a seat and enjoy our refreshments. Freddy can get anything you desire."

Although Katie may be familiar with the room, because its occupant is coming across as overly accommodating, the feeling within her edges toward caution.

With all the manners of a proud husband, Axe helps Katie into her chair.

As for Mr. Loban, he lends a hand as well. Yet instead of returning to the throne behind his desk, ever so adroitly, he takes the empty chair next to Katie's, repositioning it for a more face to face advantage.

While she leans as far back as her chair allows, Axe is forced to stand at her side.

"Freddy. Why don't you give our assistant engineer your seat?" suggests Mr. Loban ever so firmly. "And serve us with more coffee and pie."

"Yes sir, Mr. Loban," acknowledges Freddy with a hop.

Then there's Axe, whose immediate inclination is to put a trip into Mr. Loban's methods. "Perhaps, Mr. Loban, we can nibble later. We need to discuss a few things first. Don't you think?"

"I would prefer that, Mr. Loban." Katie takes the cue and leans a little forward. "And perhaps Freddy could find another chair and rejoin our circle?"

With a slight tilting of his head and a wide smile accenting his face, Mr. Loban is quick to acquiesce. "But of course, dear Katie. A wonderful suggestion."

"Thank you, Mr. Loban."

For the most part, a cue come as a sort of guide. Yet there are some versions begging to be expounded, to be received with all the tacit approvals and improvisations imaginable. As far as Katie is concerned, a cross country adventure alongside the love of her life has every appeal, to which Mr. Loban is demonstrating his ignorance. Thus, while he sits in a weak posture of cajoling, Katie advances toward negotiation.

"Well now, my dear Katie, you're looking as pretty as ever."

"Why, thank you, Mr. Loban." Katie's blush, however, is a pretense, she aware that dusting a house and riding in a roadster could only ruffle her appearance.

"Yes," smiles Mr. Loban.

An awkward pause ensues, only to be broken by a clumsy Freddy, who joins in with another chair.

"Has Axe told you of our plans?" he asks, as he adjusts himself.

"I'm not quite sure what you mean, Freddy," replies Katie with all innocence. "My head is spinning."

It's all that Axe can do to keep his eyes from rolling.

"Certainly, this is understandable," soothes Mr. Loban. "And I do apologize the suddenness."

For Katie, the word "apologize" is confirmation enough that she owns the advantage. Hence, she has the freedom to move things along.

"Mr. Loban, am I to believe that want me to drive the roadster from coast to coast?" As she poses the question, Katie's eyes are open and artless. "Such an impossibility."

"Oh, no," insists a defensive Mr. Loban. "Let me assure you, Katie, it has been done. Several times. And we wouldn't think of forcing you to drive. That will be Axelrod's duty. Your role is to accompany. For the two of you to cross the country as driver and wife."

"Do you mean I wouldn't be able to drive the roadster at all?" Shamelessly, Katie delivers a pout.

"Of course not, Katie. We would be delighted if you took the wheel of the roadster upon occasion." Mr. Loban looks toward Axe. "That would be to the discretion of your husband."

"Oh, but the hardships, Mr. Loban. And to be away from Lisbon, my home," moans Katie. "My lessons."

All the while, the husband keeps silent.

"Dear Katie, let me pledge of Loban Motor's full backing. That your nights will be comfortable at the finest accommodations, and your days will be funded and supported via the wires and railroads. We will be in constant communication." Mr. Loban gives a few nods. "Will we not, Freddy?"

"Without question, Mr. Loban."

"I do have trust in Loban Motor," replies Katie. "Bu-u-u-t?"

"Please, Katie. Understand that so much depends upon this promotion," urges Mr. Loban. "Loban Motor, its backers, its workers need this success. And I'm sure your students can manage a hiatus."

"I suppose they may, Mr. Loban," agrees Katie. "Still-l-l."

"Just tell me, Katie. How can I convince you the merit of our plans?" implores Mr. Loban, though maintaining a dose of dignity. "What sort of compensation will make you happy?"

To be sure, "compensation" has all the sounds of a business transaction. And although Katie may not be acquainted to the subtleness of commerce, she's able to recognize a golden opportunity whenever it presents itself. As it happens, one is being placed upon her receptive lap.

Indeed, Axe must flex his facial muscles in order to keep his jaw from dropping.

But then there's Katie, the focus of an undefined offer, who must contain her wide eyes, as well as conjure a reply. "Mr. Loban, whatever do you mean?"

"How can I compensate you for your time spent away from home?"

"Hmm?" reacts Katie, her lips creasing midway between a smirk and a smile. "Compensation, you say?"

While the tendencies of most minds might be to run wildly through a laundry list of possibilities, Katie's remains poised. Instead, her inclination is to calculate the parameters of Mr. Loban's offer: the low end to ignore, while the high divined. It should come as no surprise when the notion strikes Katie, that the chance to fill a personal need and an empty space is presenting itself. Thus, with no hesitation, Katie gives a reply.

"Mr. Loban. My parlor is in desperate need of a good piano."

"Oh?" responds Mr. Loban, who doesn't seem to be taken aback.

As for Axe, his wide eyes speak of his reaction to Katie's bold demand, what with subterfuge and guile being his usual employee versus employer tactic.

"Yes," confirms an unruffled Katie. "A piano would do nicely."

Mr. Loban's face lights up. "Wonderful, Katie. I have one at home that would suit your parlor well."

Yet Katie isn't one to blink when confronted with such generosity. "Might I ask the maker of this piano?"

"Oh? I believe it is a Beckwith," answers Mr. Loban, who wears the look of a seasoned negotiator.

Unfortunately for him, he's sitting opposite Katie, whose familiarity of Lisbon's cozy musical community is complete and utter. Indeed, she's aware that the melodic outcomes of the Loban family have been stifled by a mix of limited abilities and absent aspirations, meaning that all musical instruments occupying the household are little more than superfluous furniture. But in addition, there arises within Katie the question of the admitted piano's manufacture.

"Mr. Loban."Yet again, she refuses to flutter. "Surely a man of means would do better than a Beckwith? Why, I would wager there sits a lonely Kimball in your home. Hmm?" Katie pauses, only to drag out that other point. "Too bad it sits idly. Such a fine piano begs to be played. Day after day. Hour after hour."

"Perhaps it is a Kimball," accepts an embarrassed Mr. Loban, though he raises a contractual finger. "Complete the journey and it will be yours. If your parlor is large enough."

"That sounds fine," concurs Katie, while she glances at Axe. "And I'll make room. Believe you me."

A bit too impressed, Axe can manage little more than a few supporting nods.

As for Mr. Loban, his smile broadens even more, obviously elated that the Speed Six promotion can begin in earnest. "Then it seems we are in agreement. That soon, Loban Motor's fine engineer and his splendid wife will motor across the width of our country."

Certainly, Mr. Loban should be elated, in that he has secured that vital element—the Lanes—for what may be a culminating endeavor.

But Katie, too, has all the reasons to feel giddy, now that, due to her staunch cleverness, her yearning dream of piano ownership is within her grasp.

Still, there remains Axe, whose relative silence is broken by the echoing phrase "width of our country", and the realities thus implied. By the very sound of it, "width" speaks of broad expanses and an obesity of mileage, not to mention a confusion of connecting roads and the lack thereof. Suddenly, Axe remembers that America—the country in question—abounds with unmeasured distances, which some day might be calculated into thousands of miles.

"Congratulations, you two, on the bargain you've made," he interrupts. "But let me say that a piano's home should be the least of our worries. The list of which could choke a hungry goat, yet needs to be discussed. In fine detail." The engineer makes his salient point. "That recent Ohio and Pennsylvania jaunt was inches to miles in comparison."

"Of course," replies an unperturbed Mr. Loban. "But you and Flugan came through. And kept the schedule, might I say."

"Not without countless troubles," reminds Axe. "The final chapter being that drive shaft, of course. What a frustrating imbroglio."

"But Axe, you did finish your journey," counters Katie. "And the promotion was a rousing success."

"Yes, a superb and rousing success," parrots Mr. Loban.

"Superb," crows Freddy.

"You and Hugh saved the company," amplifies Katie.

"And you can save Loban Motor, again." It seems that, for at least the moment, Mr. Loban breathes un-affronted. "You and Katie both. Of this, I am certain."

"Well, Mr. Loban. I am too," assures Axe. "We just need to organize ourselves in full. Establish our ambitions, so that we might formulate our destinations. And foresee trouble."

"I see." Mr. Loban strokes his chin. "And I agree. We should leave nothing to chance."

"Superb." Axe becomes a little more animated, now that Mr. Loban is stepping into the Lane camp. "And we should begin immediately. Form our blueprint."

"Absolutely," concurs Mr. Loban.

"By gosh," furthers Axe's momentum. "We should write it up as if a contract. Leave no doubts."

It's a bold stroke from Axe, to have on paper the promises of his backer. After all, what better way to settle future conflicts than to have the present word in hand? Unfortunately, Mr. Loban seems hesitant over the suggestion, and so the ill-feeling arising within Axe. Perhaps, he thinks, he's gone a bit too far, especially when coming on the heels of Katie's piano triumph.

"Very well, Axelrod," nods Mr. Loban. "To leave nothing to chance." He looks to his business manager. "Freddy, tell Miss Charnwood to bring her pad. She has notes to take." And then Mr. Loban returns to the Lanes. "Plenty of notes, I should say."

Thus proceeds the morning in all its fits and starts, Percy Loban's office becoming a venue of disjointed ideas, while bearing the flows of approaching complications and their practical solutions. As for Miss Charnwood, she sits at her employer's side and inscribes those dictates of perceived importance. Experts are summoned—Lepper, Clappsaddle, Flugan, et. al.—and are called and recalled. And before lunchtime, a guest is invited, he being the source of sage opinions and sound judgements: Holland Snodgrass.

The discussions continue unabated, with Miss Charnwood's dutiful attention to dictation being much the same. Freddy ends a brief absence by toting a basket of edibles, his foray into Lisbon procuring the finest offerings from Morron's Grocery, Union Bakery and Heller Brothers' Meat Market. And as best he can, he sets his employer's oversized Stickley table with a generous array of cheeses and smoked meats, pickled vegetables and fresh breads—along with the appropriate silver and china.

"Very good, Freddy," observes Mr. Loban. "My friends, shall we help ourselves?"

Even as the participants migrate to the table, Mr. Snodgrass finishes an important thought. "Copies of the U.S. Geological Surveys are a must. To help you navigate from city to city, town to town. Although you will have to ask around for local directions."

Axe agrees, his experiences to Cleveland and back telling him so.

"And don't forget the railroads and telegraphs. Perhaps even the telephone exchanges," continues Mr. Snodgrass. "Vital means of communications, I should say. Never venture too far from them."

"Yes, we will compile a list of cities of interest, so that the two of you will be expected at those locations," adds Mr. Loban. "But it will be up to you to find your way between them."

"We'll do just that," assures Axe, his morning apprehensions melting away by the minute.

Amazingly, by tedious increments and quick spurts, the scheme for crossing the country unfolds. Indeed, upon mapping rough itineraries, even the promotional procedures are discussed. Certainly, Axe is a cunning salesman, the fact of which he must remind Mr. Loban. Now he'll have Katie at his side, who even in her absence proved of remarkable assistance during that Cleveland escapade, no slight to Hugh Flugan intended.

Additional witnesses are summoned, and more appear on their own accords. In fact, there happens a steady stream, the response compelling Freddy to make another visit into Lisbon's informal refreshments.

"...Miss Charnwood, what a charming choice of attire," recognizes A.W. Frew, attorney, who hovers about with a glass of porter in one hand and an abundantly-crafted sandwich in the other.

Her response is to smile coyly where she sits, and to adjust her ecru Batiste blouse and black all-worsted skirt, and then offer Mr. Loban a glance.

"By God, Percy Loban." Frew manages to redirect his attention. "If I cannot purchase the first available roadster, then I'll take it as a slap."

"Consider it a deal," assures Mr. Loban, who extends his hand.

Axe observes in wonder, of how his flawed employer and this man's litany of befuddlements can piece together the elements of sound machinery and its convincing arguments.

"Have you ever seen Frew behind the wheel of an auto?" he whispers to Katie.

"No," she replies. "I'm certain he knows nothing of working an auto."

"Then L.M. should have no trouble selling its Speed Six. None in the least," concludes a smirking Axe. "It's only up to us to cross the country. Do that deed and the other is done."

"Though some deed, Axe, I'm beginning to think," counters Katie. "Some deed."

Eventually, the period for the extended lunch fades, so that by early afternoon the quorum returns to its original five. Remarkably, even during the confusion brought on by the hungry throngs, the process has moved smoothly, with all bumps on the road being leveled. Indeed, much work has been achieved and continues so.

But then there comes a hitch—or perhaps an unhitch—a separation of sorts exposing the fundamental differences between a practical engineer and a recognition-hungry pioneer. And it's all for the sake of appearances, as good of an excuse as any to foster a conflict.

"...No, I must insist." Mr. Loban is throwing up a brick wall. "The Speed

Six must be presentable at all times. In as pristine condition as possible."

"But Mr. Loban, you're asking me to take the roadster thousands of miles with only a bare means to keep it repaired." Axe raises his voice in order to highlight his cause. "And it will break down, for sure."

"Lane, I don't consider that eventual. You should have more confidence."

"Mr. Loban, my confidence is unimpeachable," counters Axe. "But it's balanced by experience. Experience gained on the road to and from Cleveland."

"I remain aware of that particular mishap. But what are the chances of another faulty drive shaft?"

"I can't say. But who can, Mr. Loban?"

"I will." Mr. Loban is adamant. "Lane, you seem to forget that this enterprise is to promote the Speed Six. Notably, the roadster. So presentation is vital. For you to strap a spare drive shaft alongside my beautiful roadster? What message would that say?"

Silently, Katie pinches the sleeve of Axe's coat, her hint that he's close to losing his temper.

"I understand, Mr. Loban. But..."

"There can be no 'buts', Lane. You can carry spare tires and tubes atop the rumble. That is practical. And I do not want you to remove that seat for extra space. But an additional tool box can be fitted upon the running board. That will have to do for those other spare parts. Out of sight to the public. This should leave enough room for personal baggage."

"Mr. Loban," continues Axe with his protest. "I don't think you..."

"Are you writing this down, Miss Charnwood?" interrupts Mr. Loban.

"Yes sir. I am."

As much as any act, that Miss Charnwood logs the proceedings means that it becomes Loban Motor law. It's all the more frustrating for Axe, and perhaps all the more satisfying for the man who has the final say.

"What time is it, Freddy?"

"Half passed three, Mr. Loban."

"Already?" he responds. "We have put in a full day. Haven't we?"

Never mind that Axe feels he and Katie have only just begun. He takes a deep breath, ready to exhale a long list of hard facts.

"Yes, we have made a full day." Thus Mr. Loban puts the last word to his position. "Perhaps, Axelrod, you and Katie should return home. Begin your preparations. And, of course, take the roadster. After all, it belongs to you for the time being."

"If you say so, Mr. Loban," is the response from Axe's resigned lungs.

"Thank you, Mr. Loban," bids Katie, as she stands from her chair, her grip on Axe's sleeve remaining firm.

"Yes, Mr. Loban. I'll see you tomorrow," offers Axe, he taking the hint.

But as the Lanes leave the office—and with all the decorum they can muster—a graceless, Mr. Loban sees fit to push again a point.

"Pristine condition," he closes. "Always keep that in mind. The roadster should be washed and polished. Never forget what it represents."

That Mr. Loban would belabor the matter of condition and cleanliness could be taken by any conscientious engineer as a personal slight. Skillfully, Katie makes certain that her tug becomes her husband's focus, so that his building fume is taken elsewhere. In no time, the Lanes exit the building and find the roadster.

"#&@$%!"

Already, Katie has seen this coming and so has her ears covered. But with the last of Axe's breath exhausted, so too does his blood begin to cool. Safely, Katie lowers her hands.

"I can't believe he said that, Katie. Can you?"

"No. But I shouldn't be surprised. Really."

"Does he not think I'll take care of the roadster? Washed and polished? Pristine condition?"

Katie is surprised that Axe is more upset with Mr. Loban's parting than the issue of spare parts.

"And what are we to do in the middle of some God-forsaken-nowhere when the drive shaft decides to snap? Or some other unforeseen part? What does Mr. Loban expect of us then?"

Katie shrugs her shoulders and finds the passenger seat, thus compelling her husband to begin the rituals of starting the engine.

"Don't worry, Axe. You'll think of something. Remember what you always say? 'For every Loban edict, there is a Lane circumvention.'"

"Oh, yes. That. Whatever it takes to float the company." Axe, too, shrugs, as he reaches to grasp the crank. "And with only a week before we depart."

"Then we haven't a moment to waste, Axe. Not a second."

Though the beauty of a smooth crimson body and gleaming brass hardware might gather the beholder's eyes, it's the underside of an automobile stealing an engineer's attentions. But instead of meeting the dust of a street, Axe's shoulder touches the wooden planks of a Pennsylvania Railroad flatcar, where upon the Speed Six is tied and secured. A stop at the Altoona station affords the chance to leave Katie and their passenger coach, to unbind one side of a tarp cover for a quick inspection. And sure to form, that spare drive shaft feels unshakable to Axe's touch, it bolted at an angle to the frame—just one of a few Lane circumventions.

"Perfect," whispers Axe of his handiwork, as he ignores the bustle of Altoona's many tracks. He grabs the ties which bind the roadster. "Heh, heh. Budged not an inch, in spite of Horseshoe Curve. Hardly a myth."

What a whirlwind of a week it has been, muses Axe in silence, as he rises to his feet and continues his inspection. He smiles when he considers a month of preparations achieved within the span of seven days. Indeed, it was something of a miracle, made most apparent by a Dodge Brothers' windscreen, to which Axe has coated a shatter-proof experiment of clear celluloid. And then there is the collapsible canopy of a treated, black canvas, with a frame devised in haste by Willis Clapsaddle and constructed by Robert Irish.

Axe shakes his head, if only because these toppings are not to his satisfaction. Yet for the time being he understands that it all will have to stay in place, for although the journey across the country has begun, in reality it hasn't. Instead of heading toward the Pacific, Axe and Katie, and the roadster, are traveling by rail to the Atlantic. Taking advantage of the Pennsylvania R.R. will expedite time and save a little wear on the Speed Six. As it happens, east leads west—eventually—meaning that New York City will be the official start of the promotion.

This explains why Axe and Katie's departure from Lisbon saw little fanfare, though this shouldn't be the same when their itinerary returns them to said town. By then they will have crossed two states by means of the roadster. To be sure, the Lanes can expect a fitting ceremony from the citizens of Lisbon on that day, after which the couple will be free to make the automobile alterations of their choosing. Somewhere along the roads west of Loban Motor's home, the Speed Six may lose its canopy and windscreen.

"Excuse me, sir." Below stirs a voice from the station platform.

Axe turns around to see a gentleman with a suitcase. "What can I do for you?"

The mustachioed gentleman taps his bowler. "A fine vehicle, I must say. Yours?"

"Why, yes." There's no hesitation from Axe.

It's not surprising that the roadster draws an admirer. After all, perched upon the flat car, it is on display.

"Might I ask the manufacturer of your vehicle?" asks the gentleman.

"Loban Motor of Ohio," answers a proud Axe. "And this is the '08 Speed Six roadster."

"Loban Motor, you say?" The gentleman's eyes continue to cast upon the roadster. "Of Ohio?"

"That it is," confirms Axe.

"Hmm?" shrugs the gentleman. "I'm not familiar. Though your vehicle seems of sound manufacture."

Although innocent enough, the gentleman's statement digs a certain truth into Axe, that Loban Motor isn't as well known to the public as he could hope. Still, the assistant engineer is not ruffled.

"Sir, do you have a card?"

"Why, yes." Happily, the gentleman draws one from a coat pocket.

Taking the card, Axe scans its contents. "Mr. Freerdon. I'll make sure Loban Motor sends some information. You'll be impressed." And then Axe reaches to shake the gentleman's hand. "Axelrod Lane. Bound for New York and then the Pacific. To cross the country in this remarkable machine." But then Axe considers another thought. "And do so accompanied by my remarkable wife. Yes, remarkable both."

7
AMONGST STRANGERS

No longer do the Lanes have a need for trains, the end of the line being Elizabeth, New Jersey, a city of busy railyards and heaps of Pennsylvania coal. Instead, their ambitions are for that memorable beginning just beyond the Hudson River. New York City is the Lanes' next stop, and what may be a resounding success—or perhaps unseen complications and frightful excesses.

For the time being, however, this first morning of June finds Axe away from the hotel room near Elizabeth's opulent north side, at a garage where the Speed Six has spent the night. To be sure, there are some final preparations for the roadster and the short leg ahead, the most vital being the rear attachment of a metal placard: LOBAN MOTOR OF OHIO, Coast to Coast.

Then there's Katie, who remains behind in order to ready herself. But just what is the appropriate attire to wear amongst strangers—especially those of such weighty importance? There is her smart and stylish white lawn, embroidered princess dress, to suit perfectly the climate of America's smartest and most stylish city. Yet the vision New Yorkers may expect is of a young lady who's prepared for the travails and longevities of the road. And for this purpose, Katie's travel case holds a few practical blouses and skirts, a rubberized, mohair touring coat and a pair of laced, high ankle shoes.

Certainly, she's aware of how first impressions are lasting for the shallow and weak, and that New York City might be crowded with this sort. On the other hand, perhaps she should trust her own intuitions and tastes, and allow petty preconceptions to molder as they may.

"That princess dress will have to wait for another occasion," mutters Katie, as she gathers in hand her cadet blue, two-piece sailor's suit. "But I think I'll keep my corset tight all the same. For New York."

As things are panning out, Katie and Axe will be the only representatives for Loban Motor, the company's founder being far too occupied to make an easterly appearance. Indeed, it's been several months since Mr. Loban has stepped foot outside of Columbiana County, the Lanes' ongoing speculation being that he's too afraid of conspiracies and coup d'tats in his absence.

Be that as it may, their employer and his aide-de-camp, and the hired public relations firm, seem to have the situation well in hand. Contacts have been established and a vital appointment made with of all entities, the New York Times. To say the least, this is a remarkable deed, to have gained the interest of America's most estimable newspaper, the greatest chronicler known to the world! Truth to tell, most of the work is done, so that any apprehensions on the Lanes' part are unfounded. In fact, all that is required of the couple is to make the short drive north to Jersey City, take the Pennsylvania Railroad ferry across to Manhattan, and arrive at the New York Times on time. There, Axe and Katie are expected to be gracious, smiling and responsive to questions. And who knows, there may come to play some sort of commencement to the Loban Motor, coast to coast promotional journey, as witnessed by a crowd of best-wishers and curious onlookers.

"It should go well, I think," Katie assures herself, as she inhales and fastens her corset. "Whew. Yes, what could go wrong? Nothing to fear. I hope."

Quickly, Katie dons her nautical attire, highlighted by the dangle of a sailor's tie. It's atop her hair bun that she pins her straw, Merry Widow skimmer, which can be secured further with a veil. Already packed, with her goggles and gauntlets Katie is ready for the wilds and congestions of New York City.

She stands in front of the dressing mirror, making a few final adjustments to her pretty face by the aid of moistened fingers. "Axe. Where are you? We need to be on the road."

Suddenly, a knock at the door puts an end to frustration's potential. Pivoting about, Katie is met by her husband's perturbed and agitated face.

"I can't believe it!" In one hand he holds forth a telegram. "It's fallen apart! All fallen apart!"

To be sure, Axe's severe pronouncement forces a sink upon Katie's optimisms, his sparse words evoking an abrupt dread of a cancelled promotion.

"What does it say, Axe!" spills Katie's deflated tongue. "Is the telegram from Mr. Loban!"

Axe takes a deep breath and gathers his reply. "Yes, and it says that we're not to bother with the New York Times. That they have changed their minds and are no longer interested in us." Axe's anger is barely containable. "No doubt it has everything to do with that preposterous Paris race. They are the sponsors."

"Is that all it says?"

"Every one of the autos in that farce is yesterday's flivver. Nothing like our Speed Six." For the moment, Axe's concerns are over the insult to Loban Motor and not his wife's question.

"What should we do?"

"No Times for us," continues Axe. "No Times for our singular story and peerless inventions, I suppose."

"Axe!" With Katie's deepest fear aroused, she wants nothing more than to have it calmed. She steps forward and grasps her husband's arms. "What does Mr. Loban want us to do!"

"Pardon? Oh." At last, Axe's full attention is purchased. "Mr. Loban?"

"Yes. Where do we go from here?"

"Cross the Hudson to Manhattan, of course." Incredibly, and in spite of his rancor, Axe offers a shrug.

"Are you sure?" asks Katie.

"I believe so. Find another newspaper that will be interested."

Katie peers at the telegram. "But the promotion is to proceed as planned?"

"Of course. I think."

"Axe. Perhaps you should use the lobby telephone. Contact Mr. Loban and make things clear."

"I tried. But the exchange operator couldn't make the connection." reveals Axe.

"Well-l-l? Then-n-n?"

"I say there's not much choice." His shoulders relaxing, Axe frowns. "We're still crossing the country. But without the N.Y.T."

"Then let's go to New York and find another newspaper. Surely there is one of a trustworthy reputation."

"Yes. We'll do just that," agrees Axe. "But first, if you don't mind, I'd like to drop by the N.Y.T. and deliver my salutations."

In response, Katie frees Axe's arms and clasps hers around his waist. "That's my Axe."

Thus the journey proceeds. Soon, the Lanes leave their cozy hotel in trade for the street. And to mark the special occasion of a comfortable, cloudless morning, Axe has folded the roadster's flimsy top and flipped forward the windscreen. The effect is a sleeker Speed Six, even if it is packed for a long trek. Then again, and with New York City in mind, the roadster isn't carrying the full load as will be demanded by those long, lonely stretches of the western states.

Instead, that additional gear will be packed after the return to Ohio, when the first leg of the journey is completed.

"Are you ready?" inquires Axe, as Katie snuggles into the passenger seat.

"Yes."

"Here you are." Axe gives her a slip of paper. "The garage owner wrote these directions to the ferry."

"I see." Katie takes them in hand and reads the first few lines. "We should go that way," she points. "Find Spring Street and drive north."

So begins Katie's career as a navigator, the first of what should be many chartings to come.

Amazingly, those directions prove to be infallible, as are Katie's interpretations. With the Speed Six performing marvelously, the couple arrive at Jersey City's waterfront in short time. And as luck would have it, their wait to drive upon the ferry is much more brief. Yet the trend continues, when Axe is directed to park the roadster near the bow. Now, the Lanes are afforded what is essentially a front row seat upon their idling vehicle, before them standing a spectacle the likes of which they have only read.

"I can't believe it, Axe. Manhattan. Those skyscrapers. From the New World!" Katie's eyes beam in wonder. "And the Hudson. So wide and busy."

"And I thought the Delaware was a sight." Axe, too, feels awed.

Boo-o-o-h-h! Boo-o-o-h-h! The whistle announces departure and the ferry begins to lurch forward, its screw churning the water, while its stacks leave behind plumes of coal-inspired smoke. Able to avoid all obstacles, soon the ferry approaches the middle of the river.

"Cleveland has nothing on this city," notes Axe, experienced man of Ohio. "I wonder if they have a Euclid?" For the moment, his outrage over the New York Times is pushed aside.

As for Katie, a southward peer alters into a stretch of her neck and a marveled gaze, with the resulting flurry unable to suppress its discovery.

"Axe! There!" Katie clasps and then shakes his nearest arm. "The Statue of Liberty!"

"I see it," acknowledges Axe. "Impressive. Even at a distance."

Suddenly, the ferry veers northward and the limited view is lost.

"Oh, no," moans Katie. "I suppose the captain wouldn't reverse course and sail around the statue?"

"That would be the end of his post," he surmises. "But there's nothing to prevent us from driving to the tip of Manhattan. At the very feet of that colossus."

"Wonderful, Axe. I would love that."

"As soon as I'm done with the N.Y.T." With that, Axe's disgust regains its punch.

The ferry draws nearer to shore and a bustling display of commercial towers and stacked-upon dwellings.

"My goodness, it does look impossibly crowded," observes Axe. "Especially from the water."

"Mrs. Snodgrass warned me that six million people live in the city," recalls Katie. "Can you imagine?"

"Six million, you say?" responds Axe, as the engineer within congers a question of its own. "I wonder how they manage their sewage situation?"

Katie sniffs the air, as much as she dares. "I don't think they do, Axe. Manage it."

Much like the routine of a foot easing into a slipper, the ferry finds its berth. Wasting no time, the vessel releases its charge of paying pedestrians and dodgers, laden wagons and sundry motor vehicles, and an uncertain, young couple fresh from the interior. To be sure, it is a moment of truth when the tires of the Speed Six leave the wood of the deck for the pavement of Manhattan. Yet surprisingly, the transition is smooth, any bumps under wheel being a cinch for the roadster's suspension.

The rush of off-loading traffic prevents the Lanes from savoring the moment and taking stock of the environs. Fortunately, after only a block or so, Axe spots a convenient, unoccupied curbside.

"We've seen more people here than on Lisbon's busiest day," notes Katie, after catching her breath.

"It's sure to get more crowded. This is only the edge of the city." Axe's head shakes his doubts. "Somehow, we have to find its center."

Luckily for the Lanes, many of New York City's streets adhere to a number system, so that by elimination the couple should stumble upon the prescribed avenue.

"Perhaps we should angle towards the north," figures Axe.

The noises of the debarking fares blend with the city's clamor, there being no real separation. Indeed, the present impression of Manhattan is one of condensed chaos. It's as if the busy sounds have nowhere to go, their origins of internal combustions, shod hooves, boisterous disputes and unseen trolleys echoed and amplified by the manmade canyons of the neighborhood. And it promises to intensify, the Lanes' views of Manhattan's skyscrapers now blocked by the surroundings, as was not the case from the safety of the ferry.

With a worried look, Katie turns to Axe. "The north? Axe, are you sure you can keep that direction?"

"I'll try. But if need be, we can ask directions from these friendly people."

"Fine, Axe. But please, drive slowly. Keep your eyes on the street."

Axe's pivots his head, trying his best to judge the situation. A gap in the congestion looms, to which he squeezes the air bag, announcing his attentions.

"I hope there's enough wind in this city for my horn," notes Axe, while engaging first gear.

To say the least, Katie's senses are dizzied, overwhelmed by the a-rhythmic environment and a sure lack of common purpose. Yet there can be a certain fascination borne from the surface individualities, this being made plain by the sundry faces and their sundry dress, and by those odd tongues managing to find her ears.

"I wonder which skyscraper is their Tower of Babel?" poses Katie.

"By the sounds of it, all of them," replies her husband.

Yet there are the written words, bold advertisements for every sort of commerce from what seems to be every corner of the world.

"Chicken Shop," recites an astonished Katie of the establishment displaying openly at least one hundred hanging poultry corpses—feathers and all. But because she knows not an ounce of Yiddish, she cannot read on, thus missing out on a possible explanation.

"What kind of name is that?" inquires Axe, he catching a glimpse of something Cyrillic.

"I'm not sure," replies Katie. "Who knows?"

Even some of the signs of the Latin alphabet take the letters to their extremes.

It comes as no surprise when the buildings grow in height. In response, Katie tilts her head and counts beyond her fingers the stories as they come. Meanwhile, she continues to peruse the words of commerce.

"Triangle Shirtwaist Company." And then Katie speaks with a little exclaim. "Axe, I believe they sew garments at the top of that skyscraper. That horrible-looking building."

"My God." Axe is able to take an upward peek.

"Do you believe they would actually force their poor seamstresses to work up there?"

"I don't know."

"I think so, Axe."

"Well, that's something Mr. Loban would never allow. I'll give him that," assesses Axe. "But we are in a different land, Katie. Unmistakably."

Cautiously, the couple continue their way. It doesn't take long, however, before Katie's neck weakens, her eyes returning to a leveled view.

"Have you ever seen so much asphalt?" she observes from her new angle. "The streets?"

"Hmm?" considers Axe, this being an opportunity to refresh his sarcasm. "I thought they were paved in gold. Though I didn't think it would be bimetal. Like what we crave in Lisbon."

Katie smiles at Axe's comment—a mid-western sentiment out of place in a city of so much asphalt.

Soon, a few more instinctive turns are taken, as are the corrections in the forms of straight stretches. Quite by surprise, the Lanes happen upon a tonier neighborhood, this altering into residential blocks of even grander significance.

"A bit like Euclid Avenue," observes Axe. "Though more compact."

"Wasn't the president born here?" asks Katie. "Or somewhere near?"

"I believe so. We could have passed his house, already."

The blocks accumulate, and with chameleon-like eyes, the Lanes do what they can to absorb the surroundings. Unfortunately, there's as much missed as there is taken, although at least one of Katie's eyes takes a wayward glance at a corner and discovers a significant street sign.

"Axe," she shouts, while shaking his left coat sleeve. "Forty-third Street! That's our street!"

Not in position to make an immediate turn, Axe needs a full block in order to claim the street. Yet soon, he and Katie find themselves heading west on 43rd, thus leading to the New York Times—more or less.

Almost immediately, the buildings ahead loom to frightful heights—they really do scrape the sky. Nonetheless, a dutiful Axe keeps his eyes upon the street.

On the other hand, Katie is free to tilt her rested neck back on high. Once again, she counts, yet owing to the many obstacles and limited views, her arithmetic proves incomplete.

But then there arises an imposing sight, as it happens the upper floors of New York's finest building, made so familiar by a photograph as seen in Mr. Loban's office. And there's no denying its identity: the signatures of its domineering height along with a resoundingly impossible crown of columns, arches and cornices. Leaning against her loved one, Katie responds to her discovery with a wide stare and a drop of her jaw.

"The New York Times," she mutters. "The Times Building."

"Pardon? What did you say, Katie?"

"Straight ahead," she announces, pointing her left arm skyward. "The New York Times! Axe, there must be two dozen stories!"

"Really?"

Axe's lofty admirations can last only a second at a time, for his head must stay with 43rd Street and its hazards of unmindful pedestrians, carelessly parked wagons and authoritarian trolleys. And then there are the automobiles, whose numbers are proving to be remarkable.

"A Pierce-Arrow," notes Axe of a six-cylinder competitor. "A fine auto." Yet events on 43rd can alter the mood in a flash. "Maxwells?" he sneers, at what happens to be a local favorite. "Not much of a flivver."

Like an unwary mouse before a silent, watchful cat, the Speed Six approaches the New York Times. Because the block in question is one of triangles—as opposed to streets of parallels and right angles—the Times Building appears as a massive wedge, able to slice its way through Manhattan should the situation arise. And the nearer the view the more gigantic the upper story columns become, the wonder being as to how their construction at such great heights could have been achieved. It's no mystery that the New York Times is considered by most to be the greatest newspaper in the land, housed by such a grand palace.

A puffy, white cloud drifts by and highlights the topmost floor, thus rendering a swaying sensation to the entire building. It's a bid too dizzy for Katie, who can think only of the madness it must take for newspaper workers to spend the day at such terrible heights.

Skillfully, Axe negotiates the crowded pavement and confusing intersections. And in one fail swoop, he manages a bold turnabout in the middle of the street, taking advantage of a chance gap.

Katie's head swirls as the Speed Six comes to a stop, though her eyes maintain that gaze upon the top of the Times Building.

"We're here," alerts Axe, his adroitness laying claim to a perfect park. "Katie?" He taps a shoulder.

"Pardon? Oh." Able to redirect her attentions, Katie levels her head.

"We've arrived. The N.Y.T.," declares Axe, as he waves his thumb at said building.

Although the news is expected, Katie's stomach can't avoid a little queasiness. Indeed, the inevitable is occurring, that she and Axe are about to plunge into the dark innards of what must be an all-powerful titan. To say the least, there stirs a reluctance within Katie's heart and mind, a distinct desire to avoid being herded into an elevator.

On the other hand, the strength of Axe's fume continues to build, especially with its focus being so near. Because he has yet to tilt his head for a prolonged look, he's all but unimpressed. And so Axe kills the engine and sets the hand brake, and then removes his cap and goggles.

"Well. I suppose this is the moment of truth." Axe motions with his head toward the source of his current vexation. "Old Girl, let's tell them a thing or two."

"Axe." To say that Katie wears a wary face is to read the sureness of the alphabet.

And beyond doubt, there's none so literate as Axe. In spite of the noise and disruptions surrounding the Times Building, he's able to sense his wife's tone.

"Katie? Is something wrong?" Axe puts aside his disgust for the N.Y.T.

"Oh no, Axe. Nothing," assures Katie. "But I was thinking."

"What is it?" Axe's voice is as soft as the surroundings allow.

Katie loosens her googles. "Well. Would it be wise to leave the roadster unguarded? Perhaps I should stay, while you go inside and have your say?"

"Something is wrong, Katie?" His face open and wide, Axe concentrates on his wife's eyes. "Tell me, Old Girl. What is it?"

A demurred frown is Katie's reply, of which she looks upwardly to make things clearer.

Following her lead, Axe, too, gazes toward the sky—along with the nearly infinite lines of one particular manmade design. And as happenstance would have it, an additional puffy, white cloud passes by, thus creating another sensation of apprehension.

"Uhh. I see what you mean," reasons Axe. "One of us should stay with the roadster."

"You don't mind? Do you, Axe?"

"No. Of course, not. Now I won't have to worry if you've covered your ears. If I choose, I can let fly."

"Then by all means, let fly," smiles Katie.

She reaches into Axe's coat pocket for his spectacles, placing them upon their proper place. Then Katie hands him his fedora and straightens his tie, ending her fuss with a good luck peck.

"I shouldn't be long," offers Axe, as he steps onto the pavement. "The less time spent in there, the better."

"I'll be waiting."

With that, the Lanes part company. But for how long, who can say?

One thing is certain, however, that it makes little sense for Katie to remain in the passenger's seat. Deftly, she shuffles herself to the more natural position behind the wheel—with her feet at the pedals and her hands upon the wheel. To be sure, the pride of Loban Motor's creation surges into Katie, this feeling accented in that she waits alone amongst six million strangers.

Those strangers walk passed in rapid succession—mostly on the sidewalk, but with a few on the street. And it should come as no surprise when the unending horde becomes a bit too disconcerting for the native Ohioan. After all, who knows what wicked deeds certain individuals within their number could be conjuring, the possibilities being a sure matter of percentages?

They do whirr by, the citizens of New York City—some with a glance, some with perplexed glares and others exhibiting no interest whatsoever. Indeed, the rush is such that Katie cannot frame a single face, there being hardly a chance to exchange pleasantries.

"Phew," sighs Katie, as beads of perspiration form upon her brow.

"Madam."

But then there happens an encounter of sorts, one coming from the street in the form of a friendly voice.

In a jolt, Katie redirects her attentions away from the sidewalk. What confronts her are the manners of a gentleman: a tip of the hat, a bow of the head and a confident, but giving smile. Immediately, Katie's sharp intuition tells her that the man in question, who has one eye upon her and the other for the Speed Six, is not the sort from whom to draw fear.

"Pardon me, if I startled you, madam."

"Oh, but you've done no such thing. Please be assured." There's a slight quiver in Katie's voice, if only because this is her first opportunity to speak to a New Yorker.

He nods his response, and tips his hat again. "I must say, this is a splendid vehicle. A six-cylinder?"

"Why, yes." It's apparent that this admirer has some understanding of automobiles.

"Hmm? I would say that your husband has shown sound judgement."

"Thank you."

"Might I ask the name of the maker?" inquires the gentleman, who at the same instant sees the radiator emblem. "Loban Motor?"

"Yes. Loban Motor of Ohio."

"Loban Motor of Ohio," repeats the gentleman, as he continues his scrutiny. "Splendid." But then he pauses his praise to consult his pocket watch. "My apologies, madam. I am in a hurry. Time presses."

Yet before the gentleman can rush away, Katie proves to be the quicker of the two. She reaches into a small, cardboard box and produces a business card.

"Sir, if you like, write to me at this address and I'll send you information of the Speed Six. Mrs. Axelrod Lane." With a handy pencil, Katie scribbles her name.

"I beg your pardon?" The gentleman seems a bit puzzled.

"My husband is an engineer with the company, so I'm vastly familiar with the details of the Speed Six."

"Oh, I see." He's quick to recover and accepts the card. "Splendid. I will write. Thank you, very much."

"Thank you, sir. And I look forward to your letter."

No sooner than the gentleman parts, then another arrives from the sidewalk approach, though this particular replacement escorts his wife and child.

Katie doesn't miss a breath. "…Loban Motor of Ohio. The '08 Speed Six," she denotes, as she hands over another company card. "Write to me and I'll send you information. Oh, and we do have a touring car version of the Speed Six. A splendid automobile for the city, and for family visits to the countryside."

"Is that so?" replies the husband. "Though I do admire this roadster." He looks to his wife, who also seems impressed. "What do you think, dear?"

Soon, after the couple bids farewell, another interested gentleman takes home a card, quickly followed by a pair of associates who must be tired of their pedestrian ways. Not only does each accept a Loban Motor card, also they surrender their own.

"Should you need an attorney, my partner and I are available."

"Thank you."

"Thank you, and good day."

A few more potential patrons come and go. But then a gap of disinterest ensues, while the crowd of pedestrians thins in its flow. The lull is welcomed, however, if only because it allows Katie to take stock of what has occurred. To be sure, her thoughts of Manhattan are being seconded, that in spite of the cold and frightening appearances of its buildings, the people themselves are proving to be quite warm. As strange as it may seem, New York City is becoming a splendid place.

As to how long Axe has been away, her guess is no more than 40 minutes. But before Katie can consider how much more time she will spend alone, an unexpected matter steals her attention. A commotion brews, its venue being the same Times Building entry into which her husband had disappeared moments ago.

"Axe?"

By the looks of it, Loban's engineer is being escorted off the premises, he putting up at least a token resistance. And although Axe's two handlers are neat and well-groomed, the manner in which they conduct themselves might be better suited for the job of bouncing at a saloon.

"Unhand him!" protests Katie.

To which the bruisers comply—each with a decided shove. The pair stand their ground, while they fold their arms and clinch their jaws.

Quickly, Axe picks up his fedora and straightens his spectacles, though he beats a slow, watchful retreat. "You haven't heard the last of me!" he threatens. "Mark my words!" Yet, soon, he's at his wife's side, delivering his oft-repeated warning. "Katie, please cover your ears."

"Axe." However, she refuses, if only because she's more aware of the surroundings. "Hush now. These good people need not hear your foul words. Keep it to yourself."

"What?" At first, Axe is confused. But then he gathers himself. "#&@$%," he whispers, his muted words lost amidst the city clamor.

Yet in no way have Axe's expletives depleted his anger. He moves to the front of the roadster and cranks over the engine.

Katie feels the combusted vibrations. Still, she remains at her station behind the wheel.

As for Axe, he leaps upon the passenger's seat and gestures with his mighty fist toward the Times Building and its two representatives.

"All the news that is fit to be fabricated," he shouts for the whole world to hear. "Fit to be fabricated." Then Axe gives a huff, and with a certain amount of satisfaction nestles into his seat. "By all means, drive on, Katie. Let's find a rival. There are plenty in this town."

"If you say so, Axe," replies Katie, knowing that it may be wiser for her to retain command of the Speed Six. But before she releases the hand brake and presses the gear pedal, she makes a move to her husband's coat pocket. "Here. Take these," speaks Katie, as she inserts the business cards of the partner attorneys. "You may need them before we leave this city."

"What?"

The Lanes plod on, not exactly sure as to their next destination, but hoping for the best. Yet while their drive toward the Times Building had been an inconspicuous element of the city's streets, now it seems to be standing apart. Axe can't help but notice the gawks, pointed fingers and remarks between friends, all being directed at the Speed Six and its occupants.

"Perhaps in the future, Katie, you should do the driving for the cities. Leave the country roads to me."

It's no small boast to say that New York City is crowded with newspapers, meaning that the Lanes can afford to be choosy. Eventually, they stumble upon what appears to be a promising candidate, the New York Journal. After all, it is owned by W.R. Hearst. And although the daily's building is less imposing than the N.Y.T., Katie agrees to stay with the roadster in order to work the passersby.

Once again, she revels at regaling over the roadster, and once again, the Speed Six's admirers linger about in their intermittent streams.

"It took my husband only an hour to teach me to drive the roadster," explains Katie to a pair of young couples, the sisters of whom can be nothing but identical twins. "Though I do admit, prior to my lesson, I spent many hours in the passenger seat. So to say I was eager to take the wheel is an understatement." It's at this point that Katie discerns a slight crease of disapproval on the face of a husband. "Oh, but I dare not drive the roadster without Mr. Lane at my side. Goodness, no. He lets me feel safe."

Words to which the husband in question can live.

And so from her seat, Katie continues her chat with the siblings/spouses. What a delightful four are these particular Manhattanites, much like the others who have visited the roving embassy of Lisbon. Indeed, Katie could continue like this for hours on end, she being up to the task.

Be that as it may, a certain distraction does lurk. At first, Katie catches a glimpse, which alters into a lingering look, all while she maintains a friendly conversation. It seems that on the periphery of the sidewalk, a silent, meticulous man in a bowler hat is setting up a tripod, with this apparatus supporting the unmistakable box of a professional camera.

"I believe you are about to have a photograph taken, Mrs. Lane," observes one of the twins.

"I think you're correct, Mrs. Van Doorn," agrees Katie. "Oops. I mean Mrs. Leewoek."

For certain, it is a peculiar feeling to be the focus of an anonymous camera. Yet whether Katie should object, she isn't sure. After all, what she sees before her, a nonchalant photographer going through the procedures without obtaining permission, may be acceptable behavior in Manhattan. Indeed, for Katie, the real quandary is whether she should strike a pose, such as placing her left hand at the wheel and her right on the gear shift, all while bearing a look of confidence? Or perhaps she should smile, which is Axe's preference, he being the tickler behind all of their couple's portraits?

"Could that be your husband, Mrs. Lane?" spots one of the twins.

Abandoning the camera's aim, Katie looks toward the entrance of the Journal and sees her approaching husband, he being accompanied. However, in no way is Axe coerced, if only because the build and manner of the man at his side lacks the bouncer standards of the N.Y.T.

"Mr. Grimsby," offers Axe. "Allow me to introduce my wife, and driving partner."

"Please to me you, Mrs. Lane."

"Katie, Mr. Grimsby is a reporter for the Journal and will write about our journey."

"Oh, I see."

"The Journal wants our photographs," continues Axe. "With the roadster."

Katie looks to the Van Doorns and Leewoeks, who appear impressed, as do others who have gathered.

"That sounds wonderful, Axe. What should I do?"

"Stay exactly as you are, Mrs. Lane," directs Grimsby.

"Yes," agrees Axe, as he looks to Katie's visitors. "Hello. How are you?"

"Oh, Axe. Allow me to introduce the Van Doorns and Leewoeks."

"Please to meet you. Thank you for keeping my wife company."

"The pleasure is ours," replies Mr. Van Doorn. "And we do admire your automobile."

With a beaming face, Axe turns to Grimsby. "There, you have it. A ringing endorsement from some of Manhattan's stalwart citizens. I do appreciate the compliment, ladies. Gentlemen."

With that, the photography session begins, the studio being the busy, open air in front of the Journal Building. Several plates are taken with Katie behind the wheel and of Axe as passenger, and with a background of the Van Doorns and Leeboeks. And then the Lanes switch positions, posing anew.

All the while, Grimsby hovers at Axe's side. "Don't forget to keep regular contact," he reminds. "By telegram, especially of your destinations. And you have your pocket Eastman. Post a few photographs."

"Should we write to you, or even try for telephone connections?" suggests Axe, who has been doing considerable thinking on the topic. "So we might offer details for a more interesting story."

"Story?" replies Grimsby. "Details? Don't worry about that. The Journal will take care of the story. Just find your way to the Pacific and you won't disappoint our readers."

For Axe, Grimsby's off-handed remark comes as a surprise, as it would affect any competent engineer and his penchant for facts. Yet the salesman within him knows better than to press a point, that what a successful promotion needs most is public awareness. At the very least, there will be thousands of New Yorkers who will know something about Loban Motor.

"If you say so, Mr. Grimsby. We'll keep in touch by telegram."

Soon, a trio of editors make their appearance. Indeed, the moment has all of the hallmarks of a semi-official send-off, as witnessed by the onlookers and chronicled by Grimsby and his photographer.

But before long, the business with the Journal concludes and Katie rediscovers the wheel, while Axe takes command of the crank.

"Goodbye," bids Katie to her new friends. "It's been delightful to have met you."

"Good luck, Mrs. Lane."

"We look forward to reading of your adventures."

With the engine idling, Axe finds his seat. He reaches to touch her left hand upon the wheel.

"Well, Old Girl. This is our starting point. What do you say we cross the country?"

Katie responds by pushing the pedal and tapping the throttle. As they ease away, the Lanes wave to their backers and dare give rearward glances.

Without doubt, they are on their way—that daunting traverse to the Pacific Ocean. Yet although it is an occasion begging to be marked, Axe's thoughts can't be swayed away from Grimsby and the somewhat questionable approach to his profession.

"I hope the Journal doesn't put us on a back page," he notes, as they make a turn.

"Should we find another newspaper, Axe? I was told about the New York World."

"I don't know, Katie. Isn't that the disreputable rag owned by that crazed, old man?"

"Oh?"

"We may not be able to rely on the newspapers of this island. Though we might do better by the smaller ones of the hinterlands."

"Yes, Axe. We should give them all a try."

The tour of Manhattan continues southward and that anticipated view of the Statue of Liberty. Needless to say, the city's labyrinths would have the Lanes fairly lost were they not sure about the general direction. Yet uncertainties abound concerning the neighborhoods through which they must travel, the couple having read the accounts of slums and slumlords, and the associated crimes and criminals. Prudently, as the lower end of Manhattan draws near, Axe takes command of the wheel.

Indeed, as hunch would have it, the Lanes find themselves entering a more crowded and less moneyed New York City, the sights and sounds being a stark contrast.

"Axe. Can you believe it. There are Pennsylvania Dutch in Manhattan," observes Katie of the long beards and staid attire.

"I never would have guessed."

Too soon, the neighborhoods become even gloomier—and squalid and pestilent, and hopeless. It's all Axe can do to keep up his speed and dodge passed the accumulations of the street, including a dead horse—likely shot upon reaching the end of its usefulness.

"My God, Axe. How could they allow this to happen?" questions Katie, as she holds her handkerchief to her nose. "These people. These poor, unfortunate people. And their ragged, little children. In the streets. So near, yet so far from Manhattan's riches."

"I can't believe it either. The greatest city on Earth?"

"But I wonder how the president would allow this in his city?" continues Katie.

"Maybe it matters little where a man is from, but where he's going."

"What do you mean, Axe?"

"Well. Is he going to heaven or hell, for instance?" poses Axe, his eyes keeping to the street.

"Axe, how could you say such a thing?" protests Katie. "Talking about our president, like that. No, I think he would want to change the city to his liking. But some New Yorkers thought otherwise and had him evicted. So now he lives in the White House."

"Hmm? That does makes sense, Katie."

"Oh, Axe," sighs Katie, her mood having taken a topple. "I really don't care about the Statue of Liberty. Let's turn westerly. Find the ferry and leave this city behind."

Another night is spent in Elizabeth, and another day is spent leaving New Jersey. But anxious to return to Lisbon and not so keen to dally in another crowded metropolis, the Lanes give Philadelphia a wide berth. As it happens, their decision is a scrupulous one, if only because said city is not a part of Mr. Loban's agenda.

And so the Lanes re-cross the Delaware, and find the artsy burg of New Hope and silken and woolen Doylestown to their liking. The morning has Katie and Axe in another textile center, Lansdale, after which a few too many wrong turns lead them to the footsteps of the state lunatic asylum in Norristown. Fortunately, the couple regain their sanities, and upon asking for directions, find the straight road.

"Do you think it possible to teach those folks to drive the Speed Six?"

"Perhaps, Katie. After I could get to know them for a while."

That the Lanes are traveling through God's country may be an understatement, His fields of fertile beauty being nothing more than a representation of Heaven. And although the profusion of sound, mud-free roads may be confusing, God's amiable children are all too happy to point the way for the Ohio-bound. Soon, in spite of an oil leak and four tire punctures, the couple reach Downington. And because this is a town of boilers and brick, there is an interest in manufacturing and invention, along with some incomes to pay for such. An extended demonstration is in order, the reward being that an early dinner is on the generous citizens of Downington. How fortunate for the Lane's to have found this town, and with enough remaining daylight to make it to a Coatsville hotel before nightfall.

Axe and Katie do find a cozy night at the aforementioned steel and foundry town, the result being that they're able to make a dawn's early departure. And when eventually they cross the line into Lancaster County, the ground remains dewy, with the morning sun sparkling its jewels upon a perfected countryside.

"Axe, will you look at those fields. What are they growing?"

"I can't say." Axe glances upon the landscape and rummages through his internal roster of agricultural possibilities. "Young tobacco plants? Hmm? What precision. Like each was sewn by hand."

"It's beautiful," deems Katie. "As if sheets of music. Can you imagine how more wonderful when it matures?" To be sure, Katie's gifted passions are moved by the precisions of man and nature, and their joint cause. "Definitely, I'll bring my violin and mandolin. When we leave Lisbon, again."

"So that's how they raise tobacco," nods Axe, his inclinations for exactitudes allowing him to share the fascination. "I wonder if I should take up that habit? Smoking. Snuff. You know, I've heard good things."

"I've heard the same too," returns Katie. "Maybe I should give it a try?"

"Well-l-l? On second thought."

Upon the Lancaster lanes the Lisbon Lanes press on, passing additional fields of tobacco, along with many more of wind-waving wheat and hay grasses. To say the least, this is as far-removed from the vertical ambitions of Manhattan as it gets. Yet Lancaster County, Pennsylvania, does share a few things in common with New York City, such as their reliance upon indispensable beast of burden.

"Look at that man over there," observes Katie of a bearded farmer behind a plow. "I never would have thought we'd see a Russian Jew in the middle of Pennsylvania."

Thus it's on to the county's namesake city, beyond which lies the Susquehanna River and further, the Alleghenies. Although this may sound simple enough, those mountains are a barrier, the Pennsylvania Railroad's mastery through its slopes being nothing short of a major engineering accomplishment.

"I believe when we find the mountains, we should stay on the roads parallel to the rails," discloses Axe of a long-simmering thought. "That should get us to Altoona. Pittsburgh will be downhill from there."

"And then Lisbon," adds Katie. "Lisbon, will be duck soup."

8
HOME…

"I promise, Axe," snaps a vigilant Katie. "One more yawn and I'll have you pull to the side of the road. We'll spend the night out here, if need be."

"We're almost home, Katie," pleads Axe, who forces his eyes to gaze upon a distant light. "Must be only a couple of miles away."

Three point two, to be precise. That is to say, the distance it takes to reach the Speed Six's birthplace, beyond which lies a Pine Street address empty of its homesick inhabitants.

Hardly has there been a darker night, and rarely does there exist a sleepier town. The only lights in Lisbon are the lanterns of its handful of night watchmen, scattered as they are amongst the south side industries. Then again, there does glimmer American Tin Plate, the factory providing just enough luminescence to accommodate its skeleton nightshift.

It's toward this beacon that Axe and Katie have been guided for what seems like dozens of rolling miles. Granted, the roads from East Liverpool may be familiar, but owing to the late hour, the normal hazards are multiplied—even with the additional confidence of the roadster's kerosene lanterns. Dirty and worn though they may be, instead of finding accommodations earlier, the couple is finishing their leg.

Before long, the Lanes pass the structure at Lisbon's southeast limits, a certain factory which should be dim and dark because it lacks a nightshift.

"Axe, is that a light, upstairs? Mr. Loban's office? Are he and Freddy working?"

"Maybe." Axe offers a glimpse. "Though that wouldn't be like Mr. Loban."

"Should we stop and tell them what happened? Our telegrams were brief."

"Do you really want to, Katie? I would rather see a hot tub and a soft bed than Mr. Loban."

"Of course. What am I thinking?"

By the time the Lanes make it home, the idea of a bath loses its warmth. After all, it does require considerable effort to heat and haul water for the cellar tub. On the other hand, the dust of the road, lubricants of the roadster and sweat from the glands have been accumulating on nearly every surface inch known of the human anatomy. Some sort of cleansing is in order, and the quicker it comes, the better. Yet the solution may be simple, needing little discussion and hardly any ado.

"…Well, then if it's fine with you, it's fine with me," agrees Axe to Katie's suggestion. "And we can unpack in the morning."

Thus the bath is by the bucketful, upon the unlit kitchen porch for all the world to see—except, of course, the immediate neighborhood, now fast asleep.

"Oh-h," shivers Katie to the first dowse.

"Shh. You'll wake the neighbors."

"As if they don't wash themselves like this," whispers Katie.

"What?" replies Axe. "How would you know?"

"I just do," answers Katie, who in turn takes the bucket and its remnants.

"Oh-h. It is cold," responds Axe.

The light of the morning goes unnoticed, as does the sun's warmth. Yet ignored equally are the raps upon the front entry. To be sure, Katie and Axe have earned a late morning. However, when a frustrated fist pounds the door, the demonstration cannot be denied.

"No, let me," insists Axe. Grogginess aside, he dons his robe and finds the front entry. "Mr. Loban?" To his surprise, Axe opens his door not to a salesman or a neighbor, but to the man behind his salary. "Freddy?"

"So you have returned," greets Mr. Loban.

Unfortunately for Axe, there are no further words written upon his employer's face, nothing to decipher nor an expression to offer a clue.

"Uh-h-h. Good morning, sir."

"It is that. If only just."

As Mr. Loban speaks, Freddy checks his watch, thus accenting the fact.

"Let me guess. You arrived sometime during the night?"

"Just after midnight." Although Axe looks at Mr. Loban, he can't help but notice a spiffy blue roadster parked curbside. Production must be gathering momentum—in the color of Chagrin's Cleveland.

"I was right, Mr. Loban," notes Freddy.

"How did you know?" asks Axe with feigned concern.

"Someone told me this morning."

"Really, Freddy?" speaks Axe, disapprovingly, to hide a tripped curiosity. "Who then?"

"The Swift boy. I saw him while leaving the Hostetter," explains Freddy. "After breakfast."

"I see." Axe's face exudes a bit of pride, of how well his hireling is performing his task. "Jimmy was keeping an eye on the house. He must have walked passed earlier."

"Never mind about that," interrupts Mr. Loban. "What matters, Lane, is that you are not expected here."

"Pardon?" Axe is confused. "Mr. Loban, is something wrong?"

"Something is very wrong, I should say."

With these words, Axe feels an alarm.

"You seem to be at a loss." Now, Mr. Loban appears confused. "You really have no idea."

"I'm afraid I don't," replies Axe.

"Did you not receive our telegram at Ebensburg?" asks Freddy.

"No," replies Axe. "We had to veer around Ebensburg, because of a strike. They blocked a bridge and weren't obliging. Katie and I spent that night in Johnstown."

"I see." Mr. Loban looks to Freddy. "That explains our problem."

"Problem?"

"Yes. Problem. You and Katie are not expected in Lisbon until noon." At last, Mr. Loban offers a detail. "We've planned a reception in front of the courthouse, with the Buckeye covering the event. And Bennett's agency is sending the news across the state."

"We even hired Will Morron and the Red Onion to provide refreshments," adds Freddy.

"So there it stands," continues Mr. Loban. "A recipe for a grand celebration. Except the only people unprepared are its subjects. You and Katie."

"I see." Or perhaps Axe doesn't. "Mr. Loban, what should we do?"

"There's no choice but for you and Katie to load the roadster, sneak out of Lisbon and return at noon."

"If you say so, Mr. Loban." In truth, Axe expected worse from this unexpected visit. And because the roadster remains packed, Mr. Loban's directive is hardly a bother. "Do you want us to look surprised when we arrive at the square?"

"Lane, this isn't a birthday celebration," delivers Mr. Loban. "Just be timely, and, later, we'll discuss New York in detail. Hmm? I must say, that you engaged a Hearst newspaper is impressive."

"Yes. Impressive," joins Freddy.

To which Axe offers a shrug of modesty—or perhaps a subtle gesture to the contrary.

Noon arrives in Lisbon, as does the roadster for the second time. And although the Speed Six seems a little worse for wear—dust-coated and with a shattered windscreen—the automobile remains in sound condition. Remarkably, the roadster's occupants appear to have suffered much less from the road, even to the point of being cleaned and groomed.

"You think they would have donned their goggles," mumbles Mr. Loban, as he stands at the head of a crowd in front of the Columbiana County courthouse.

But at least Katie and Axe are all smiles when the Speed Six comes to a halt amidst the rousing cheers of a hundred of Lisbon's citizens. Arm in arm the couple traipse to the steps of the courthouse, urged further by salutes of more personal natures.

"Congratulations, Mrs. Lane."

"Atta boy, Axe!"

Fortunately for Mr. Loban and his long wind, the accolades fade quickly and he's able to take command of the proceedings. "Ladies and gentlemen. My dear friends and neighbors. Let me be the first to welcome home, at the end of the first leg of their momentous…"

In all probability, Mr. Loban could prattle on for the better part of an hour. Yet he should know an eager crowd when he sees one, and just might want to keep his part brief.

"…And with that, allow me to re-introduce my engineer and his lovely wife, Mr. and Mrs. Axelrod Lane."

"Speech! Speech!" is a hail from the crowd, which urges others.

Axe isn't in the mood for a keynote, however. And although part of the crowd may be avid for a few words, a hunch tells him that because it's lunchtime, a greater portion may be hungry.

"Good citizens of Lisbon. On behalf of my wife and Loban Motor, I thank you. And as a token of our gratitude, we invite you to our table." Axe gestures toward the public square. "Let us dine."

The homecoming takes up all of the noon hour, ending at the moment when the refreshments deplete. It's just as well, for there's work to be done, a first leg to assess and strategies to adjust.

And so the Lanes divide their labors, Katie at home to begin her campaign of letters and Axe at Loban Motor to file his report and contribute to the critical discussions.

"Gentlemen, I am puzzled," speaks a miffed Mr. Loban, as Miss Charnwood records. "Of that Swift boy at the fete. Twice I shooed him away from the beer keg. Yet even after I had you stand guard, Freddy, I spied him with tumbler in hand. I'd like to know the name of the scoundrel who foiled my actions."

A brief silence ensues.

"Never mind for now," redirects Mr. Loban. "We need to hear from you, Lane, about your journey. Especially of how the Speed Six performed."

"Splendidly, Mr. Loban." Axe's response is immediate. "I'm fairly happy with the carburetor. Though I think we can do better, still. And I'm certain were it not for a leak, we used less oil." Axe plops the driving log upon the table. "I'll make the calculations."

"That is splendid news," comments Mr. Loban.

"Splendid," parrots Freddy.

"Yes. Modifying our carburetor is a continuing effort. Right, Kimble?"

"Day and night, Mr. Loban," replies the chief engineer.

"I must say, I was mildly shocked the drive shaft held its own," continues Axe. "Though I would like to replace it before we depart again."

"Of course," agrees Mr. Loban. "Have someone see to it, Flugan."

"Oh, don't bother, Hugh." Axe is quick to intervene, if only to protect the secret of the spare drive shaft. "I'll do it, myself. Your boys are too busy."

"Very well," agrees Mr. Loban. "So, then, tell me of the windscreen."

"That happened this side of the Susquehanna," explains Axe. "The screen shattered after a farmer threw a stone at us. I suppose he became peeved when the engine noise startled his livestock. He missed me, but struck a horse, which kicked up an uproar of projectiles when it rushed passed."

"I see." Mr. Loban appears to be surprised at the windscreen's failure.

"So I was forced to keep the windscreen lowered, and with it the canopy. What a nuisance it had become. Not very compatible to the open road"

"Umm." Now, the look on Mr. Loban's face is one of disappointment.

"Though the lack of a top wasn't terribly inconvenient. When it showered, we just parked and unfolded the tarp."

"Hmm?" considers Mr. Loban.

"We had quite a few punctures. As many as Hugh and I suffered on our Cleveland trip. But, oh, those Alleghenies." Axe pauses. "It was while crossing those mountains that my lingering fear was realized."

"Fear? What fear was that?"

"Of how the fuel tank is fixed too low to feed the engine on an incline. Several times we nearly stalled upon a mountainside.

"Really?" Mr. Loban appears to be taken aback by this unforeseen problem.

"Yes," continues Axe. "Can you imagine the difficulties when we confront the Rockies?"

There's a moment of silence at what may be an insurmountable barrier to Loban Motor's scheme.

But leave it to Axe to come up with a solution, this being of a design at its most simple.

"If the fuel tank can be elevated, this could make all the difference in the world. Defeat the forces of incline with a better angle of our own."

"Would that not displace the rumble seat?" counters Freddy.

"Likely," answers Axe.

"Oh, no." Mr. Loban is quick to object. "The rumble seat will remain as is, for the country to appreciate."

"But Mr. Loban, it is a monumental problem," protests Axe. "Uphill?"

"Nonsense, Lane. How should this matter, with the Speed Six conceived as an automobile of the farmlands and cities?" Mr. Loban shrugs away a serious design flaw.

"This is news to me." Axe raises his voice. "Mr. Loban, why even attempt the Rockies?"

"Because we are committed. Bound and determined to cross the country."

Axe should be forgiven if he considers such a statement to be somewhat outrageous.

"Don't worry, Axelrod. I'm sure you and Kimble will find a way to elevate the fuel tank an inch or two," allays Mr. Loban. "That may suffice. And you could find a surer route across the Rockies."

"Hopefully, Mr. Loban."

"But don't you see, Axelrod," cajoles Mr. Loban. "That by pushing the Speed Six to its extremes, this will enable us to realize its potential. Why, I never would have guessed that New York City would have been swept away by our roadster had we not sent you there. And like you said before, Axelrod, New York loved our crimson and its lines. Much different from Cleveland's blue. Might we assume, Willis, that each region will develop its own tastes for the Speed Six?"

From Axe's standpoint, the words "swept away" may be taking his and Katie's Manhattan experience a bit far. Although, he cannot argue against the crux of Mr. Loban's logic.

"Who can say what is learned by the time you reach the Pacific?" continues Mr. Loban. "Along with the notoriety coming with your deed." He pauses, with his face and eyes becoming somewhat dreamy. "How I envy you, Axelrod. To be young, but to have such an opportunity. And to be able to take the comforts of home with you. Sad to say, I am passed all that, or I would take the roadster myself."

"I believe you would, Mr. Loban."

"Thank you, Axelrod. And by all means, enjoy your adventure. Relish every moment of it."

Axe nods his head and stretches a smile, he knowing that there are no genuine doubts to the promotion's motives. Indeed, only minor details are the points of contention, insignificant snags such as conquering mountain roads of 30-degree inclines with a 25-degree, fuel pump-less automobile.

Thus the discussion is able to rage on toward other topics and concerns.

Meanwhile, an auxiliary portion of Loban Motor proceeds in her own sublime atmosphere. To be sure, Katie takes her association seriously, the reason why she sits at her cherrywood, slant top desk—a wedding gift from her maternal grandmother. Upon having settled, she wastes no time, plunging herself into her list of new acquaintances, each of whom has shown a bona fide interest in the Speed Six. Into a bottle of Sanford Gloss Black Ink, Katie dips her ten karat gold pen by its fancy twist, cut pearl holder—a graduation gift from her maternal grandmother. And it's onto a page of Irish linen stationery that a stream of Ohio eloquence and its heartfelt sentiments begin to flow:

> Dear Mrs. Leewoek,
>
> As you can see, those best wishes from my new Manhattan friends have guided my husband and me to a safe journey home. Though we burned the midnight automobile oils to reach Lisbon, I feel no worse for wear, so eager am I to begin my correspondences. What a kind happenstance to have met you and your sister and your husbands. Could there ever be a pair of more gracious couples on this earth? I think not, though I must say that our brief tour of Manhattan afforded us several encounters with its amiable citizens. That the Leewoeks and the Van Doorns proved to be people of civility came as no surprise, these notable traits being the tenor of your great city
>
> I hope, Mrs. Leewoek, that your husband will find the brochures and photographs of the Speed Six to be satisfactory. The drawings and the water color print were produced by our gifted chief draftsman. Lisbon,

Ohio may not be a grand metropolis of culture and commerce, but out little town certainly holds its own when it comes to manufacturing and mechanical advancements. I, myself, cannot explain why this is so, why my quaint burgh attracts men of talent and innovation. It certainly has lured Mr. Lane, and with him, yours truly. Nevertheless, whatever the circumstances may be in creating the Speed Six, even a stubborn skeptic cannot deny that it is a remarkable vehicle: powerful and sturdy, yet trim and stylish and responsive to the commands of its driver (even we who belong to the weaker sex). It is no small boast to say that our automobile is a joy to drive, as well as being a proud vehicle upon which to be seen. As it happens, I believe our Speed Six is perfect for the streets of Manhattan (this being a surprise to myself, and I am certain not the intent of Loban Motor's staff of engineers and designers). What a coincidence, I should think, that the inventions of Lisbon, Ohio marry so well with New York City, New York. Nonetheless, upon second thought, is it so strange that an exchange of Manhattan culture and Ohio industry should find a mutual satisfaction? Of course, it will, because already it has.

Allow me again, Mrs. Leewoek, to offer my gratitude for the welcome given by you and your sister and your husbands. Though might I extend my thanks to all of your city, where the obligations of a stubborn schedule forced us to leave before our wishes. May the Leewoeks and the Van Doorns find pleasant roads ahead.

With fond regards,
Mrs. Axelrod Lane

And so one letter is composed, the first of what promises to be many. But then immediately, a second letter begins, its sentiments being the same as its predecessor, although with a different mix of words:

Dear Mrs. Van Doorn,

It seems like only hours ago that my husband and myself were so fortunate to have met…

By early evening, Axe is free to return home and render assistance.

"Why don't we send the laundry to Maine's?" he suggests.

"Suits me fine," agrees an overwhelmed Katie, whose list of chores goes well beyond writing letters.

"Are we still dining out?" furthers Axe. "The Hostetter?"

"Absolutely."

Soon, a dinner of roast pork and vegetables proves to be filling and savory, with the conversation being a stream of business and pleasure.

"…I do admit, Katie, sometimes I can see genius in Mr. Loban's methods. That he may be one to admire."

"You know, Axe, you said something like that three times while we crossed Pennsylvania. But now you seem adamant. So then it must be true. Mr. Loban is a genius."

"Really?"

There's a little daylight left when the Lanes leave the Hostetter and begin their stroll homeward. But as luck would have it, Mr. Nace is keeping a late hour, meaning that his pharmacy remains open for business.

"Jimmy," shouts Axe, when he happens to spot a friend down the block. He waves his arm and offers an invitation. "Ice cream!"

Soon, Mr. Nace's last three customers for the day are dipping their spoons into bowls of frozen vanilla, chocolate and peppermint.

"Mmm. Gee this is sure awful nice of you, Axe. Mrs. Lane."

"Our pleasure, Jimmy," returns Axe.

"When are you two leaving again?" asks Jimmy.

"Three, maybe four, days," replies Axe.

"I sure wish I could tag along."

"Maybe in a few years' time. When you're done with your schooling."

"Mmm," continues Jimmy. "Beer and ice cream in the same day. You sure are a friend, Axe."

"Axe?" The innocent revelation draws a sharp reflex from Katie's elbow. "Beer?"

"Uhh?" responds a clumsy Axe. "Eat your ice cream, Jimmy. It's getting late."

To be sure, three or four days isn't much time, as the pace of events hastens.

"Why don't you get dressed and see for yourself?" suggests Katie to her restless husband, as they both lie upon their bed. "It could be that Hugh and the shop remedied it late in the day."

Although weary, the persistent thoughts of the fuel tank are stealing away Axe's ambitions for slumber. But Katie's proffer is a sound one, that the elixir for a good night's sleep is to take his bicycle to Loban Motor and scrutinize the roadster for himself.

"I'll be quick." Thus Axe springs out of bed.

Unfortunately, there's not much of a moon to shine his cycling way, while the faint glows of a midnight Lisbon fade upon his back. Yet although Axe expects nothing but the shadows of Loban Motor to help pedal him along, soon, and to his surprise, he spies a distinct light.

The mystery pans even further when Axe closes the distance. If a light is shining at this particular hour within Loban Motor, then logically its source should come from one of the shops. Yet there is no mistake, that somebody is busy in the second floor office area, where a somnolent Clarence seldom ventures.

"The blue roadster?" mutters Axe, when he sees the light glowing upon the parked Speed Six.

He eases his pedals and then stops altogether, while his eyes stay fixed upon Mr. Loban's office. After settling his bicycle to the ground, Axe fiddles through his pockets for his legitimate means of entry.

"My keys. Damn it," he whispers, as he jiggles the locked front door. "I forgot my keys."

But fear not, for Axe has been informed of a secret point of access. Around Loban Motor, he sidles. And when Axe discovers one particular, unlocked basement window, he slips through without hesitation, as if being swallowed into the bowels of a colossal beast—perhaps to a fate unknown.

Because the boiler is not up to steam, the generator is not up to electricity, meaning that the darkness surrounding Axe is absolute. Fortunately, although Axe may be forgetful about his set of keys, he isn't with a box of matches. He strikes a light, and almost immediately discovers a Fury Four and one of its handy, removable kerosene lanterns—perhaps the same type of hardware illuminating Mr. Loban's office. And so it's toward the stairway Axe seeks, and, cautiously, it's up to the second floor he proceeds.

The higher he climbs the slower his steps become, his ears keening to any report. Suddenly, a hint of murmurings reaches Axe, while a glint of the other source of light allows him to set his lantern upon the topmost step. As best he can, he calms his heart and leans toward the source, concentrating his capacities to absorb the faint hints of a congruous nature.

The open entry enables Axe to peek around the corner with little risk. Following the trail of pants and purrs, he reveals part of his face and all of an eye—the vanguard of a dutiful employee and curiosity-seeker.

Axe's suspicions have run rampant. But one by one, they're eliminated, until only a sole survivor remains. To be sure, Axe's confirmation brings a sure shock, a gasp contained only under extreme duress.

Perhaps it shouldn't be unexpected to find Mr. Loban in his office—regardless of the hour. But that he has his secretary pinned against his desk forces a disturbing vision, this innocent being menaced and groped by the man of whom Axe has been coming to admire.

"Oh, Percy. Percy, my love."

Or could it be the other way around, for not only is Miss Charnwood putting up no resistance, she seems to be relishing the moment, with her exposed right leg wrapping itself around the left of her employer's. And then there are her hands, which take no dictation, but instead are delivering a message all their own.

"Oh, Charlotte."

To say the least, any indecision as to whether Axe should rush to a damsel's aid is squelched. Now the question arises as to how he can escape without detection. On the other hand, Miss Charnwood's aloof charms are an established source of interest for all but a handful of males, and the promise of an unfolding vision could be worth a prolonged glance. But then there happens her partner, Mr. Loban, an overweight, over-bearing glob, who lacks the feminine curves and whose galluses are being freed at this very instant.

The picture gauges too heavy for further contemplation. Slowly, Axe backs away his overburdened head, and then reverses his steps altogether, all while doing his level best not to produce a peep. Never mind that the participants around the corner can be in no state to pay heed to anything short of a riot.

Still, Axe is cautious with his jittery feet when he finds the stairs, taking each step so that scarcely a creak is produced. Without a single trip, he finds himself on the basement floor, and quick as he can, returns to the Fury Four. Dowsing his lantern, Axe crawls through the window, freeing himself from the fear of being discovered, though guiltless he may be.

When he picks up his bicycle, he doesn't pause to look upward, but instead speeds away. In fact, Axe's exertion becomes so furious, that soon it fuels his indignation, thus replacing those initial feelings of shock.

Poor Mrs. Loban, he thinks, she being the true damsel in distress, who seems to be paying the price for setting up a second residence in order to be close to her two sons and their Columbus prep school. But as lonely as Mr. Loban may find himself, his current circumstance is no excuse for his present indiscretion. Indeed, Axe is regretting that he would spend any of his confidence upon a man lacking in strength.

"#&@$%!"

Because Axe isn't concentrating on the pitch black road, the front wheel of his bicycle discovers a pothole, resulting in an involuntary tumult.

"Ugh-h-h."

Fortunately, the points of impact are the palms of Axe's hands and not his head. And since there is a rush of pain, there seems to be no crippling blow. With his spectacles remaining in place, Axe is able to gather himself and proceed as before. Soon, his perturbation builds anew—although at a much steadier rate.

Eventually, Axe manages to lumber home. By the kitchen light, he's able to view the damage to his hands and, as well, discovers the torn knees of his trousers.

"Damn," winces Axe, as he washes in the sink his dirty, slightly bloody palms.

There are nursing hands at the ready, however, Katie's restless sleep being alert.

"Axe? You're back so early?" she notes upon entering the kitchen.

He turns around and reveals the damage done.

"Axe! My goodness! What happened!" Katie rushes forward and grasps both of his hands.

"It's nothing, Katie. A slight mishap."

"Oh, Axe." Closely, she examines the wounds and finds a handy cloth for a soft rub.

"Ouch," reacts Axe. "Really, Katie. It's not so terrible." He lets out a sigh.

Yet Katie is not one to miss such a subtle signal—as profound to her as a shock of lightning. "What happened, Axe?" She continues to doctor. "Is something wrong?"

He hesitates, not really sure how to word the episode as was played before him.

"Something is wrong. Axe, you've turned all parchmenty. Like you've seen a ghost."

"If only I had," he smirks.

"Axe?" Katie's voice bears some reluctance. "What did you see? Tell me?"

"Katie. I don't know if I can."

"Maybe you should try."

"Well-l-l. I don't know if you should hear of it." Like a good husband, Axe is protective.

"Axe." Suddenly, Katie's mood becomes insistent. "Now I have to know."

"Very well. But you have been warned." Axe takes a deep breath. "I saw them, together. By accident. Mr. Loban in his office. Mr. Loban a-a-and." His depiction sputters short.

But leave it to Katie to complete the sentence, her suspicions bolstered by what she's heard as town gossip. "Mr. Loban and Miss Charnwood? Compromised?"

"Compromised? Yes." Axe is all too happy to exhale. "They were about to compromise all over the place. Before I sneaked away."

"Oh, my God, Axe." But then Katie gathers herself. "So it must be true."

"True?" Axe is astounded at what in effect is a revelation.

Katie shrugs her shoulders. "From what I've heard. I suppose."

"Heard? Katie, how come you haven't told me about this?"

"Axe. I didn't know it was true," she explains with all genuineness. "And besides, I figured you're much too involved with your work to be bothered with such trivial gossip."

"It's not trivial gossip now," counters Axe. He feels the exhaustion and takes a seat at the kitchen table.

"Oh, Axe. There is no doubt? Is there?" Katie takes her chair and scoots it to his side.

"None, Katie." Axe slumps into his chair, as the evening's episode becomes too much to bear. "And now that's all I have. Doubt."

"Axe." Katie arms smothers her husband, her sympathies melding with his uneasiness.

"What am I to do?" he asks. "How can I carry on as before? To cross the country in that man's auto?"

For at least the moment, Katie is left without a reply, what with the account arriving during the dead of night. Yet her strengths are such that she's not one to allow an extended impasse. Swiveling herself in order to look at her husband eye to eye, Katie places her hands upon his shoulders and offers a little shake.

"Axe, you don't mean it," contends Katie. "His auto? Mr. Loban may own the company, but is the Speed Six really his child? Need I remind you of whose idea it was to develop the company's own six-cylinder? Who pushed for vanadium steel? Did Mr. Loban design and test the frame? What of the carburetor? The crimson red? What of the other designs you and your co-workers have made? What of them, Axe?"

Once again, he inhales deeply, but with his jaw firmed. And then, in a steady rhythm, Axe gestures his head forward and backward. Forced by the brunt of sound logic, he has no option but to disavow his late night conversion to pessimism, reconfirming that pragmatic faith to which he has been both born and wed.

"We should face the truth," continues Katie. "The Speed Six's success means more to Axelrod Lane than any other person."

The nodding continues, accompanied with a raised brow.

"And all your friends, who are depending on you, Axe. Lisbon, too, for that matter," adds Katie with a greater measure. "Mr. Loban? Humph. He's at the bottom of the list."

"Yes," agrees Axe. "For certain."

"So we'll cross the country for the two of us. First and foremost."

"Yes. All the way to the Pacific."

Katie smiles broadly, and then wraps her husband in a hug.

"But Katie, we should be more watchful of Percy Loban. No more the trustworthy. Who can say if his support for the promotion might flag? By God, if the situation comes where we're forced to cross the country by our own devices, then so be it."

Under no uncertain terms, Axe's lapse is being overwhelmed by his ongoing faith, to which Katie's response is to tighten her wrap ever more.

"We know what we have to do. What our path should be." It's as if Axe is mounting the pulpit. "If Percy Loban thinks we're going to mind his every word, then he's in for a shock. Prescriptions and proscriptions, my eye. We know better of how to conduct business. Who is he, after all? Who elected him to office?"

"Absolutely, Axe. And we always have known better. Surely."

"Absolutely. Though still-l-l."

"What's wrong now, Axe?"

"What's wrong is that I have to face the man. At a morning staff meeting in his office. The scene of the malefaction! God, what horrid visions will be forced into my head when I see him at his desk! That desk!"

"There, there. You'll be fine," soothes Katie. "Poor Axe. The things he must endure."

"Endure, I must, I suppose. My burden. But my God, that man. That dirty, filthy man."

Indeed, the aforementioned meeting is an ordeal for Axe. But as well, those co-workers present might say the same, the moodiness of the assistant engineer being apparent. Axe's replies to Mr. Loban's questions are short and snappish—without the usual elaborations and considerations. That his immediate wish is to be elsewhere, he offers little effort to conceal.

"Excuse me. But I promised to help Katie prepare," begs Axe's indulgence, this after Mr. Loban informed the staff to install a new windscreen and canopy top. But because these encumbrances can be discarded at a later date while on the road, the want to argue the point doesn't exist. "Good day."

And so sets the tone for the next couple of days, mere hours if one is inclined to make the tally. As far as Axe is concerned, his business is to make ready for the long road ahead, and not cross paths with Mr. Loban.

9
...AND HOME, AGAIN

AT LAST, KATIE AND AXE ARE BACK on the road, plunging through the morning mists of Carroll County and its snaking roads. In no way, however, does this land compare to the Pennsylvania Alleghenies' steeper grades, Ohio's undulations being mere foothills. With this in mind, although cautious as they wind their path, the Lanes don't expect the limited scope of the fuel tank to be a problem within their home state.

"How ready will gasoline be in Wyoming, Axe?"

"Who can say? But if need be, we'll alter our route through Montana. Or another state."

There did occur a modest amount of ceremony for the Lisbon re-departure, it taking place at Loban Motor. Of course, this suited Axe just fine, the brief hoopla having offered less opportunity for Mr. Loban's noise. Still, posing for the camera while shaking his employer's hand required a bit of resolve, such as grinding his teeth to forge a smile.

"How is your jaw, Axe?"

"Still a bit sore."

For the time being, Axe has folded down the wind screen and the canopy top, the Lanes protecting themselves with goggles, coats and brims. And the roadster isn't loaded to full. With a planned reception at Columbus' capitol being less than two days away, appearances are important, so that unsightly baggage is kept to a minimum—the spare tires and tubes atop the rumble seat notwithstanding. As planned, Delaware is where a goodly portion of the cross country gear and provisions will await, delivered via the railroads almost at this very moment. And so it's on to Carrollton, New Philadelphia, Coshocton, Newark and hopefully, Columbus. To say the least, timing is vital, for a late arrival will not do, and to find the capitol too early could appear awkward. Because Ohio's middle city has been a good customer for Loban Motor, Axe is determined to maintain that status.

Only five tire mishaps mark the first day out of Lisbon, this leg being punctuated instead by an aggressive farm rooster losing a duel to the death with the right front wheel. Yet no rocks are thrown nor hard feelings extended, if only because of Axe's timely compensation of nineteen cents.

By evening the couple reaches Newark, it lying east of Columbus' doorstep. Almost immediately, it becomes apparent that the Lanes are entering a beer town—or to be more precise, a small city of beer bottle manufacturing. And it's before they discover their hotel that Axe feels the inspiration, his practical mind conjuring a solution against those impending, impractical horizons.

"Beer bottles?" he notes, when his eyes admire yet another factory. "Perhaps we should purchase a couple of cases as a hedge against possible Anti-Saloon League territories?"

"But do we have the room, Axe? Especially, when taking on baggage at Delaware?"

"You made room for your violin and mandolin, Katie?"

"Yes, Axe. But you agreed. Even insisted. Remember?"

"Oh. Yes."

"Don't worry, Axe. When we finish packing in Delaware, you can stow your bottles about the roadster. That is without my parents' knowledge. There should be enough room inside the spare tires."

"The spare tires? A brilliant solution," judges Axe. "And those Anti-Saloon Leagues won't have a clue."

Because the Lanes have managed Newark, they should be afforded a calm morning. Barring an unforeseen catastrophe, Columbus' noon engagement should be a cinch.

"It's 11:55, Axe," notes Katie of her watch.

"Perfectly timed," exudes Axe, as he guides the roadster upon Main Street.

The Speed Six is in meticulous order, as are the Lanes, with Katie clad in her princess ensemble.

"What should we expect in the way of dignitaries?" inquires Axe, who up to now has had other concerns.

"Possibly the governor," replies Katie. "Should there be no conflicts to his calendar."

"Uh-h-h?" Axe is stirred. "Harris?"

"Yes, Axe. Governor Harris. Before we married, as a favor to Father, you voted for Mr. Harris? When he ran for Lieutenant Governor? Harris, the temperance supporter? Remember?"

While Axe keeps his eyes upon Main Street, the look upon his face turns undeniably blank.

"Axe. Don't tell me you voted for Mr. Houck?"

"I think I may have. Accidently."

Katie lets out a sigh. "Well, then it will have to be our secret. Axe, no one should know."

"Fine with me, Old Girl. But who told you the governor will be there?"

"Mr. Loban."

"Hmm? Mr. Loban. Don't you find it odd he couldn't make the trip ahead of us? I wonder if Mrs. Loban will show. And I wonder if she suspects."

"Axe, let's not sour the moment. Mrs. Loban had sent me her regrets. She'll be at a cousin's funeral."

"That's too bad." Yet Axe manages a smile when he spies a signature rotunda of columns. "There she lies. It's time to be festive."

Truly, if democracy demands its tokens, then there's no better way than to pay homage to its origins. And so, decades ago, the people of Ohio erected a Doric capitol—replete with Doric capitals—located in the heart of their state and the middle of Columbus.

"Look, Katie?" A line of sight is achieved, Ohio's resplendent and dignified, grey-stoned capitol coming into plainer view. "There must be a hundred people. The governor and his toadies."

"Gulp," responds Katie. "I hope I see someone I know."

Already, Axe feels the inspiration from Ohio's main edifice, which causes him to grip the wheel even firmer. The steps to the first floor of the capitol number little more than a dozen, though the incline is fairly steep. Yet they make for a mountain begging to be scaled, and a risk to be taken.

"By God," announces a determined Axe. "Let's see how the fuel tank works now."

With a toot on his horn, Axe enters the capitol grounds and takes an inappropriate turn. Yet fortunately for the populace of Columbus, and the future of Loban Motor, he's able to spot a convenient gap.

Immediately, Katie is able to divine her husband's intentions. "Are you sure? Will it work?"

"Yes, I am," he answers with a determined grin. "And yes, it will. I think."

There's a collective murmur from the crowd, accompanied by a few cries of disbelief.

But as far as Axe is concerned, they're all shouts of encouragement, the combined hubbub demanding an impromptu display of showmanship. The gap widens, ready to be exploited and begging to be plugged.

Together, the front tires touch the first step. And with a little urging from Axe, the engine groans and helps them along. Well within its strengths, the Speed Six lurches upward and that initial rise is topped.

"Gracious alive," declares Katie, she hanging for dear life.

"Hold tight," comes the belated advice.

The ascent proceeds, the roadster overcoming the terraced slope with relative ease. In quick time, the Lanes reach the summit and Axe is able to park the Speed Six between two columns. Upon pulling the handbrake and killing the engine, he stands upon his seat and waves to the applauding crowd. And in a dashing move, Axe leaps to the other side of the roadster and renders assistance to Katie. Arm in arm they parade toward the clutch of dignitaries, his free hand extended toward the man in charge.

"Nice to meet you, Governor," he announces in a proud voice. "The best candidate I've ever voted for."

To Katie's horror, however, a complication presents itself, one threatening the roadster's triumph over the capitol steps. She tugs at Axe's arm and nudges her face to his ear.

"That's not the governor, Axe," she whispers discreetly. "He's the Speaker of the House."

Regardless, Axe is quick to react to the sharp swerve. "That is to say, our future governor, Mr. Speaker. And my vote you shall certainly have."

In spite of the faux pas, the gathering proceeds, for how often do a native son and daughter attempt to traverse the continent with an indigenous invention? Indeed, those who find themselves on the capitol grounds are participating at a moment in history.

Be that as it may, unlike the return celebration at Lisbon, there are no refreshments on hand, meaning that the event is doomed to a short duration. After all, speeches, as given by self-serving politicians, can provide only limited diversions for a noon crowd.

Yet this suits Katie and Axe just fine, they being anxious to reach Delaware. When the crowd thins and the dignitaries depart, the Lanes are able to back down the steps.

"Whew. I had my doubts about that tank," confesses Axe, as he steers the roadster upon High Street. "I could feel the engine bleeding dry at that top step."

"My goodness, Axe," responds Katie, surprised and relieved at once.

As it happens, High Street leads directly passed an old haunt of Axe's—a diversion of narrow lanes and open boulevards.

"I took all of my mathematic courses, here," points Axe at but one of Ohio State University's notable structures. "What an odd calculus professor I had. Wore the same suit and necktie each day to class." He shakes his head. "I could never figure out the circumstances behind that."

"My goodness," reacts Katie. "We would never hear of such a thing at Wesleyan."

The brief tour continues through the nearly deserted campus.

"Now how did it come that you never joined a fraternity?" provokes Katie, after passing a few houses.

"Oh, I considered it," retells Axe. "But I wouldn't put up with their abuses. And I suppose they of me, after I punched a pair of noses. That had me banished from the Greeks. Heh, heh."

Katie offers a giggle. "Sounds like my Axe."

"It seems like so long ago," he continues with a little dreaminess. "And only yesterday."

"I know what you mean, Axe."

He lets out a sigh. "What do you say we speed away? Get to Delaware and your parents?"

"By all means," replies Katie. "There's not much here we haven't seen already. And besides, I don't think your calculus professor is about today. Probably gone to visit his tailor."

"Where else could he be?"

The following pre-dawn darkness finds an agitated Axe sitting up in bed. After all, there's too much to do and he's marooned within a Winter Street household of strict rhythms and regimentations, the threat being that the morning hours will idle by.

Katie, too, succumbs to the same antsy affliction, though she knows better than to tussle with her frustrations. "What time is it?" she yawns.

"Sixteen after five." Axe has been keeping track.

"Easy now. Remember. When in Delaware, we keep banker's hours."

"Uh-h-h," is the response from one who isn't afraid to dirty his hands.

Delaware, Ohio, population 8,500, remains the same as when the Lanes last visited Katie's hometown of light manufacturing, weighted education and

Apennine architecture—not to mention the location of at least one presidential birthplace. That was four months prior, when the couple chose the expediency and reliability of the rails over the chancy outcome of a borrowed Fury Four. Yet the times are changing, that is to say the circumstances of Katie and Axe and their current means of transportation.

"If only we were allowed to get dressed, have breakfast and get on with our lives," protests the husband, while trapped in his wife's former bedroom. "Katie? Might you slip into the kitchen and cook for us?"

"Oh, no, Axe. I couldn't," squelches Katie. "To take charge of the kitchen would so upset Mother."

Regardless, a different solution enters his head. "Perhaps we could slip away to that hotel? You know? The one with the castle tower?"

"The Bee?"

"Yes. The Hotel Bee. Surely, they could offer us a fine breakfast."

"Axe. For goodness sake. That would surely hurt Mother's feelings, were she to find out."

"Then what can we do?"

"Wait for Mother to awaken us. Nothing more."

"I wish we could stay at your sister's house," pouts Axe. "Frances wouldn't be afraid to accommodate her guests. Frances and Robert both."

"We have to stay here. You know that."

Katie's assertion is nothing less than hard reality, the familial complications being absolute.

Although Axe understands this truth, in no way does it soothe his restrained wants. Indeed, wide awake and restless, he needs to spend some of his morning zest. With nothing else to do, Axe takes a pleasant whiff of Katie's flowing hair, her auburn tresses having had a thorough wash during the previous evening. He entangles his fingers, only to carry his curiosity beneath the covers and upon her smooth, feminine curves.

"Axe," protests Katie. "Don't you dare. Not with my parents in the next room."

"Why not?" he counters. "They're sound asleep. Banker's hours?"

"But we'll awaken them, Axe. You know how we are."

"We'll keep quiet." His wayward hand continues its mischief. "Just this once."

"No we can't." Katie grasps her husband's wandering appendage and applies a slap. "We'll have to wait until we're out of Delaware. Not a moment before."

"None too soon," replies a dejected Axe, who, nonetheless, continues to sniff the divine atmosphere.

Eventually, Axe receives his breakfast, albeit with condiments of thin criticisms and disapproving sermons—and with the promise of more of the same for those other mealtimes. That the Kanes have not been happy with their youngest daughter's adventure, not to mention the choice she made for a husband at the outset, is of no surprise to Axe. Indeed, Dr. and Mrs. Lane's unbridled affection for their daughter-in-law stands as a continuing contrast.

"That was so enjoyable, Mrs. Kane," compliments Axe, while wiping his mouth.

"Thank you, Axelrod," responds Mrs. Kane, from whom her youngest child has received few traits. She remains at the table and delivers a command. "Katie, might you clear the dishes?"

"Yes, Mother." To which the daughter hops.

"Perhaps you may begin washing them? Use that pot of hot water on the stove. For the sink."

"Yes, Mother." To which the daughter hops even quicker.

While Katie gathers the plates and silverware, Axe gulps down the last speck of scrambled egg. He senses an ambush, this one coming well before the anticipated hour.

"Let me help you, Katie." Axe stands while holding his plate.

"Oh no, Axelrod," insists Mr. Kane, from whom his youngest child has received his eyes and hair, and little else. "Katie can see to the dishes. Please, stay seated."

Axe does just that. Yet at the same instant, he feels within himself the stubborn need to forestall the impending challenge, what should be the Kane's condemnation to their daughter's haphazard tour of America's western wilderness. Axe surrenders his plate to Katie, and when the swinging kitchen door closes behind her, he clears his throat and gathers his resolve.

"Mrs. Kane. Mr. Kane. Thank you for being so accommodating. Such is a comfort in the middle of our journey to stay with family. Though our travels haven't seen hardship. To the contrary. Our automobile is very sound. Why, it all but drives itself. And the people we encounter have been awfully friendly. So much so, that Katie's spare time is filled with writing letters of gratitude."

"Is that so?"

It's difficult for Axe to read his mother-in-law's comment, and so he continues his plod. "With these experiences, and because we are well-funded, Katie and I see no difficulties ahead. Why, I wouldn't be surprised if we reach the Pacific within two weeks with a quicker return home by rail."

Two weeks! Instead of listening to the sounds of hot, splashing water, Katie's left ear is pressed against the kitchen door.

"And the hotels we'll be staying are well-regarded by the railroads' preferred travelers. Though I do suspect we may be invited as guests into the respectable homes."

"Hmm? Two weeks, you say?" reacts Mr. Kane to the bold declaration. "Two weeks to the Pacific?"

"Two weeks or less, sir," continues Axe. "Although I do wish it would take longer. If only to allow us to spread more the Loban Motor word."

"Yes. I see what you mean," nods Mr. Kane. "Hmm? Spread the word."

"Yes," echoes Mrs. Kane, as a slight smile angles upon her face. "Spreading the word."

"Tell me, Axelrod, more of your Mr. Loban," furthers Mr. Kane. "What sort of man is he?"

"A greatly admired man." Axe doesn't hesitate, even if this particular topic has been broached on previous occasions. "For certain, a staunch Ohio Republican. And I admire him greatly for that. And for the fact that he is an unfailing family man."

From Katie's hands, a coffee cup bolts free from her grip and fractures upon the floor.

"Is everything all right, Katie?"

"Yes, Mother."

"So then, Axelrod, you will make frequent stops along your route?That is, beyond those needs of normal, automobile travel?"

"Why yes, Mr. Kane." Axe feels somewhat hesitant, if only because he detects a slight change in tone. "Most likely at every sizeable town we come upon. Especially those with a newspaper."

"That would be very astute of you, Axelrod," notes Mr. Kane.

Upon receiving what seems to be an unqualified compliment, Axe's ears become astounded.

"Yes," agrees Mrs. Kane, whose tone alters as well.

With this chorus, Axe's senses are all but paralyzed with confusion.

As for Katie, that she might begin washing the dishes any time soon is a wishful thought.

"There's really nothing so astute, Mr. Kane. Mrs. Kane," protests Axe, as if preferring his in-law's history of belittling. "Our plans have endured thorough reviews. By co-workers and investors both."

"Of course, dear Axelrod," counters Mrs. Kane. "But with your contributions at the lead."

Such astonishing words from his mother-in-law Axe has yet to hear. To be her target of a term such as "dear" he would never expect—not in her lifetime, or his. Although it may appear that the reason for Katie's kitchen exile is to separate Axe from his staunchest advocate, he's beginning to think otherwise. He looks at Mrs. Kane's stiff smile, and then veers to Mr. Kane's almost benignly fatherly expression.

"Achem." There's nothing in Axe's throat, not a speck of breakfast to be cleared nor a trepidation to be gulped. Instead, there is the realization that something he said is making an impression upon his in-laws.

"Axelrod. I believe Mrs. Kane and myself are convinced that your trip to the Pacific is a worthwhile endeavor, and that our Katie will not be endangered nor face hardship."

"Certainly not, Mr. Kane," asserts Axe. "Not while she's under my protection."

"It seems you will chance to greet many people. Crowds of the curious, for sure, yet those of influence."

"Yes sir. So far this has been true."

"Then it shouldn't be too much of a burden, Axelrod, that while Katie and yourself engage with these people, you might distribute some pamphlets and placards."

"That is a splendid idea," joins Mrs. Kane. "And such a wonderful favor it would be to us."

"Of course, I can." His mother-in-law's enthusiasm catches Axe unbalanced, and without the chance to right himself. "What sort of pamphlets did you say?"

"Why, those of the Anti-Saloon League. Of course."

"Oh. I see," perceives Axe, who should have seen this coming. After all, when it comes to their pet social cause, the Kanes are like a damaged phonograph record. Yet Axe has no choice in the matter, to be a soldier for what he considers is a nonsensical ideal. "I'd love to scatter your pamphlets about the countryside. Like any devoted son-in-law, you can count on me."

Crash! And an innocent saucer meets its end upon the kitchen floor.

Instantly, the issue of available space becomes more complicated, especially when Mr. Kane produces four boxes of Anti-Saloon League material. With the gear sent from Lisbon not yet stowed upon the roadster, Axe isn't sure about accommodating his in-laws.

But soon, the work will begin, with Katie lending an able hand. First things first, and that'll be to remove the bothersome wind screen and the folding canopy top, to be stored in the Kane's attic. Then there will come an inspection of the engine and other unseen components, along with reapplications of fluids and lubricants. And when this is done, Axe and Katie can take the roadster into the countryside for a test drive, after which they will be able to load the Speed Six for that anticipated, long journey to the Pacific.

Two days it has been, two days toiling and tooling at the automobile, not to mention packing for the roadster's needs and those of its occupants. But then there arrives those familial obligations, the arduous labor of those evenings spent with the Kanes and the associated trials to a man's patience and pride.

"...If you don't mind, Axelrod. We don't use that word in this household."

"My apologies, ma'am." Although the offending tongue has no idea what utterance is the crime.

Yet it all matters little to Axe, if only because the morning will find the Speed Six back on the road and away from Delaware. Indeed, there persists but a minor chore to perform, albeit one which Katie will not allow before dusk for fear of being discovered. Tactfully, using the excuse of testing roadster's lights, the Lanes beg away from the parlor.

It comes as no surprise to find downtown Delaware all but deserted, when Katie and Axe turn upon Sandusky Street in order to keep a clandestine appointment. Carefully, she looks about to see if any of her parents' friends are out for a wayward stroll.

"Don't worry, Old Girl," assures Axe, as he parks the roadster in front of the Anthoni Brewery. "Mother and Father will never know."

Soon, and much to the delight of the assistant brew master, the spare tires are stuffed with bottles of liquid instead of tubes of air. But as well, each nook and cranny of the roadster receives its baptism of contained amber—all to a clever excess.

"Axe. Don't you dare," warns Katie, as she reads her husband's mind. "Don't you dare throw away those pamphlets and use their boxes for your beer."

Before long, the final phase of preparation is completed and the Lanes are able to leave Anthoni's. However, instead of driving directly to Winter Street, Axe steers the roadster upon a circuitous route. As much as anything, the couple is making a goodbye tour of Delaware, and, by intent and proxy, bidding farewell to their home state, never mind that the boundary with Indiana is several horizons away. The moon is a mere sliver and the backside of Delaware appears black and drowsy. Yet the Speed Six finds its way, what with both carbide gas and kerosene a-blazing.

"I wonder, Axe, where we will find ourselves this time tomorrow?"

"Fort Wayne, Indiana, perhaps. And, hopefully, a day later we'll reach that Merrillville bank."

"Yes," remembers Katie of the city in question. "Where our funds are forwarded."

"Exactly. Mr. Loban's means of control. Forwarding our funds by piecemeal."

"Axe, that is a terrible way to put it. Though it is true."

A few more minutes upon the dark lanes should do it for the Speed Six.

"Take this street, Axe," guides Katie. "It leads to Winter."

"We should have an early start, tomorrow," reminds Axe. "Not let the banker's hours frustrate us."

"They'll not. I promise."

"Katie, if we can't have breakfast, then so be it. We can always nibble along the way."

"That sounds perfectly fine," agrees Katie. "But to think, tomorrow we'll be crossing the country." She nestles up against her husband, glad to be leaving Delaware with the air of tranquility and parental approval.

The Speed Six purrs along, illuminating the way for all to see.

"Axe, I see something?" The corners of Katie's eyes catch sight of a potential obstruction. "Slow down."

Easing back on the throttle, Axe squints through his spectacles. "Can you believe it? Someone careless has lost their load. Either that, or a half-wit is ridding himself of his rubbish. Foisting the burden."

Although the heap may be relatively small, because it rests in the middle of the narrow street, it cannot be sidestepped. And since the rear of the Speed Six is lit so poorly, Axe is reluctant to reverse path.

"I suppose I should move it aside," he remarks. "I hope that pile isn't too disgusting."

Ah, but perhaps it may be.

"Axe, are you sure it's rubbish?" notes Katie, while her husband steps upon the street. "Be careful."

Taking a kerosene lantern in hand, he approaches the heap. Almost instantly, Axe comes to a conclusion.

"Katie. It's a person. Still breathing." Stretching his left arm, Axe shakes a shoulder. "Hello, sir. Are you all right?"

The only response is a bellowing snore, which happens to be something of a signature.

"Oh, no." Katie's heart sinks with resignation. "Axe, it's Uncle Henry. Poor Uncle Henry has fallen off the wagon."

With the confirmation of kinship thus established, Axe slaps at a cheek and opens an eyelid.

"Henry. Wake up. It's your nephew, Axe. I've come from Lisbon to take you home."

"Axe," chides Katie. "Don't be that way."

Yet her husband can't resist. "Henry, would you prefer that I drop you off at your brother's house?"

"Stop it, Axe!" snaps Katie, who abandons her seat and rushes to her uncle.

The snoring ceases and becomes a series of groans. And perhaps because the darkness has been altered into light, and that Henry's head is cradled by loving arms, the patient's stupor eases a bit.

"Katie?" His hazy eyes begin to function.

"It's me, Uncle Henry."

"Katie," he perks, touching one side of her face and giving the other a gentle kiss. "Katie, my favorite."

She takes the compliment to heart. "Oh, Uncle Henry."

Eventually, with a Lane holding each arm, he's able to come to his feet. But Uncle Henry is too far gone to engage in a real conversation, let alone make mention of Katie and Axe's visit only yesterday afternoon.

"Where is Sophie? Is she with you?" speaks Henry of a failed, childless marriage, which had sputtered away five years prior.

"Aunt Sophie had to visit her ailing mother. Remember, Uncle Henry?" concocts the thoughtful niece. "This is why we're here, to take care of you."

"My sweet Katie."

Before long, with a bow to practicality, Henry is positioned in the passenger seat, held in place by Axe who sits high upon the backrest. Meanwhile, Katie takes the wheel and steers the roadster toward Henry Kane's boarding house address.

"You know, Katie. Your parents may have a point," observes Axe of the obvious, while making sure that Uncle Henry's head is tilted away from his favorite niece. With his left hand, Axe pries into an Anti-Saloon League box. "Here you go, Henry." He stuffs a pamphlet into the drunkard's coat pocket. "This will do you more good than the bottle, I think. Or Aunt Sophie, for that matter. Ugh-h. Thank God, I've never had to deal with a Sophie."

Katie takes an upward glance. "Nor shall you ever." Her vow comes with an air of disdain.

Upon reaching the boarding house, it requires considerable effort to carry Henry to his upstairs room. Yet his keepers are able to deliver him safely, even to the point where he's tucked into bed.

"Sleep tight, Uncle Henry," bids Katie. With her fingers, she brushes back his hair, as would any mother to her sickly child. "Wish us luck."

"We'll see you when we return from California, Henry," adds Axe, although he knows full well that his goodbye is not being received.

"We can go now, Axe. He's fine. But my parents must not know of this. Understand?"

"Of course."

"No, I'm afraid Father is of little help," sighs Katie. "Uncle Henry is a much more apprised man. He's going to have to solve this on his own."

As had been hoped, the Lanes are ready before the crack of dawn. But as had been predicted, an early breakfast in the Kane household is not forthcoming. Still, it's just as well, for it lessens the chance that the couple will be forced to linger.

Soon, Axe has the Speed Six started and parked in front of the Kanes', while Katie bids the last of her farewells before taking the passenger seat. But before Axe can put his foot to the pedal, his father-in-law walks to his side and offers his hand.

"Good luck, Axelrod."

"Thank you, sir."

"Be advised to use all caution. You'll be amidst strangers, after all."

"I understand."

"By the way. Where is your shotgun?"

"Packed away, Mr. Kane. On the left fender."

"As I thought. Not of much use in an emergency, I should think."

"I suppose not, sir."

"Here. You should take this." From an inside coat pocket, Mr. Kane pulls out a small frame revolver, a Hopkins & Allen, and from his trousers he frees a box of .32 caliber cartridges. "I would suggest you keep this on your person at all times. Did you hear that, Katie? Make sure Axelrod does just that."

"Yes, Father."

"Thank you, Mr. Kane." Axe tucks away the revolver and cartridges. "Then I suppose we should be off."

"We'll keep in touch. Let you know where we are," informs Katie, yet again. "And when we return to Lisbon by train, we should make a stop here."

At last, Mrs. Kane backs away from her embrace, thus allowing Axe to push the gear pedal. And so with their vigorous waves, the Lanes leave behind Winter Street and head toward the edge of Delaware. Shortly, the couple are beyond the bounds of the city, itself, drawn into the countryside and that eventual goal of the Pacific. But while the feeling may be one of intoxicating freedom, there exists the sobering thoughts of driving alone toward the promises of vast, empty spaces.

The road to Marysville proves to be relatively smooth, scarred by only a smattering of potholes and rills. Yet after only a few miles out of Delaware, a sense of discomfort begins to tap at Axe's inner recesses. He pulls the roadster to the side of the road, and guides it toward the shade of an imposing hickory.

"I'm starving," explains Axe. "What do you say we share a can of peaches?"

"I was about to make that suggestion, myself. Peaches would be divine."

10
AN ACCUMULATION OF MARGINS

"King Iron Bridge Company of Cleveland, Ohio," reads Katie, as she drives the roadster across the small, trussed span in question. "Just how many of these have we crossed, Axe?"

"Too many," he replies, looking up from a map of the U.S. Geological Survey. "Too many and one."

A few more uneventful miles are logged in a land of busy agriculture: maturing grains and infant fruit. Soon, a metal placard upon another small trussed span is spied, though differing from the established routine.

"Indiana Bridge Company of Muncie, Indiana?" reads Katie.

"What?" reacts Axe to the shocking disclosure. "By God, we may be in Indiana."

"Goodness," returns Katie. She eases the roadster upon the bridge's planked floor. "Another margin."

"Get used to it, Old Girl. These margins will come without warning. Possibly unrelenting."

The change of states is confirmed upon entering Monroeville. Meanwhile, the Speed Six's tank thirsts for fuel, the reason why the Lanes stop at what appears to be a former stable and current garage.

"I've never seen one of these," approaches the young, bespectacled owner, while he takes a rag to his greasy hands. "Loban Motor? This isn't a Fury Four?"

"Exactly. This is the new Speed Six." Instantly, Axe takes a liking to the man, as he abandons his seat and reaches for a hand. "Axe Lane. Engineer for Loban."

"Arnie Holcomb."

"And this is Mrs. Lane. Katie."

"Ma'am," tips Arnie. "What can I do for you two?"

"We need to top our tank." Katie, too, finds an affinity for the proprietor, if only because he's taking no undue notice of a female driver.

"I can do that. Hmm? A six-cylinder," marvels Arnie. He moves about his head, absorbing several angles. "Sound." But then Arnie backs away a bit. "Say, you two aren't part of that Paris race?"

"Absolutely not," avows Axe. "We're driving to the Pacific as a part of a promotion."

"Thank goodness. Those people passed north of here a while back. Probably in Siberia, by now."

Shaking of his head, Axe explains further. "Those autos are modified for that race. Impractical for the public. No, this is a production model. The only genuine modifications being no windscreen and canopy."

"I see." Arnie continues his scrutiny. "But by the looks of it, I'd say your roadster would be ahead of the field, had you entered."

"You think?" replies Axe.

"Of course. It's more impressive than the Thomas. And I should know, I've worked on one."

"You have?"

To be sure, a bond is being formed—one of kindred spirit and mutual respect.

"I'd say you have a pretty fair business, Arnie," admires Axe, as he takes note of the garage's interior. "Is that a Stearns? Massive, with double chains. Some disciple in this town has money."

"Yes, indeed," nods Arnie. "Mr. Stark."

"And a Premier. Of course," continues Axe, as he spots the Indianapolis make. "I wouldn't mind dirtying my hands on that. Is it fine to work with?"

"Sometimes. But mostly they're irritating. Not at all like that Olds buggy or that Ford."

Katie knows full well that this talk over shop can dawdle to no end. And beyond this, a delay can become endless were Axe to don his coveralls and lend a hand, as threatened. To the contrary, Katie's thirsty eyes are cast upon a Bowser cart pump, her thoughts centered toward that flexible appointment at Fort Wayne.

"Say, Mr. Holcomb," she interrupts. "What is the source of your gasoline?"

"Oh, it comes out of Whiting. A reliable grade."

"For certain, Arnie," persists Axe. "I'd like to work on that Stearns and that Premier."

Katie's hint falls upon deaf ears.

"By all means. Help yourself," offers Arnie.

Wearing a child's candy store grin, Axe turns to Katie. "Do you think that would be fine?"

"I suppose so, Axe," relents Katie. "Fort Wayne isn't all that pressing. We could use a rest."

And a rest the Lane's should have. Soon, Axe is up to his elbows in grime and a defective Stearn's transmission. But just as well, Katie becomes occupied when Arnie takes her into the tiny house behind the garage and introduces his wife, Anna, and their twin two year-old boys and infant daughter. Delighted to lend a hand, before long she finds herself a storyteller to a tugging pair and a lullabiest to a tranquil angel.

"Goodness gracious, Katie," observes Anna, while she feeds her Sunshine cook stove from a coal scuttle. "I do think my babies have taken to you."

Sitting upon a kitchen chair, Katie's response is nothing but a smile, words being far too inadequate for what is the most supreme of compliments.

When the stove returns to heat, Anna places into its oven a pan holding a sizeable hen, and then proceeds with the rest of dinner's preparation. Meanwhile, with little Alice nestled safely upon Katie's lap, the Holcomb children receive their first violin lesson. Already, Katie has played a little Brahms and is in the middle of a medley of gentle Irish airs.

"Oh, if only you could play for us every day," yearns Anna, as she peels potatoes. "I've never seen my boys this still for so long."

Katie glances upon Abner and Adam, their captive heads swaying to the waves of her bow. Then there's Alice, who has every excuse to slip into a tranquil nap, yet has her eyes and ears open to the recital's charms.

"I wonder if the boys can hear you?" mentions Anna. "If they're enjoying the afternoon as much as us?"

Whether Axe and Arnie are receiving the music, who can say? Yet it is fortunate that what is said inside the garage does not carry into the kitchen.

"#@%! Will you look those worn teeth," points Axe. "Those chain-drives do jim the transmission."

"You should hear the clatter they make when the ratchets bite the chains." Arnie shakes his head. "Sure drowns out that agreeable engine sound."

"I'm not surprised."

Because parts need to be ordered, work on the Stearns is set aside. Now it's the Premier's turn for a fix.

"I suspect we'll have to replace a valve spring. If not all."

Axe is quick to accept the offer. "Let's leap into it. Premier looks to be a stubborn competitor in a year or two. Possibly sooner."

Thus the Premier's valve springs are tended—along with its hand brake. Yet again, Axe takes advantage of the chance to examine a rival company's handiwork.

"You know, Arnie. Loban Motor is always looking for new dealers. Have you ever thought of selling autos out of your garage?"

'Hmm? Sounds interesting, Axe."

"You certainly can repair them. At least you should be one of our recommended mechanics."

"Very interesting, Axe."

To be sure, the work progresses smoothly and could go on like this for several hours more. But then there comes an interruption by four visitors, who arrive via the rear door.

"Dinner will be ready in an hour," announces Katie, she cradling Alice, while the boys attend her train.

Looking away from the Ford Model N, Axe's eyes become stunned by the rays of a late sun shining passed his wife and her charges. Indeed, the angle of the moment serves to highlight a heavenly presentation.

"You should see what Anna is preparing. Roast chicken. And sugar cream pie for dessert." With that, the lady and her angels part.

"Hmm, Axe. I'd say that your Katie is a picture of motherhood. A natural."

"Isn't that the truth." Axe stares at the glow still retained by the open door. And fearing that the vision might fade before its time, he offers an off-the-cuff proposition. "I don't suppose you would allow your babes to accompany us?"

Arnie pats a shoulder. "Don't worry, Axe. You'll get there soon enough. Heh, heh. But what do you say? That we finish with the Ford and Olds, so that you can show me the details of your Speed Six? I need to know, after all, if I'm to become a Loban dealer."

"Of course." Axe's gaze is broken. "Quick as we can."

The tour of the Speed Six begins just before dinner, only to reconvene immediately thereafter, the climax being road tests with Arnie at the wheel and assortments of Holcombs as passengers. Thus closes a day of lasting impressions—from both sides of the street—a profitable period had by all.

Night follows, and because the Holcomb's neat and tidy house has only two bedrooms, there's the need to double up in order to accommodate the Lanes.

"Do it," chorus Adam and Abner.

To be sure, it is a tight fit—the twins' bed—if only because their guests are tucked in as well.

"Axe, no more bubble tricks. It's getting late and the boys need their sleep." Katie looks at the twins, who are squeezed between herself and her husband. "Sleep tight and Uncle Axe will show you how to blow bubbles in the morning. How's that?" She gives each a gentle kiss and then motions with her head. "Can you dowse the light, Axe? We need our sleep too."

"As you wish, Aunt Katie."

The boys remain asleep when the Lanes rouse themselves during the early morning. As for the ensuing goodbyes, they come with staunch vows to keep in touch and maintain associations.

The Speed Six idles in place. But just as Axe is ready to engage the gear pedal, there arrives a possible delay. It's not so much an approaching Shire and master that draw notice, but rather the lifeless weight they pull: an empty-hooded Cadillac and its enormous single-cylinder engine beneath the front seat.

"Axe. We really need to be on our way," reminds Katie.

"Of course," concurs Axe, his temptation squelched. But as his foot presses the pedal, he shakes his head and airs a thought. "I hope we don't fall to such indignity. Relying on a beast of burden."

And so the Lanes resume their tour across northern Indiana, stopping at the Fort Wayne Daily News, but regaining the road in quick fashion when the questions repeat themselves. Upon reaching the Whitley County line, the dew remains upon the morning ground.

Yet in spite of the pleasant air, Axe is perturbed, his grip on the wheel being overly firm.

"We needn't worry," remarks Katie. "We should have enough funds to reach Merrillville."

"Oh, I'm not troubled with that. No, I'm still fumed at that reporter's fuss over the confounded Paris race. And can you believe his editor, asking why L.M. failed to enter that farce? He didn't know that even Packard declined, which speaks volumes."

"He had no idea. Goodness, the expense of it all. L.M?" Katie pauses. "How is your lip?"

"Still sore, somewhat."

"Next time, try not to bite it so hard."

"I'll remember, Katie. But it is certain we are in that race's shadow. And the closer we follow its path, the more the annoyance."

Katie frowns at what is becoming her source of irritation, as well. "It just may be that we'll have to alter our route and get away from that confounded shadow."

"Really? Those are your thoughts?" asks Axe.

"Yes," replies Katie.

"Wonderful. Because they're mine too."

The people of the Kosciusko County countryside have obliged their directions upon two, potentially lost interlopers. Yet for the moment, this kind assistance is of little use. With hardly a warning, the skies of northern Indiana are unleashing an accumulated fury, meaning that Katie and Axe are compelled to unfold and prop their tarpaulin by a roadside patch of woods.

"Thank goodness there's less thunder," notes Katie, her jitters easing to the pitter-pats of rain.

She clings to Axe and his calm demeanor. It seems Katie is forgetful of his engineering background and his previous employment with electricity, that there's little to fear so long as rubber tires are underfoot.

"Axelrod Lane will see you through, Old Girl. My worry is of sloppy roads." Katie snuggles closer. "Mmm. Nice and cozy. To what do I owe the pleasure?"

"My company, of course." There's a bit of nervousness in Katie's voice.

"It's been some time, don't you know?"

"Axe, for goodness sake. At a time and place like this? You have friskiness on your mind?"

"My mind is always frisky with my lovely bride at my side. Besides, we are safe and snug, and secluded."

The rumbles of thunder continue, those telltale sounds of lightning shocks probing the sky. Katie shivers at the thought, but also she's provoked by the sure touches of her husband's hands, which probe as well.

"Oh, Axe," she coos, responding to a well-placed nibble.

As it happens, the only obstacle to connubial bliss is the steering wheel above Axe's lap. But leave it to the engineer to find a swift, tacit solution, he needing only to abandon the driver's seat and slip into that of the passenger's—a reapplication of the original design.

"Axe, you Hun," plays Katie, as she finds herself face to face upon his lap, thus beginning the tantalizingly slow process of disrobing.

Ka-boom! Now the electric sky heightens the cause, adding a thrill upon what has yet become routine.

But eventually, the frenzy ceases, as does the passion of the weather. Their obligations done, the Lanes are free to return to the road. Of course, Axe is the first to make himself decent, not that this matters, the stand of maples being quite isolated. He picks up his side of the tarp, to take a peek at the road and the degree of mud it has become. But quickly, the subject of quagmires loses its hold, when Axe spies an object of a more consequential sort. The start causes him to drop his flap and turn to Katie with his look of embarrassment.

"What is it, Axe?" she asks, while trying to adjust her corset.

"Uhh," is the immediate explanation, though this will not suffice.

"What!"

"Shh, Katie. We're not alone. There's an auto parked beneath the tree behind us."

"What?" whispers Katie, sharply. She ignores her corset and covers the conundrum with her shirt waist. "Dim the lantern, Axe."

To which he complies.

"Who are they?" Katie does her best to control her panic. "No, don't look now. Wait 'til I put on my skirt. And my stockings."

Axe budges not an inch, although his mind feels confused. "You had taken off your stockings?"

Never before has Katie dressed so quickly, a remarkable feat when considering the cramp conditions. She even manages to bun her hair and pin her skimmer, making herself presentable to the point of innocence.

"What are they doing, Axe?"

Carefully, he takes another peek. The first thing Axe sees is a semi-octagonal radiator, along with the sullied white body of a touring car and its inadequate canvas top.

"Crapo Durant," interprets a sneering Axe.

"There's a Buick?" responds Katie, who knows the language. She lifts up her side of the tarpaulin, and gathers a look. "My goodness, Axe. They're a family. Just behind us."

"Well-l-l," shrugs Axe. "Could it be any different had we been in a hotel room?"

"For shame, Axe," protests Katie.

"They're not so close as that," replies her husband, who with a wink reaches to grasp the horn's wind bag.

Honk! Honk! To which there comes an immediate retort.

But to the Lanes' surprise, the acknowledgement harkens from the opposite direction of the Buick, from another automobile parked ahead of the Speed Six.

"A Franklin?" notes Katie of the radiatorless vehicle.

Hopefully, the storm's outcome will prove an inconvenience rather than a genuine obstacle. Soon, after cranking the engine, Axe pushes too much throttle, the result being fantails of mud. He adjusts his speed and allows the roadster's fenders to do their work. Instantly, the '08 flings less.

"I hope we find drier roads ahead," complains Axe of the reduced speed.

"And I hope someday you and L.M. fix passenger doors for future roadsters," complains Katie, as she wipes the dollops of mud from her duster.

As it happens, the roads ahead become much more negotiable, although no less confusing. Still, the Lanes manage to keep to the spirit of the northwest compass point, nudging the wake of the New York to Paris race.

Before the Lanes left Lisbon, Axe had developed a hunch for a potentially fruitful diversion, of a region situated north of the route between Columbia City and Warsaw. This is Indiana's lake country, a land of summer resorts catering to families from the cities. And by experience, Axe knows that the majority of this ilk has yet to enter into the realm of automobile ownership, thus making themselves viable targets.

"Shall we visit the lakes?" he asks, while slowing at a crossroads.

"Certainly. But which lake? And how do we get there?" replies Katie.

Axe hesitates, but then takes a right turn. "We'll follow the first tracks we come upon. It should lead us to North Webster, or Oswego. Or thereabouts."

Soon enough, the Lanes discover the lake country. And it's from one body of water to another they wander, the quandary being where to make a genuine stop.

"This should do," determines Axe of a gathering of Detroit and Indianapolis makes, before taking notice of the Patona Hotel and its Tippecanoe Lake. Indeed, it's as if he's picked up a gauntlet of sorts. "We'll show the train-bound who has the better auto."

The resort hops with activity—by guests of a wide range of ages and a precise social stratum. To be sure, after entering the lobby, the question thrusted upon Katie is of affordability.

"I wonder of the cost, Axe?"

Bing! Bing! Axe taps the bell at the check-in counter.

"Sir, may I help you?" asks a cheerful clerk.

"Yes, you may. My wife and I would like accommodations for the night."

“One night?”The clerk’s pleasant demeanor alters. “May I assume you have no reservation?”

“Is that a problem?”

For certain, it is. After leaving the Patona to seek refuge elsewhere, the Lanes discover that the lake resorts of Kosciusko County are meant for extended visits and not overnight stays. Indeed, this is a playground for the exclusive-minded of Detroit and Indianapolis, and not meant for interlopers from Lisbon, however innovative their inventions may be.

“I wish Hugh were here,” notes Axe, after he and Katie are rejected from another inn without a room. “He would make an impression on this crowd. Heh, heh. That is, if I plied his thirst with a little exuberance.”

“Goodness gracious, Axe,” whispers Katie. “How the two of you stayed out of jail during that Cleveland escapade remains a mystery. Thank God, it’s me at your side and not Hugh.”

Frustrations aside, the road beckons still. And it’s to this task that the Lanes reacquaint themselves, their enthusiasm not stymied by a horizon of unattainable accommodations. To be sure, although empty rooms may be scarce, the sublime roadsides are aplenty, made luxurious by the pitch of a tarp and the spread of a ground cloth and blankets.

“Mmm,” responds Katie to the moonlit night and the creaking crickets, and the snuggle of her husband. “This is much better than the Patona, and all of its sort.”

“Absolutely. But what a wild goose chase that came to be. A colossal waste of time.”

“It won’t be the last such episode, Axe. I’m sure there lurks more such disappointments.”

“Yes,” agrees Axe, as he firms his wrap around his wife. “Speaking of which. I’m becoming bored with the herds, those bourgeois people and their ideas of work and play. I prefer the resourceful and spontaneous. Like the Holcombs. We should find more people like them.”

“I miss them already,” adds Katie. “And I do hope we can return to Monroeville, some day.”

“We will,” assures Axe. “But for now, we need to rediscover the route to Merrillville and our king’s ransom. Or whatever sum our esteemed benefactor deems necessary.”

“Axe, I’m sure Mr. Loban will fund us sufficiently.”

“He had better.”

“Axe, settle down. Remember, the staff and employees are the true company.”

"Of course. I like the way you think, Old Girl. And that I can always rely upon you."

"Of course. But you have no choice, do you? No choice, whatsoever."

The sediment bulb beneath the fuel tank must be drained, and the oil changed and the spark plugs cleaned. But upon seeing to these needs, Axe discovers that the engine is loosening from the frame and that two wheel spokes need to be replaced at a local livery. Because of the nuisance of a few other repairs, there happens a stay at Walkerton with its unexpected expenses.

So goes the delay. Yet so ensues the recovery and a return to Indiana's confusing roads.

"Excuse me, ma'am," inquires Katie of a lone pedestrian, who comes from the opposite direction. The engine idles while an anxious question is posed. "Is this the way to Wanatah?"

"Where?" replies the young lady, she holding a willow basket.

"Wu-nay-tuh?"

The look upon the pedestrian's face is befuddled, as if no such town exists.

Meanwhile, the feeling within the Lanes sinks decidedly, the fear being that they are hopelessly lost on the northern boundary with Michigan or somehow have reversed course toward Ohio.

"Wu-nay-tuh?" repeats Axe, in a weak attempt to clarify.

"Hmm? Wu-nay-tuh?" mutters the Indianan, who puts a hand to chin. "Wu-nay-tuh?" But then she perks, as if a spark is conceiving a flame. "You mean Wan-i-tah."

"Yes!" speak the Lanes in unison. "Wan-i-tah."

"Oh, it's only two miles straight ahead. You can't miss it."

"Much obliged, ma'am," acknowledges Axe, as he tips his hat and nudges the gear pedal.

"Thank you very much," adds Katie.

As they continue down the road, the confused Lanes turn at one another.

"Just how many Wanatah-sounding towns can there be, Axe?"

He maintains his expression. "Quite a few, it would seem. Perhaps someday we'll do a tour."

None-too-soon, the Lanes reach Merrillville, albeit with a few dollars to spare. Although situated just south of Gary's burgeoning steel and Lake Michigan industries, the town's flavor is decidedly rural, meaning that it ministers to the various agricultural trades. Yet as far as Axe and Katie are concerned, the burgh exists for only two purposes: the Merrillville Bank and its proximity to Chicago's auto-starved populace.

Almost immediately, upon finding an empty curb space, the spectacle of a packed, placarded roadster draws a coterie of the curious. And it's the duty and pleasure of the Lanes to explain it all, to tell of Loban Motor's motivations and of their own road experiences.

"Why, New York must have half of the world's skyscrapers," recalls Katie.

"And half of the world's dead chickens," amuses Axe.

Without a doubt, the regaling might go on just short of forever. But it seems that a gathering held in front of a bank is something of a commotion to those in charge. A vice president is sent to investigate, leading to a few questions and, hence, an introduction.

"Axelrod Lane. Mrs. Lane. I was expecting you, three days prior," reveals the bank officer. "Your funds are in my desk. And there is a recent message from a Mr. Loban. Possibly urgent."

That a few words might follow Mr. Loban's money comes as no surprise. But because the message is being referred to as "urgent", there billows a concern. Quickly, the Lanes are escorted into the bank.

"Sixty dollars in five dollar bills, Mr. Lane."

But Axe doesn't care to count, his concerns focusing upon the message. With Katie looking over his shoulder, he mumbles aloud.

"Proceed to Springfield and not Chicago. Breakfast reception with their automobile club and chamber of commerce. Important. Be there on the twentieth."

"The twentieth!" blurts Katie. "Axe, that's tomorrow!"

Her panic spreads, the realization being that there's no time to waste, assuming that enough exists. Thus Axe stuffs the twelve bills into an inside coat pocket, the same cubby where is concealed Mr. Kane's revolver.

"Thank you, sir. My apologies, but we must be off."

"Mr. Lane. Please sign here."

To which Axe complies. Thus, with a farewell shake, the Lanes flee the scene.

"Tomorrow morning?" Axe grasps the crank. "I hope we can make it."

"So much for Chicago," notes Katie.

"So it seems." The engine starts and Axe rushes to the driver's seat. "But it does make some sense, if only because Mr. Loban carries an unexplainable grudge for that town."

"Yes." Katie's memory is jogged. "What Mrs. Snodgrass told me, who heard it from Mrs. Brown, who heard it from Mrs. Pritchard, who was told by Aunt Lucie."

"What?" asks Axe, while he urges the roadster onto the street.

"Chicago is one of those places where he was expelled from college. Years ago."

"And Springfield is his excuse to keep L.M. away from there," frowns Axe. "But it's all the same to me. At least we shouldn't hear the clamor of that Paris race."

"Amen, Axe."

"Unfortunately, we have a long drive ahead of us. Possibly two hundred miles. There'll be some night driving. Are you up to it, Katie?"

"Do we have a choice?" There's a bit of trepidation in her voice.

"We always have a choice," replies Axe. "Like a telegram to Springfield with our regrets."

"Oh, no, Axe. Let's not do that." Quickly, Katie sets aside her misgivings. "Let's give it a try. We shouldn't disappoint those nice people in Springfield."

"There should be no problems. We'll hop from town to town, keep southwest into Illinois. And with a little luck, stumble upon Springfield in time for breakfast." Axe nudges the throttle. "Hmm? Now let me see? Which way is southwest?"

11
AN ACCUMULATION OF MARGINS

WITHOUT FANFARE, BUT WITH FAMILIAR ambiguity, a state line is crossed and the Lanes enter Illinois. To no surprise, the land is strikingly similar to Indiana, although the green corn and amber wheat must be viewed at a blur given the circumstance. But at least Axe has found that southwesterly direction, the confidence building that the Springfield invitation will be kept. By the looks of it, only a mechanical breakdown or a scarcity of available gasoline can prevent the Lanes from breakfasting in the capital city.

And so beyond the caution of keeping the fuel tank topped, the towns of Sherburnville and Kankakee are given little regard—likewise for Ashkum and Roberts. What had been the remnant of the afternoon is now miles to the rear, with nothing but dusk and darkness lurking ahead. When the Lanes reach Gibson City, with Katie behind the wheel of the lamped and lanterned roadster, the clear sky is lit by distant stars and a half-hearted moon. Yet at least there shouldn't be any navigational difficulties, for by following the roads parallel to the Illinois Central tracks, Springfield cannot be missed. Clever are the Lanes.

"Katie, why don't you let me drive into the night?"

"Fine with me, Axe."

Much of the country remains to be electrified, meaning that most of rural Illinois dowses its kerosene lights at relatively early hours. Thus these beacons fade into the blackness, contributing mightily to the cause of isolation for those travelers who dare to motor passed. As strange as it may seem, the sensation as perceived within Illinois' abundant spaces is decidedly claustrophobic.

"Can you go a little faster?" urges Katie, who up to now would have preferred a slower pace.

Able to dodge the roads' potholes, though not the occasional facial-impacting swarms of insects, the Lanes accumulate an impressive number of miles. Regardless, the isolation of the flat countryside carries into the sleepy towns and communities, where less and less stirs with the growing hours. As the Lanes near Clinton, their genuine concerns are for the fuel tank, and of how to get it filled.

"I don't think we're going to get near Springfield, Katie. Even with the spare cans."

But as luck would have it, upon entering Clinton the first establishment the Lanes spy is a garage, one with a curb pump sitting atop its underground tank. Fortune continues to smile when Axe pulls the roadster alongside, finding the self-measuring Doran unlocked. He jumps into action and replenishes the roadster's thirsty tank one gallon at a time.

"I've read about these Doran pumps," remarks Axe. "Ingenious."

Soon, the deed is done, requiring but a token to complete the transaction. Rounding up the bill, Axe wedges a silver dollar into the pump's handle.

"That ought to do it. Springfield should be a cinch."

Indeed, the capital beckons, with no foreseeable complications obstructing their way.

"Axe! Wake up!"

It seems that the driver of the Speed Six has become distracted by the urge to fall asleep.

"Huh?" In a flash, Axe's eyes widen, and his hands guide the roadster out of a potentially disastrous veer.

"Axe. Find a place to park. You're too tired. We're both too tired."

Although now wide awake, Axe offers no resistance. Instead of racing toward Springfield in the dead of night, he stops at the first suitable site.

"We'll have to wake up well before dawn," details Axe, as the couple begin to set camp.

"Of course," grants Katie, while rummaging through the baggage. "The alarm clock. Axe, I can't find it."

"Oh?" he replies. "Never mind." Reaching into a handy toolbox, Axe grasps a bottle of Anthoni's. After popping the crown by aid of a file, he takes a substantial gulp, ending the deed with a satisfied grin. "Ah-h-h. We'll leave the matter to my own alarm clock."

"Axe," responds Katie, who grabs the bottle and repeats the act. "Ah-h-h. Now we have two alarms."

The Lanes make an early morning return to the road. And by the time the sun eases over the horizon, their Springfield arrival looms at well under an hour. Thus the couple has an opportunity for a little preening, to make more presentable not only the Speed Six, but themselves.

"You look splendid, Old Girl," strokes Axe. "Just a little soap and water and you're as pretty as ever."

"I still feel filthy. My hair and every part of me beneath my face."

"Believe me, Katie. The Springfield autos and commerces will be charmed. But when we're done with them, we'll find a hotel and have a thorough bath. And have our clothes laundered."

"I'll look forward to that."

"And who knows, perhaps we'll have time to tour Springfield. Rumor has it, it's the town of Lincoln."

"Really? Lincoln?" Katie returns with some mock absurdity of her own. "Will he be at the breakfast?"

"Hopefully."

"Hmm? Axe, what sort of auto do you suppose he owns?"

"I can't say. But we'll sorely do our best to sell him an '08. Even offer a drive."

With nothing to hinder their way, the Lanes manage to find the outskirts of the small city of Springfield. And there could be no greater beacon than the unrivaled capitol, itself, the edifice's dome piercing the sky to an astounding 361 feet—or more. Seated behind the wheel, a captivated Katie must struggle to keep the Speed Six on the road.

"Goodness, Axe. Such a great height. Manhattan would be proud."

"Gargantuan," agrees her husband, while he keeps an eye for potential hazards. "Watch out for that dog."

"Oh." Katie eases the throttle and then returns to thing's grander. "Now Axe, no matter the opportunity, we're not driving upon the capitol steps."

"Fine," comes the disappointed reply.

From the east, the Lanes enter into Springfield proper, the first impressions being of prosperity and industry—a promising recipe for the likes of Loban Motor. To be sure, the city is ringed and punctured by an impressive array of railroads, coal mines and factories. Yet within, Springfield is a place of contrasting neighborhoods, clustered together by remarkably slim margins.

Like the strangers they are, the couple wander through the streets, the inevitable being that soon they enter an undesirable section of town. And because of Axe's navigator status, he's free to observe unhindered. To the right he glances, catching sight of a nondescript, two-story frontage. Edging close to the street, the building appears to be something of a house and less of a business—or perhaps vice versa. But then its purpose becomes somewhat plain when a man in a suit and no tie exits the front entry, draped by a young woman attired in a tawdry, shamelessly-exposed manner. The encounter unnerves Axe, though his instincts remind him that Katie's purer sensibilities should be diverted.

"Look at that house," he alerts, pointing in a nick of time to the other side of the street.

Unfortunately, a similar scene is being played out as with the house's neighbor, except that at this address there are two women in a brazen state of semi-dress.

As nonchalantly as he can, Axe peers to his right to monitor Katie's reaction, hoping for the best. But what confronts him is not her look of trauma and revulsion, rather it's one with a decidedly sharp smirk.

"Goodness gracious, Axe," comments Katie, as her eyes return to the middle of the street. "That's the fourth brothel we've passed already. Just how many do they need in this town? And all the saloons? Some are still open for business. What a filthy place Springfield must be."

To say the least, Axe is taken aback by Katie's reaction. Yet more so, he's relieved that her sensibilities are tempered by her cool, analytical side. Thus he's inspired to put into use his own version of the same ability, as honed by his background in engineering logic. Indeed, if Katie's numbers are close to accurate—and no doubt they are—then there must exist a sure degree of tolerance. That two motorized strangers from Lisbon, Ohio can make the observation means the sins of Springfield are an open book. Yet the truer implication must be of a city government and police force making allowances for audacious vice—a crime in its own right. Such an atmosphere could never occur in Lisbon, considers Axe, although perhaps he should consult Katie before coming to a conclusion.

"I don't believe we should trust the people here," he reasons. "The city's politicians. Its police."

"I suppose the tales of Illinois politics are true," concurs Katie. "Do we really want to sell them our autos?

"Vice, liquor and possible corruption," continues Axe. "A volatile mixture."

The informal and haphazard tour of Springfield continues, as does the search for the venue of the breakfast reception. To their delight, the Lanes find a path to the capitol. And it's of this monument to democracy that Katie circles—

four times over at a low, sputtering throttle. Only when her neck muscles become strained does she steer to the right and returns eastwardly.

"Where to now, Axe?"

"That's up to your discretion, Katie. Anywhere but Madison Street."

From two disparate directions Springfield seems to be stirring: the dubious who have been up all night and the decent who are beginning their days. And it may be inevitable that there should chance a mingle, though a more incongruous amalgamation there could never be.

Enter the Lanes. Although Axe had managed to shave himself earlier by the light of kerosene, a nearby barber's pole draws his attention. Yet it's what occurs just beyond which gathers the brunt of concern. At first there appears little more than a gathering of individuals, possibly like-minded workers beginning their morning parade to their factory.

"Axe! Look!" Yet Katie's attuned eyes discern that no such march toward a noble trade is taking place.

There's considerable pushing and shoving, followed by a succession of punches, all being applied with no restraint. To be sure, the violence is shocking and clearly one-sided: three young brutes delivering their blows upon a victim, who is middle-aged and black.

The roadster is quick to shorten the gap, though the moment feels like eternity. As it happens, the uneven confrontation is taking place at the side of the street and so could be avoided by passing at the opposite edge. Yet this convenience means nothing to Katie, who nudges back the throttle and takes her foot off the gear pedal. With that, the roadster rolls to a stop, thus compelling its driver to make some sort of commitment. But as to what this should entail, Katie hasn't a clue, only that at the very least something should be said.

"Leave him be!"

Axe, too, isn't sure as to what he should do, though at least Katie's protest could be repeated. "Yes! Leave him be, I say!"

But the shouts of outrage have no effect on the assailers, who appear to be enjoying themselves at their victim's expense.

"Axe!" panics Katie.

The temptation within her husband is to continue their way and ignore the proceedings. After all, what business is it of theirs if three Springfield toughs wish to beat upon a black man?

"Unhand him!"

Be that as it may, Katie's words ring of a familiar episode.

"Yes! Unhand him!" echoes Axe.

"Leave him be!" This time Katie accents her demand with several toots on the horn.

The assault pauses and the attentions of the toughs shift upon the occupants of the Speed Six. "What did you say, woman?" comes a question from the stoutest of the three.

Axe might swallow a lump of trepidation, were his throat muscles not so stiff.

"I said, leave him be!" Katie's throat is just loose enough.

For a couple of seconds, the assailants seem confused. But then the mangiest one looks directly at Katie and delivers his objections with both a smile and a snarl.

"Now you just shut your mouth, woman! Keep your mouth shut and get yourself back to that house on Madison Street! Where you belong!"

The insult flies passed Katie, but like a punch in full flail lands squarely upon Axe's jaw. He stands from his seat—an aggressive move difficult to reverse. Indeed, Axe's rising rancor leaves him with few choices.

"You! Apologize! Apologize to my wife! Immediately!"

"Axe. Sh-h-h." With the realization of this sudden escalation, Katie's eyes bulge forth and her face becomes as stiff as a statue. "Sit down, for goodness sake."

But Axe doesn't. "Apologize!"

"Gander at the four-eyes, boys. 'Four-eyes' wants me to apologize," huffs the mangy one, who then takes a sinister gaze. "Hey, 'Four-eyes'! Just how are you going to make me do that!"

A perfectly fair question, which deserves an answer in kind, if only Axe knew what that could be. Yet there's little doubt he's finding himself in the position of defending his wife against three toughs, so that "by any means possible" may be perfectly fair.

Although Axe's knees are not buckling, they do exhibit a definite quake, which causes a shiver throughout the rest of his frame. And it's because of this, that a certain, heavy object in his coat pocket rattles against his ribs, this tickle not bringing about a laughing mood.

"Cover your ears, Katie," instructs a determined and reinforced Axe.

Instinctively, she complies, readying herself for a volley off a foul tongue.

"#&@$%! Apologize or you won't live to regret it, you #&%!"

Certainly, Axe's threat holds a margin of bluff, he being of the non-criminal kind. Yet it also contains a certain validity, this weight coming from forged and machined steel, walnut grips and lead-ended, brass cartridges.

The mangy one takes a couple of steps forward, followed by his friends.

But as far as Axe is concerned, they're as much as a dozen steps too many. He reaches into the pocket, and grasps Mr. Kane's revolver.

"Come a little closer, you #&%! Make it easier for me!" And to punctuate his intentions, Axe takes the unnecessary step of cocking the double-action revolver.

Almost in unison, the three take a step back. But there they stop, staring at their threat as if assessing the situation. In no way, however, are any apologies spewing forth.

Axe means to have a satisfaction of some kind, make no doubt. But fearing that the local constabulary may not favor the side of a law-abiding stranger, he must tread carefully. Instead of pointing the revolver, now he aims it, finding a target to make an impact upon these stubborn toughs. Holding his breath and firming his jaw, slowly, Axe squeezes the trigger.

Bang!

Momentarily, Axe's eyes flinch. But when they reopen, to his amazement he sees that the bullet has struck its target—the patch of street in front of the toughs.

Yet they linger, perhaps stunned or holding on to the belief that the threat is not genuine.

"Damn it, I missed." Quick with his thinking, Axe puts on a perturbed air. This time he aims at the nose of the mangy one, and cocks the revolver.

Fortunately for all persons present, the grumbling toughs accept the hint and haste away—without so much as a word or an apology.

Now that the three are showing their backs, Axe redirects his aim.

Bang!

With another shot closer to foot, the toughs accelerate their skedaddle.

"Axe, please stop! They're going away! You don't have to shoot any of them!" pleads Katie, who in fact realizes the embellished response and so abets ably.

Still, the temptation persists to shoot at least one of the toughs in the back, and in doing so, make permanent the gratification.

"Axe, that poor man," points Katie. "We should help him."

"What?" Thus Axe's thoughts are redirected, and the desire to spend another cartridge removed.

He's sprawled upon the ground—this victim of blatant crime—his vest and shirt torn and his pockets turned inside out.

Katie is the first to approach, though she stops several feet short—afraid of the result of brutality's stamp and, as well, of the racial divide. But then she distinguishes the familiar, of a favorite uncle who from time to time may find himself under similar circumstances.

"Axe, do something. Please, help him."

He's quick to obey, dropping to his knees in order to offer assistance. Putting aside his own misgivings, Axe produces a handkerchief and applies it to the man's injured face.

"Mister, can you hear me?"

A few blows to the head will render even the sturdiest of men groggy, let alone those of smaller frames and advancing years. Yet this one particular fellow seems to have resilient strengths, as he lifts his head and steadies himself with arm and elbow.

"Uh-h-h." He draws a deep breath and manages to sputter forth. "Those animals. Those damnable animals. Are they gone? Are they gone for good?"

"Yes," assures Axe. He looks about. "They went down another street."

"Yes. They're gone," reassures Katie.

"Thank God. Thank the Almighty. And thank you, too. Bless you. Bless you two."

Sincere gratitude owns the capacity to move mountains, never mind the leanest of hills. With that, Katie produces her own handkerchief and applies its tender mercies.

For certain, under such deliberate care an initial recovery can be swift. Before anyone can realize, the Lanes have the man sitting up, followed shortly by helping him to his feet and exchanging introductions.

"My keys." The victim looks toward the ground.

"Here they are, Mr. Burton." Katie hands him his set.

"And your spectacles." Axe has expanded the search. "Sorry, they're broken."

"Do you want us to walk you home, Mr. Burton?" offers Katie.

"Oh no," responds Mr. Burton. "This is my shop, here. If I just slip inside, I can rest up fine." Although beaten and worn by the ordeal of being put in his place, a brave Mr. Burton appears to want nothing more than to stand his ground within his place of business. "Fix up myself."

"But Mr. Burton. Shouldn't we summon the police?" insists Axe. "A crime has been committed. Those animals shouldn't be allowed to get away. Why, I've half a mind to hop into my auto and chase after them."

"Don't you dare do that, Mr. Lane. Don't you dare chase after those animals and look for trouble on my account. And you might not bother with the police, too, if'n 'cause they don't care about peoples like us. Always siding with the animals in this town."

"But how can this be, Mr. Burton?" Katie is upset by such an astounding revelation. "In the city of Lincoln, of all places? Where are the Republicans?"

"Oh, Republicans don't matter, Mrs. Lane. Not to us colored folk. Peoples is peoples, but bad is bad. And it's the bad ones who always throne over us. Mayor Reece and his like."

Axe nods in agreement, his initial assessment of Springfield receiving a sound confirmation.

Katie, too, pivots her head, albeit from a different angle.

"Thank the Almighty for decent peoples like the two of you, Mrs. Lane. Mr. Lane. If'n only strangers like you could come and populate this town. It sure would be a more likeable place. But the two of you best be forgetting all you seen. Forget it now and be on your way. You done shot your gun to protect a colored man. And that just won't do in this town."

"Oh, Mr. Burton. How can we leave like this?"

"You just have to, Mrs. Lane. This state and its city is just too crooked for the likes of you. Honest folks don't stand a chance."

Reluctant and resigned, soon the Lanes part ways with Mr. Burton, with Axe guiding the roadster toward the courthouse and downtown.

"How horribly they must treat their colored people." Katie's expression is pained, her emotional strengths sapped. "Like some backwater town of the Deep South."

"My thoughts precisely. And how sharp to ask about the Republicans. They must either be criminals to a man or absent altogether."

"Oh, Axe. I don't want to be here any longer. I don't care about that breakfast with the auto club or a hotel bath. Let's rid ourselves of this hellish place."

Katie's oath brings a mild shock to Axe. But it also serves to highlight her anxiety over the setting, the sentiment of which he pays heed without reservation.

"Of course, Katie. We should put Springfield behind us."

"Thank you, Axe."

"I'll concoct an excuse to satisfy Mr. Loban. He'll believe we hadn't set foot in this town."

Katie let's out a sigh of relief. Yet before she can relax further, her cautious eyes catch sight of a prominent banner displayed in front of Harry Loper's restaurant, this being Springfield's finest and most spacious establishment.

"Axe. Over there. That banner."

"What?" As he continues driving, Axe locates the banner and voices its message. "Welcome Loban Motor." His eyes widen somewhat. "So this is the place. We are expected."

Katie's heart readies itself to take a plunge.

"But I'm afraid they'll have to eat breakfast without us. Sorry folks."

Axe's apology is a quick bolster for Katie's spirits, especially when he taps the throttle.

"God help Springfield, Katie. It's a simmer ready to combust. This I fear."

"My fear too, Axe."

What a ramble Springfield has been, yet another needless digression imposed upon the Lanes' transcontinental ambitions. Still, what a well-timed happenstance this particular tangent has become for one Mr. Burton, he being spared from a possibly abrupt fate. At least now, the barber can look forward to a much-extended future.

And so it's a return to the countryside and to what alters into a familiar northwesterly direction. In regards to this, the Lanes shouldn't be blamed when they take frequent rearward glances, for their nerves have yet to resettle. This may require several miles on the open road, for the capitol building, which only a short time before served as a beacon, now looms menacingly as an unfriendly reminder.

Luckily, the route out of Springfield becomes less complicated with each minute gained. And thank God for the surety of Loban Motor engineering, in that its products can extirpate themselves from touchy situations. Although exhausted, the Lanes realize that it will require a few of hours to be at a safe distance from Springfield. Only then can they find a hotel and take advantage of a hot bath.

By all appearances, it seems as if the Lanes are making good on their getaway from the scene of the crime. The Park Hotel of Beardstown is a brick solid structure. And impressive is one particular room, its exterior marked by a balcony above a sidewalk and shaded by a lofty elm. Inside, the furniture is highlighted by a Herter Bros., double bed, along with a parlor suite of satin damask and a Roycroft dresser. The tapestry carpet and lace curtains are nothing if not Belgian, melding fluidly into the wallpaper's floral theme, with the vertical also supporting an oil rendition of a beardless Abraham Lincoln before his undivided throngs.

Embellishments aside, what most distinguishes the room is that it contains its own plumbing—especially hot water—meaning that the Lanes can cleanse themselves in absolute privacy. Indeed, Katie indulges herself in the process, soaking in her comforting bathwater, while removing the filth from the morning's troubling events. Already she's had her hair washed by her loving attendant, who at this moment is on a laundry and telegram errand, expected to return shortly.

Knock! Knock!

Suddenly, Katie's eyes perk open, although this interruption arouses no objections.

"It's me, Katie!" announces Axe, who enters the room by aid of a key.

"Back already?"

He steps into the bathroom and takes a chair by the tub, and then gives gentle strokes to his wife's cheeks.

"The laundry was nearby. And they promised to have our clothes sent here before six."

"That soon? Wonderful."

"And I did send a telegram to Mr. Loban. Explaining things."

"Do you think he'll believe your story, Axe?"

He frowns and even shrugs his shoulders. "Well-l-l, I didn't concoct a story, so much as told the truth."

"Oh?"

"Katie, we have nothing to hide. We did nothing wrong. And is Mr. Loban worth the effort of a lie?"

"Precisely." Now it's Katie's turn to stroke a cheek, albeit an uncleaned one. "Hand me that towel, Axe. I think I'll draw a new bath. It is your turn, after all."

Not being one to delay such an opportunity, Axe is naked in the tub before Katie has a chance to refill it. Soon, he finds his stained skin being scoured unto cleanliness by loving, gentle hands.

In due time, every atom of dirt and grime is released from the attraction of Axe's skin and sent down to the Illinois River. Yet he's not done, for the tub is filled anew, its warm waters serving not to cleanse, but to soothe. It's only when Axe's feet and hands turn prunish that he gives up the idea of extending his bath.

Yet the Lanes do not remain in a state of towel for long, for the Park Hotel has an additional draw.

"I saw the dining room," reports Axe. "It looks nice, so we need not search for a meal."

"Sounds fine to me. Though how about a stroll before we eat?" suggests Katie.

"Peachy," agrees Axe. "We can check on the roadster."

To be sure, the walk through Beardstown proves to be restorative, the burgh being far removed from Illinois state politics—precious are the miles. It is a calm, pleasant town, after all, especially since the meager winds for the moment are blowing its nickname, Porkopolis, toward another direction.

"A house divided cannot stand," quotes Axe, as the couple amble along. "I wonder, were President Lincoln alive today, would he prefer Beardstown over Springfield?"

"Likely," replies Katie. "Though his crazed wife might choose otherwise."

The Lanes continue their lazy stroll, striking up a few casual conversations and even making a purchase at the drug store. What follows is a filling and satisfying meal of stuffed pork chops, etc. at the Park's dining room. Yet even more appreciated, and needed, is an uncomplicated night on that Herter Bros. double bed. If a sound sleep is what Katie and Axe want most out of Beardstown, then it's a sound sleep they should have.

Knock! Knock! Knock! Rudely, the wakeup call is early, never mind that it comes at the requested hour.

"Six o'clock, Mr. and Mrs. Lane. Breakfast in the dining room."

After dragging themselves out of bed, the Lanes are able to take that breakfast. Soon, they pay a visit to the telegraph office, where unexpectedly no message from Lisbon awaits. Thus, with indifferent frowns, Katie and Axe are free to crank up the Speed Six and begin another leg of their journey.

A few city blocks later the Lanes end their visit to Beardstown by the unceremonious transaction of a twenty-five-cent toll. And so Axe steers the roadster upon the State Street Bridge—an impressive four span structure over the sedate Illinois River and its serenely wooded banks. Indeed, the moment begs to be extended.

"Axe. Let's stop for a while."

In the middle of the bridge pauses the Speed Six, thus allowing its occupants to absorb the rippled and riparian scenery as offered by the Illinois. To be sure, the margins are dominated by a leafy verdancy. Yet green also best describes the river's early morning waters, the gentler angles of light affording more color and less reflection. In the distance a plume of smoke flags the approach of a sternwheeler and its barge. But the river's commerce includes other occupations, as demonstrated immediately below by three men, who tug ashore an enormously long seine. By the looks of their struggle, the morning's first catch must be bountiful, meaning that a day's honest toil is off to a good start.

There's no hurry for the Lanes, the tranquil moment prolonged due to the lack of traffic.

"What a shame Beardstown doesn't have an auto club," notes Katie, as she gazes. "We would have avoided Springfield, altogether."

"Springfield?" Axe, too, feels the calm. "We'll never see that place again. And I hope nothing like it."

first catch must be 'Jonathan,' meaning that a day's honest toil is off to a good start.

There was no hurry for the Lanes as the tranquil moment prolonged due to the lack of traffic.

"What a shame Richard two doesn't have a chance to do this more," Kate says. "We would have avoided Springfield, altogether."

"Springfield? Absolutely," tells the captain. "We'll never say that [illegible] and [illegible] nothing like it."

12
WELCOME TO THE WEST

PART OF AXE'S TELEGRAM from Beardstown informed Loban Motor that he and Katie should arrive at Keokuk before the end of the day. Thus comes a certain trepidation as the couple approach said Iowa town and an expected message from Lisbon. Still, first things first, and that is to cross a mighty barrier with Katie behind the wheel and her apprehensions times two.

"Goodness, Axe! That bridge! And the river!" wonders Katie, whose awe for broad waterways is discovering a new cause. "It must be half of a mile wide."

"Careful now, Katie. Keep your eyes on the road."

The Lanes find themselves approaching the Keokuk and Hamilton Mississippi Bridge, the title of the structure revealing its purpose. As noted by Katie's rough estimate, the nation's greatest river is all of half a mile in width, spanned at this point by a decades-old railroad bridge, which connects two cities, two states and the two divisions of a country.

"Slowly," guides Axe, as a nervous Katie nudges the Speed Six upon the wooden roadway positioned to the side of the tracks.

Yet there's little to fear, if only because the bridge's construction is of obvious sound engineering—in spite of its age. Although the planks may rattle under the weight of the Speed Six, Katie's perceptions tell her that the structure's overwhelming size and height are the reasons behind the false sense of danger.

"It's not all that petrifying."

"No, Axe," agrees Katie, whose burgeoning appreciation is allowed a majestic view.

Unfortunately, there's no chance to pause, the afternoon traffic of wagons, pedestrians and even another automobile assuring the need to keep steady the roadster's throttle.

"I can't believe we're crossing the Mississippi," comments a steadier Katie. "Whew."

The traffic plods along, while Keokuk, Iowa beckons.

Soon, the couple locate the telegraph office, only to have their anticipations thwarted by the lack of a message from home. Indeed, it is perplexing, if not troubling, as the couple return to their parked roadster.

"I hope this is not because of Springfield," airs Katie of a gnawing fear.

"I doubt it. Mr. Loban just may be too occupied at the moment."

"You mean, Axe, he can't spare a few minutes on our behalf, and for the promotion's? Or have someone do it for him? If we shouldn't worry about Springfield, then perhaps we should over Lisbon." Katie pauses to catch her breath. "What are we to do?"

"Same as always, I suppose." Axe grasps the crank. "Find a newspaper and tell our story."

With that, the Lanes follow their routine, cruising about for a newspaper, any one of which will suffice.

"The Daily Gate City?" reads aloud Katie of some brick-embedded lettering, as she slows the roadster. "Does that sound like a newspaper?"

"Looks like one," notes Axe of the style, size, situation and even the smell of the building in question. "Yep. There's that odor of whiskey we've come to expect."

"Then we'll give it a try."

"Yep."

Apparently, the Lanes' ability to make a good first impression is nearing perfection, for no sooner do they enter the building then they're shuffled away to the editor-in-chief's office.

And apparently, Mr. Howell is something of an automobile enthusiast, who comes as an interested listener and a none-too-shy contributor. "The Speed Six, you say? I like the sound. Mine is a Moon Model A. Of St. Louis. For the family. Though I do have an eye for a lively roadster. For myself."

Regarding Moon, Axe recalls that it assembles rather than manufactures, with most components made by contractors and then shipped to St. Louis. Of course, Loban Motor is committed away from such a conservative approach and, of course, Axe harbors a disdain for those companies which are not.

"Does your Moon use a Rutenber engine?" he inquires.

"Why, yes," replies Mr. Howell. "A four-cylinder. Though now Moon produces its own."

"We're fairly familiar with the Moon touring cars. And well-built autos they are," notes Katie.

"Yes." Axe adjusts his condescending attitude. "Four-cylinders are quite sufficient for touring cars."

Mr. Howell appears to be a man enjoying his company. Still, the editor is in the newspaper business. Thus a reporter is summoned, so that a story might be gathered and/or concocted.

At first, the questions asked by both editor and his reporter are of the hum-drum, technical nature, the replies of which Axe's expertise is eager to fill, and fill in detail.

"Have you met any troubles along your tour?" injects the reporter during a carburetor lecture.

No one knows better than Katie that her husband's engineering rants and tangents might drag on forever, the risk being of an audience lost. "Uh-h-h." Perhaps this is the moment to add a little spice into a dull interview, thinks Katie, that is if she can summon the nerve. "Well-l-l. Yes. We have. In Springfield."

Immediately, Axe ceases his sermon.

"Springfield, Illinois?" asks the reporter, who must be gathering Katie's serious tone.

"Yes."

"What happened, Mrs. Lane?" furthers Mr. Howell, as he chomps at the bit.

"Well." Katie's caution is losing its punch. "My husband came to my defense in the face of three toughs."

"Toughs?" asks Mr. Howell.

"Three drunken toughs. Yesterday," replies Katie. "Under the very shadow of their capitol."

"There were three?" questions the reporter with an air of doubt.

"Yes. Three brutish animals."

The reporter turns to Axe. "Just how did you manage that, Mr. Lane?"

Axe hesitates, but then with a sly grin he takes up from where Katie has left. Demonstrating with his right hand, he points the barrel of his forefinger and cocks the hammer of his thumb.

"Simply, I showed those animals the error of their ways. And that I meant business. Burning a little powder and flinging some lead in the process." As Axe's drops his mock Hopkins & Allen, his demeanor turns more serious. "No man threatens my wife and gets away with it. No man impugns her honor without me setting him straight. Let that be said."

A brief pause ensues, only to be broken by the editor and what seems to be his ballooning enthusiasm—or admiration. "Grimlee! Take this down! This is tomorrow's front page!"

"Yes sir, Mr. Howell," confirms the reporter, who reconvenes his scribble.

"By God, Springfield will hear the exploits of our brave couple from Ohio," avows the editor, of this golden opportunity to cast disparaging words across the Mississippi. "The entire country, if I can help it."

With all the subtlety each can muster, Katie and Axe exchange their crafty smiles.

"Watkins! Harvey!" commands Mr. Howell through the open door of his office. "Contact city hall! I want a ceremony! With plenty of photographs! And I want it done quickly!"

And quickly it all plays out—astonishingly so for the Lanes. While Grimlee scrawls every word, the couple are hustled away a few blocks to city hall, the hierarchy and underlings of the Daily Gate City being their entourage. Before they know it, Axe and Katie are introduced to the mayor of Keokuk, as well as enough of the city fathers to make for a passable quorum. They're even presented with a bronze key, this token of municipality allowing the couple to do as they please, or so it implies.

"You people are so kind and generous," declares Katie to her devotees. "If only Springfield had been the same. I would not have suffered."

Be that as it may, in due time the newspaper's Carlton camera performs its task, the last plate of film being exposed in front of Keokuk City Hall. And it's here that the impressive gathering begins to go its separate ways. Soon, along with their Daily Gate City escort, the Lanes find themselves walking back to the newspaper and their parked roadster.

"But of course, the two of you will be my guests for the overnight," invites Mr. Howell. "Mrs. Howell and the children would be delighted."

"We would love that, Mr. Howell," accepts Katie. "How wonderful of you to ask. Axe?"

"Yes. Exceptionally generous, sir."

To be sure, the fears of repercussions from Springfield are all but forgotten. But as well, there comes a certain relief to have procured accommodations for the evening, although this does little to soothe the building concerns over the loss of contact with Lisbon.

But before Katie can ask about the competency of Keokuk's telegraph office or pose a question concerning the reach of the telephone exchange, her ears detect a distant, familiar sound.

"Stars and Stripes Forever?" she whispers in response to the approach of blaring brass, a thunderous bass drum and rattling snares—all with a curious lack of crashing cymbals.

On the other hand, the reaction from the newspapermen isn't one of appreciation for the work of John Phillip Sousa. Rather, their wrinkled chins speak of their dandy story in danger of losing it exclusiveness.

"The County News, I'll wager," grumbles Grimlee.

"Of course, the County News." Mr. Howell shakes of his head. "And another insufferable parade."

It's not long before the cavalcade comes into view, with Katie's ears tuned to the music and Axe's eyes sharpened upon the vehicle at the head.

"A Packard roadster, I see," he mutters. "Model L."

"McGrath," chorus several in the Daily Gate entourage, whose disdain must be for the driver of the car.

Quickly, the Lanes realize that the County News is a rival chronicler. Yet at the same instant they marvel at the speed of how news spreads in Keokuk and that, expeditiously, a parade has been organized. Although some of the musicians haven't had the time to don their uniforms and the band itself is absent of its director, coupled with a fantail of what must be the local automobile club, this procession makes an impression.

When the Packard comes abreast to Katie and Axe, it halts the parade.

"Mr. and Mrs. Lane, I presume." The driver tips his hat. "My name is John McGrath, acting editor of the County News. Welcome to Keokuk. May I congratulate you both for your momentous achievements."

"Thank you, sir," replies Axe.

"Would I be too forward to ask of you, Mr. Lane, Mrs. Lane, to join our celebration? To mark your crossing of the Mississippi? If you please, start up that marvelous Loban of yours."

Certainly, Axe and Katie are hesitant toward the invitation. After all, they've been engaged.

"Howell?" Mr. McGrath directs his plea toward his adversary. "You don't mind, do you?"

"Of course not," answers the editor of the Daily Gate with a surprising amount of resignation.

Apparently, there's a division of labor between the newspapers of Keokuk: one domain being city hall proclamations and the other downtown parades. The Lanes have no choice but to accede to the established norms of the Iowan city, that avoiding conflict must be a key to Keokuk's pleasant bearing.

Soon, the Speed Six joins the parade behind the Packard and in front of the band, to march through the business district and even a few neighborhoods. And all the while the Lanes prove to be gracious visitors, as they wave their hands and blow their horn at the curious onlookers.

"It just occurred to me, Axe," notes Katie, while commanding the wheel.

"We should stop at a confectioner's shop. So we could toss candy to the children."

"Yes. And bottles of whiskey from a saloon. For the newspapermen."

Ultimately, the parade comes to an end, doing so at the foot ofThe County News. Refreshments are offered and interviews taken—as a pair and then by piecemeal. Indeed, the atmosphere is convivial and fairly professional, abetted by the presence of several automobile enthusiasts, Mr. McGrath included.

"So the Speed Six has a touring version?" inquires the editor. "I've been considering one, for the family."

"Our touring Speed Six will suit your needs perfectly, Mr. McGrath," assures Axe, as Katie rejoins his side. "It has ample room, believe me."

"Yes. Plenty of room," she confirms. "The measurements are in the brochures."

Mr. McGrath nods with approval. But then he stops, as if he's conjuring a brilliant idea.

"Say," he announces. "The two of you will have to be my guests for the overnight. Why, Mrs. McGrath and the children will be delighted with your stay."

Thus a controversy emerges, one which could upset the delicate balances of Keokuk. For at least the moment, Axe and Katie are tongue-tied.

Eventually, the Lanes concoct their excuses and apologies, something about the need to take advantage of the remaining 116 minutes of daylight and push into the interior of Iowa. For at least the time being, the peace between two rivals is left intact. As far as the night's accommodations are concerned, the first town harboring a telephone exchange will do just fine.

As it happens, it takes only 59 minutes to reach Donnellson and its communications to the outside world.

"Lisbon, Ohio, you say?" repeats Mr. Cumrie, owner of the telephone exchange. "As it happens, my cousin operates the Lockington exchange. A connection should be no problem. To whom, may I ask?"

To whom, indeed, for Axe and Katie have given little thought to the question. Yet the implication is that Loban Motor, where the office at this moment may be vacated for the evening, is too obvious a connection.

"Should we call a friend instead of Mr. Loban?" asks Axe. "Someone we trust?"

"Yes." Katie is quick to agree. "But who? Who owns a telephone? Mrs. Snodgrass?"

"Perhaps," replies Axe.

"Achem," pushes Mr. Cumrie, who must be anxious for dinner.

With that, Axe snaps his fingers. "I know. Hugh Flugan has a telephone."

"Of course," excites Katie. "Mae Flugan charges her neighbors a penny per call."

Remarkably, it requires a hungry Mr. Cumrie under an hour to place the call. "Speak loudly, Mr. Lane."

"Hugh? Is that you? This is Axe." His ear is glued to the receiver. "What do you mean, 'Axe who'?" He pauses, signaling to Katie to cover her ears.

"Mr. Cumrie," she warns, as she cups her hands.

"#&@$%!", Hugh Flugan! Put down that bottle and listen to me!" Yet just as suddenly, Axe calms himself. "Hugh, we're here in Iowa, and have had some difficulty contacting Loban Motor. We've had no telegrams, no reply to our messages."

It's at this point that Katie tugs at Axe's sleeve. "Tell him we're going to run low of funds."

"I'm afraid the Speed Six is due for some repair work, Hugh. The transmission for a start. We lack some parts, so we're pinched for money."

Katie nestles to the receiver, although she does manage to glance at the exchange owner. "It's safe to put down your hands, Mr. Cumrie."

"Hugh, what is the problem with Mr. Loban?" continues Axe. "Or Freddy, for that matter?"

Katie holds her breath in wait for the reply.

"Oh, my God. How is she doing?" responds Axe at the news from Lisbon.

"What is it, Axe?" Katie's heart skips a beat.

He listens intently to each word before removing the receiver from his ear. "Katie. Aunt Lucie has suffered a stroke."

"Oh, my God!"

"But she is recovering." Axe listens further. "Say again, Hugh." Axe repeats the message. "Rumor has it, she's looking to sell her share of L.M. And Mr. Loban lacks the funds."

The implications are plain, that control for Loban Motor, and its promotions, may be in doubt.

Once more, Axe presses the receiver and sucks in every ounce of the dispatch. "Oh, my God!" he declares, yet again. "Mrs. Loban has returned from Columbus! She's moved back to Lisbon!"

Although the night's accommodations are comfortable, the Lanes have trouble settling themselves.

"I wonder if I should have asked Hugh to probe Mr. Loban, or Freddy?" questions Axe.

"No," assures Katie. "I think you were right to have him ask around. Especially Willis. And the Snodgrasses. They should have a clue. And be truthful about it."

"Umm." Axe offers a frown. "Just what is happening in Lisbon? That is the question."

"All heck and confusion," figures Katie. "Possibly."

"Yes," agrees Axe. "But you don't suppose, do you?"

"What?"

"You don't suppose?" Confronted by the unknowing, Axe is reluctant. "This could be the end of us?"

"The end of us? What do you mean?" Although not at a panic, Katie's voice sinks.

"Don't worry. L.M. is safe. I just have doubts that Mr. Loban will stay keen for our journey. It wouldn't surprise me if he cancels the promotion."

Instantly, Katie's face draws wider. "Axe, you can't mean that. Cancel? After all we've been through?"

"I'm sorry, Katie, but we may be told to return home."

"Axe, don't say that. I don't want to hear it."

To say the least, Axe is surprised at Katie's response. Yet at the same moment he's profoundly proud. As a tear begins to tumble down her troubled cheek, he moves to embrace her.

"You really do want to see the Pacific. Don't you?"

"Yes, I do," muffles Katie, what with her face buried into her husband's neck.

"So do I. But my fear is genuine. We have to be prepared. The next time Mr. Loban wires us money, it may come with a message sending us home."

"But how can he, Axe? We're halfway across the country."

"More like a third, Katie. Remember, the states grow wider this side of the Mississippi."

"Oh, Axe," moans Katie. "I don't care. We've come so far to give up now."

"Yes, we have." Axe offers a sigh, as the potion of sincere tears rubs into his exposed skin.

"I know we could find the Pacific." Katie pulls away from Axe's neck and gazes into his eyes. "Never mind what confronts us."

"I assumed that from the beginning." With a gentle thumb, Axe wipes Katie's cheeks. "Why, together we could take on the world, if need be."

Katie forces a smile. "Yes, we can, Axe." But then she raises her brow. "So who's to say we can't confront L.M., if need be?"

Perhaps, Katie's suggestion appears weak and vague. Yet she knows it contains enough hint, if only because she knows her Axe.

"Do you hear what you're saying? Strike out on our own? What would Mr. Loban say?"

"Axe, what do you care what Mr. Loban says? Or would do? He's six hundred miles away."

"But six hundred miles with our bankroll," counters Axe.

"How much money do we have?" Katie's stubborn streak accelerates.

"Forty-seven and change."

"Plus the ten dollar bill sewn into the liner of my duster," notes Katie and her optimism.

"Including that ten dollar bill."

"I see." But Katie isn't one to give up easily. "That should see us across Iowa. Hmm, Axe?"

"That's a mighty speculation, Katie. Remember that the gears feel a little worn, and fairly soon we'll have to purchase tires. Hefty expenses."

"Wouldn't it be a hefty expense were we to return to Lisbon?" responds Katie. "Don't you think Mr. Loban would send us enough money to make our way home?"

"Yes. That is if he doesn't have us ship the roadster by rail. As we were to upon reaching the Pacific."

"But Axe, even that would use a goodly amount of funds. Funds better spent continuing westwardly."

Axe's reaction is a disapproving look.

"Change that frown, Axe," insists Katie. "There's nothing dishonest about using Loban money to stay true to the plan. We would not be spending it on ourselves. It would all be for the better of L.M. You know that. More so than Mr. Loban."

In the face of such logic, what can Axe do?

"Besides," continues Katie. "Should we allow Percy Loban and Freddy Brothers to prevent our goal?"

"Well-l," ponders Axe, briefly. "I admire your pluck. If you're willing, then so should I. But Katie, we will have to cut costs. More camping and less chances for hotels."

"I'm fine with that, Axe."

"Fewer restaurants and more cooking over an open fire."

“That would be perfect, Axe,” assures Katie with her building enthusiasm. “You could use your shotgun and shoot a rabbit. Or a duck.”

“My, aren’t you the pioneer.”

“Yes, I am. And our dream is the Pacific. The devil to those who get in our way.”

Such a shocking declaration coming from a devout Methodist, yet so sincere a sentiment arising from a singular Wesleyan. Truth to tell, Axe leans toward the promotion’s cancellation forthwith, so that he and his persuasive bride might conquer the west by their own devices.

“Hmm? I wonder. Our account at People’s Savings?”

“We can’t touch that money, Axe,” reminds Katie. “The mortgage payments? And our bills being sent to the bank?”

“Yes. Though should it matter if we can’t use those funds?”

“No, Axe. Not at all.”

Thus a decision is reached, and a country is to be crossed regardless of the uncertain horizons. And with this comes a sure calm, meaning that there’s a fair chance for a gainful slumber.

Before departing Donnellson, the Lanes make a return visit to Mr. Cumrie. This time their call is directed to Loban Motor, to let them know of their intentions. Unfortunately, Mr. Loban and Freddy are unavailable and Axe is forced to leave a message with Miss Charnwood’s replacement. As far as Loban Motor is concerned, their representatives afield are progressing as normal and will make a stop at Bloomfield, said town being the perfect place to wire money.

The morning continues, with the Lane’s having reduced significantly their anxieties over what may await. As it happens, the road out of Donnellson points perfectly westward, with the nearest barrier being a simple crossing of the Des Moines River.

“Such a beautiful, little river. Don’t you think?” notes Katie, as the couple leave the valley.

“Yes, but such a primitive road,” grumbles Axe, while he drives. “I sure hope it improves.”

But improving roads are the constant hopes of every long distance traveler, this coming against the harsh terms of reality. The further the Lanes drive the worse become the conditions, never mind that they’ve told this is the most reliable route. The Speed Six struggles to notch another mile, its driver putting his shoulders into the steering wheel, while the passenger clings to her seat. Still, all three do manage to conquer the latest minimal hill, where Axe stops in order to survey the situation.

"How do we manage that?" alerts Katie of the stretch ahead. "Do the Good Roads people know of this?"

Gumbo it's called, a natural amalgamation of loam, clay and moisture capable of being altered into the wildest of configurations. Although already the calendar has beckoned summer, the rains remain plentiful enough to keep the roads wet and slippery, and extremely pliable. Indeed, far too many of Iowa's byways are little more than potters' tables, the random designs maintained by the traffic of farmers' heavy wagons and plodding hooves. As for those runs which have been kilned by the sun, they resemble a bed of amorphous ceramics more than a legitimate road.

Regardless, the Lanes will not be thwarted. Recovering from the shock, they prime their resolve.

On each side of the "road" are fields of young corn—for miles on end. Yet between the edges of crop rows and the river of gumbo lie two parallel spaces, narrow ribbons consisting of weedy growth, shallow ditches and occasional fencing. Perhaps this is the truer path to Bloomfield, to bob and weave on either side of exposed gumbo while dodging the manmade barriers of wooden posts and trenches.

"Straighten your goggles and hold on tight," proclaims Axe. "We're pushing through."

Indeed, the Speed Six plunges ahead, like a honey bear invading a hive. But whereas Axe is able to avoid the stings of fences and ditches, he cannot steer the roadster's edges away from stretches of unprotected corn stalks and gumbo road. The results are swarms of mud and chaff flinging upon the Speed Six and its occupants, coming alternately from the left and then the right, and the left again. To be sure, this is a filthy process—as well as exhausting. Yet it is a forward movement, westerly so with the realistic ambition that Bloomfield will be reached and that subsequent portions of Iowa should be crossed, eventually.

The fifty miles it takes to find Bloomfield from the Des Moines Valley requires all of seven, sapping hours. Dirty, hungry and worn, the Lanes are as sad a sight as their roadster. First things first, however, and that is to locate the telegraph office, putting aside the wants and needs of making themselves presentable.

"You must be Mr. and Mrs. Axelrod Lane?" presumes the clerk.

"Yes, we are," replies Axe, somewhat surprised at the intimation of a Loban Motor response.

"Sign here, please." The clerk presents a pen and receipt.

With the trade of his signature, Axe is handed a thick envelope.

"Thank you, Mr. Lane."

With their path delineated, Axe and Katie make their way toward the door. Yet strangely, there follows a certain reluctance to push through, to leave the comforts of the office for the outside world.

"Perhaps you should open it, Axe. We need to know."

Thus encouraged, Axe pries apart the envelope. Immediately, his eyes are impressed by the wad of cash. Yet quickly, his attentions become diverted toward the typed missive. Handing the money to Katie, Axe unfolds the message and begins to read silently.

"What does it say, Axe?" asks Katie in mid-count.

Axe's heart sinks as he reads on. Nevertheless, he feels no shock from Lisbon's brief words. Finished with the telegram, Axe looks to Katie and raises his brow.

"We're on our own, Old Girl. For better or worse, we're on our own."

Katie pauses, as she reaffirms Axe's expression. "Need I say 'I do' all over again?"

Axe's response is to drop the telegram and take his bride into his arms, burying his face into a cheek and lifting her feet off the floor.

"Achem," asserts the clerk's sense of decorum. "Sir, do you wish to send a reply?"

To which the Lanes calm themselves. "Absolutely not," they chorus. "Have a pleasant evening."

And so it's back to the struggle of Iowa's gumbo, albeit with a largesse of seventy-five dollars cash.

The gumbo rages on, as do the Lanes. Yet there comes a point where the determined forces are sure to meet head on, with the eventual outcome demanding a winner and a loser.

Katie is at the wheel, alternating between first gear and the reverse pedal, hoping to achieve a rocking action. And struggling in his shirt sleeves is Axe, putting every fiber of muscle and most of his weight into the rear of the Speed Six.

Vroom! and the roadster frees itself from the active suctions and smothering depths of gumbo.

But where there was a point of reliable resistance, now comes an instant brace of empty air. Suddenly, Axe's push against the Speed Six becomes a nosedive. Yet swiftly, his instinctive arms pry loose his face. However, temporarily blinded by the loss of focus and a thick coat of mire, Axe is all but helpless.

But leave it to Katie to rush to his side after securing the roadster. Ignoring that her husband is dressed in gumbo and appears only half-human, she helps him to his feet.

"Go ahead, Axe," winces Katie, as she covers her ears. "Let it fly."

Yet Axe is too exhausted to voice even the mildest of expletives.

"My spectacles," he squints, followed by a futile wipe with his sleeve.

"Here they are." Katie reaches down into a facial mold of gumbo. "Ugh. They'll need a cleaning, much like you. Forget a bath, Axe. You need to be doused by a fire hose."

"Doubtless," agrees Axe, as he gathers himself. "But I did push us free. That feat should merit a kiss."

"Later, Axe," declines Katie. "Heavens. Not the trousers to your blue serge suit. Axe, if only you were wearing your khaki."

Before long, the Lanes return to the task at hand. But it is certain that with each westward mile and every added minute of summer's heat, there should arise drier conditions and, hence, easier driving. While Axe scrapes away at his muddiness, a skillful Katie steers clear of obstacles.

"Axe, I can't find first again," she grumbles after another stop and restart. Katie jerks and jams the shift, and then she pumps at the gear pedal—all to no avail. "Ugh-h-h!"

It's not an unexpected complication, that the gear's teeth are losing their bite.

"Try the second gear, but with a little more throttle. Andante the pedal."

Eventually, the Lanes limp into Centerville, to lay over in a town noted for its skilled machinists and casters. The Speed Six is in good hands, Axe's included, and undoubtedly will return to working order. As to how much money the Lanes' pockets will carry when they leave Centerville, who can say?

As it happens, three days are spent at Centerville, time needed to repair the transmission, connecting rods and a camshaft. To be sure, the process is costly, with those parts made from scratch putting a painful dent into what may be the last of Loban Motor funds.

Yet there have been some deposits to the Lanes' bankroll. It seems that Centerville is a town starving for musical instruction, with Katie happy to fill the void—piano, violin and voice. She's even sat in with the local mandolin orchestra, although the only profit gained from the recital is a share of coinage. So goes the Centerville stay, with but one chore remaining.

"Will proceed to Pacific as originally planned. Axelrod Lane," reads the telegraph operator of the first morning message out of Centerville. "Will that be all, sir?"

Axe looks to Katie, who clutches at his side. "I believe that says it all."

"Very well, sir. That will be eighteen cents."

From his pocket, Axe delivers the exact change.

"Have a nice day, sir. Ma'am."

And so the Lanes return to their spanking clean roadster.

"I suppose the die is cast and we're crossing the Rubicon," notes Axe.

"No looking back," interprets Katie. "But do you think Hugh might send parts when we need them? On the sly?"

"It would be cheaper. And Hugh would help us. Likely, all the shops."

"Wonderful, Axe. Then we'll reach the Pacific yet."

Thus the Lanes' route is mapped. With a little surreptitious aid from home, the couple should earn and persuade their way across the rest of the country, and, if need be, return their roadster to Lisbon.

13
BLESSED NEBRASKA

AXE AND KATIE MAY VERY WELL be the first drivers in the history of Iowa to traverse the state without the aid of horse teams, such is their triumph over gumbo. But upon crossing the wide Missouri, there loom other obstacles: vast, empty distances. For more than sixty years, America's pioneers have made the daunting trek, lugging with them every last possession of their lives. Now there arrives a certain couple from Ohio, who follow those trails of uncertainty and the promise of similar, if not identical, conditions.

The Lanes keep well to the south of Omaha, Nebraska, if only because the city is a known stopping point for certain New York to Paris autoists. Instead, they travel upon a less tainted region of the state, into a pin-neat expanse of genuine inventiveness and practical living. Through Otoe and Gage Counties and toward the Big Black River the Lanes proceed, passed newly created fields of wheat stubble and row upon row of green corn. And although the roads are of the same haphazard design as in Iowa, at least in Nebraska these country lanes are drier and, thus, easier to negotiate.

"Oh, the heat," grouses Katie, who has folded her duster and must face the road particulates unprotected.

As much as anything, Nebraska is homesteaded ground, a carrot luring people from faraway lands, while maintaining holds on their progenies. And with these unicameral Nebraskans come their many tongues, English being the foremost, but there including the waggles from Europe's other corners and many middles.

The necessity to economize is now a driven fact. And so if an opportunity for a little profit arises, then the Lanes must be quick to the task. Yet before dealing with those never-ending requirements of food, shelter and gasoline, there comes the more basic need of potable water. Fortunately for Katie and Axe, the wells of Nebraska are abundant, while their refreshing issues are free for the asking.

The Speed Six pulls to a stop in front of a likely source—yet another farmhouse of expanded and flawless construction. And no sooner after the engine sputters into silence then the Lanes are greeted by the apparent master of the farm, whose eyes are occupied by the example of Ohio machinery before him. Quickly, Axe's request in perfect English is answered by an enthusiastic, Czech accent. Before they know it, the Lanes are having their containers filled from an outdoor hand pump, manned by the farmer while the members of his extended family hover about in amazement.

"You mean to say you are crossing the country in your vehicle?" asks Roman Pesek, his right arm not missing a beat at the handle.

"Why, yes," assures Axe. "As a promotion for my employer, Loban Motor of Ohio."

Instantly, the younger portion of the curious family becomes further excited by this revelation, while Roman's parents and grandmother must wait for the translation.

Regardless, in the midst of the Slavic/English amalgam, Katie and Axe hear the word "gasoline", and observe the nods of acknowledgement from the elder Peseks. But then Mr. Pesek prattles away to Roman, mixing in more recognizable words such as "Russell", "steam" and "Ohio." Shoulders are shrugged and brows raised—not only by father and son, but by wives, the grandmother and the children. Something is up, it being plain that Axe and Katie's simple request for water may be leading to something more consequential.

"Mr. and Mrs. Lane, if you please," speaks Roman, as he ceases pumping. "Might I show you something? It should not take long."

Before they can realize, the Lanes are ushered to the farm's sturdy, red barn. And because the structure's enormous door is wide-open, it becomes plain why Roman is so anxious to show his guests of what must be the spectacle of eastern Saline County.

"What a brute," remarks Axe, though he speaks not of a flesh and blood Clydesdale or Percheron.

Instead, said brute is a bright and shiny, wheeled machine, its engine powered by steam, as revealed by the red cylindrical, universal boiler.

Although somewhat awed, Axe is able to recognize a yellow trademark symbol, and can even make a quick estimation. "A Russell tractor. Why it must be eight tons."

Katie, too, feels the surprise, but as well is able to gather her senses. "The Russell and Company," she reads of the lettering stenciled upon the bin. "Massillon Ohio USA." And then she glances at her husband. "Did Hugh Flugan ever work for them, I wonder?"

"Hmm?" Axe considers the question. But then he returns to the matter at hand and looks toward the host. "Do you own this colossus?"

Certainly, it is an obvious question, of how a modest farm could afford a costly piece of farm machinery.

"Oh, no, Mr. Lane." With his family standing about him, Roman is immediate, if not embarrassed, with his reply. "This Russell tractor belongs to our farmer's society. My neighbors, who share its use."

Thus explains Roman, of how he and his family, and their Czech associates, have scrimped, saved and made-do-without in order to purchase a metal-wheeled Russell tractor. It seems at least one corner of Nebraska is recognizing the need to modernize.

And no couple appreciates this kindred spirit more than the Lanes, never mind the differences of internal combustion versus external.

"We cut and shocked our wheat as we always have," continues Roman. "My neighbors and myself. Even after we received our Russell tractor and towed it here."

Immediately, Axe realizes the problem. "So you've had trouble operating your Russell."

"Precisely. And you can see our threshing machine, there. It is powered by our Russell's belt." But then Roman's enthusiasm pauses. "Well. Sometime soon, we hope."

Sometime soon, indeed, especially since the bound wheat of Roman's neighbors is no doubt hardening and will need the thresher's appointments.

"And I suppose you want me to help you operate the Russell? For your society, Mr. Pesek?"

"Yes. And teach us. And please call me Roman, Mr. Lane."

"Hmm?" Axe looks at an acceptable Katie, and then at the gathered, expectant audience that is the Pesek family. "Hmm?" as he scratches his chin.

"But of course, as president and treasurer, I am permitted to offer a fee."

"Fee, you say?" Axe's interest wastes no time at being piqued. Again, he glances at Katie and her agreeable smile, only to gaze upon the Russell and its challenges. "If you don't mind, Roman, please call me Axe. And please bring me the manual."

Axe does have a history with steam. After all, what competent mechanical engineer doesn't? And so the complications of the manual are but problems to be solved. First things first, and that is to become intimate with the gauges and their tolerances. Then there are the urgencies of lubrication, as well as the need to grasp the workings of the over-mounted engine. Soon, Axe should make dry runs with the steering wheel, gears and friction clutch, and then see that the boiler tubes are filled with water. But with a little luck and before the end of the day, he may put a match to the wood already in the firebox and, hence, produce a little steam.

Meanwhile, Katie has her own interests, and is getting acquainted with the rest of the family: the three Mrs. Peseks—including Roman's wife, Marie—daughters Mary and Sara, sons Martin and George, and baby Teddy. Before long, she's learning all about the wonders of a multilingual setting—not just English and Czech, but also splices of German and Hungarian—and is introduced to the sumptuous inventions of fruit-swirled kolaches and stuffed-cabbage cholupchis.

Indeed, it is a busy kitchen, the largest room in the house. And because the three Mrs. Peseks are present, with the oldest, chore-able siblings being Mary and Sara, there is no shortage of labor. Along with the boys, all that's required of Katie is to sit back and observe, and add to the pleasant conversation as she sees fit.

"...So Mrs. Pesek, where were you born?" asks Katie for her pertinent portion.

"Oh, I born in Praha," replies Roman's proud mother, her fingers engulfed in dough. But then Mrs. Presek's face lights up even further, as she delivers a correction of sorts. "No. I really born in Nelahozeves. Near Praha." She renders a Czech version of her response to her equally-occupied mother-in-law.

"Ah, Tisnov," nods Babicka Pesek, who points at herself and repeats her birthplace. "Tisnov."

"And I was born in Wilber," joins Marie Pesek. "Wilber, Nebraska." To which all the Presek in-laws giggle in harmony.

"Where you?" asks Mrs. Presek.

"Me? I'm afraid I was born in Ohio," answers Katie. "In a boring town called Delaware." Because Katie's attentions have been diverted toward the wilds of Europe, she's lost all interest of her hometown. "Could you tell me something about Nelahozeves? Tisnov?"

And so the tales of the old country are unleashed by means of rapid, foreign tongues and slower interpretive English. As for the regalee, Katie is all ears.

"...A ano ja touzit ten podivuhodny Katina," reminisces Mrs. Pesek. "A ten vune od ten sosna lesni."

"Ano," agrees Grandmother Pesek. "Ja zapor od can mit Karel pestorat jeden sosna."

"They miss the pines and hills," translates Marie. "And complain that Papa Presek will not plant a pine."

As if to accent her pinings, Grandmother Pesek begins to hum a tune from her homeland, joined by her daughter-in-law, the pair not missing a beat to the kitchen chores at hand.

To say the least, there are inspirations aplenty from the Pesek hearth. With Teddy in her arms, Katie slips off her high stool and hands the baby to his oldest sister, Mary.

"Excuse me. I'll be back in a moment," she explains, as she exits through the rear door.

It's to the Speed Six that Katie rushes, ignoring all of the activities concerning the Russell. And it's from beneath the passenger's seat that she pries loose her violin case. By the time Katie reenters the kitchen, she's wielding her bow while plucking her strings.

"Ahh! Ona vykonati ten housle!" chorus the two elder Peseks.

"You play the violin!" echoes Marie.

Indeed, Katie does. But more to the point, she finds herself amidst a perfect venue for her love of Antonin Dvorak. Smartly and instinctively, Katie reaches for a piece from the composer's Slovanic Dances.

"Ohh!" Not only do the three Pesek women respond to a recognizable strain, so, too, do the children bounce with a discernable glee—including a wide-eyed Teddy.

The results are feet springing upon the kitchen dance floor, even while the miraculous hands manage their chores. Yet Katie accepts the challenge all the same, revving up her bow to swifter strokes. Soon, Babicka and Mrs. Pesek abandon the table altogether, joining hands in a mutual display of girlhood memories. And while Katie's violin maintains the rhythm, it's assisted by the spontaneous percussions of Pesek handclaps—even Teddy's. By the joy of it, dinner may be late at the Pesek household.

But eventually the music must stop, be it by shear exhaustion or the interruption of a cooler head or…

Too-o-o-o-t! Too-o-o-o-t!

In mid-stroke Katie halts her bow and in mid-step the Peseks cease their dance.

Toot! Toot! Toot!

There can be no doubt as to the source of the sudden uproar. Yet in no way are the kitchen participants taking the resounding signals as a disruption. Quite the contrary, for each Pesek face is as lit as would any neophyte's toward a fulfilled prophecy.

"The tractor!" announces Marie. "They've figured out the Russell!"

Sara is the first out the door, followed by her brothers and mother, grandmother and great grandmother, and lastly, her youngest and oldest siblings. As for Katie, she's blithe to tail along, her husband's conquest over the Russell coming as no great shock.

Still, the tractor does make for a grand spectacle, as it creeps its way out of the barn. Mounted upon its cab is the proud chevalier Axelrod Lane, ably accompanied by squires Mr. Presek and Roman. There's much steam, as well as the clamor of piston machinery and oversized wheels cleating into the ground.

"Mama. Mama," cries Martin, as he and George retreat to the safety beneath Marie's skirt.

The other Peseks, too, are stunned by the vision of an unleashed, animated beast, even if the Russell moves at a bare crawl.

Regardless, Axe's self-satisfied grin makes for a reassuring proclamation, that all is well with the tractor.

And so the Lanes spend a few days with the Peseks. But also the couple is shuffled to other farms, where society implements are stored and where the Russell is put to use. In addition, the Sulak and Marek farms become gathering places for society members, to bear witness to practical demonstrations and to feel the intense lessons of safety and maintenance. As he interprets the functions of recent inventions and devises practical ways to integrate the old, Axe discovers a new arena in which to revel. Certainly, it is strenuous work—sometimes backbreaking—and certainly it is everything satisfying.

It's fortunate that the Marek house owns a spare bedroom—a rarity in this part of Nebraska. Cleansed and well-fed after a tiring day, the Lanes are none too happy to melt into their bed and its forgiving mattress.

"How is your arm, Axe?" asks Katie, as she cozies up to her husband's side. "Seven stitches?"

"Mmm," groans a sleepy Axe. "It's fine. Doesn't hurt so much."

"Thank goodness it wasn't worse. Remember, the doctor said keep it clean."

"I'm sure you'll see to that, Katie."

"Of course." She shifts herself and looks toward the ceiling. "Ah-h-h. So comfortable after such a busy day. And such wonderful, new friends."

"Mmm," continues the groan.

"Axe?"

"What?"

"Try not to say Bohemians. They prefer Czech."

"Mmm."

"Can you believe it, I learned today another way to make kolaches," prattles Katie. "And I really do think I'm beginning to love sauerkraut and pork dumplings. My goodness, all the polkas and waltzes I've learned. Mazurkas. I could write a book, if I weren't so busy with my correspondences. Hmm? I suppose I should write a lengthy letter to Mr. Loban. He might deserve an explanation." Katie takes a breath. "First thing when we return home. I'm going to order an accordion."

"Mmm."

"Axe, for goodness sake. Please be more careful," continues Katie. "Who would ever think to leave the seat of a moving disc harrow? Promise me you'll never be so careless again. Axe?"

Glancing toward her husband, Katie sees that he's fallen into a well-deserved sleep.

"Oh, Axe."

With her fingers, Katie strokes one of his cheeks, and with her gentle lips she pecks at the other. But then she looks toward the wound in question, only to reach down and deliver a tender kiss to Axe's bandaged arm. Although this may not be the most antiseptic of medicines, it is the best curative all the same.

"My sweet Axe," whispers Katie.

Saturday, the Fourth of July, arrives, and with it concludes a busy, gainful week. That the day comes replete with the spirit of celebration, this should be of no surprise. However, the Marek family has every reason to stack another joy upon this particular day. By choice planning, Hannah, the eldest daughter, is to be wed, and by delighted consideration the Lanes are invited guests to the ceremony.

Never before have Katie and Axe done so much kneeling—when in Saline County, do as the Salinians. But as they occupy a section of the rear pew within Saints Cyril and Methodius' , the discomfort to their genuflected knees is soothed by the diversion of the church's interior. Without a doubt the Lanes are dazzled by the overt and subtle symbolisms of their surroundings. There's much in the way of statuary, this being of the inspirational saints and, naturally, of the Messiah who started it all. But then there is the artistry of the painted, vaulted ceiling, its starry, heavenly sky heralded by a host of trumpeting angels and supported by wooden columns of a clever, faux marble. And it's all lit through Gothic windows, these covered by stained-glass panels not only of Biblical lessons, but of old country memories.

Still, although Katie is touched by the spirit, she feels a squirm, if only because her church attire is taking a bow to the hardships of the road.

"Don't worry. Your hat isn't all that terrible," whispers Axe.

Clad in her princess dress, Katie lets out a sigh. "Yes," she agrees, all the while hoping that her last-second festoon of dried flowers is covering the shame of her once smart skimmer. Yet the wonder of the moment still exudes, as she murmurs into her husband's ear. "How could they build such a church? How could they have found the means?"

Indeed, the answer may be found only through the determined sacrifices of a vibrant community, a parish bound by limited funds, though not by a faith unfulfilled.

Soon, a final sign of the cross is delivered by the priest. And followed by a tender, binding kiss, a surname is changed, thus concluding this most holy of ceremonies.

"Oh, Axe," exudes Katie, as she clutches her husband's good arm and leans upon him. "Oh, Axe," with her eyes fixed upon the joined couple.

So it's on to the beckoning trumpets of the Zapadni Cesko Bratrska Jednota lodge/dance pavilion, the venue for the celebration. And it's during their short stroll that the Lanes no longer feel the need to whisper.

"What did you think, Katie? About the wedding? The ceremony?"

"I liked it. So much Latin. And there was no wickedness to it, which is what I've been told all my life. In fact, it seems a very musical religion. In a staccato sort of way, but within a sanctuary every bit fortissimo."

"Hmm? I think I see your point, Old Girl."

As they near the white, octagonal Z.C.B.J. building, the sounds of music and busy feet rush through the propped open windows. This comes as a surprise to the Lanes, that the brass/woodwind band and celebrants are wasting no time. Regardless, Katie's feet cannot help themselves, their stroll altering to the beat.

Yet they stop in their tracks, when her eyes cast upon the sudden vision of female merry-makers lining up in front of a beer keg. And there is no doubt, when the light of the afternoon sun glistens through a heady, amber glass as held by Mrs. Pesek.

"What's wrong, Katie?"

"Look, Axe. At what they're sipping. The women."

Up until today, Katie's impression of women who drink openly, and who also seem to dance freely, are those of the objectionable, loose kind—harlots, in other words. Yet now she knows to the contrary, that the females she's encountered in Saline County are nothing but virtuous and hard-working, their characters being unimpeachable. Apparently, within their surroundings and upbringings these fine ladies are not shy when it comes to having a good time. And so why not do the same, reasons Katie? Why not blend with this crowd of contented women and their liberating ideals?

"Axe? Could you fetch me a glass of beer? That is after we have our first dance?"

Delighted, Axe takes his wife's hand and escorts her to the floor in question, to swirl about and romp to the cadence of an uproarious polka.

As it happens, Katie may have to wait for that first glass of beer, for no sooner does the band end its polka than an eager, light-footed Roman Pesek taps her husband upon the shoulder.

Axe is not at all reluctant to surrender his bride into the arms of a trusted friend. Instead, he's happy that Katie, herself, feels the vivacity of the air, which includes the freedom to dance with others. Unfortunately, for at least the moment, Axe is left standing alone—partnerless amidst the opening strains of an accented, 3/8 waltz. He pivots around and spots the Pesek table, where Marie sits temporarily unencumbered from child-rearing by the presence of her mother-in-law and babicka-in-law. Eye contact is made, with the beam of her face saying that the offer is accepted before Axe can make it. Soon, the Lanes and Peseks are dancing side by side, with each individual melding their short steps into that of the waltz's.

Thus the celebration hastens into the evening, whizzing passed by the aid of the whirling dance floor, where the children occupy the middle, while the adults circle about in nonchalant supervision. And then there are the contributions of the kegs of beer and bounties of tasty edibles. Regardless, the Salinians are a hardy people—both young and old—and are able to take the wedding celebration in stride.

On the other hand, there is that Ohio couple, whose Saturday nights have never been taxed to such extremes. Katie becomes exhausted from her intense, hands-on and feet-upon study of Czech dance music, as ably assisted by an endless parade of partners, including all of the Pesek children. Yet because she's tipsy, she doesn't realize her fatigue, quite the opposite in that she's in the mood for a little mischief.

"Axe! They want me to bring my violin for a shivaree!" Katie puts her finger to her mouth. "Sh-h-h. Don't tell anyone! We're going to surprise Hannah and John! Sh-h-h."

Previously, the Lanes decided that Sunday morning will mark the end of their stay in Saline County. And suspecting that a Czech shivaree might last well into the wee hours, Axe decides to take the matter in hand.

"Why don't we walk to the Marek's and fetch your violin?" he suggests, knowing full well that by the time he and Katie reach their current hosts' home, she'll be primed for a deep sleep.

"Wonderful, Axe! Let's go! Sh-h-h."

But as Axe leads Katie toward the open door, he waves his farewells to their many friends, and even manages a few passing handshakes.

"Goodbye, Roman. Marie. It's been a real pleasure. Katie and I have never had a finer week. Never."

Thus the Lanes leave the celebration, to get their rest before the promise of a hazy and confused morning.

For several days, Katie and Axe have avoided the annoyances of the New York to Paris race. But sooner or later, they'll need to veer northwestwardly and merge into its stream. This is the best route, after all, to traverse the Rockies.

Beyond the town of Holdrege and across the Gosper County line, the Lanes motor cautiously into the evening. Already, it's been apparent that the region is more spare. Now, the lamps beginning to light the homes are far between and few in number.

"Axe, I don't think we're near any town. No hotels, for sure."

"We'll have to make do, Katie. Find a place to pitch our tarp and then..."

Pop! Suddenly, an all too familiar sound interrupts. Pop! Followed instantly by another.

With some struggle, Axe manages to bring the roadster to a safe stop.

Hiss-s-s-s.

"Not again," complains Katie over the loss of pressurized air to her immediate left.

Axe leaves his seat for a quick inspection. "Can you believe it? Both tires. Horseshoe nails, I'll wager."

"Will they ever invent tires stronger than horseshoe nails?" Katie shakes her head.

"I doubt it. Far simpler to put the dobbins out of business."

"Are they repairable, Axe?" asks Katie, as she leans from her seat for a look.

"They should be." He stares at the front, left tire, and then sighs.

"Leave it for the morning, Axe. We should camp by the roadside. Build a fire."

"Hmm?" Standing from his crouch, Axe looks about and surveys the dark surroundings. "There's a light over there. Might we impose ourselves? They may offer us a bed."

Katie turns her head toward said beacon. "Should we bother?"

Certainly, it is a dim light. And that it's been obvious for many miles the Lanes have been crossing a rougher region, Katie has every reason to cast her doubts.

"They may not have the means to take in guests, Axe. They could be impoverished."

"Well, if that's the case, we'll share what we have. The sausages, potatoes and sauerkraut. And we could offer them a dollar for their trouble."

"Oh, very well, Axe," yields Katie, her gut feeling notwithstanding.

Guided by a lantern, the Lanes inch their way toward a strange cluster of small, dark and ramshackle farmhouses and onto the porch of the lit one.

"Should we, Axe?" whispers Katie's reaction to the eerie surroundings.

Knock, knock, knock! Her husband's reply is abrupt.

Yet it seems that Axe's raps upon the door are slow to be answered. He repeats the process and then looks upon Katie.

"Axe," she alerts.

Through a window, it's plain that the beacon of light is moving, apparently approaching the door. Footsteps are heard, while the apprehensions grow as to what may come and of whom might open the door.

The knob jingles from within and a crack between door and jamb widens a bit. The Lanes hold their breaths and then take hold of one another. Suddenly, an eye peeps through the crack, it being both piercing and bleary. But then it becomes excited, as if losing the want to be reticent. The door swings open, exposing a thin, disheveled man of about 45 years, he wielding a parlor lamp.

"Mike? Mary? You've returned!" Obviously, the man is confused. "Oh? You're not Mike and Mary."

"No," confirms Axe. "I'm afraid not."

Yet this does little to soothe the man's confusion, so says his puzzled face.

"My apologies, sir. My name is Axelrod Lane, and this is my wife, Mrs. Lane. We're autoists who have run afoul of horseshoe nails on your road and..."

"Horseshoe nails?" interrupts the human of the house. "I have no horses."

"Oh, no, sir. Pardon me," excuses Axe. "I'm not casting blame. We're merely stranded and saw your light, and thought that..."

"You're stranded." The man's face lightens. "How, uh-h-h, unfortunate. Please come in."

In spite of Katie's subtle tugs, Axe accepts the invitation, dousing his lantern as he steps forward.

The portion of the house into which the Lanes are led isn't so much a formal parlor nor a relaxed family sanctum, as it is something of a stark, gathering room. So speak the plain, multi-leaved table and its assortment of a dozen chairs. Meanwhile, two of the walls are occupied by functional book cases, the shelves crowded by volumes of what is likely non-agricultural subject material. As for those other vertical spaces, upon them are pinned and hooked a menagerie of artwork and posters seemingly of a political nature. In addition, because of an overwhelming lack of children's furniture, the front room where Katie and Axe find themselves probably has nothing to do with family dining.

"Brother and Sister. Er, uh." In a nervous flutter, the host corrects himself. "Mr. Lane. Mrs. Lane." He places his lamp upon the table and adjusts its wick. "Please have a seat."

"Thank you," replies Axe. He pulls out the chair next to the head of the table.

As for Katie, she takes the seat at her husband's right and away from their host.

"My apologies. I should introduce myself. Jack Sinclair." After shaking Axe's hand, he seats himself at the head chair. "Can I get you something? A bite to eat? A drink? Gin?"

"We're fine, Mr. Sinclair. Thank you," declines Axe. "We just…"

"Oh, yes. Your tires. So you own an automobile?"

"Well, yes. In a manner of speaking. We're on a…"

"Perhaps the two of you need a place to spend the night," interrupts Sinclair. "And of course, you've come to the right place. For we have ample room at Social Farm. Uh, formerly New Society Farm. But now, Social Farm. Where we never turn away a stranger. Where we freely share what we have." There's a definite boast to Sinclair's tone.

Glancing beyond a stack of Mother Earth magazines, Katie tries to make sense of her surroundings. That Sinclair speaks of his property as a farm seems a stretch, the kerosene lantern's approach having caught no indications of tillage or livestock. And then there's Sinclair's curious use of the plural "we" when by all cursory indications he should utter "I." The bookshelves are a mystery, Katie's hope being they remain as such. As for the artwork attached to the wall, their simplistic, alliterative slogans of class struggle and sinewy images of the wild-eyed are an attack upon her aesthetic sensibilities and love for subtle beauty. In subtraction, because of the sepia curtains and less-than-minimal frippery, Katie feels appalled by the lack of culture and by the disdain for familial order.

"Are you comfortable, Mrs. Lane?"

"Hmm? Pardon?"

"Are you comfortable, Mrs. Lane? Should I find another chair?"

"Oh no. Thank you. I'm fine," replies Katie to her host's courtesy. "Perfectly so."

Maybe there is nothing to fear from Sinclair, he being in the company of no one amidst a fairly disordered setting. And so Katie is able to relax somewhat.

"We're suited to accommodate visitors for prolonged periods," continues Sinclair. "Months on end, if you please. Years, should the need arise."

"I don't think it could come to that. Our repairs are minor and we have commitments," explains Axe. "But thanks all the same. Very generous of you."

"But at least, I should give you a meal. Or that drink. As an obligation to my brothers and sisters."

Axe shrugs and accepts. "If you insist, Mr. Sinclair. We might have a sip. If it's no trouble." Regardless that during the non-sobrietous segment of his life, Axe has never sampled any sort of a watery-clear intoxicant. "A little gin might do us some good."

Meanwhile, Katie's discovers a particular mark, which she finds both hideous and captivating. "Could that be your mother, sir?" she asks of a framed photograph and its frightful image.

"Who?" replies a somewhat surprised Sinclair. "Oh. You mean Emma. Emma Goldman. No. She's not my mother. In fact, I believe Emma and myself are nearly the same age."

"Really?" To be sure, Katie is more astonished than embarrassed.

"Yes." On the other hand, Sinclair appears to be more flattered than appalled.

Be that as it may, there remains a reluctant request the host seems all too eager to serve. Soon, three surprisingly clean, crystal tumblers are place upon the table along with an uncorked bottle of St. Louis gin.

"Here's to your healths, Brother and Sister."

Sinclair is quick to quaff, while the Lanes are slow to sip. The gin is both cheap and stimulating—something of a trial for the newcomers, but apparently an old friend to the resident.

"Ahh," finishes Sinclair of his glass. "So you're motoring through Nebraska?"

"Yes. We spent some time in Saline County. Helping the farmers adapt to their new machinery," reveals a proud Axe. "Clever, hard-working people, we found them."

"Do you mean you were staying with those Germans? Or rather those Bohemians?"

"Yes," confirms Axe. "For a week."

"Our friends in Saline County prefer 'Czechs'." Katie is insistent. "Not 'Bohemians'."

"I see." Though perhaps a bewildered Sinclair doesn't. "So you've come to Nebraska to help the farmers? All the way from-m-m? Where did you say, Mr. and Mrs. Lane?"

"Ohio. Lisbon, Ohio."

"Really?" Sinclair's perplexity appears to be gaining strength. "All the way from Ohio?"

"Oh. No, Mr. Sinclair." Axe senses the confusion. "We haven't come from Lisbon to assist the Saline farmers. Mrs. Lane and I are on a journey. Crossing the country in our Loban Speed Six roadster."

"Yes," assists Katie. "Our stay with our new Czech friends was a happy circumstance. They needed my husband's engineering expertise, and we were too glad to help."

"Really?" It's almost as if Sinclair is salivating, as well one should when an opportunity comes knocking. "Drink up, Brother and Sister. Let me pour more. We have plenty."

"We're fine, Mr. Sinclair," declines Axe. "Thank you."

"So you own a Loban roadster?" continues Sinclair, as he tipples more gin for himself. "Quite a fancy vehicle, it sounds. Must sell for a considerable sum."

"Well-l, that's not entirely true. In fact, our Loban comes at a fairly reasonable sum," explains Axe. "Within the means for many people."

"Oh?" Sinclair's tone exudes a bit of disappointment.

"This has always been our goal at Loban Motor. We take great measures to lessen the costs of production, while delivering an inventive auto." A prideful Axe can't help himself. "Our use of vanadium steel for a solid frame. Our six-cylinder engine. The three-speed, sliding gear transmission. And the…"

"Excuse me. Did you say 'we'?" Apparently, Sinclair is focusing on one of Axe's words.

"Yes. I'm the assistant engineer for Loban Motor. Mrs. Lane and I are on a promotion. Crossing the country."

"I see." Sinclair sighs and pours more gin—a reasonable reaction when in the presence of unenlightened, capitalist lackeys of modest means. He keens an eye and swallows his inspiration.

Bit by bit, Axe is gaining a sense of the surroundings. And so he's beginning to regret that he followed the light of Social Farm, as opposed to Katie's sounder intuitions.

"My employer is a fairly progressive man, I should say. Who pays a decent wage, in an industry which does not exploit women and children."

As for Katie's response, she's a bit astounded—not from Sinclair's subtle censure, but at her husband's defense for Mr. Loban. Still, there does brew a confrontation, of which she's in no mood to witness.

"Achem. Mr. Sinclair. Tell us about Social Farm. For instance, what crops do you raise?"

"Pardon? Raise?" Sinclair appears confused.

"Yes. Crops." Such an uncomplicated question, although Katie feels the need to simplify further. "Do you grow crops? Grains, vegetables, livestock? Do you farm at Social Farm?"

"We don't really. Not for a while."

"We?" questions Axe—of the obvious.

Once again, Sinclair lets out a sigh, followed by a gulp of gin. "Yes, we were a genuine farm at one time, I suppose. In the beginning. And we were, often times, content. Sometimes too content. It was the Haymarket Massacre that shook our ways. We missed that tumultuous opportunity, and it tore our society apart. I was so young, back then. Full of fervor." Sinclair refreshes his glass. "But those members who left were in time replaced by the refugees of the city. Bright and well-versed. Ah, yes. Young, oppressed women, who were opening their minds. Oh, how they loved it when Big Bill Haywood would extend a stay. Look, there hangs his photograph."

Axe and Katie are rendered a-gasp by the latter revelation. Together, they down their gins.

"Before long, we organized a C.D.A. A Central Direction Authority. And Social Farm regained its prosperity. Its passion."

A pause ensues.

"What happened then?" asks a reluctant Axe.

"Hmm? Oh." Sinclair shakes his head. "We lost our support, I suppose. Especially Mary Hathaway. Our Mayflower heiress, she switching her curiosities toward archeology. Egyptology, was it?" There's more than a hint of disdain in Sinclair's explanation. "And then the C.D.A. refused to support Daniel DeLeon for Eugene Debs. The reformist over the revolutionist." Now, Sinclair's tone alters toward the bitter. "Debs. That poodle in the lap of dilettantes."

Neither Katie or Axe has ever bothered to form an opinion of Eugene Debs, be it high or low. And so they shouldn't be faulted if they can't concoct one on the fly.

"The miseducation, led by false movements, forced stagnation and diffidence," continues Sinclair. "Which led the kangaroos of the C.D.A. to bow to the pressure! To dissolve the proceedings, so that the comrades might return to the cities and educate the ignoramuses and fakirs of the proletariat!"

Phew!

"It sounded like your C.D.A. may have opened the doors of Bedlam," urges a shameless Axe, he recovering his sense of humor. But then he speaks from the side of his mouth. "Those poor cities, Katie."

Yet it's as if Sinclair is clueless to the true intent of Axe's words.

"To think, we could have done the same as the abolitionists and their Republican Party. It took them only six years to elect a president." Sinclair shakes his head. "Six short years."

"Tell me, Mr. Sinclair?" continues Axe's curiosity. "Where do you find your funding now?"

"Oh." Sinclair shrugs his shoulders. "Mostly we sell what we have at Social Farm. And sometimes we get the surpluses from a few of our neighbors, I suppose." He calms himself with a nod as he gazes into his tumbler. "But I shouldn't complain. My poverty allows me to imbibe in my work. To continue my education, as I did during my college years."

"Really?" Now it's a turn for Katie's curiosity. "What college did you attend?"

"Oh, I went to several," confesses Sinclair. "Usually I studied philosophy. Although there was that semester when I was drawn to theology. Hmm? Now where was that?"

"Does it matter?" assists Katie. "The particular college? So long as you kept what you learned."

"Exactly," agrees Sinclair, who then toasts his tumbler, briefly. "Ah-h-h. Yes. So tell me, Brother and Sister. You're motoring across the country. Where did you begin? Ohio? Lesbos, Ohio it was?"

"Oh. No, no. We didn't begin in Lesbos," corrects Axe—to a point. "Actually, we began in New York City. We're driving from coast to coast."

"New York, you say. Yes, New York." Sinclair's seems to reminisce. "I should return to New York, soon, and dynamite the place. Set the town on fire."

Certainly, he's speaking in metaphors, wonders a stunned Katie.

"I hope you mean that metaphorically," airs Axe.

"Uh-h-h? Metaphorically? But of course," assures Sinclair, somewhat. "Though you have to admit, no man could ever do the harm that town inflicts unto itself."

To which the Lanes can do nothing but nod in unison.

Sinclair draws a deep yawn, while his eyes weigh heavy, enough signs to say that his head has received its daily allotment of gin. Nevertheless, his hand refuses the message and pours anew.

"How long do you plan to stay? If you like, park your vehicle in the barn and make your repairs." Again, Sinclair yawns. "Help yourself to whatever is on the farm. Treat it as your home." He pats his empty shirt pockets. "Say, Brother. You wouldn't have any cigarettes?"

"Sorry. I don't smoke."

"Too bad." Sinclair rubs his face and then points at a door. "We keep a soft bed in that room. You're welcome to it. And the kitchen has a sink and pump. Like I said, this is your home."

"That's very kind of you, Mr. Sinclair," acknowledges Axe.

"Yes. Thank you," adds Katie.

The talk lumbers on, though it wanes, thanks to the late hour and those other influences. As could be expected, Sinclair's slouch becomes more pronounced and his participation eases toward the sporadic. Soon, his head limps to one side, while the lids of his eyes close involuntarily.

"Axe," whispers Katie. "I believe he's fallen asleep."

"Mr. Sinclair. Sinclair." Axe's right hand gathers its knuckles, yet it stops short of delivering a rap to the table. "He's asleep, all right. Better to leave him to it, I suppose. Hmm? We should return to the roadster."

Willingly, Katie follows Axe when he leaves the table and reclaims the lantern, only to make for the front door. But as to whether they're returning to gather their effects for an unspecified stay, she's unsure.

"We can patch the tires and be out of here before that self-sanctioning radical becomes aware," details Axe. "Though I'd wager he'll sleep through the night. Probably a late riser too. Like your father."

"Yes. We should hurry all the same," agrees a much-relieved Katie.

In a flash, the Lanes tend to the Speed Six, with both lanterns lit and the roadster's injured side propped.

"Can you imagine the ways of the flesh at that place," comments Axe, while he applies the air pump to a tube. "Sordidness and wretchedness. The truer reason behind its establishment."

“I can’t imagine spending a night there. In that ‘soft’ bed.” Katie shivers at the thought. “All the nonsense of the alienists.”

“Heh, heh. Better the hard ground,” agrees Axe, who ceases his pumping and listens for a hiss. “Perfect. A patch well done.”

Soon, the second tire is put in place and the engine is cranked. At last, with Axe behind the wheel, the Lanes are able to sidle away from the environs of Social Farm.

“I suppose he can’t cause any genuine harm. So long as people don’t take him seriously,” notes Katie of the obvious. “Or his sort, for that matter.”

“For sure,” concurs Axe, as he shifts gears. “But can you believe I was defending that ridiculous man?”

“What? Our poor, misguided fire-eater?” asks Katie. “Mr. Sinclair?”

“No. Not him,” clears Axe, as he shakes his head. “Mr. Loban. I was standing up for him.”

“Oh, that ridiculous man,” considers Katie. “Yes. What are we to do with Mr. Loban? This I wonder.”

14
PEAKING THE ROCKIES

Once again, the Lanes find themselves at a telegraph office, their present setting being the town of North Platte, Nebraska. However, their message to Hugh Flugan lacks urgency in that no parts are broken, only an anticipation of what may come: Send carburetor and flywheel to Rawlins Wyoming—Fear breakage soon—Short of money so please pay shipping.

"You really should contact Mr. Loban," urges Katie, as the couple leaves the office. "Speak to him on the telephone. Or someone who can influence him."

"Perhaps." Axe stops at the sidewalk.

"At least, ask Mr. Loban to forward portions of your salary, if he will not send funds."

"Salary? Katie, I wonder if I'm still employed?"

"Oh, Axe, you don't mean that?"

"The possibility is genuine."

A brief silence of reality ensues, only to be broken by a greater, determined force.

"Well, I don't care, Axe. We struck a bargain with Mr. Loban, so that when we reach the Pacific, he owes me a Kimball. That contract will bind him."

Enough said, as the Lanes step upon the sidewalk and resume their venture.

North Platte wedges a fork of sorts, this being of its namesake river. From this point exists paths of varying directions and destinations: decades-old, wagon wheel ruts from previous pioneers and the rails and associated roads of their followers. Indeed, what better ways are there to bind a country's past and present? As for the Lanes' choice, there really is none, the gentler grades sought by the Union Pacific's surveyors being the only sure route for the fuel pump-less Speed Six. Due west it is, the hope being that the parallel roads are not too terribly steep.

A night camped just north of the South Platte River leads to a day driving through Sutherland and Ogallala, and then passed those towns of a prairie dog nature.

"How many burrows must those creatures create? Thousands?" marvels Katie at the latest rodent metropolis. "My goodness, our groundhogs have nothing on these busy, little beasts."

The sky plays host to a smattering of clouds, meaning that the sun is free to dry the air and bear the dust, and raise the temperature. As for the country roads, they're proving to be functional and so are not much of a challenge to the Speed Six. But the result of too much dust means that in addition to bleeding frequently the drain cock, the carburetor requires a thorough cleaning every sixty or so frustrating miles.

"By God, someday I'll devise a filter system," vows Axe, who is up to his elbows in a filthy, six-cylinder engine. "And end these delays. Ugh. I can't wait for Rawlins, so I can toss away this crusty carburetor."

"How I miss Iowa's gumbo," complains Katie. "My poor lips. Where's that jar of petroleum jelly?"

The Lanes encounter fewer farms while traveling through western Nebraska. Thus when they cross into Wyoming, it comes as no start when this state offers scant signs of tillage. As Axe and Katie are quick to discover, this is a land reserved for non-native bovines and the native short grasses to be grazed, where vast, fenceless ranches dominate. To be sure, the initial impressions upon the strangers are of frightful emptiness and forlorn isolation, never mind that owing to the Union Pacific, this particular corner of Wyoming is its least sparse. Unwilling to trust their survey maps, the Lanes cling to the tracks, keeping them within sight, especially when the primitive roads veer toward questionable directions. If from time to time they're forced to drive the roadster across the open range, then so be it.

"Moo-o-o. Moo-o-o," are the gentle sounds of an early dawn, as opposed to the uproar of a night train.

"Um-m-m. Um-m-m," are the stirrings of peaceful slumber.

The lows gather strength, as more cattle mingle into the vicinity of the Lane's campsite. Nevertheless, it takes the piercing whistles from human lips to rouse Katie.

"Axe. Wake up." She sits up from their bedroll and looks outside of their tarpaulin overhang. "Someone is approaching," warns Katie in an excited whisper. "Axe!"

The whistles continue—possibly as a duet—and are backed by even more lows.

"Over there. Cowboys on horseback. I think." Katie has every reason to doubt her eyes. "Axe, I believe they're girls! Dressed in trousers and riding astride!" As best she can, Katie maintains her whisper. "With hair down their backs! For sure, long, brown hair!"

Yet it seems that Katie's depiction is falling upon deaf ears, those belonging to Axelrod Lane. She reaches beneath their blanket and grasps a fistful of shirt.

"Wake up, Axe!"

Thus he finds the motivation to sit up as well. "Gosh. Have you seen those cattle, Katie?" observes Axe, while he gathers his senses. "And look at those cowboys."

"Axe. That's what I've been trying to tell you. They're not cowboys. Look at their hair."

"What?" He rubs his eyes.

"They're cowgirls, Axe."

"Really? The devil you say."

As they close the distance atop their mounts, each cowgirl waves a hand, thus indicating that the eventual encounter is to be friendly.

The response from the Lanes is to wave in kind, and to rise upon their feet, this deed made conveniently respectable because of Axe's trouser-clad status. As for Katie, her faith in her perceptions takes a leap as she stands exposed in her chemise.

"Hello!" she greets, as the cowgirls and their mounts amble to within earshot.

There is no doubt that the approaching pair are females, but it's also plain that they're sisters, separated by hardly more than a year. Dressed in baggy trousers and oversized slouch hats, while wearing neater coats, it's apparent that their range attire is a mix of what has been borrowed and what comes from the wardrobe.

"Good morning," speaks the elder of the two. "Did you have a good night?"

"Yes. Thank you," responds Katie. "Hope you don't mind our camp. It's just for the night."

"Oh, you're perfectly fine," assures the elder sister, whose age couldn't be beyond sixteen years.

"Yes," agrees the other.

"That's nice of you," thanks Katie. "By the way, we're the Lanes. This is my husband."

"We're the Drydens. And this is my sister. Please to meet you."

Katie is somewhat at a loss, as she reaches for the blanket to wrap away the morning chill.

"I'm sorry, but this is our first chance to meet cowgirls," she explains, never mind that she and Axe haven't had much experience with cattlemen of the other sex.

"Oh. Well you see, we have no brothers. Just six of us girls," shrugs the elder Dryden. "So from time to time Father must borrow some of us from Mother. We're the oldest."

"I see," replies Katie, who spots another unusual sight. "Is that a rifle by your saddle, Miss Dryden?"

"Why yes." With obvious pride, the elder sister pats the buttplate of her firearm. "My Ideal Stevens. Father insists I carry it."

"Heavens," reacts Katie. "Are things that dangerous?"

"No," assures the elder miss. "Not so long as I keep my Stevens by my side."

There's a pause, as the Dryden sisters turn their attentions to the Speed Six.

"Say, you two wouldn't be a part of that Paris race?" asks the elder.

"Positively no," insists Axe.

"We didn't think so, Nora and I. Those people passed through way back in April," continues the first born, as she steadies her mount. "Why, you two would be terribly behind by now."

"Hopelessly behind, Nellie," agrees Nora.

"Yes. We have nothing to do with that race," furthers Katie. "In fact, Mr. Lane and I are alone. Driving from coast to coast to promote this Loban Motor auto. He's their engineer."

"Oh, I see," acknowledges Nellie. "My goodness, such a remarkable task. Why, Mr. Lane, you must be terribly tired from all of that driving. Thousands of miles I should guess."

"Not so much," assures Axe. "Since Mrs. Lane does much of the driving herself."

"Really!" Nellie looks at Katie and then turns to Nora. "Did you hear that!"

"I did!" It seems that Nora is equally excited.

"How often do you drive, Mrs. Lane?" asks Nellie—still wide-eyed. "How many miles?"

"As often as I like. But I can't say for certain the exact number of miles. We only keep a log for total miles and for when a part needs replacing."

Nellie nods her head, as does Nora.

"But it should add to five hundred miles by now," judges Katie. "Or close to it."

"We had no idea automobiles could travel so far," notes Nellie.

"Or that young women could drive them," adds Nora. "So many miles!"

This time it's Katie's turn to offer a shrug.

And so the conversation between mutual admirers continues, with the Lanes standing beside their mode of transportation and the Drydens remaining atop theirs.

"...Gosh, how I'd love terribly to see what the ladies are wearing in New York City," wonders Nellie, after hearing Katie's brief account.

"I never saw so many picture hats and ostrich feathers in my life," recalls Katie.

"Just think how fetching we could be while working Father's cattle," giggles Nellie. "Why I could..."

Like all pleasant encounters, unfortunately, this one cannot last forever, interrupted by the day's agendas.

"Nellie, we have to pen this drove," reminds Nora. "Remember? Father wants to teach us the ecraseur."

"Oh yes. And then he said we can shoot prairie dogs afterwards. Before lunch." Nellie turns to the Lanes. "I'm terribly sorry, but we must say goodbye."

"We understand," assures Katie. "You two have your tasks and so do we. Our way west."

"And our way on our spread," returns Nellie, who then guides her mount away from the campsite. "It was terribly nice to meet you," she speaks, while twisting upon her saddle.

"Yes. Terribly," concurs Nora, she, too, looking rearward.

Quickly, the sisters carry away toward their father's wayward cattle.

"All the creeks and draws flow east to west. So there's little to bar you through the open country," continues Nellie with some parting information, she raising her voice proportionally. "It's terribly flat all the way to Burns. Possibly to Hillsdale. Perhaps to Cheyenne. Wouldn't you say, Nora?"

"Yes. Terribly flat."

"Goodbye!" bids Nellie.

"Goodbye!" waves Nora. "Good luck!"

"Thank you! I hope we meet again!" Katie's farewell spreads across the prairie. "So long Nellie and Nora Dryden!" She takes a deep sigh and then directs her voice to Axe. "What a wonderful pair. Don't you think? Gosh, I wonder how many more Annie Oakleys we'll encounter? Axe?" With no answer forthcoming, Katie looks to her husband.

He appears perturbed, his arms folded as he gazes upon the backs of the Drydens.

"What is it, Axe?" smirks Katie.

"That race. That humbug, Paris race. I thought we were rid of it, once and for all. But to think that it came through this very place."

"Is that all, Axe?" questions Katie. "What we've been through and what lies ahead? Humbug, indeed."

After driving across country to Burns, the roads become more east to west and, hence, surer all the way to Hillsdale. As for the mostly treeless terrain, it's dominated by modest undulations, as vegetated by grama, Junegrass and buffalograss and occasional clusters of wild sunflowers. And although there is a slight gain in elevation, as detected by the attuned Lanes, the driving elapses unhindered, so much so that they approach the environs of Cheyenne before noontime.

"I think I see something," alerts Katie from behind the wheel. "Straight ahead."

"There's a dome of some sort," squints Axe. "Surely, the capitol?"

Indeed, it is the looming capitol, as powerful a guide as can be. Yet it seems the Wyoming prairie may hold greater strengths, that being of expanse and an insufferable indifference to time. To be sure, the more the Lanes gaze upon the dome, the slower it grows in size, meaning the longer it will take to reach Cheyenne.

"Axe, why don't I stop at the first newspaper we see and not bother with the others?"

"Please do."

Eventually, the Lanes close in on the capital and Katie locates the Cheyenne Leader. Not in the mood to tarry, the couple rush through the thrust of their story, bidding their goodbyes within half an hour. Still, the Lanes do manage one diversion before leaving town, that being the capitol's dome.

"Where do they find the means?" asks Katie, her head tilted upward.

It's a fair question, when admiring the building's stately height—never mind its modest, but expandable, girth. So far, the Lanes have encountered little population and scant wealth within Wyoming, meaning that to pool the state's resources in order to erect this capitol must have required considerable finagling.

"Perhaps their government sold off portions of itself. Like L.M.," replies a sarcastic Axe, as he guides the roadster for a few circumnavigations.

Soon, he breaks free from the circle and steers toward the compass point of the Union Pacific. It doesn't take long before the Lanes put Cheyenne miles to their rear.

"I can still see that dome, Axe," complains Katie, after yet another glance over her shoulder. "I do believe that thing is following us. Ugh."

Inevitably, the Lanes lose themselves of Cheyenne's dome—though in trade for far loftier heights. At last, the Rocky Mountains and their feared slopes loom, shadowy figures marking the far end of the Great Plains.

"I wonder how distant they are, Axe?"

"At least twenty miles."

"Then they're sure to grow before we reach them." Katie's eyes remain fixed ahead.

"And those are just the front ranges. The taller peaks should lie further. Out of view."

"Then just how are we to cross them, Axe?"

"Slow and steady. Which must be the Union Pacific's method." Axe softens his voice. "And ours, if we can find a road that cuts through those peaks."

"Did you say 'if'? Axe, I don't know. It looks like a solid wall, with not enough room for a road." Katie shakes her head. "Too much mountain."

The couple presses on, hoping for the best as they rise in elevation with each accumulated mile. Yet while the slopes of the Rockies continue to pose their threats, by noticeable increments the mountains appear to display a sure weakness. There can be little doubt that the Union Pacific and its parallel roads are bearing toward a sizeable breach, which by the Lanes' increasingly favorable angle seems to be widening. To be sure, the meticulous efforts of the railroad's early surveyors are nothing short of remarkable.

"Granite, Wyoming. Elevation 7,336 feet," reads Katie of a railroad depot's sign. "Axe, we've climbed 1,800 feet since Burns!"

"Odd," he considers, while driving passed the depot. "It didn't seem that much of a climb."

Be that as it may, the carburetor feels the gain so that an adjustment is necessary, Granite being as good a place as any.

It's at the far end of town where Axe parks the roadster and opens the hood. And it's here that the Lanes learn of what lies to the immediate west, as informed by the curious and friendly citizens. Indeed, there does loom a favorable split in the front range: Green Mountain to the north and Mound Mountain southward.

"...Thank God. Though I still hope a new carburetor awaits at Rawlins," worries Axe. Now that the external frets have been calmed, the internal perils take lead.

One thing is certain, however, that being the need to buy gasoline at every opportunity. When challenging the Rockies, a topped tank feeds an engine more efficiently than one only half-full—or for that matter, three-quarters. Fortunately, Granite is wet with fuel and it's been assured by at least two local autoists—one a Fordist, the other a Moonist—that the route all the way to Laramie, and even Rawlins, is much the same. Nevertheless, the Lanes have been warned of rough, variable conditions, and of how the roads paralleling the Union Pacific at some points veer away to parts convoluted. Better that the couple seek more advice ahead and, if possible, draw detailed maps.

Steadily, the Lanes continue their climb, making frequent stops and inquiries. All the while, the landscape alters, advancing from grasses to scrub, junipers to a few pines.

"Will you look at the size of that boulder, Axe."

The depot sign at Sherman gives the elevation at 8,247 feet. Astounded, Katie and Axe pause for a sigh of relief. Yet there's even cause for celebration, when, once again, he reviews a portion of his U.S.G.S. library.

"I'm almost certain," Axe almost asserts. "Katie, this is probably the highest point we'll see in Wyoming. From here on out, it's downhill for the rest of the state."

"But how can that be, Axe? We're still in eastern Wyoming?"

"It just happens," he shrugs. "I'm fairly sure."

As often is the case, the Lanes and their circumstances become a center of attraction. Of course, there does come the usual jumble of questions, this rewarded by a harmonious duet of well-rehearsed replies. Yet as luck would have it, when the local curiosity begins to fade, Katie's open inquiry concerning the westerly path is received by what may be an amiable expert.

"Why, my beauty, I would be favored to aid the pair of you. For I know the way like I know the calluses of my hands," reveals an older gentleman of short stature and Cornish accent, he tipping his hat. "Daines Pentreath at your service. Night caretaker at the roundhouse."

"Oh?"

"But formerly a digger of the silvery rock. A Cousin Jack scooping his way through this portion of Wyoming. Territory and state. Borrascas and bonanzas."

"Oh-h-h."

Almost immediately, Katie produces pen and paper, to which Mr. Pentreath wastes no time, using the hood of the roadster as his desktop. With the Lanes looking over his shoulders, the Cornishman begins to draw his map, and as well, offers an expert narration.

"You will travel near to five and three-fourths miles, 'til you meet this wee fork. 'To the south,' tell yourself to choose and the goings will be cinchy."

"Oh-h-h."

With surprising detail, Mr. Pentreath continues his mapmaking. "…And that be where to find that wee shaft of '89. Too wee for bear or cat, yet may suffice for a handsome and his beauty. But be wary not to err for the shaft some six hundred feet 'yond. Lord knows what beasts dwell there. By the morn', do seek…"

Eventually, the Lanes have all the information they need and are ready to be on their way.

"How can we thank you, Mr. Pentreath?" asks Axe.

"'Tis my pleasure, my handsome. But that you aver, might we pleasure a whiskey at yon' establishment."

The Lanes turn around to spy a saloon—unmistakable in its design and intent.

"Mr. Pentreath? To take my wife into a saloon?"

"Oh, but sure you may take your beauty. Mrs. Farley would never mind."

"Who is Mrs. Farley?" Simultaneously, Katie and Axe pose their question.

"She be the saloon's keeper. Respectable, you should know. Why, Mrs. Farley would fancy to meet my beauty. And for you, my handsome, likewise also. Come. Favor me to present the pair of you."

"Oh-h-h."

And so the Lanes are able to pay their gratitude to Mr. Pentreath, and in the process find Mrs. Farley to be quite convivial. There's but one regret in that their stay at her saloon proves brief, the necessity being a return to the road and its remaining sunlight.

Cautiously, Axe proceeds, dodging rocks and holes, and steering clear from precarious outer edges. All the while, Katie keeps her nose to the Cornishman's map, and, as well, looks ahead for vital landmarks. But as the Lanes drive well out of Sherman, it all makes sense, as prescribed by Mr. Pentreath. Thus there's no surprise when the couple come upon a certain slope and its "wee shaft." Indeed, it proves to be an ideal location to make camp, the Lanes beginning the process immediately.

"Do you really want to shoot a bear?" questions Katie, while she watches her husband ready his weapons.

"Suppose, instead, I'm preparing for Springfield toughs, who insult my wife?"

"Oh. Well if that's the case, Axe, you may shoot as many as you please."

After spending a bear-free night, the Lanes make an early start in spite of the frigid air. And true to Mr. Pentreath's word, before noon the couple roll into Tie Siding and regain sight of the Union Pacific's tracks, which they should not lose all the way to Rawlins. All in all, things are moving splendidly, save for the routine of tire punctures and a broken, running board bracket. As it happens, the Lanes may have conquered Wyoming's worst, never mind that they're far from finished with the state.

"Axe, we should have the running board repaired," urges Katie, as the injured roadster nears Red Buttes.

To say the least, a drooping running board is unsightly, especially when coupled with Axe's unworkable fix of knots and rope. But because this brief plain serves as a platform for baggage and essentials, there lies the possibility of losing valuable possessions. With the obvious laid to bare, a solution must be found.

"BLACKSMITH'S BLACKSMITH SHOP," reads Katie of the sign above a local business, though it takes a few seconds for all of the message to sink.

"Oh, I see. Then I suppose the man's occupation was predetermined," notes Axe, as he parks the roadster.

Yet his assumption couldn't be more incorrect, although it's not terribly apparent at first. The shop, itself, is typical—of rock wall construction, with a wide entry. And the clanging sounds and wafts of coal smoke are expected. As the Lanes approach, they see nothing unusual of a boy manning the bellows, nor do they find a forceful hammer forging hot metal out of the norm. However, because the Mr. Blacksmith in question is of a slight build seems a bit peculiar, and that he wears a skirt is nothing but queer.

"Axe," whispers Katie, as she tugs his sleeve. "Mr. Blacksmith is Mrs. Blacksmith."

"Oh?" he responds. "Thank God."

"Afternoon," offers the blacksmith, while keeping her focus to the matter at hand—clang, clang. "What can I do for you?" But then she speaks to her son. "Johnny, go look in on your sisters." She ceases her hammer and with her tongs drops the piece of iron into a bucket of water. It's then that the blacksmith removes her gloves, wipes her brow and extends her hand. "Polly Blacksmith, at your service."

"Axelrod Lane."

Unfortunately, both Axe and Katie remain under the sway of their minor shock.

"To what do I owe the pleasure?" rephrases Mrs. Blacksmith, who, in spite of being begrimed and perspired, owns a decidedly feminine face.

"Oh. I beg your pardon," recovers Axe, adjusting, once again, to the ways of Wyoming. "Our auto needs a bracket for the running board."

"I see," replies Mrs. Blacksmith. "Do you have the broken one?"

"Yes."

Together, the three walk to the roadster.

"I left it in place," explains Axe, while he locates a wrench and begins to remove the bracket.

"A beautiful vehicle," admires Mrs. Blacksmith, as she takes her views. "Solid, yet trim."

"Yes, it is," agrees Katie, her tongue un-stilled.

"Are you two new to town?"

"Yes. In a manner of speaking. Just passing through, Mrs. Blacksmith," details Katie. "My husband and I are crossing the country to promote this auto. For Loban Motor."

"Really? How adventurous."

"All the way to the Pacific," furthers Katie. "We hope."

"But not before I forge a new bracket, Mrs. Lane."

"Precisely."

Before long, Johnny is back at the bellows and his mother forges a copy of a Loban Motor bracket. In the meantime, the conversation continues, and with it an explanation given.

"…It was so sudden, my husband's passing. Poor Henry. A good man and a good father." Like any seasoned blacksmith, while she talks, Mrs. Blacksmith concentrates on her work. "But I have a family to feed and Red Buttes has the business. Fact is, the town could use another smith. So we've stayed on."

"I admire your pluck, Polly Blacksmith. I don't know how I could carry on without my husband."

"Yes, you should be commended," agrees Axe. "This is masterful. Mr. Blacksmith would be proud."

"Why, thank you."

Four bits finishes the transaction, and after Axe installs the new bracket, the Lanes continue to Laramie.

"She really did make a fine bracket? Hmm, Axe?"

"Of course. In fact, Mrs. Blacksmith could work on the second floor. That is, were it not for Mr. Loban."

The dozen miles northward to Laramie are nothing if not uneventful, what with the Union Pacific serving as a faithful guide and the elevations coming at slight, steady descents. Much like Cheyenne before, the towers of Laramie loom, drawing the strangers from faraway like adrift sailors to dry land.

"Where do they find the means?" admires Katie, as the roadster enters the shadow of the Main Building's spire—the sandstone, Romanesque Revival beacon for Wyoming's namesake college.

"I can't imagine," concurs Axe. "But the size of the U.P. machine shops. Impressive. As is Laramie."

Indeed, there's nothing insignificant concerning Laramie: industrial, institutional and cultural. But because the Lanes have taken advantage of the town's wealth of provisions—notably a stack of tires and bundles of stationery—there's little in the way of currency to exploit further the present setting. Precariously, the Ohio couple are down to fifteen dollars and change, a paltry sum to see them through to the Pacific.

"We need to find a way to get some funds, Axe," airs Katie of their dire situation and with Laramie behind them. "You need to contact Mr. Loban. Or failing that, my parents."

"No, Katie." Axe is adamant. "Though what about my parents?"

"Absolutely not." She's at least as stubborn.

"Then we better find something, Katie. If we don't want to become stranded."

"Yes. Think of something. Something in a state sure to become less dense with opportunities."

With little choice, the Lanes continue their journey—into a land grassy and shrubby in some places, while rocky and fossiliferous in others.

After only an hour north of Laramie, Axe spies a sign marking a small, dusty town. "Wyoming, Wyoming? Hmm? Did they give enough thought into that name?"

"Perhaps too much thought," counters Katie. "But I wonder? Is there an Ohio, Ohio?"

"I'd like to think not, Old Girl. One Ohio is enough."

With hardly any reason to pause, the Lanes decline to stop at Wyoming-squared, continuing toward Lookout and Rock Creek.

And so the day wanes. But almost too quickly, Axe and Katie's ready cash alters into fourteen dollars, the blame being the priority of the fuel tank. To be sure, this is a monumental blow to the couple's coffers—percentage wise—thus stealing enough of their resolve. In spite of three hours before dusk, the Lanes make camp beneath the shade of Carbon Creek cottonwoods somewhere between Medicine Bow and Carbon.

As Katie and Axe greet another bleak morning, they consider themselves fortunate to have spent another night in bear country without an encounter. Still, there did happen beyond their campsite considerable howling and yelping during the pre-dawn hours. The commotion was something of a wild canine matter, though whether the sources were timber or prairie wolves, the Lanes cannot make a distinction.

Yet through the night and into the morning, a more prevalent growling occurs, this troubling source coming from empty stomachs.

"I'm as hungry as a bear," complains Katie. "I could eat a bear. If only you could shoot a bear, Axe."

"If only one would present itself," he replies.

It seems that the readily available foodstuffs are depleted and any that cache of can goods is buried at the foot of the rumble seat. To say the least, an inventory is in order, regardless of how reluctant the Lanes may be to realize the direness of their situation.

"Two cans of white cherries, two of egg plum, two of muscat grapes, two of wax beans, two of succotash," recites Axe, while he and Katie repack the roadster, this following a thorough search for anything edible.

"Don't forget two of marrowfat peas and two of broiled mackerel in mustard sauce," reminds Katie. "And two of olives."

"Two of everything? Was it Captain Noah who packed our pantry?"

Down the road, the Lanes continue—sans one empty can of cherries—their frets over impending starvation being a real traveling companion. Yet before the couple can ponder further, there arrives a diversion to their miseries—a timely coincidence if nothing more.

"Percy? Percy, Wyoming?" utters Katie of a roadside marker. "That town is called Percy?"

"So it is."

"I wonder, Axe, if Percy Loban would be impressed? Perhaps he should establish himself in his namesake stop? Take command and become its ruler?" provokes Katie.

"Then I pity his subjects," responds Axe. "We should warn Percy, Wyoming of the danger."

The Lanes choose not to tarry, doing the same at nearby Elmo, thus ignoring their routine of buying gasoline at every opportunity, if only because of their reluctance to spend any cash. The pleas from their stomachs cannot be ignored, however, and so one can of muscat grapes and another of succotash are devoured along the way.

"If it comes down to it, I could hire on in Rawlins," considers Axe, while he drives. "At one of the shops. For a week or so."

"And perhaps I could give lessons. Or-r-r." Katie hesitates with her suggestion. "I could sell my princess dress, and a few other things."

"No, Katie. Not that dress. I want to see you wear it at the Pacific." Axe shakes his head. "I won't hear of it. We'll sell what I have. By God, I'll go naked before my wife sells any of her clothes."

"But Axe."

"No, Katie," he insists. "Besides, doubtless it would be for pennies on the dollar. No chance for a fair trade under duress."

Katie knows better than to press the point, especially when Axe evokes his right as husband and protector.

"I suppose you're correct. And if it comes down to you and your nakedness, then so be it. I just hope, Axe, you keep a pair of drawers."

The longer the Lanes press ahead, the more fretful becomes their fuel situation—the acceptable result of an irrational rationality. Twice, Axe pulls the roadster to a stop in order to tap at the fuel tank, and twice, he convinces himself that the percussive report tells of enough gasoline for a Rawlins' replenishment.

"Immediately, when we reach Rawlins," mentions Axe for the third time. "Gasoline and oil."

Twelve or so miles later and Axe proves true to his word, coming to a halt at the first available garage and filling the roadster's tank as well as the auxiliary cans for both gasoline and oil. Now, at the very least, the trek can continue well beyond a hundred miles.

Doubtless, the town of Rawlins is worth a linger, the signs being aplenty even from faraway. Soon, by meandering happenstance, the Lanes find themselves rolling upon Maple Street, surrounded by what can be described only in Euclidean terms: ornate homes and mansions featuring thick turrets with conical roofs, geometric adornments and imaginative asymmetry.

"I would call this a compact rendition of Cleveland's best," admires Axe.

Before long, the couple come upon the old territorial prison—tall and robust, with its version of turrets and conicals.

"I wonder if it ever had a moat and drawbridge," airs Katie of the obvious comparison. "Or archers?"

The grand tour continues, it being little more than a brief diversion away from the inevitable communication from Lisbon—or worse, the lack thereof.

"The Ferris Hotel," pines Katie of the three-story establishment. "Oh, how I'd love to spend a night in such a palace. If only we had the funds."

But then the roadster passes a Greek-inspired building on the next block.

"Elks Lodge," reads Axe. "Imagine, those mammals having migrated all the way to Rawlins."

The Lanes encounter even more man-made wonders. Positioned in a perfect row are the high school, courthouse and masonic lodge—some hipped and pilastered, some belvedered, some towered—each bursting to size in reddish brick walls. Once again, the Lanes are impressed, and once again the moment is ripe for what has become their obligatory comment.

"Honestly, Katie." This time it's Axe's turn. "Where do they find the means?"

Regardless, Rawlin's aggrandizements do have a limit, and in short order play out. Reluctantly, Axe veers the roadster to where he last saw the post office and its cross-country packages.

"...Please sign here, Mr. Lane," directs the clerk, who has just presented a cardboard box of about two feet cubed, only shortly arrived.

Axe takes possession. "Thank you, sir."

That there exists a package in the first place raises hope for the Lanes, and that it comes with no postage due furthers the feeling. There's no sense waiting, as Axe places the weighted box upon the floor.

"Katie. The return is Hugh's address."

This is an optimistic sign, taken as such by Axe, who falls upon his knees and whips out his pocket knife. Quickly, the contents are revealed: a packaged carburetor along with a flywheel. But atop of these rests a sealed envelope, taken in hand by Axe.

"Open it. See what it says, Axe." Katie, too, rests upon her knees.

He wastes no time and pries it apart. Immediately, the first impression is of green. Stunned, Axe gathers himself and hands the cash to Katie, his concerns shifting upon the letter.

"We hope you and Katie have reached Rawlins safely," reads Axe. "The flywheel is the same as old. But the carburetor is the newest. Lepper tested this one for two days in Loban's own roadster before I switched it. Just for you. The boys in the shops are behind you. So we took a collection behind Loban's back.

Even his pet monkey, Freddy, has no idea. Loban is riled you can be certain. But because Mrs. Loban is back in town and the investors are tugging his sleeves, and the factory is busy like never, he does not have the time to fuss over you two like he would want. But do not feel you are on your own. Lisbon is proud, you can be sure. And hopeful you can meet the Pacific. Good luck to you and Katie. Sincerely, Hugh Flugan."

"Oh, Axe," reacts Katie. "I could kiss Hugh's head. And every cheek at L.M."

"What wonderful friends we have," concurs Axe. "As true as can be."

Indeed, there can be no greater truth. But as the Lanes stare into each other's eyes, there is clutched by Katie's right hand a wad of desperately needed cash.

"I wonder how much?" The first to recover, Katie poses the obvious.

"I suppose you should count," answers Axe.

"Me?"

And so Katie tallies, with not a bill slighted. "Fifty-three dollars, Axe! Can you imagine!"

"A fortune. To think, we can spend a night in that Ferris Hotel."

Yet Katie seems hesitant, as her smile alters into a frown. "Should we, Axe? Spend a night there? This is our friends' hard-earned money. To coddle ourselves just might be shameful."

Axe, too, frowns, and then nods in agreement.

"Besides, Axe. We can always bathe ourselves from our pot of hot water. Like we have."

"Then so be it. A pot of hot water instead of a bathtub it shall be."

With scant delay, the rejuvenated Lanes put Rawlins behind them. In doing so, they find themselves entering into a vast, strange region known as the Great Divide Basin—a land of times geological.

To the east of the Continental Divide, all waters flow eventually into the Gulf of Mexico, while those west make it to the Pacific Ocean via the Colorado, Snake and Columbia Rivers, et. al. Yet within the Basin, all rainfall and snowmelt gathers into local creeks and draws and contribute nothing to the country's aggregate flow. Although it may seem pointless, the waters of this 5,000 square mile region remain trapped by ridges, hills and mountains, thus making the land something of a self-contained entity.

And the further the Lanes travel, the starker the landscape becomes.

"Are we in a desert, Axe?"

"I'm not sure," he replies. "It's at least as close as it comes."

By the time the Lanes reach the U.P. stop of Fillmore, the land becomes nothing more than dry, rolling hills of scrubby vegetation and sparse, short grasses. Yet the joy of a distant playa lake is spotted—no doubt of alkaline chemistry—while the low buttes of sedimentary construction offer a few diversions.

"Will you look at that one, Axe. Over there. It must have a name. Don't you think?" The sculptor in question is nothing but the winds within this arid land of few breaks. "If only the folks back home could see this. Could see us now."

At tiny Creston, the couple stop only to purchase gasoline and to stretch their legs. Soon thereafter they encounter sand dunes—just north of the tracks and of several acres in area, but with no seascape in sight! Meanwhile, the native rocks are getting more purple and red by the hour, contrasting greatly to Cheyenne and even Laramie standards.

"My goodness, those are the strangest cattle," observes Katie of a thin, distant herd.

Indeed, said animals are peculiar, so much so that Axe takes his foot off the gear pedal. He squints and then scratches his head.

"Katie, I'm not sure those are cattle. And I don't believe they're any kind of deer."

"What could they be, Axe?"

Then it hits him. "By God, they must be antelope. Imagine that. Wild, American antelope."

Although it's been a long day, a significant portion remains, too much to let it go to waste. The new carburetor awaits to be installed, a vacant lot on Wamsutter, Wyoming's only street being a suitable locale.

"This is a work of art," marvels Axe. "I can't wait to test it."

"Not today," protests Katie of her husband's enthusiasm. "Have we not reached our daily quota of miles?"

"I suppose so," replies Axe. He leans over the open-hooded roadster and seats the carburetor. "It can wait for the morning." Axe wields a wrench. "We could pitch camp here. I don't think the people would mind."

"Of course. Wyomingians are nothing but accommodating."

As it happens, Katie's opinions of her newly-planted state may be nothing short of astute. No sooner than her husband tightens the last bolt that the first of the curious begin to gather. Because Axe remains busy with other adjustments, it's up to Katie to greet their guests and make them aware of the world of Loban Motor.

"…And I'm please to make your acquaintance, sir. Ma'am. Nice to meet you, Mr. Tate. And you, Mr. Kiel. You too, Mr. Grunch. And yes, as you surmised, Mr. Harlow, my husband and I are that couple. I really am flattered that you are so well-informed."

"Well, it wath Mth'th. Harlow, who hath kept me apprithed," confesses Mr. Harlow, while his wife grasps his arm. "Her reading of your ethploith."

"Oh. Why, thank you." Without a flinch, Katie is able to interpret through Mr. Harlow's impediment. "So surprising to know of us this far in advance."

"Oh, yeth," elates Mrs. Harlow. "I wath lucky to have read an Omaha newthpaper. A Deth Moineth one too. Both menthioning you and your huthband. Why, every perthon in Wamthutter knowth of the Laneth."

"Re-e-e-ally?" With the same impediment being voiced from two sources, Katie must force herself to maintain a pose. "Uh-h. How delightful. Yes. If only because we hadn't visited those cities."

"Thomewhat thrange," notes Mr. Grunch. "But then newth can travel fatht."

"Uh-h-h. Yes, Mr. Grunch," agrees Katie. "It is strange."

Soon, Mr. Tate and Mr. Kiel join in with their kindred comments.

"Do you do any driving, Mth'th. Lane?" inquires Mr. Tate.

"Why, yes. A goodly portion, if I may be immodest."

"Moth prathworthy, Mth'th. Lane. Don't you agree, Karl?"

"Of courth, Timothy. Motht outthanding."

Meanwhile, because Axe is engrossed with the Speed Six, he's oblivious to the confusions of speech.

A few other pedestrians mingle, joined by a pair on horseback. And it's Katie who fields their questions and furthers their curiosities.

"…How astute of you to note, sir. If you might look more closely. Excuse me, Axe. Look closely to see that the engine has six cylinders. Very powerful, you can wonder. Why, on good roads I've sped above fifty miles-per-hour."

"Very imprethive. Yeth, thith ith a winthome automobile."

"Why, thank you, sir. Its design and lines are both trim and sharp," boasts Katie, who then raises her voice to address the others. "Yet powerful within and sound under floor. Very capable and dependable, I should say. Able to take on a variety of situations, from the gumbos of Iowa, to the crowded avenues of New York City, to a long night through Illinois. Even a riot in Springfield. The Speed Six, with its strapping engine and vanadium steel frame and suspension has conquered, and continues to conquer. Mountains and all! To carry the citizens of this great country to places where before they could only have dreamed!"

A brief pause follows Katie's crescendo, only to be broken by the handclaps of her audience.

To say the least, she's taken aback, although her recovery toward this unexpected reception is speedy. After all, Katie's becoming quite accustomed to the ways of Wamsutter.

"Bravo, Mth'th. Lane. Bravo."

"Thuperb."

The gathering continues to blossom—and elongate. Soon, Katie is asked about her immediate plans.

"Oh, no. I won't hear of it Mth'th. Lane. That you and your huthband would be forthed to thpend the night under a tarpaulin would be my dithgrathe," asserts Mr. Grunch. "The two of you thall be the gueth'th of my wife and mythelf. I inthitht."

Immediately, a good portion of the crowd's faces turn dejected, as if Mr. Grunch has beaten his fellow citizens to the invitation. Yet just as quickly, there emerges a counter of sorts.

"Perhapth we might have a dinner?" suggests Mrs. Harlow. "In honor of our gueth'th."

"Oh, thank you. Thank you, so much. You are kind. So wonderfully kind." Then Katie looks toward her occupied husband. "Did you hear that, Axe? Our new friends are so wonderfully sociable and kind."

With his name thus mentioned, Axe breaks away from his engine. "What is it, Katie?"

"Axe. Mr. Grunch has offered us accommodations. And Mrs. Harlow has suggested a dinner in our honor. Can you believe it?"

"Why, yes I can," replies Axe, who turns to face the assembly—greasy hands and all. "Like my Katie has mentioned on several occasions. You Wyomingians are people who are nothing but accommodating. The salts of the earth as we have come to discover. To our delight."

Though not as impressive as Katie's applause, Axe, too, receives a round.

Soon, with his work done and his hands wiped clean, Axe cranks the engine, while Katie sits behind the wheel. But instead of taking the passenger seat, he offers Mrs. Harlow the honor.

"Why, thank you, Mithter Lane. But could there be thpathe enough for Mary and her Martha to join me?"

"Of course, ma'am. That seat has plenty of room."

Along with toddler, the ladies squeeze in, while Axe steps onto the running board and secures himself.

"Gentlemen," he urges. "Find yourselves a foothold and we'll have a little jaunt."

The response is an immediate avalanche, the result being a contorted crowd posing upon an automobile designed for no more than three people.

"Where shall we go, Mrs. Harlow?" inquires Katie.

"Hmm? Now let me thee?"

Beyond the saloons and private houses, tiny Wamsutter doesn't have a proper venue for a celebratory affair, be it grand or otherwise. Yet it does possess an endless array of wide, treeless choices, the best of these located behind the hiatused schoolhouse. On to said grounds the overloaded roadster is guided, this being yet another informal trial passed with flying colors.

No sooner than the Speed Six comes to a halt, that its passengers hop off and flee toward their houses. What ensues is a steady stream of light, portable furniture and practical dinnerware. Indeed, in busy time, an open air reception hall is concocted along with liquid offerings both strong and soft. And by sure increments, the edibles begin to make their appearances: at first, the fresh and already baked, followed by the hastily cooked. Before long, all of Wamsutter is making both its presence and contributions felt.

The fare proves impressive with its breads, meats, poultries and pies, as are the lemonade, coffee, beer and whiskey. And although tables have been set, they serve only as resting places, the celebrants being of mind to stand with their plates and tumblers in hand.

It seems that Katie remains the center of attraction. As for her husband and escort, upon having his fill, he's content to demonstrate and instruct, to take the roadster on brief excursions and return to the reception for his next group of pupils. By the time the sun nears the horizon, half of Wamsutter has taken the roadster's wheel, with the remainder content at being passengers.

"Why, I've never had tho much fun, Mth'th. Lane," excites Mrs. Grunch, upon returning from her very first driving lesson. "Oh, how I with to potheth a Thpeed Thikth."

Because Mrs. Grunch is among the last group of pupils, Axe's return to Katie's table is short in coming.

"My, how happy you look, Axe," comments Katie.

"Happy, but a bit thrown," he replies.

"How's that?" asks Katie.

"Well-l-l." He nestles to her ear and offers a whisper. "Have you noticed the accent here in Wamsutter?"

"Uhh?" But then Katie speaks aloud. "Why yes, Axe. There is a singular sparkle within Wamsutter."

That the Grunch's spare bedroom is cozy means that Katie and Axe have a restful night. This, of course, after the couple finish their speculation over the cause behind Wamsutter's "accent."

And so the pleasant morning to follow. In no time, the Lanes are dressed and find themselves at a filling and conversational breakfast.

"Yeth, by all meanth, Utah ith an agreeable thtate," advices Mr. Grunch. "Though you mutht be alert for their ruleth and regulathionth. They can be very thtrange over their ruleth."

"Yeth," agrees Mrs. Grunch. "Thrange and thometimeth peculiar."

Soon, breakfast is done and the time for the Lanes to part company nears. Before they're able to thank their hosts, however, a sudden knock interrupts. Quick to answer the front door, Mrs. Grunch invites into her home what sounds like something of a delegation. With hats in hands, five gentlemen enter the dining room.

"Oh, pleath thtay theated," urges Mr. Harlow.

"We're quite finithed, Harry," assures Mr. Grunch. "What can I do for you?"

"Thank you, Garrett. Mithter and Mth'th. Lane," continues Mr. Harlow. "If you don't mind. My friendth and I would like to have a word."

"Certainly," replies Axe. "You gentlemen seem to have something in mind."

The delegation's members look at one another with their nodding heads.

"That we do," concurs Mr. Harlow. "Achem. Ath Garrett ith well aware, there ith movement afoot to incorporate Wamthutter by the lawth of the thtate of Wyoming. We need that thtatuth in order to inthure our future prothpecth and prothperity."

"So I see. A sound solution, I should say. Superb and sagacious."

"Thank you, Mithter Lane. But ath you may well thurmithe, thound leaderthip ith ethential to the thuctheth of thuch an endeavor."

"Surely so. Sufficiently said."

"We're glad you agree, Mithter Lane. Achem. What I'm about to athk may theem a bit forward. But pleath give it conthiderathion. An incorporated Wamthutter will need a mayor and the only candidate to emerge thuth far ith Louetta Parker."

"Yeth. Louetta Parker, who ath a juthtith of the peathe in Johnthon County, onthe thententhed her huthband two weekth for publick drunkeneth," furthers Mr. Grunch.

"Yeth," returns Mr. Harlow. "But what we have in mind ith that you, yourthelf, might conthider..."

To say the least, Axe is stunned by the offer about to be made. More so, he's immensely flattered. Indeed, to make such an impression upon strangers only confirms his suspicion that he owns a winning personality.

"...Achem," continues Mr. Harlow. "That you yourthelf might allow Mth'th. Lane to be a candidate for mayor. Yeth indeed, we've come to the concluthion that Mth'th Lane would make a thplendid mayor. Haven't we, gentlemen?"

"Yeth. Yeth," are the immediate reactions.

Now it's Katie's turn to be stunned—and truly flattered. She looks to her husband, who puts up a brave front for his damaged feelings.

"What do you thay, Mth'th. Lane?" Now, Mr. Harlow addresses the candidate directly.

"Well, I-I-I-I," sputters Katie. "I hadn't realized you have suffragists in Wyoming."

"Thuffrigith'th? In Wyoming?" replies Mr. Harlow, as he looks to the others in the room. "We don't have any thuffrigith'th. Do we, Garrett?"

"I've never theen any. But doeth it matter?"

"Thertainly not," asserts Mr. Harlow. "Mth'th. Lane, it matterth not."

"Oh? You don't have to be a suffragist to run for office?"

"Not in the thtate of Wyoming."

"Really?"

From Axe, it takes every bit of clever determination to free Katie from her situation—diplomacy and gratitude for Wamsutter's citizens, and logic and loyalty for the non-suffragist. And so it's a return to the road, bound for Bitter Creek, Salt Wells, Rock Springs, Green River and, with a little luck, Evanston and the state line of Utah.

"They sure are mightily progressive here in Wyoming," notes Katie from the passenger seat, her head still in the clouds. "I never would have guessed."

"Neither would I," agrees Axe. "And I'd wager they wouldn't, either. No, they're merely practical, and don't burden themselves by the petty arguments of back-east philosophies."

"I believe you're correct. Yeth, you do have a point."

To say the least, Axe is rendered silent by his wife's reply.

"Mmm. But to think. Me. Mayor Lane," she wonders aloud. "Yeth. Her Honor Katherine Marie Lane."

15

DESCENDING UNTO DESERET

IT CAN BE A COMPLICATED ISSUE, the Wasatch Mountains. Within Utah's broad contribution to the Rockies, the Union Pacific branches into other lines, as do the accompanying roads and pathways. And although the Wasatches may not be the grandest of mountains, they do provide a source of confusion for motorists, especially those who seek friendly gradients. But also, Axe sees fit to change the flywheel, requiring the pulley and a sturdy Douglas fir. Thus the reason behind the Lanes' extended stay amidst Utah's alpine forests and meadows, along with bleating flocks of sheep—more of the ovines than in all of Ohio.

"What day is it, Katie?" wonders Axe, while he drives.

"Thursday, I'm fairly certain."

"And the date?" he poses.

"July 16th." But then Katie hesitates with the rest of her reply. "Uh-h, 1908?"

Before long, the Lanes encounter yet another ridge. However, when Axe guides the roadster upon a crest, he and Katie are confronted by Utah's undeniably signature feature.

"My goodness," gasps Katie, she gazing at the vastness ahead.

An infinite flatness waits beneath a clear sky, this dominated by distant, glimmers of water.

"It can't be the Pacific, Axe? Tell me we're not that terribly lost?"

"No. Not an ocean, Katie. But for certain a lake. The Great Salt Lake, by God!"

"Amen!" agrees Katie. "My, oh my."

For a moment, the Lanes become entranced, while specks of sunlight sparkle off the faraway lake. The worn roadster sputters in neutral, its handbrake set in ready for an intransigent interlude. Yet before time on this particular Wasatch perch becomes stretched, other diversions begin to play.

Like columns supporting a ceilingless sky, several plumes of smoke rise in an almost perfect verticality—the obvious signs of rampant civilization.

"Look, Axe. There's a town," notes Katie, as she glances toward the northeast. "A city."

"Ogden," reckons Axe. "And look at the rows of trees. Orchards. When have we last seen that?"

"I was coming to think never again."

To be sure, these familiarities of home are a comforting vision, albeit from an elevated and parched view.

"That is a destination. Ogden," delineates Axe. "Shall we introduce L.M. to the Saints?"

"By all means." But then Katie rises from her seat in order to get a better look. "But how do we get down there? Do you really think this pitiful trail will suffice?"

Once again, the Lanes backtrack the Wasatches. But eventually, they do find a safe descent into the valley of Deseret. Thus Ogden becomes a brief diversion for the couple, especially after they make contact with the Ogden Standard and an automobile agent with an unwavering enthusiasm for the Paris race.

Before long, the Ohioans course southerly toward Salt Lake City, leaving behind, yet again, that matter of international motoring competition. But also they abandon the comfort and safety of the Union Pacific, a new friend having served them in more ways than one. Truly, the Lanes are becoming more and more exposed upon their rapidly dilapidating automobile, and with their rapidly depleting resources.

Although green, the peaches have attained full size, thousands upon thousands dangling from neatly-pruned trees. It's beneath these fruited umbrellas where the Lanes have situated themselves—just off the Salt Lake City Road and precisely between two adjacent properties. Certainly, the air is dry and clear, thus forgoing the need for the tarpaulin. And so a night is spent in the open, where the couple is dazzled by the shimmers of a million stars and the gentle motions of just as many peach tree leaves.

"Mmm," moans a bleary Katie, as she rolls upon a shoulder. "When do we rouse ourselves?"

"Mmm," responds a drowsy Axe. "Never again."

A faunish sleep is assured—the greatest reward for an exhaustive day. And so the night hours flit by, interrupted only by the briefest of dreams and the minor shifts of slumbered poses. Who knows, with a little luck the Lanes may never again have to rouse themselves.

Regardless…

Honk! Honk! Honk! What a rude awakening comes the morn. And it seems to arrive via the uninvited squeezes of the roadster's horn.

In a jolt, the Lanes sit up, rubbing their eyes to lose the blur and clear the confusion.

"Brush runabouts?" mutters Axe of two parked vehicles. "State of Utah?" he reads of official ownership.

"Turn around, Axe," breathes the cautious voice of Katie.

Before the Lanes stands a bowlered figure, who leans against the roadster and displays no apparent humor. But as Katie and Axe gather themselves further, they see that the man has three friends—two fedoras and a short Stetson—none of whom offers even a smidge of a smile.

Surrounded and at a disadvantage, Axe has no choice but to turn to his affable side. "Good morning, gentlemen. What can I do for you?"

There's no reply.

"Axelrod Lane. Of Lisbon, Ohio." While Axe introduces himself, Katie clings to his side. "And this is my wife, Mrs. Lane."

The bowler and fedoras glance toward the Stetson, who places his hands upon his hips.

"A beautiful state, your Utah," continues Axe's chatter. "We've been awed by…"

"So you're from back-east?" interrupts the Stetson.

"Why, yes," answers Axe. "As I mentioned, Ohio. Lisbon."

"And where are you headed?"

In the face of what is an interrogation, Axe hesitates. "Southward. And then a turn westerly."

To Axe's surprise, his innocent response is met by raised brows.

"So then you're going to Bingham?" continues the Stetson.

Not quite sure of the local place names, Axe shrugs.

"Tell the truth." Incredibly, the Stetson's scant demeanor becomes more stern. "Are you agents for the A.F. of L? The U.M.W? Are you friends of Mother Jones? Are you agitators for the I.W. of the W?" In rapid, bewildering combinations comes the alphabet, as if the letters have been recited by the man beneath the Stetson on a constant basis. "Do you work for the W.F. of M?"

As they turn to one another, the Lanes acknowledge their mutual perplexity.

"Just who do you work for?" demands Mr. Stetson.

"The L.M. of O., of course." As calmly as can be, Axe gestures toward the roadster. "Who or what else?"

In no way, however, does Axe's simplistic clarification soothe the moods of Utah's officialdom. Quite the contrary, in that the state's present representatives harden their poses.

Katie firms her grip on Axe, and through this he can sense her apprehensions. His obligations aroused, he has no choice but to come to his wife's defense—never mind the odds.

"See here, gentlemen," asserts a raspy Axe, as he rises to his feet. "You have no business with us. Mrs. Lane and I are law-abiding citizens. Pillars of our community." He glances down to Katie. "Are we not?"

Her reply is a succession of nervous nods.

A hopeful Axe turns to Mr. Stetson, though he comes to the quick conclusion that a logical and honest approach is not making an impression.

Stetson snaps his fingers. "Murphy. Search him."

"Yes, Captain."

Not only does Murphy rush forward to begin the process, so, too, does an eager accomplice.

In a flash, Axe finds himself being manhandled. "Tell me, have you two ever worked for the New York Times?" he manages to quip, while his arms are grasped and his trouser pockets rifled.

"Axe," chides Katie in a harsh whisper. "Hush."

In rapid order, the search continues, down to the pillow which is Axe's rolled-up coat. It's because of this, that a discernable lump lodges into his throat.

"Look at this, Captain," announces Murphy of his discovery.

Almost cracking a smile, the captain accepts the Hopkins & Allen revolver. "I take it, this belongs to you?" he asks, as he examines the weapon.

"Well, not entirely," replies Axe. "It's a loan from my father-in-law. Mr. Kane of Delaware, Ohio." But as he reads the puzzled look of the captain, he feels the need to stress a point. "My wife's father."

"You said your name is Lane," counters the man of authority.

"I did. Axelrod Lane. And this is Katherine Lane. And her father is Mr.

Kane." Axe speaks slowly. "Kane. Lane. Though they may rhyme, they're not one of the same."

"I see," responds the captain with a doubtful look. "And he's from the state of Delaware?"

"Delaware, the city. In Ohio." Axe's frustration stops short of blurting out his true sentiments.

The captain pauses, and then motions with his head, this signal sending his underlings to swarm over the roadster and its contents.

Carefully covering herself in her blanket, Katie stands beside Axe, her only comfort being that now he can wrap his arms around her.

"Allow me to explain in detail, and I'm sure you would be happy to see us on our way," suggests Axe.

But his words of reason are squelched by the discovery of the shotgun, only to be followed by a half-empty bottle of rye—a gift from Wamsutter.

"Captain." It seems that Murphy has come upon some pamphlets. "The Anti-Saloon League?" he reads. "These are temperance bills."

"What?"

"No doubt about it, sir."

The captain looks squarely at Axe, only to do the same to Katie. "Labor agitators and temperance people?" he questions with no lack of confusion. "Armed and liquored? Just what are you up to, anyway?"

To which Axe can offer little more than a smirk. "Why, we're trying to reach the Pacific. Though tired and worn we may be. We have a country to cross."

The search continues and comes up with more incriminating evidence: telegraph receipts, a bronze plaque from the machinists of Centerville, Iowa, a can of Greek olives and a rosary from the Peseks. Yet what most ensures the Lanes' immediate fate is Katie's list of addresses, beginning with the people of NYC all the way to and passed a Cornish miner.

And so the reason why, soon thereafter, the Ohio couple and their roadster are escorted southward to Salt Lake City and the offices of the state attorney general.

As he guides the Speed Six at a crawl, Axe has nothing but contempt for the twin Brush runabouts to his fore and aft. Indeed, how simple it would be for him to shift to second gear and then third, and be rid of Captain Stetson and his ridiculous authority.

"Axe, don't you dare speed away," intervenes Katie, the talented reader of faces. "I don't want to become a fugitive, again. We're not guilty of a thing, and soon these people will be made to realize. Understand?"

"Very well."

It seems, however, that the Lanes are lawbreakers, for no sooner after they arrive at Salt Lake City, then the charges compile. Firstly, the couple has no state automotive permit, nor have they registered with the counties where they have traveled. And because the Speed Six is loaded to excess, they should have attained a supplemental commercial license along with a second rear light. In addition, since the Lanes entered Utah with a full tank of gasoline and a couple of spare cans, a state tax—or tithe—is required.

But then there remains the matter of trespassing on two properties, although Axe and Katie doubt that the farmers in question have filed complaints. Beyond doubt, along with that bottle of rye and a list of several other, less serious offenses, the outsiders from Ohio are nothing if not hardened outlaws.

The result is that Axe and Katie are released from custody, but separated from their roadster. Indeed, the Speed Six is being held hostage, the ransom of which is well beyond their means.

For more than three days the Lanes have languished in Salt Lake City, their new address being the rented room of a kindly Mormon family's modest home, itself situated on the edge of the Greek and Italian neighborhoods near the railyards. And with no resolution in sight, the couple have been forced to take practicality to extremes: Katie having sold her princess dress at a decent price and Axe doing the same with his pocket camera and shotgun—though not the revolver still under state possession. Regrettably, Katie's cherished violin and mandolin are next on the list of barterable goods.

Needless to say, for an industrious couple to be stranded in a strange land is an unsettling turn. With little to do on an unforeseeable horizon, the Lanes must be content to stroll about Salt Lake City in order to waste away their frustrations and find amusement. Unfortunately, since they've become overly familiar with the city, there remains little to discover, try as they might.

"I still can't make the distinction between the Temple and the Tabernacle," confesses Axe during an afternoon walk. "Which is which, and just what is the difference?"

"Remember, Axe?" points Katie. "The Temple has the spires and the Tabernacle, there, is domed. But as to what is the difference? Well, you'll have to ask the Eastwicks."

"That I will, Katie. This evening at dinner. With all diplomacy."

The stroll veers onto North Temple Street, where a side glance from Katie spies a man in the distance.

"I see Murphy is shadowing us. I wonder what became of him, yesterday?"

"He probably became lost," replies Axe. "That jester really should ask for directions."

"We might write an itinerary."

"Yes. But in very plain language."

Ambling around the corner, the Lanes lose sight of their tail, which gives Axe an idea.

"Shall we stop and wait for him? We should say 'hello'."

"That would be polite."

By the time Murphy's shuffle can be heard, the Lanes stand ready to greet, even to the point where their unoccupied hands wave their chumminess.

"Afternoon, Murphy. Pleased you could join us, today," greets Axe.

The response from the snoop is one of dimmed surprise.

"We were worried, yesterday," resumes Axe. "I hope you weren't confused when we left by the kitchen."

"Oh," replies Murphy. "I see."

An awkward pause looms, though thankfully is squelched by Axe. "Well, we must be off, Murphy. And we promise to leave through the front entry from here on out."

"Yes," joins Katie. "And give our regards to that wonderful, sensible captain of yours."

The walk resumes, but with Murphy left behind, conspicuously befuddled as to whether he should follow.

Eventually, the smiles fade and a few blocks further the Lanes find themselves on an unacquainted street, one surrounded by a campaign of vigorous construction.

"My goodness," observes Katie. "It's like a boomtown."

Suddenly, Axe recalls a warning given by Martin Eastwick. That this particular district, known as the "Stockade", is a place to avoid. Understandably, Axe picks up the pace.

"Axe," protests Katie. "Why the rush?"

"Uh-h-h." He does his best to avoid a trip. "Remember Madison Street?"

"How can I forget?"

"Katie, I believe we've stumbled upon Utah's version."

"Goodness!" To which she shuffles her feet even faster.

Thus, with every haste, the Lanes free themselves from the arena of wickedness. Only when they're blocks away do they catch their breaths.

"S.L.C. has too much in common with Springfield." Axe is first to mention the obvious. "Who would have thought?"

"Oh, Axe. I'm tired of this God-forsaken city." Katie gathers more air. "Remember last night, when you talked of finding a job to earn our way out of here? I'm sorry, Axe, but I won't stand for it. I want to be rid of this place. To be back on the road, where we belong. Tomorrow. And I don't care what it takes."

For the remainder of the afternoon, the Lanes bide their time at the Eastwicks'. The house itself is mostly empty of family, the two daughters married into homes of their own and two of the sons having summer jobs. Then there's the eldest, Samuel, whose dusk to dawn position at the Salt Lake Tribune demands that he sleeps into the afternoon. As for his father, Martin, he, too, works at said newspaper as the day typesetter. Because Alice Eastwick keeps busy with housework, Katie and Axe find the home all but silent.

Fortunately, the Lanes' lassitude is broken when Samuel is roused out of bed. And shortly thereafter, daughter Ruth and her Eastwick grandson pay their daily visit. Soon, the other members of the family should file through the kitchen entry, to share their days' events amidst the aromas of a developing dinner.

Ruth's husband's position as a railroad inspector takes him far a-track, thus the reason why she dines often at the home of her upbringing. "...Goodness, to have that man still following you," she remarks, while helping in the kitchen. "How genuinely eerie for you and Axe."

"Poor, Katie," joins Mrs. Eastwick.

"He's not so bad as that," replies the stalker's subject. "In fact, we've had some fun at his expense."

"For shame," giggles Ruth.

"Yes. Shame on you, Katie," agrees Mrs. Eastwick. "Tee-hee-hee."

Soon, all is ready, except that Martin Eastwick is somewhat late—no doubt, things are busy at the Tribune. But eventually, the head of the house makes his unceremonious return, so that, after a sincere grace to God, the dinner of roast mutton begins in earnest.

Happily, the Eastwicks are a loquacious family, so that their evening repasts offer more than basic sustenance. Even while the mutton is carved and bowls of vegetables are passed around, the dinner conversation starts with Martin Eastwick's latest in rumor and report.

"Axe. Katie. You may be interested in what the city editor and his reporters told me. Moments ago."

Instantly, Katie stops spooning the peas and Axe sets down his tumbler of milk.

"There's no doubt that state authorities consider the two of you to be radicals," resumes Mr. Eastwick. "Sent from the East to help foment the labor troubles."

"But that's untrue," protests Katie. "There's nothing faintly radical about us."

"We know that, Katie," assures Mr. Eastwick. "Clearly, the state authorities are blind. And more so, stubborn. Yet the city authorities seem to be warm to the pair of you. The problem being that our mayor is often at odds with the state. Both sides are always looking for a conflict. Today, that cause is the Lanes."

"Oh, dear. Axe, what are we to do?"

"I'm not sure, Katie."

"It may not be so much the fault of the powers that be—Mayor Bransford, Governor Cutter, his attorney general—who are likely little informed. No. Probably, it's their underlings, eager to make an impression." His slicing done, Mr. Eastwick begins to distribute the mutton. "They're to blame for your predicament."

"What should we do, Mr. Eastwick?" appeals Axe, as his plate receives its portion.

"The city editor is sympathetic, though things remain tricky," draws Mr. Eastwick. "Not only do we have state and city, but also the Church. The omnipresent Church. Axe, if you can't find the money to pay those ridiculous penalties, then you'll have to find a power to bear its influences on all three factions." Mr. Eastwick frowns. "Either that or abandon your automobile and flee the state in the dead of night."

"Oh no, we won't do that, Mr. Eastwick," insists Katie. "Will we, Axe?"

"Flee?" he responds. "Not without the roadster. Bu-u-u-t"

"No, Axe. No. I won't hear of it."

Not unexpectedly, the Lanes' night proves restless, alternating between the bed and the floor. Along with the couple's uneasiness comes a concerted discussion, the topic having been forced upon them.

"We need to know what's to become of us," whispers Katie, aware that the Eastwicks must have their sleep. "And where you stand with L.M."

"I'm aware of that, Katie."

"Will we even have a home when we return to Lisbon?"

"We will, Katie. This I guarantee."

"Of course." She takes a breath. "But Axe, I want to become apprised."

"I feel the same."

"Then you have to contact Mr. Loban, Axe. Speak to him at the earliest. Please. For me."

To be sure, "Please, for me" are words rarely uttered by Katie and so carry considerable weight.

"I will, Katie. First thing, tomorrow."

Katie reaches to embrace her husband. "Thank you, Axe. It will work out well. This I guarantee."

"Absolutely. But we should go back to bed. Get at least a few hours' sleep."

"Whatever you say, Axe."

Yet as soon as the covers are pulled, he airs a misgiving. "What will I say to him? I have no idea."

"You'll figure something, Axe. Thinking what you're going to say is much worse than actually speaking to Mr. Loban. Whatever comes into your head will do." Content, Katie nestles her head. "No one can steer him better than you. It is your talent, after all. Convincing the pigheads and fools to see the light."

"Oink, oink," comes the immediate response.

"Mmm. That's my Axe."

"Although that talent doesn't seem to carry in Utah."

"Sh-h-h, Axe. Sleep. We need sleep."

Before the crack of dawn, the Lanes are up and about. And although the couple accumulated little sleep, in no way do they feel sluggish—quite the contrary. Unfortunately, the nearest telephone exchange doesn't open its doors until eight o'clock.

"What time is it?" asks Katie, when she and Axe arrive at the exchange's locked door.

He checks his watch. "It's 8:01."

"They're late," she notes, as she peers through a window.

The wait seems interminable. But eventually, at 8:03, the door is opened.

"We wish to make an urgent, distant telephone call," requests an abrupt Katie.

"Oh? Of course," replies the manager, who seems taken aback. "May I ask the city in question?"

"Lisbon, Ohio," details Katie. "Which is south of Youngstown, which is southeast of Cleveland."

"Ohio?" replies the manager. "I'm afraid a connection for such a distance is a bit unfeasible."

Katie's face wilts, her raised expectations taking a resounding deflation. Nevertheless, a look of utter hopelessness does possess a certain power, perhaps enough to stir great deeds.

"Hmm? Though there could be the off-chance," reconsiders the manager.

Perking into action, he summons a nearby employee. "Miss Tansie. Remember that matter we discussed? Concerning the new amplified 'phone? I think we may have a test case. All the way to Ohio."

"Ohio!"

Soon, an eager Miss Tansie puts a switchboard into play. Meanwhile, she warns the Lanes that to place a call to Ohio may require several hours—if at all possible. Better that the couple leave and go about their business, and check the exchange every hour or so. And to sweeten the suggestion, Miss Tansie assures that she'll keep an open line all day if be, just in case the Lanes find themselves diverted.

Yet again, Axe and Katie wander about Salt Lake City, to reacquaint themselves to its streets, though not to stray too far away from the telephone exchange.

The morning creeps passed ten o'clock and still no connection with Lisbon. Hence, the Lanes are burdened with more superfluous time, the only available cure being to splurge at the nearest available drugstore and its soda fountain.

"Oh, this lemon soda tastes so wonderful," considers Katie, as she loosens her straw. "I wish they could make this at Nace's."

"Mmm," agrees her husband from his seat at the counter.

"The way things are happening, we may have to return here after lunch," continues Katie.

"It is a long call. But I am curious." With that, Axe looks away from Katie and turns to his right. "What do you say, Murph? Does it take long to connect the eastern states?"

The Utahn stops slurping his soda. "I can't say for sure, Axe. All my out-of-state calls have been to California, and were fairly quick. East of the Mississippi?" Murphy shakes his head and then resumes his slurp. "Mmm, this is the best. Thanks again, Axe. Sure is nice of you."

"Think nothing of it."

Upon finishing their sodas, the three return to Salt Lake City's sidewalks. But it's after only a few blocks that Murphy remembers a previous appointment: something about an ongoing investigation of a state employee who may be swindling the government in order to support his suspected polygamous ways.

"Perhaps we'll see you later, Mr. Murphy," bids Katie.

"Yes, we should return to the exchange," tells Axe.

"Good luck, you two," wishes Murphy, as he offers a wave.

Once more, the Lanes' visit to the exchange comes up short of Lisbon. And because of the approaching noon hour, they return to the Eastwicks' for lunch with their sympathetic hosts.

"There's more of Ruth's apricot pie, Katie," encourages Mrs. Eastwick.

"Thank you, ma'am. But this is delicious enough," speaks the much-diverted guest.

"I can use another piece," solicits Mr. Eastwick, whose plate has received already two wedges.

"Never mind that, Martin," insists Mrs. Eastwick. "You need to hurry, before the Tribune misses you."

Shortly thereafter, the Lanes find themselves making a dutiful return to the telephone exchange. Yet, almost immediately, they're met by the sparkle of Miss Tansie, who, as she works her switchboard, motions for the Lanes to have a seat.

"Mr. and Mrs. Lane! I've just made the connection! It's a miracle! Loban Motor of Ohio!"

At first, Axe is reluctant, standing in his tracks. But then Katie urges him forward and all but escorts him to the empty chair by the switchboard.

"Here you are, Mr. Lane," instructs Miss Tansie. "Speak into this 'phone. Loudly"

It's a moment of truth, as Axe takes the receiver in hand, with Katie's reassuring hands set upon his shoulders. He takes a deep gulp and edges his mouth toward the transmitter, while his head struggles to come up with the first words.

"Hello, Mrs. Loban," alerts Miss Tansie into her transmitter. "I have Mr. Lane on the line."

Katie's fingers dig into Axe, such is her shock.

Yet he feels no pain, he being stunned, too, by the revelation of Mrs. Loban's name. Still, Axe has no choice other than to speak into the transmitter and press the receiver against his ear.

"Hello, Mrs. Loban. This is Axelrod, in Utah." He looks up to Katie for encouragement. "How is your day?" Axe's head bobs upon hearing the reply. "That's very nice, Mrs. Loban." He continues to listen.

Meanwhile, bending down, Katie snuggles in order to capture a portion of the receiver.

"Yes, Mrs. Loban, I agree." Finally, Axe is able to wedge a word. "Mrs. Loban? Is Mr. Loban available? I have an urgent message."

Unfortunately for Katie's ear, Mrs. Loban's return comes muffled. "What did she say?"

"Oh, he's busy," repeats Axe. "He and Freddy are on the assembly floor." Again, Axe concentrates on the receiver. "Yes, ma'am. Yes, I see."

"Ask about Aunt Lucie," whispers Katie.

"Mrs. Loban? How is Miss Loban?" As before, Axe bobs his head. "So she's doing fine. That's good news." But then there's a further disclosure, one which cannot be contained. "My goodness!"

"What is it, Axe!"

With a hand, Axe covers the transmitter. "Mrs. Loban's family has bought Aunt Lucie's share of L.M!"

"My goodness!"

Rest assured, Mrs. Loban's eye opener comes as a genuine start. Yet in spite of this, Axe is able to read further, that the wife of Loban Motor's founder now holds a small, but critical, portion of the company's majority. In more ways than one, Mrs. Loban may be flexing her muscles.

"Mrs. Loban," he resumes with a newly-found confidence. "As you may be aware, Mr. Loban and I have had our differences, the result being that Katie and I are stranded." He pauses to hear her response. "Yes, ma'am, and we've struggled to reach this far on behalf of Loban Motor. So you can imagine our frustration from Mr. Loban's lack of support. Why, the stories I could…"

The conversation lasts a good fifteen minutes, more than enough time for Axe and Katie to conclude that Mrs. Loban remains warm to the promotion. Indeed, as the Lanes leave the exchange, they have the confidence that, soon, their misunderstanding with the State of Utah should be resolved and the journey to the Pacific will resume. Only a bit of patience is required.

As it happens, the following day proves to be a test for the Lanes' perseverance, especially in light of the promise that efforts on their behalf will be made. And so their customary, afternoon stroll has a distinct droop to it, the expectation for this Wednesday being that news should have reached them by now.

"I wonder if you should go to Miss Tansie and ask her to reconnect us to Mrs. Loban?" suggests Katie, as she and Axe take a break on a bench beneath a storefront awning.

"Perhaps," replies her husband, who then looks to a friend. "What do you think, Murph?"

"I'd wait for tomorrow." Murphy pauses. But then his sympathetic smirk alters into a smile. "Things will turn out. But I tell you what. How about a lemon soda, along with vanilla ice cream? The treat is on me."

"Thank you, Mr. Murphy. I'd like that." Almost noticeably, Katie's spirits rise. "You're so very kind."

Thursday's breakfast hits its stride when at last Mrs. Eastwick takes her seat. But as she dishes herself a helping of scrambled egg, there interrupts a knock at the door.

"Please stay seated, Mrs. Eastwick," volunteers Katie. She leaves the table, returning in less than a moment with a slip of paper and a perk upon her face. "There's a message waiting at the telegraph office. What do you think it means?"

"It means our prayers have been answered," replies a smiling Mrs. Eastwick.

Thus the Lanes' breakfast ends abruptly, as they excuse themselves and rush through the door.

"That way?" points Axe, as he and Katie overtake the message boy.

"Yessir," he responds, only to shout the last of his directions. "Turn left at the shoe store."

Katie and Axe have no trouble locating the telegraph office. And as luck would have it, they're the first patrons for the day. As presaged by Alice Eastwick, the news from Lisbon begins eventfully.

"Two hundred fifty dollars, Axe," exclaims Katie, as she reads over her husband's shoulder.

"And we have L.M.'s full support!" furthers Axe. "All the way to the Pacific!"

Yet there's more, one seemingly insignificant item at the bottom of the telegram.

"Look, Katie. Look who sent the telegram."

"Percy Loban? My goodness. I would have thought that this is Mrs. Loban's deed."

"Hmm?" Axe stares at the telegram. "But you know it is, Katie. I think now Mrs. Loban has her husband performing her deeds."

"Of course," agrees Katie. "And I wonder, should we now deal with Mrs. Loban in our messages?"

"Absolutely," concurs Axe. "Just like they have it in Wyoming. Mrs. Loban has my vote."

After stuffing his pockets with the $250, Axe leads the way out of the office. But before he and Katie can discuss the matter of their impounded roadster, they're stopped on the sidewalk.

"Axe! Katie! Mrs. Eastwick said you would be here!"

"Murph?"

"Mr. Murphy! Have we good news for you!"

"Have I good news for you!"

"Loban Motor has sent us funds!"

"Your roadster is released from custody!"

Quickly, the three calm themselves and Murphy is able to deliver a sketchy explanation.

"…A senator?" poses Axe. "On our behalf?"

"A Washington senator?" queries Katie.

"Yes. Senator Smart, so I heard," relates Murphy. "Who's also an apostle in the Church."

"Oh-h," chorus the Lanes, as they look at one another, beginning to understand how events could move so swiftly. Yet there remains a further question. "Why?"

"Could be you have an angel who knows how to push his influence," he suggests.

"Mrs. Loban?" wonders Katie.

"Or the Snodgrasses?" considers Axe. "Or their associates in Columbus? Or Washington?"

"I suppose, Axe," agrees Murphy. "Oh. By the way." He reaches into his pocket. "Here's your revolver."

Moments later, it's all the Utahn can do to keep up with the Lanes, as the three hurry to where the Speed Six has been kept dormant. By the time it takes the ten or so blocks to reach one particular state maintenance facility, Murphy is an exhausted wreck.

To the employee in charge, the final act for vehicular emancipation requires but a signature. Soon, the Lanes and a gasping Murphy are lead toward the clangs of a smithy, where there stands a white barn.

"It's parked beyond the last stall," directs the state employee. "Be sure to close the gates behind you."

Too eager to contemplate the shame of having their roadster stabled with beasts of burden, the Lanes rush to the Speed Six.

"Still looks the same," notes Axe. "I doubt it's been out for a drive. Umm. You think someone would've been curious."

"Is there anything I can do, Axe?" Murphy appears eager.

"Let's move these hay bales and crank it over?"

Soon, after some sputtering and spewing, and a few spooked horses, the

Speed Six is able to escape its ignoble confinement. When the last gate is shut behind them, the trio is free to use and abuse the streets of Salt Lake City, such are their pented dreams and unflexed muscles.

"Hang on, Murph," warns Axe, as he ignores a slow 90 degree turn for the speedier arc.

"Jumping Joseph," exclaims the Utahn, who clings at Katie's side, his feet firmed upon the running board. "You could have easily outrun our Brushes! Yahoo!"

Needless to say, Axe is not one to waste an opportunity, to thumb his nose at the laws of the land while under its protection.

"Yahoo!" continues Murphy's enthusiasm. "I can't wait to wrap my hands around that wheel!"

Eventually, he does, following Axe's re-acquaintance with the roadster. Now it's the Utahn's turn to take those speedier arcs under his own impunity, while his hosts squeeze together in the passenger seat.

"Honk! Honk!" comes Murphy's elated warning to his fellow citizens.

"I think we need to take this into the countryside," advises Katie into Axe's ear.

"Murph! What do you say we find an open road!"

"You got it, Axe! Yahoo!"

To which the Lanes respond with mutual grins.

"I wonder how the Eastwicks will react!" wonders Katie. "Remember, Axe! You promised a lesson!"

"That I did! And that I will!"

More than anything, the rampage through Salt Lake City's streets marks a re-beginning, that in more ways than one, the Lanes can get back to the business of crossing the country. Thus nears the end of their Utah sojourn, never mind that the nearest western border approaches two hundred miles away. But if Katie and Axe can skirt around those uninhabited deserts and find those occasional, passable roads, then Nevada and the Pacific beyond loom as real possibilities. Hopefully, their Speed Six roadster has a few more miles in it, yet.

16
FOLLOW THE COMPASS

WITH SALT LAKE CITY WELL to their rear and the lower tip of Utah Lake immediately east, the Lanes are primed to make a consequential, hard right turn. Indeed, from here on out with only minor variances, the direction should be profoundly west, especially upon reaching Nevada.

As for provisions, the couple has purchased and packed enough can goods, including Greek olives, to last all the way to the Pacific. They've even found a source for coffee, tea and intoxicants, and will not have to wait for a Nevada town. But as well, the Lanes have managed a visit to a Salt Lake City milliner, purchasing a sand-colored Stetson sombrero and a red ribbon, leghorn flat, straw hat: vital, wide-brim replacements to deal with the promise of hot, cloudless skies. Furthermore, because they will leave railroad-supplied civilization until at least Ely, they've obtained an additional five-gallon container of gasoline. More so than ever, fuel looms as a constant concern.

To be sure, the Lanes do have their compass, this enhanced by a detailed map courtesy of the Attorney General's office, which in turn has satisfied a thorough Eastwick scrutiny.

"There, Axe," alerts navigator Katie of a road sign. "Eureka! We've found it! Turn here."

And so the couple begin their crossing of Cedar Valley to said town, thus taking the quickest route out of the state of Utah, albeit one with no guarantees.

Now that their coffers have been replenished, the Lanes' can afford the price of a hotel room. Be that as it may, the available accommodations of the Rush Valley community of Vernon appear scant if not shoddy.

"They don't seem to be terribly difficult, those peaks," views Katie of the not-too-distant Onaqui Mountains. "In fact, they look quite pleasant. And they are on our route."

"Then there awaits our hotel." Axe takes the hint. "We'll have ample time to cook a filling dinner."

Soon, amidst the pinions and junipers, the Lanes make camp, where they prepare a stew of potted beef, fresh potatoes and canned tomatoes. Before long, dinner is consumed, and following the clean-up under a descending sun, Katie and Axe are ready for bed by aid of a nightcap.

"Mmm. I think I may get used to St. Louis gin," she sips.

"Mmm," concurs her husband. "To think, if Jack Sinclair knew he could find his liquor in a state of secluded polygamy. It would suit his politics perfectly."

"For shame, Axe. Heh, heh. Oh, that poor, misguided man."

The following day, the couple leave behind the comforts of the Onaquis for what should be a trying stretch of mileage.

The word "desert" owns several definitions, the foremost being a severe limitation of annual precipitation and its logical measure of less than nine inches. With this, of course, comes a conspicuous lack of native vegetation, associated with a bothersome abundance of dust. It's in between the parched territories that the Lanes find themselves being squeezed—with the Great Salt Lake Desert to the north and the Sevier to the south. But as the land of sagebrush and cheatgrass alters to the more stark, so, too, do those encounters with human habitation. Take a wrong turn and the Lanes could run short of gasoline and, eventually, water.

"What do you think, Katie?"

Because one primitive lane has ended at the intersection of another, a decision must be made.

"I hardly call that a road," she avails.

"But look. Those wagon ruts," insists Axe. "This has to be the way to Nevada." Once more, he peers at the map as wielded by Katie. "We have no choice. East means a wide circle and west means the border. I don't want to wander like we had to in the Wasatches."

"Very well, Axe," surrenders Katie. "I trust your intuitions. Mine are tired and worn."

And so the Lanes veer leftward, to enter upon a route where the ruts owe a partial lineage to the Overland Stage, and where some of the chips and shards were created by the hooves of the Pony Express.

"Do you think this land will ever become civilized?" poses Katie, after a few arduous miles.

To which Axe swallows his pride and faces the truth. "Not until they forge a railroad."

Never have the Lanes been subjected to such dust, and never have they endured such heat—the results of a harsh land and an unrelenting July sun. Yet the Speed Six forges onward—sans passengers or express—in spite of several stops to clean spark plugs, clear the float chamber, repair tires and rest the overheated engine.

Perhaps it should come as no surprise that, after crossing a brief range of rocky hills, Axe and Katie enter a land almost devoid of vegetation. Indeed, it's as if an arm of the Great Salt Lake Desert is imposing its bleakness upon two determined travelers, whose misgivings have every excuse to emerge.

"This map and these directions must be accurate," asserts Katie. "If only because they don't syncopate from the compass."

"Yes, of course. But I wonder? Have we driven to the moon? Where's the man?"

"Why, he sits next to me," replies Katie. "And he's driving me to Eden."

Her bold statement might come as a prophecy were it not for the map upon her lap. While Axe must keep his eyes upon the unforgiving road, Katie is free to look about and scan ahead.

"Over there!" In the distance, Katie spies an anticipated beacon. "Fish Springs! It must be Fish Springs!"

The name itself speaks plenty: "Springs", like eternal hope and "Fish", as with the aquatic creatures of pristine waters and not a Great Salt Lake. As the Lanes draw near, they're awed by the mirrorr of flat, tranquil ponds—a clear indication of their shallowness. Then there are the lazy, breezy waves of shoreline vegetation—rushes, sedges, etc.—another clue revealing a profusion of freshwater. Such are the invitations of Fish Springs, the foremost being that they beckon from the middle of an arid, nearly trackless land.

"Oh, Axe. Let's spend the night here," suggests Katie. "I know there's enough day to reach Callao. But I'd rather stay here. Beside a pond."

"Of course." To his credit, Axe realizes an Eden when he sees one.

By securing one side of the tarp to the roadster and the other to a pair of Wasatch pine limbs, the Lanes erect a protective shade. And by coupling their kerosene lanterns they've produced a suitable cookfire amidst a cordless region. Thus Katie and Axe situate themselves, two happy peaches who lounge upon their ground cloth, while the dinner pot simmers leisurely.

Suddenly, from far across Fish Springs comes a faint clanging of metal upon metal.

"It looks like a settlement over there. Maybe a couple of miles away," observes Axe. "Likely a mining camp. They won't be a bother."

"I doubt they'll even know of us," concurs Katie. "Though I hardly care."

Eventually, the Lanes have their early dinner at their secluded campsite. And shortly thereafter, Axe finds that bottle of gin. Soon, one sip leads to another.

"How I could use a bath," airs a complaint.

"By all means, Old Girl. Before you awaits a sublime tub."

Although Axe's remark is somewhat a dare, Katie alters it into a full-blown endorsement. Before he can utter a single protest, she stands away from the tarp cover and begins a strip to match her bare feet.

"Katie!" But in no way does Axe offer a protest. "Where did you put the soap?"

From the bowels of the earth issue the cool waters of Fish Springs, the first sensation bringing a shiver to the Lanes. But huddled together, their systems adjust, and so their mutual ablution begins in earnest.

"What a paradise," opines a lathered Katie.

Several times over, the Lanes wash one another, such are the needs and demands. Yet even when the couple are cleansed thoroughly, after Axe tosses the bar of soap ashore, do they remain in the water—to swim and frolic, splash and swirl.

To the west, the dust-filtered light of a Titian sun nestles upon the Fish Springs Hills. But it also dabs its color upon the mirrored canvas of gentle ripples, aided so adeptly by the blues from a rapidly changing sky.

"Oh, Axe. I wish I were an artist," pines Katie, she gathered in her husband's arms. "Then we would have an excuse to stay here, forever."

By the time Katie is carried ashore, she and Axe are all but dry from the effects of Utah's arid air. And its upon their ground cloth they choose to lie, gazing silently at nature's artistry and inspirations.

"Why Katie? Here in the open? Such a sin?"

"But there is no sin in Eden, Axe. You should know that."

To be sure, a desert morning compels a no uncertain chill—even with two layers of blankets. But Axe and Katie are hearty souls, inured to the hardships of the road. Thus they continue their nakedness—through a breakfast of canned apples and connubial bliss.

Clang! Clang! Clang!

"Uh-h-h. I suppose we should don our fig leaves. The world beckons."

"Must we, Axe?"

Reluctantly, the Lanes dress and pack, and otherwise prepare to be cast out of Eden.

Soon, they rediscover the road, which curves northwestwardly around the wide waters of Fish Springs toward the source of the metal upon metal alarm. From a distance, there doesn't appear to be much in the way of a community, just a few functional houses and the trappings and dross associated with minimal mining activity. Then again, as the Lanes draw nearer, one particular building manages to stand apart.

"FISH SPRINGS AMERICAN MERCANTILE," reads Katie of its sign. "We should stop and see. They may have something we need."

A bell tingles when Katie opens the door, followed by Axe. Her first impression of the store's interior is of orderliness and precision, and that the shelves are not stocked fully. And another sweeping glance tells Katie that the goods for sale are typical of a small community's general store, although this particular example does carry prominent displays of canned fish, bottled sauces and sacks of rice.

Meanwhile, Axe's nose whiffs something pertinent.

Suddenly, a door to what must be the private residence opens, and through it emerges the proprietor.

"Good morning," he offers in a polite and enthusiastic manner. "What can I do for you, madam? Sir?"

"Oh? Well, uh-h-h?" That she can't recall her perpetual shopping list, Katie is blameless, if only because she's taken aback by the unexpected.

"Please, have a look," speaks the proprietor in perfect, though accented, grammar.

The keeper of FISH SPRINGS AMERICAN MERCANTILE, who although is dressed in Western attire, owns a Japanese origin.

Yet because Axe's first sense maintains its sniff, the birthplace of the proprietor is the least of his concerns. "Is that gasoline I smell? Do you actually sell gasoline?"

The proprietor's response is to throw up his palms and bear a wide grin. "Yes, I do!"

"Excellent." Axe knows a genuinely friendly reaction when it's thrusted upon him. He lunges forward and offers his hand. "Axelrod Lane. And this is my wife, Katherine Lane."

"Please to meet you, Mr. Lane." The exuberance doesn't fade. "I am James

Okyo. And I, too, have a wife." He turns around toward the rear door. "Dolley! We have customers! Mr. and Mrs. Lane!"

Almost instantly—and certainly without a peep—the wife in question enters the store. Clad in a simple, brown and white plaid skirt and a plain blue shirt waste, and with her hair captured by twin pigtails, Dolley begins to bow demurely.

"No, no," whispers James in a remindful way, he extending his arm in a mock handshake.

"Oh." To which she approaches Katie. "Meesus Wane. Pweese to you meet."

"Thank you," shakes Katie, who remains a bit stunned.

And then Dolley takes her graciousness to Axe. "Meester Wane. Pweese to you meet."

"The same to you, Mrs. Okyo."

"Mr. and Mrs. Lane wish to purchase our gasoline."

"Ahh!" Dolley beams with a pronounced glee. "You gasoween buy!"

Luckily, the shocks of the moment fade, and Axe is led to a corner where a five-gallon, corrugated, spout can awaits. Although he has his doubts, Axe unscrews the top and unceremoniously samples its air.

"Is it good gasoline?" asks James.

"It smells fine," judges Axe. "I'll take it. Every drop."

At thirteen cents a gallon, Fish Springs gasoline may seem a little steep. But when considering the trouble to procure the fuel for such a remote location, it's worth every penny. After the transaction is made, James is eager to help refuel the Speed Six.

"Such a fine automobile to be our first gasoline customer," marvels the proud proprietor. "A sign of good fortune." And when the last drop is relinquished, James looks toward an approaching Dolley, who along with Katie, carries the Lanes' purchase of fish, sauces and rice. "We need to order more gasoline!"

"Ahh, yes! More gasoween!"

Such a fine couple are the Okyos, as pegged by the expert Lanes. So when a humble request comes at the moment of departure, Katie and Axe are happy to cooperate—never mind the problem of accommodation.

"I suppose he can sit atop the spare tires. Above the rumble seat," figures Axe, as he turns the crank. "What do you think, Lincoln?"

The passenger in question is the sixteen year-old, Okyos' employee, who is involved in the construction of two additional rooms to the household. As it happens, Lincoln is a Paiute, raised by a family of Goshutes. And he needs to reach Trout Creek in order to be a part of his adopted sister's wedding, this ceremony being sanctioned by the graces of the Latter Day Saints.

Lincoln nods eagerly, and with his belongings slung upon his back, he scrambles atop the heap of tires.

"Hold on tight," warns Axe. Following a wave to the Okyos, he engages first gear.

"Goodbye," gestures Katie.

Thus the Lanes and their passenger leave Fish Springs, to venture again into that finger of the Great Salt Lake Desert. But little do Katie and Axe know that with them travels a supreme navigator. Soon, after they negotiate around the Fish Springs Range, there comes a fork, the plan being to veer right for the Callao road.

"Go left," announces a previously quiet Lincoln from his perch.

"Are you sure?" questions Axe.

"Yes. Much shorter. Through the lava field."

"Lava?" Katie, too, has her doubts. "Is it safe?"

"Yes. Very safe."

"Very well. If you say so, Lincoln," trusts Axe.

Only two hours later and the trio make it through the hazards of the lava field, where the road and all of its shortcuts and detours are well-known to the seasoned foot-traveler Lincoln.

Yet today's arrival to Trout Creek for the sixteen-year old comes via the most modern of conveyances and atop its highest pedestal. The roadster slows as it enters the tiny community, and a small trail of curious onlookers is able to tag along. Understandably so, Lincoln appears reluctant to abandon his throne.

Bringing the Speed Six to a stop, Axe is quick to grasp the situation. "Lincoln, we couldn't have done it without you," he announces, as he abandons his seat and reaches to shake the young man's hand. "Why, you saved our lives, the way you guided us through the desert. Mrs. Lane and I are forever grateful."

"Yes, Lincoln," assists Katie from her seat. "You will always be my hero."

Nevada and its mining towns of various ores loom. But without any reliable signs, the Lanes can't be certain when a boundary is breeched. Nevertheless, after they begin to climb in elevation, with all the trepidations thus accrued, there can be but one overwhelming conclusion.

"This has to be Sacramento Pass. No doubt, Axe," determines Katie from her navigator's seat. "Yes. We've entered Nevada. And that peak we've been watching is the state's highest."

"Thank God. We'll send a telegram to Mrs. Loban, that we've put Utah behind us."

Thus the Lanes continue to snake their way through the Snake Range and onward to the railroad salvation which is Ely, Nevada. And how fortunate for them that their road seems well-traveled, there existing less ambiguity with a worn path.

The only reason to dally in Ely is to tap into its supply of gasoline. And because Katie and Axe spent the night camping at Connor Pass in the Schell Creek Range, a stay within a comfortable hotel room will have to wait for another occasion. Before noon, the couple is ready to depart.

"I thought he was a very kind editor," notes Katie of the Ely Daily Mining Expositor.

"Yes, he was. And informative," nods Axe. "So those sheepherders we encountered were Basques. And their sheep we waded through were Spanish Merinos. I didn't think they were native-born. What with their peculiar-looking wagon and dress. Basques? Hmm?"

More importantly, the Lanes have been told that the road to Eureka is a sure one—all the way to Carson City, near the California border. However, the editor cautioned that the way west of Eureka—in all its simplicity and single-minded direction—may be the loneliest and most exasperating road in the world. Indeed, the Lane's resoluteness is to be taxed, on a route stretching just short of infinity.

Once again, Axe and Katie camp in the wilderness, this time at Pancake Pass. And once again, they arrive at a hotel town too early in the day to take advantage. But at least Eureka's merchants' are fairly stocked, in spite of the fact that a decades-old depression of silver prices has not quite righted itself. To this, the Lanes make a couple of visits, purchasing a few vital items in order to shorten the long road ahead.

"Axe, do you really think we'll need twenty-four bottles of beer?"

"Absolutely."

Soon, after several post-Eureka curves and undulations, the road alters dramatically into the straight and narrow. With that, the forewarning of vast starkness comes true.

"I don't suppose we could find a route through those mountains?" aspires Katie of some distant 10,000 feet peaks—too far to the south.

"We can't afford to become that desperate."

Fortunately, desperation can be avoided altogether if timely measures are taken. Thus Katie reaches for her instrument of choice.

"What's it going to be, Old Girl?" smiles Axe, who is in the mood.

"Hmm?" considers Katie, as she chins her violin. She listens to the churns of the roadster and then makes a decision. "I believe a polka may do the trick. This is not the proper circumstance to grind out a waltz."

And so Katie fiddles away, as best she can. But the bumps of the road prove a fierce handicap, rendering her bow too clumsy for a polka—never mind, a waltz. Frustrated, Katie switches to mandolin, strumming through a succession of safe chords.

Gradually, the Nevada miles compound. But the slower rate produces greater distances, the sum of which may be beyond the roadster's capacity. Abandoning her attempts to make music, Katie clings at Axe's side, and stares ahead at the endless, parallel ruts of the ground. But as well, the futility of keeping the engine tuned to her perfect pitch has not been lost, making the powers of isolation all the more potent.

"I wish we could find a hotel for the night," she mentions. "Or better, a Fish Springs."

Eventually, the sun shows its wane. And wishing to beat this conclusion, the Lanes set up camp at the first available site. As luck would have it, they find themselves on the gentle, eastern side of the Toiyabe Range—at a cool spring and its trickling stream, and beneath towering ponderosas.

"I hope we don't get confused here, like in the Wasatches," notes Katie, as she stirs the pot.

"We shouldn't," assures Axe. "These mountains lack the girth."

Soon, the Lanes are left with a starry, moonless sky and a minimal campfire. With dinner elapsing into memory, all they can do is sit back and behold the stark isolation closing upon them. Indeed, all is black, as the couple gaze into the distance, be it a hundred miles or one hundred feet.

"There's no light, Axe. Nothing out there," clutches Katie. "If only I had a moon to sing to."

"Hard to imagine. But we were warned."

"Whew. Who knows what lurks?" Katie firms her grip.

"You can't deny our perfect camp. You did ask for another Fish Springs."

"Fish Springs had its lights. Here there's nothing."

"Don't worry, Katie. If you like, I'll feed the fire through the night and keep a dim lantern."

"Will you, Axe? I would appreciate that." Katie breathes a sigh of relief. "I'll be able to read my watch."

Dawn has the Lanes wakening to the brisk scents and whirring sounds of wind-animated pines. But also there echo the rapid hammers of feathery flickers and industrious sapsuckers, meticulous creatures marking their signatures upon the ponderosas. Thus provoked, the couple rush through their morning rituals, and reconvene their climb upon the Toiyabes.

As it happens, their route through the range offers little in the way of hardship. Although the Speed Six's engine coughs and backfires its way through the chill air, shortly it gathers enough heat to tackle the road's forgiving incline. Before long, Katie and Axe top the range.

"My goodness, Axe! Down there! Steeples!"

"What? A town? Let me see that map."

As with any item made of paper, creases do occur. And with this, rips and tears will follow, which explains how a place name can fall off the face of the earth.

"I suppose it's possible. There could be a town."

"Axe? Steeples? What else?"

Down the slope the roadster coasts—in first gear and low throttle. And it's to the unanticipated town that the Lanes proceed, the road's twists and turns impairing the view for only brief moments.

"Austin. Of course," announces Axe, as he and Katie near the edge of the Toiyabes. "Remember how that Ely editor mentioned Austin?"

"I think so," replies Katie. "But he said so much."

Shortly, the Lanes confirm that steeples do exist in Austin, Nevada, these supported by inviting sanctuaries of Catholicism, Methodism and Episcopal. Indeed, it is a town of solid foundations, built of granite and ponderosa pine, by all appearances settled and living life as it sees fit.

"To think, we could have spent the night in that cozy hotel."

"Oh, don't feel bothered, Axe. But we could ply a couple of hours here, if you don't mind. I sure would like to visit those beautiful churches. See if one has an organ."

And so Axe parks the Speed Six for a morning sojourn.

"St. Augustine," she observes, as they stroll to the nearest church. "In this city of God."

What an oasis tiny Austin turns out to be, a pleasant surprise of tidy houses, tastefully ornate, commercial establishments and churches with their multiple keys of piped music—the results of a golden past and turquoise present. Yet too soon do those two hours elapse. After making a dutiful visit to the Reese River Reveille, the travelers compel themselves to leave.

"Goodness gracious, Axe. A castle?" notes Katie, upon passing a thick, three-story, medieval tower.

"No doubt built when a nabob came into his wealth," reasons Axe. "Hmm? I wonder if Mr. Loban will ever build a Lisbon castle?"

"If Mrs. Loban allows it," quips Katie. "We shall see."

Immediately following their Austin respite, the Lanes return to that lonely road and those qualms of separation—a repeat of the previous day's leg. Soon, they lose sight of Austin's steeples. Eventually, even the Toiyabas melt into the eastern horizon.

Yet because of the isolation, any hint of civilization can be seen from miles away. It can't be smoke—the sign from afar—in that it appears nonstationary, at what must be a crawl.

"Road dust," discerns Katie. "Someone is coming our way."

There can be no doubt of an encounter, unless one party takes an unlikely tangential course.

"Oh, for a telescope," bemoans Katie, as the impending merge moves at too slow a pace.

Still, the opposing plumes of dust do draw near, though mostly because of the roadster's efforts.

"A team and a wagon," spies a sharp Katie. "They may be a family. Oh, Axe. Let's stop and say 'hello'."

To be precise, the husband, wife, three children and apparently half of their worldly goods are the Bennetts. And it seems they, too, have succumbed to the road's lonely extremes, for no sooner after they introduce themselves does each member leap from their market wagon and surround the roadster.

"Axelrod Lane at your service. And this is my wife, Katherine."

"My, what a beautiful vehicle you have, Mr. Lane."

"And might I say, what a beautiful family you have, Mr. Bennett."

Any existing ice melts by the honest terms of mutual admiration. But the obligations of automobile stewardship force the Lanes to reveal first their story, although quickly, thereafter, under Axe and Katie's insistence, the Bennetts tell theirs.

Very simply, Fred Bennett is a mining engineer. And although he and his family reside in Austin, from time to time his work takes him elsewhere. After spending six months divining the gold and silver ores of Chalk Mountain to the west, the calendar is urging the Bennetts homeward.

"We have a bag of lemons," announces Katie. "And plenty of water and sugar. And a bounty of Utah fruit. Shall we have a soiree!"

And so amidst the bitter Nevada interior comes sweet lemonade. But as well, after Harry Bennett makes a subtle, sudsy comment, a swift Axe produces a few bottles of Eureka beer. Indeed, when Katie breaks out her violin, the impromptu wayside takes on a festive atmosphere.

Yet amazingly, the celebration grows, when, minutes later and seemingly out of nowhere, a certain Mr. Brumsley accepts the invitation and ties his horse and pack mules to the wagon. And the dust barely settles when a Mr. Black, who's returning his empty freight wagon for a load of Austin lumber, is lured by a refreshing waltz and, hence, the enticing refreshments. Before long, to the rhythms of a Czech polka, the assembled help themselves to a second round.

"Whom might they be?" inquires Axe of an approaching four-seat surrey and its five passengers.

"Oh. Those are the Bartles and the Brussards," answers Mrs. Bennett, while waving. "They have a wedding to attend. In Eureka. Where there may soon follow a funeral."

The roadside social continues in all its friendly conversing, partaking and occasional dancing. It seems that the country's loneliest road is now blocked to all traffic.

Thus the celebration erodes a couple of hours, with Katie excusing her music so that she might join the mingle. But when the late-arriving Brittons and their Buick join the revelry—this after motoring from Ely and spending a night with relatives in Austin—the erstwhile hostess becomes somewhat nervous.

"Axe," she whispers. "You should have bought more Eureka beer. We're running low."

"Perhaps we can convert them to Sinclair gin?" comes Axe's off-handed solution.

The day is at its hottest when the participants agree they've had enough of a good time. Soon, the horses and their masters head east, while the motorized vehicles take the opposite direction. But because the Speed Six leads the way, there does arise an unwanted complication.

"I hope the roadster functions well," confesses Axe. "I would hate to be passed by a Buick."

For the rest of the afternoon, the Speed Six performs as best it can, requiring only a few of the usual maintenance stops. But the same must be true for the slower Buick, its dust plume becoming increasingly distant. As for the road, it continues much of the same as before: avoiding the mountains and plunging through a scrubby desert, while maintaining its lonely reputation.

Yet it all comes to a sudden, surprising end, if only because the Lanes'

U.S.G.S. map was printed in 1905 and that their festive conversations with their latest acquaintances hadn't brought up the matter now at hand.

"Smokestacks? Axe? How can that be?"

Indeed, it is a curious spectacle, to encounter in the middle of nowhere the same sort of sky high belchers of eastern, heavy industries. Then again, there have been those recent sightings of a western influence.

"Is it all that unusual from what we've seen before, Katie? The Eurekas?"

With their eyes gleaned upon the portents of civilization, the Lanes close the distance.

"I wonder what they call this place?" asks a wide-eyed Katie.

"I think you already know," replies Axe, who is just able to sharpen his focus. "Look. Written on that smokestack. Wonder, Nevada."

At last, the Lanes roll into a town before dusk, their timing being perfect for a hotel stay. Most obvious are the smokestacks and their mill, situated beyond the edge of Wonder, and spewing out not only the grimy issues of burning coal, but the steady, calamitous sounds of massive crushers and stamps, and oscillating vanners. And then Katie and Axe enter the town proper, soaking in what it has to offer, their ambitions being for clean sheets and a hot bath.

To be sure, Wonder is a busy place, albeit one of lumber and canvas as opposed to quarried rock, bricks and mortar. Indeed, its signs of infancy offer the cries of a boomtown. Granted, Wonder's establishments may sell a world of goods, but so much of it seems to cater for specific clientele: miners who have yet to send for, or even establish, their families, and the seedy sort who prey upon their wages.

"I think I might have found a new diversion," concludes a quick Katie.

"What could that be?"

"Counting saloons and gambling halls. Brothels," she grimaces. "There's no sport to counting churches."

The Lanes continue their wondrous tour, but with Axe's right hand ready to shift to second.

"What are the odds that any of those hotels have vacant rooms?" he presents.

"What are the odds that I would agree to spend a night here, regardless?"

Enough said, as Axe's right hand tugs—along with the corresponding movements of throttle and pedal.

"Wonder Mining News," he reads, as the couple pass a concern. "Can you believe it? They already have a newspaper. With the convenience of a saloon for a neighbor."

"I've seen enough public groping. Let's not bother with them, Axe," urges Katie. "Better to find a camp in the desert before it becomes cold and dark. Axe, we're done with our penance, here."

After an uneventful night, the Lanes plunge into an early morning, guiding and urging the roadster through a land of sinks, alkali flats and dry lakes. And then there dominates the stark vegetation of minimal cacti and extremely spare grasses. For certain, this region is proving to be the most foreboding the Lanes have encountered, thus making their efforts to keep the Speed Six in working order more of a struggle.

Once again, they find themselves at the side of the road, with Axe occupied in engine repair and Katie tending to a tire puncture.

"I never could have dreamed of so much sin before Wonder," she reckons.

"Now I can see how Utah and Nevada are neighbors, Katie. The two fit hand in hand."

After pumping air, she lifts the mended tire into place. But before Katie tightens nuts to bolts, she stands apart in order to wipe her brow.

"How more barren can a place be?" declares Katie of the glaring. "Other than reptiles, I think we're the only creatures about."

"Reptiles?" replies Axe, his nose buried in engine. "When have we last seen a reptile?"

Fallon, Nevada is a substantial town. And because it's served by railroads means that gasoline is no problem. But as the Lanes discover beyond, their ordeal through the limitless barrens of Nevada, and those of western Utah, comes to a sudden, resounding end.

The Carson River isn't much of a stream, its short duration coming at an ignoble end into a series of remote sinks. But that it issues from the eastern ranges of the massive Sierra Nevada guarantees a steady flow of water amidst an exploitable valley.

"My God," observes Katie, after she guides the Speed Six upon a hill. "Such farms."

To be sure, the geometry of earnest agriculture is an undeniable placard—even from afar. And when the road takes the Lanes into the Carson Valley proper, they can witness at hand the careful calculations of lengths and widths, angles and segments, quadrilaterals and a smattering of arcs, all nurtured by the dividing lines of irrigation canals. There're fields of growing corn, decaying wheat stubble, purpling alfalfa, sugar beets and potatoes, along with orchards of apples. But then the roadster passes the occasional scene of trellised vines of a heretofore unrecognized crop, no doubt being of vital importance.

"Hops," concludes Axe. "By God, that must be hops and those farms Czech. So neat and precise. Splendorous."

There's nothing hyperbolic about Axe's statement concerning yet another paradise. However, his assessment does contain a tincture of inaccuracy, surfacing when the few non-English signs and markers are of the Teutonic tongue and not the Slavic.

"Suppose they have any societies in need of Russell tractor expertise?" yearns Axe.

"Or wedding celebrations wanting a fiddle?" responds Katie with her own pine.

The Lanes glide through their comfortable setting, as does the roadster upon a road amazingly devoid of horseshoe nails. In this corner of the world, all valleys lead to the capital, Carson City, the smallest of the country's such municipalities. Be that as it may, because the town is the seat of state government, also it must be a center of efficient communication. Yet as well, Carson City looms as a pivot point upon which the couple must make a momentous decision, perhaps the most important since their first departure from Lisbon.

To the north and to the south, mountains of minor stature bound the Carson Valley. But as noted, the Sierra Nevada awaits—a domineering spectacle even from a distance. More and more, it seems impossible, the range having the promise of besting the Rockies. Indeed, that sense of foreboding is returning to the Lanes, this bolstered by the information gathered during a stop in Dayton, that the New York to Paris competitors chose to take the long, taxing loop south through the Mojave Desert and around the Sierra.

"I'm not so sure, Katie," shakes Axe's head.

Short of Carson City, the Lanes have pulled to the side of the road, to take a break and gather their senses. Their U.S.G.S. map spread upon the hood, Katie and Axe take another gaze toward the Sierra Nevada.

"For our roadster to make that trek through the desert? It's just too many more miles, and we have so few left. We're reaching our limits."

"But surely we can find a way through the Sierras?" counters Katie. "We did outwit the Wasatches?"

"Only just." Axe returns to the map. "Hmm? Look here." He traces with a finger. "This Lake Tahoe Wagon Road looks promising. All the way to Placerville, California."

"Yes," studies Katie.

"Still, those Sierras look to be cunning and stubborn," continues Axe with some resignation.

"'Cunning'?'Stubborn'?" The words draw from Katie a degree of resistance. "Tell me when Axelrod Lane was bettered by 'cunning' and 'stubbornness'?"

"Well-l-l?"

"Never, it seems. Axe, if you, the engineer, believe the roadster cannot survive the longer route, then I trust you. Just don't tell me we can't find a way through the Sierras. Look at the map. The Pacific is not that far. I can almost smell the salt!"

Axe takes a deep whiff, affirming Katie's assertion, while he stares down the Sierra. "By God, that ocean isn't that far away." He folds away the map. "We should make a telephone call to Mrs. Loban? Tell her that, do or die, we're taking on the mountains?"

"Thank goodness, Axe. No more deserts. I've had my fill of torrid dust."

"If she wants a ceremony by the Pacific, it will be at San Francisco and not Los Angeles."

In due time, the Lanes find Carson City.

"…Sir, so you say you're unable to place a call to Ohio?" interprets Axe of an assertion made by the telephone exchange manager.

"Yes. That you made the connection from Salt Lake City is nothing short of miraculous. But to stretch a voice even further west?"

"Yes, of course," realizes Axe.

"I'm afraid from here on out, the two of you will have to make do with telegrams," points the manager.

"Hmm? We'll do just that," recognizes Axe. "Then push on to the Lake Tahoe Wagon Road."

"The Lake Tahoe Wagon Road, you say?" questions the manager even further.

"Yes."

"Then you haven't heard, Mr. Lane. There's been a large rockslide. The road is blocked to traffic. For several days at best."

"Oh?"

The Lanes are caught in mid-stride, as the message of a granite solid delay sinks, that Carson City may be the venue for an extended stay.

"I fear another Salt Lake City, Katie."

"Oh, Axe. I don't know." Katie is disinclined to tarry for even a moment.

"Why not try Reno? Send a telegram to Mrs. Loban to contact us there? Then we might find a northerly route through the Sierras."

"Yes. That seems reasonable enough," agrees the manager. "With a little luck."

Once again, the routines of camp are followed—in spite of a pocketful of money. And for this occasion, the Lanes are blessed by the tranquility of a lake—Washoe, to be exact—its cool waters providing a quick, shivering bath. But as well, the ground is softened by a pallet of gathered pine needles atop of which rests their bedroll. As for dinner, Axe's unsuccessful bid to hook Washoe trout is rescued by Katie's previous purchase of Carson Valley German sausage, making his frustration very short.

"Axe. Save some for breakfast."

Because of the chill, there's a reluctance to greet the dawn. However, there do exist creatures who fear not the morning's short temperature, if only because they bear coats of warm fur. Indeed, they are active, leasty/beasty chipmunks not a bit shy to scamper about and even upon the drowsy Lanes.

"Shoo now! Shoo, if you don't want to become my breakfast!" warns an irritated Axe, though not to the desired result. "God, what a nuisance!"

"Is that you, Axe?" awakens Katie to the crude alarm. "Woo-ooo, it's freezing. Be a saint and feed the fire. Brew some coffee."

To their credit, the Lanes rise to stoke their furnaces, even before the morning sun can do the same to the day. Soon, they're on the way to Reno, leaving behind the used grounds of coffee, to be picked over and, perhaps, further agitate the natives of Washoe Lake.

Coupled with the upper altitude and wear and tear, the roadster takes a few miles to adjust. But eventually there comes a lessened wheeze from the engine, thus allowing the Lanes to sit back and enjoy their drive.

"Happy anniversary, Axe," announces Katie's sly grin.

"What?" responds her husband, while his head fumbles through the consequential dates. "Anniversary?"

"Yes. August, the first," hints Katie, but to no immediate avail. "Axe, it was two months ago that we left New York City. Remember? June, the first?"

"Oh. That anniversary," absorbs Axe. "Two months? Seems like yesterday. Hmm? The Van Doorns and Loewoeks. Katie, you should write them. Tonight. Let them know of our progress."

"Yes. I'll do just that."

By far, Reno is the largest city in Nevada, and should continue so forever, if only because of its proximity to the precious metal mines and serving railroads, and the California border. Indeed, the city is an admirable place, especially to a pair of road-weary travelers arriving from the wilderness. And it is a busy Friday within this municipality—a Manhattan in miniature, although without the unabashed displays of poultry massacres and severe poverty.

"We could really sell the Speed Six here."

"Amen, Katie."

More importantly, however, Reno is a city rife with wires, perfect parallels streaming above the roofs of the older buildings, yet beneath those of more recent construction.

Soon, a visit to the telegraph office results in a message received by two eager Ohioans. Thus it reads, of how Mrs. Loban is proud of Katie and Axe, and of her two sons having prayed for their safety. But then there is the news of a Pacific shore ceremony, to be arranged by the publicity agency -- with of all things Mr. and Mrs. Loban in attendance! Could a rendezvous be made at San Francisco in five days? Indeed, the train fare from Ohio to California requires only four. Because the Lobans can depart almost immediately, an impending merge may be short in coming.

"Mr. Loban coming to greet us?"

"Yes, Axe. It is his right, after all. But with Mrs. Loban to escort him. Do you suppose she will ever again let him out of her sight?"

"You do have a point. But I wonder?"

"What's that, Axe?"

"If when we next see Mr. Loban, will he be in chains? Heh, heh. What a vision."

"Axe," responds a frowning Katie. "Though some chain, I suppose. But can we do it? Five days?"

"We can give it a go. Let's send a return, that we'll try for San Francisco in five days, and they should contact us in California a-a-at. Achem. Excuse me, sir, where would you suggest?"

"Where?" considers the patient telegrapher. "For certain, Soda Springs. And beyond that, Dutch Flat."

Thus the Lanes send their return telegram and so, shortly, reclaim their roadster.

"Which way?" inquires Axe from behind the wheel.

"Straight ahead," details Katie from a map. "We should find the Southern Pacific."

Yet it may not be as simple as that, to exit Reno, if only because of the city's diversions. It seems that Nevada's chief burgh is a setting for an astounding number of newspapers, these being too difficult to ignore.

"I suppose we are obliged, Axe," yields Katie, when they come upon the office of the Progressive West. "Let's be done with it."

That happenstance has made the choice matters little to the Lanes, who are satisfied with the convenience of the moment. But as they enter through the door, instantly, Katie and Axe are able to assess the stark setting. Upon introducing themselves and relating the purpose behind their journey to a seemingly uninterested editor, the couple see fit to drop a name or two.

"Could that be yourself with Bill?" observes Axe of a framed photograph, while he and Katie sit in front of the editor's desk. "Big Bill Haywood?"

"Why, yes," answers the editor, whose face takes on a proud beam.

"We've never had the pleasure, though we do have mutual friends," joins Katie.

"Really?"

"Jack Sinclair, for one," she reveals. "We recently spent some time with him. At Social Farm, Nebraska."

"Yes. Jack Sinclair." The editor seems to be recalling names. "Social Farm. Hmm? How are things?"

"Quite hospitable, it was," assists Axe. "Although it wouldn't surprise us if Jack returned to New York for an extended stay. To perform his calling there. And be closer to Emma Goldman."

"Yes. They do make a fine couple, don't you think?" recalls a sure Katie.

"Uh-h. Yes. Quite accordant, as I remember." By the looks of it, the editor is scratching his inner recesses. "In their letters they always mentioned one another." Rubbing his chin, he pauses, as if reconsidering. "Hmm? So tell me, Axelrod and Katherine, if you don't mind."

"Of course," comes the duet.

"Tell me more of your automobile and your journey. Loban of Ohio?"

"Why, yes," replies an eager Axe. "Loban Motor of Ohio, where our promotion tour is being sponsored in part by the unexploited workers, who, themselves, control the means of..."

Eventually, the Lanes finish their chore at the Progressive West, and are on their way. Yet, the lures of Reno present themselves, again, stopping the Speed Six short of the Southern Pacific.

"The Plaindealer," reads Axe of a more substantial newspaper's proclamation. "Shall we?"

"If we can do it quickly," agrees Katie. "Plaindealer? I think it may require a different approach."

"Certainly. But we can handle them. Adjust on the fly, like always."

"Which goes without saying. But I wonder, Axe. Do you suppose there are people here who read both newspapers?"

"God, I hope not." Axe raises his brow. "Although, should it matter?"

"Hardly. By all means. Let's have a little fun."

Inevitably, the Lanes find those Southern Pacific tracks, which adhere to the forgiving grades of the Truckee River Valley. And it's to the immigrant trails and subsequent service roads the couple seeks, the foremost being the Old Donner Lake Road.

For several miles, Katie and Axe have been skirting the Sierra Nevada. But at last, they're plunging headfirst into the mountains and its confusion of routes. From the Truckee River Valley branch a few, including the Auburn Road, the Henness Pass Road and the Beckwourth Trail, the latter looping northward and consuming far too many miles. To be sure, in order to spare the Speed Six and make their arrival to San Francisco timely, Axe and Katie must forgo the luxury of excessive backtracking. Thus the need to ask for directions at every chance.

Soon, the Lanes approach Verdi—Nevada's westernmost settlement. By and large, the town appears to be one of a single road, this being the tracks of the Southern Pacific, around which situate a community of retail establishments, hotels, churches, houses and what may be a brewery. Then there are the enveloping foothills, for the most part denuded of their lofty, native conifers.

"Look, Axe. A millpond. Stacks of lumber. Now I see. Verdi is for logging."

As if on cue, the Lanes pass a railroad siding, where rest a flatcar load of rolls of steel cable and another of two, shiny steam engines.

"Donkeys," figures Axe. "Those are Dolbeer engines. They take them into the forests to drag the logs to the railroad tracks. And then to that mill."

Yet, immediately, the roadster approaches another telltale sign of the logging industry: a gang of lumberjacks packing crosscut saws, falling axes, mallets and wedges into two mule-hitched wagons.

"Excuse me," greets Axe, as he halts the Speed Six. "Do you gentlemen know of the road to California?"

To be sure, they are a group of rugged lumberjacks, who appear to be shifting their work to another site. Yet their immediate response to Axe's uncomplicated inquiry are looks of puzzlement, as each man turns toward one member of the gang.

"Pardon?" asks their apparent leader.

"My wife and I are driving to California and wish to know if the roads are safe?"

"Oh, I see," replies the lumberjack, who then translates a rapid French to his friends.

Almost in unison, the men nod their heads, only to follow with shrugging shoulders.

It's not exactly the favorable reply sought by the Lanes. But if they crave clarity, Axe needs only to reach for the item resting upon Katie's lap, this being the appropriate U.S.G.S. map.

"Ah, excellent," lights up the English-speaker, when he nudges against the idling Speed Six and scrutinizes the displayed map.

And likewise do his friends approach the Lanes, all doffing their slouch hats.

"Bonjour, madam."

"Bonjour, messieurs."

"We believe this is the road we should take." Axe's forefinger traces the route.

"Hmm?" considers the English-speaker.

The lumberjacks comment amongst themselves and use their own fingers to delineate the route ahead. Yet what seems to be baffling to those not attuned to the French tongue alters quickly toward the hopeful, especially when the last, doubting head ceases its shake.

The English-speaker turns to the Lanes. "Yes, the two of you should have a safe journey. But be aware of these divergences, here and here. And here. With caution, maneuver the curves. Especially here. So many switchbacks. Yet most especially, select this left divergence, here."

The Lanes absorb every word, with Axe penciling the pertinent points upon the map. And so their confidence builds, that the Sierra Nevada is a conquerable range.

"It's been a pleasure, boys," bids Axe, as he reaches to shake several hands. "Thanks aplenty."

"Au revoir. Au revoir."

The roadster begins to creep away.

"Bon voyage, mon ami! Mon amie!"

"Merci beaucoup," waves Katie.

"Se revoir, madam!"

"Adieu, mon amour!"

While Axe negotiates the road, Katie continues her wave.

"Goodbye! Adieu and se revoir!" With that, Katie snuggles into her seat. "Such fine gentlemen. In spite of their rough appearances. But Frenchmen at such a wild occupation? Who could have imagined?"

Thus continues the Lanes' brief tour of Verdi, passed its assorted structures and its sidings of flatcars laden with sweet-scented logs. Yet when they reach its far edge, Axe brings the roadster to a crawling stop, to gaze upon the beckoning granite massif.

"There they await," he observes of the no longer distant Sierra Nevada. Axe takes a deep breath. "Well then. Are you ready, Old Girl? Ready to take on those mountains?"

"As ready as can be," replies Katie, as she gazes upon the Sierra. "Ready for one more state."

17
ONE MORE STATE

Already, the Lanes have been introduced to the wonders of the western forests, inspired by ponderosa pines and stands of even loftier Douglas fir. But now, as they ascend into the Sierra Nevada, there comes into the mix another towering species, a good number having avoided the lumbermen's tools.

"Will you look at the size of the pinecones, Axe. Over a foot long, if not two."

"Spectacular. We should collect a few and take them home."

"The sweet scent," enjoys Katie. "And have you ever seen a more vivid aqua?"

"That color was defined by these pines."

The forest rises and then disappears altogether into the mountain mists, the peaks of the Sierra shrouded in mystery for at least the time being. Yet the road beneath the Speed Six appears to be doing much the same, as it begins to diverge from the Southern Pacific and the Truckee Valley. Indeed, the Lanes' route contains a troubling incline—much sharper than the railroad's grade.

Be that as it may, the wheezing Speed Six pushes stubbornly, while Axe guides it through some petrous miles, eventually penetrating the haze.

"I wonder if this is rare?" he poses. "Fog on the eastern slope, the desert side?"

"It's not all that soupy, Axe," counters Katie. "Not like Ohio's."

"It still strikes me as odd. I hope we don't miss that fork."

The engine skips a beat, only to follow with a succession of sputters, a clear indication that it's losing its flow of fuel. The Lanes have no choice, that in order to defeat further inclines, they need to top the tank.

"We'll be quick, Old Girl."

With the engine idling, Axe unbinds a gasoline can, while Katie wanders off in search of fallen pinecones.

Minutes later, the tank is filled. And upon securing the can, Axe looks about for his wife.

"Katie?" He's spotted an approaching figure, who evokes confusion. "You're not Katie."

Certainly, she is a young lady, this stranger who has managed to sidle her way into Axe's midst—through the mists. Her sunny, curled hair dangles unbound and her eyes glisten in a crystalline blue, with her nearly six-feet, barefooted frame covered by a white linen, lace trim dress. And she stands silently with her arms at her side, gazing softy—not so much at Axe, but as if straight through him. Ever so calmly, the young lady curves the slightest of smiles and then raises a portion of her brow.

"You're not Katie," repeats Axe of the obvious.

A pause ensues, made brief by an apparent need to clarify.

"No," responds the young lady at just above a whisper. "My name is Califia. And this is my home." With her hand, she gestures off to her left.

Through a patch of mist, Axe discerns the outline of a structure—modest in size and possibly of a pin-neat, board and batten construction.

"Oh, I see," he acknowledges.

Yet Califia offers a further surprise, she glancing over a shoulder. "And here are my sisters."

Indeed, from behind a sugar pine, two young ladies of linen dress and flowing hair emerge.

"Oh, I see. Uh-h-h?" stumbles Axe, although he manages a recovery. "Allow me to introduce myself. Axelrod Lane. Please call me Axe."

"I'm delighted, Axe," returns Califia, whose charming demeanor shows the pearliness of her perfect teeth.

As for her sisters, they cover their lips with their soft hands, as if muffling their coy giggles.

Were it not for gentlemanly constraints, Axe might titter himself. Still, there's no harm for genial repartee.

"My, Califia. What pleasant surroundings for you and your sisters," espouses Axe, who breathes deeply. "Intoxicating." But then Axe gathers himself and reaches for another glimpse of the environs. "Hmm? It is surprising there aren't others who have settled here."

Califia's immediate response is but a short shrug, though she does follow with an enduringly subtle look of bewilderment. "My sisters and I have thought the same. Though we are rather new to these mountains."

"Oh. I see."

The sisters giggle on, while not abandoning their sugar pine.

"Hmm? What a fine vehicle, Axe," admires Califia. "We don't often see such in the Sierra." She tilts her head and twirls at a lock. "Nor of your sort, I'm obliged to say."

"Yes. It is a very fine auto. Thank you," responds Axe. "Uh-h-h? The Loban Motor of Ohio, '08 Speed Six roadster. Using vanadium steel and the most advanced innovations of engineering designs. Uh-h-h?"

"How remarkable," continues Califia. "What means it must take to own this splendid auto."

"Means? Yes, I do have resources," confesses Axe.

"And you must be terribly clever," comes Califia's conclusion. "This I can tell."

With all modesty—false or otherwise—Axe smiles and gestures with his hands. But as he continues looking upon Califia, he notices a not so slight change to her facial expression, as if her mood is being deflated somewhat. Suddenly, a well-defined interruption to the current pleasantries is forcing itself, this coming in the form of several taps to Axe's puffed-up shoulders.

"Oh?" He recognizes the hand in question. "Katie."

"Axe. Might you introduce me to your friends." Her terms are persuasive.

"Yes." Axe turns to the Sierra Nevadans. "Califia. Ladies. Allow me to introduce my wife. Mrs. Lane."

"Please to meet you." She moves to her husband's side, wrapping one arm around her prized possession. "Call me Katie."

"Oh." It seems Califia may be caught unprepared. "What a pretty name."

"Thank you, Califia." Yet before an awkward interval gains ground, Katie pushes it aside. "Axe, have you asked these ladies if we are on the road to California?"

"Oh, but you are in California, Katie. Axe," informs Califia. "And have been for several miles."

"I see," responds Katie, who isn't surprised. "So my husband and I are on our way to San Francisco?"

"For certain, you are," affirms Califia.

"Such a comfort," replies Katie. "And the road is safe?"

"As safe as a cradled babe," assures Califia even further. "Though you must be mindful of the next fork in the road. Just beyond where it swerves around the double-humped rock."

"Please, tell us more."

"There's hardly more to tell, Katie. Except that you and Axe need only to favor the right fork. The first northerly road beyond the rock. Favor the right and your way through the Sierra will be true and peaceful."

"Hmm? And to think we were considering the left fork," confesses Axe. "Why, Califia, you and your sisters may have saved us considerable hardship. We are grateful."

The pleasantries might continue. However, because Katie has her pinecones, there's little excuse to dally.

"You must pardon us. My husband and I are in a hurry," she explains. "We really must be off."

Wisely, Axe offers no resistance. "Yes, we have a schedule."

Soon, Axe takes the wheel and the Lanes wave to a collected Califia and her sisters.

"Those California girls sure are alluring," mentions Katie, when the subjects are no longer in sight. "I believe I may have seen Califia's likeness on a bottle of hair curl elixir."

"Imagine that," comes the cautious response. "I suppose they are alluring." But then Axe considers further. "It is rather strange. The circumstances of our encounter."

"But I wonder more, Axe. Of how those sisters manage to support themselves?"

Axe glances at Katie's impeaching face. "For goodness sake," he counters, as he shakes his disapproving head. "We're not in Springfield or Salt Lake City. Or Wonder, for that matter. The conduct of those young ladies was unforward at the most. You saw them."

"I'll give you that, Axe. Still-l-l."

"Still?"

"Axe, just how do they support themselves? Miles from Verdi?"

"Why, their parents, of course. Who are busy elsewhere. Busy earning wages. Somewhere."

"That may be true, Axe. Though, I wonder."

As if on cue, Axe catches view of a promised crag. "Look, Katie. The double-humped rock."

The Speed Six plods along, while the Lanes discover that, indeed, the road does seem to swerve around said landmark. Meanwhile, as they draw nearer, the still air gains a little huff, meaning that the Sierra is losing some of its misty cloak.

Smooth and curvy is the mass of posed granite, almost as if figured by an inspired sculptor. And it appears to be casting a shadow upon the road. With the path beginning to loop around the massive rock, Axe slows the Speed Six, thus allowing for prolonged gazes.

"It must be forty feet," estimates Katie. "As smooth as polished marble. Or perhaps a gentle maiden's skin."

"Yes," agrees Axe. "Polished marble."

The couple enter into the shadow and its temporary darkness, only to emerge within seconds to the glaring sun. But the Lanes' eyes adjust quickly and are able to gather their impressions of the other side.

"Hmm? Now that's interesting," notes Katie of her discovery, that this work of natural artistry is only half-complete. It seems that the opposite side of the double-humped rock is rough and jagged, common and dilettantish, and falls well short of inspiring. "That is to say, uninteresting," she corrects of herself.

Katie's criticism is enough of a signal for Axe to give the throttle a nudge. But no sooner does the roadster finish the swerve then it comes face to face with that anticipated fork in the road.

"Stop, Axe. Stop here." Katie's firm tone conveys her doubts. "Look at the map. Once more."

This Axe does, for he, too, carries a doubt. "Here we are," he notes with a finger on the map. "Hmm? Califia did say the right fork? To the north?"

"She did, Axe."

"But the U.S.G.S. says otherwise. As do my Verdi pencilings. This is strange."

"Yes, it is." Katie stands up and looks down upon the fork and the roads beyond. "The right seems to be less-traveled, which makes little sense."

"No sense at all, Katie. I wonder if Califia was mistaken?"

"Mistaken? Perhaps." Katie's words are careful.

"Very well." Axe acquiesces—a bit. "We'll follow the left fork for a mile or two and see what happens."

Thus satisfied, Katie regains her seat. "Slowly now. With every caution."

As the couple proceed, they find the surface of the road to be drivable if not somewhat safe. After a mile, the Lanes even become comfortable with their choice, though they remain perplexed with their directions.

"Califia said the right fork?" scratches Axe. "The north road?"

"Yes. I'm certain. And so are you."

Stopping the roadster at an open space, Axe looks off to his right at a steep, narrow canyon. "That north road should be in that direction. Like on the map."

"Yes. Over there, across the canyon," points Katie. "Hmm? I think I see something. A road?" She focuses further and in a blink is able to spy something strange. "I'm not sure, but it seems as if it comes to an end." And then a shock surges into Katie. "Oh, my God! A precipitous end!"

"Where! Where!"

"There! There!"

Instantly, Axe is able to spot his wife's discovery. He turns to Katie and matches her astounded face.

"You don't suppose?" The words draw slowly from Axe's mouth. "That they-y-y?"

With her wide eyes and open mouth, Katie nods at what may lie unseen at the canyon floor.

The couple freeze in place, gazing at one another and allowing a genuine possibility to sink.

"What should we do?" poses Axe after a partial thaw.

But Katie remains frozen.

Although there are plausible actions a responsible man could take, the strange circumstances force a dilemma upon Axe's flooded head. And so the inconvenience of indecision threatens.

"Shall we move on?" suggests Axe. Right or wrong, any decision bests vacillation. "And not look back?"

"Yes," insists Katie, who, nonetheless, can't help but cast an eye over her shoulder.

For the next couple of miles, the Lanes have little trouble fleeing the scene, the road being accommodating for such purposes. But then, not so subtly, its grade alters toward the more sheer, which in turn leads to a troublesome complication. Ominously, the roadster's engine begins to sputter, the obvious cause being gravity and its powers over the badly-situated fuel tank.

"Axe. Don't tell me the road is too steep."

The incline rises another two degrees, thus stopping the flow of gasoline and killing the engine altogether.

"What are we to do, Axe?"

"The tank is practically full. A few ounces of gasoline won't make a difference."

"Axe!"

"We'll coast down to a level spot."

Thus Axe rolls in reverse the roadster, setting the handbrake when he finds a favorable patch of road.

"Axe, do you think we can make the climb?"

Certainly, the Lanes are in no mood to reverse course and find another route across the Sierra with all the inherent delays. But more so, they dread another encounter with a sinister Califia and her sisters.

"Is there another way?" Katie's question comes as a plea.

Indeed, her entreaty forces Axe to pause and dig into his treasury of resourceful engineering. Then the idea strikes him, he leaping from his seat to take hold of the crank.

"By God, I do have a way, Old Girl!" proclaims Axe. "And a simple solution at that!"

When the engine kicks over, Axe returns to the driver's seat. This time, however, in a series of reverses and forwards, hard lefts and harder rights, he guides the roadster into a position so that it faces the direction from whence it came. Yet instead of looking toward the front of the vehicle, Axe turns around to the rear.

"If we have to reverse our way through the Sierras, then so be it," he declares.

"So be it," approves an eager Katie, to which she shifts herself rearward upon her knees.

And so the Lanes resume their ascent—slowly and not so surely—though now with the fuel tank leading the way via its elevated position. But at least the couple are moving forward, so to speak, not only putting some distance between themselves and Califia, but inching their way to their Pacific rendezvous, as well.

The Lanes have set a cautious, beaconless campsite, meaning that without a fire their night proves chilly. So stirs their morning, as they huddle beneath their blankets.

"I'll gather some wood and build a fire for breakfast?"

"Why trouble yourself, Axe? I would rather be on our way."

"Yes. Better to spend the effort starting our frigid roadster."

"Will that be a problem, Axe?"

"Probably. Though not insurmountable."

Having not made a proper camp, the Lanes pack for the road in swift order. Soon, Axe forces the crank, repeatedly, resulting in a few, non-lasting sparks. The work is draining, with the need to take a break.

"California is a beautiful, alluring state," notes Katie, as she stands behind her husband and kneads his shoulders. "Oh, but what really occurs beneath its charms? This Cloud Cuckooland?"

"Umm"

"Remember stark Wyoming?" continues Katie with her rub and thesis. "Yet how wonderful its people?"

"Of course," agrees Axe.

"I would even say that Manhattan was a stark place in its own way. Yet how warm were most of its citizens. And the people of Nebraska, Iowa and Indiana were very sweet."

"What of Utah?"

"Oh, Axe. The people of Utah were kind to us. It was their authorities who ran us afoul."

"Amen to that. But what is your point, Katie?"

"Well, Axe. I have this feeling about California. That there may be too much Springfield in this state."

Axe clinches his shoulders, while Katie ceases her rub.

"I can't argue with your beliefs," he accedes. "Perhaps we should regard California like we would Springfield. Keep our contacts brief."

Katie resumes her massage. "That makes sense. Utter sense."

Following another round of cranking, the engine gathers a cough, with Axe controlling the sparks into sustained wheezes. Soon, there's enough power to regain the road, so that, once again, the Lanes back their way through the Sierra, or spin to forward whenever the inclines alter.

Out of view to the south, the tracks of the Southern Pacific and its Truckee Valley grade forge onward. But where the river takes a loop elsewhere, the railroad must continue a westerly direction by its own devices. In a way, so, too, do the Lanes, albeit without a payroll's worth of mechanics and supply staff.

Somewhere, north of Soda Springs, the Lanes end their day of travel, never mind that there remain a few hours of sunlight. But driving vice versa and vis-a-vis can be a tiring business on both man and machine. Still, there is no rest, when the late afternoon finds Katie cleaning spark plugs and carburetor and Axe under the jacked-up left rear end changing a spring.

"God help us if we break another," he warns of the depleted stock.

Yet the mechanics wage on, patching the Speed Six so that it might motor for another day.

It takes a while for the eastern sun to peek over the Sierra's peaks. Yet at first ray, the Lanes are quick to roust themselves, doing the same for the Speed Six, shortly thereafter.

"I sure hope we have a telegram at Soda Springs," reminds Katie after a few curvy miles. "Lisbon needs to know of our progress, and we of them."

As luck would have it, Soda Springs holds a positive message from Loban Motor, and enables the Lanes to send a return in kind. Also, there are the telegraph operator's encouraging words, that by reaching Soda Springs by way of Donner Pass, the worst of the Sierra Nevada is behind them. When the couple resume their trek, the feeling is that the tired reverse pedal can be put to rest, that they've found the western slope.

Yet what the Lanes learn shortly, is that the Sierra is not finished with them, as it continues to heap abuse. Although the inclines favor a forward movement, only the first gear is needed for the surface conditions and its snail's pace demands. Indeed, along some stretches the Lanes are compelled to dismount and rearrange the crude road.

"That should do it," figures Axe, after he and Katie fill a portion of a rockslide into a growing pothole.

As exhausted the couple may be, at least they can draw inspiration from the promise of a Dutch Flat telegraph office—only thirty miles west of Soda Springs, though likely hours upon agonizing hours away.

By discernable increments, however, the Lanes discover a more merciful road surface, accompanied by somewhat cooperative mountainsides. And so they're able to dodge between darts and flit around minor obstacles, making good time and accumulating mileage.

"Careful, Axe," warns Katie of an impending hazard: a blind curve around a steep outcropping.

He throttles down accordingly, for although the traffic has been remarkably sparse, one never knows.

Screech! grind the sudden brakes, with the roadster avoiding a catastrophe.

"Oh, my God, Axe," exclaims Katie. "Will you look at that!"

"Uh. What a lulu. I thought we were done with this."

It seems that the Sierra massif has lost some of its grip, the result being an impossible/impassable rockslide, the mountain debris making up the lack of accumulated volume with individual size. Boulders three they are, each one too large to be manhandled and each one positioned in the middle of the narrow, precipitous road. But as the Lanes leave the roadster for a more immediate look, they're confronted by the inconvenient fact that the pulley's rope is lengthy enough to stir vehicular weight and not masses of granite.

"Perhaps we can forge a path through the forest." Axe hopes for the best. "With some luck."

"Oh, Axe," moans Katie, all whipped and subdued.

Yet the Lanes have no real alternative, and after mustering a portion of resolve from ruinous defeat, they strike out on foot in hopes of blazing a trail for the Speed Six.

"Perhaps we should go this way," suggests Katie, when, soon, the going becomes too rugged. "Or that way. Or-r-r." Her head stops panning. "Axe, is that a tarpaulin?"

Cautiously, they stumble toward the shelter, and upon hearing the unexpected bray of a mule, slow their advance even more.

"I wonder, should we impose ourselves?" whispers Katie. Indeed, the memory of Califia retains its sting.

"Why not?" replies Axe, who carries a certain resistance. "They own a mule, for pity's sake."

Yet before the Lanes step further, the clicks of manipulated metal break through the whirrs of the pines.

"Stop right there!" greet the words of a threat. "One more step and I'll blast away!"

Immediately, Katie becomes petrified and so accedes to the demand.

And then there's Axe, whose dulled, confronted senses recall the working sounds of a lever action rifle—the reason behind his buckling knees. But it can't be helped, that in order to save himself from a tumble, he takes an instinctive step forward.

Crack! as the sound of a rifle's shot and the bullet's impact occur within the same instant. From above, sylvan fragments cascade upon the innocents, with the pines deferring their whirrs for the blast's echoes. While Katie trembles, Axe flinches, although to his credit he feels behind and forms shield.

Perhaps this is a gesture-received, for a better, second shot is slow in coming—if at all.

"Who are you!" arrives the question after a brief, but boundless, pause.

"Don't shoot!" begs Axe's shaky voice, he realizing that a reach for his revolver could be a tragic mistake. "We mean no harm!"

"Who are you!" repeats the unseen shooter, who may be growing impatient.

"Axelrod Lane! Along with my wife!"

"Your wife?" The shooter resumes his shout. "State your business."

Yet it is a hopeful sign, that the Lanes are being allowed to explain themselves.

"My name is Axelrod Lane! We are autoists, crossing the country to promote our roadster! A rockslide has barred our way!"

There's no prompt reply, only the faint sounds of footsteps scuffling upon the rocky ground.

Meanwhile, Katie's grips on Axe's arms become a tourniquet.

But then a figure is glimpsed, a man who appears to be concealing his approach behind the trunks of the forest. That he wields a rifle is no surprise, though it is a comfort to see the weapon pointed skyward.

"We mean no harm!" pleads Axe. "Let me assure you! We're from Ohio!"

Before Axe and Katie can realize, a slouch hat and its perch peer from around a sugar pine.

"We really do mean no harm," chorus the couple.

The man with the Winchester reveals a little more of himself, staring at the Lanes as if sizing up the pair. Slowly, he abandons more of his cover, until he's almost as exposed as the Ohioans.

"You're not a shadow for the S.P., are you, Axelrod Lane?"

"I beg your pardon."

"A hired gun for the railroad? A Southern Pacific detective?"

Astonished, Axe looks back at Katie and then turns toward his inquisitor. "I'm nothing of the sort. Like I said, my interests are purely automotive. I design and test automobiles."

"And I teach music," confesses Katie, as she pokes her head from behind her husband.

"The railroads are a Frankenstein to the public," furthers Axe in all earnest, while he flutters the blood back into his hands. "How often do you read of death and injury from train collisions? But automobiles are a perfection for civilization. The chances for injury being remote."

In response, the shooter nods approvingly and offers a further friendly gesture by re-posturing the buttstock of his Winchester upon his shoulder, thus pointing the barrel downward. Now, the shooter's face and stance show the humbled signs of embarrassment.

"Please accept my apologies, Axelrod Lane. And you especially, Mrs. Lane."

"Oh?" sound the couple, now arm in arm and looking to one another. "Think nothing of it."

The shooter takes a final few steps forward and extends a hand. "Henry Patrick. A rockslide, huh? Barring the way of two passionate autoists? Perhaps I may be of service."

What a span of emotions forced upon the Lanes—from sudden terror to utter relief, all within a matter of minutes. And so, after gathering themselves,

Axe and Katie lead the way to the roadster. But while the Lanes must struggle to retrace their route through the unaccommodating terrain, Henry Patrick takes his steps with seasoned agility. Thus, as Katie and Axe pant, their "captor" is able to prattle.

"…I know you must think it odd, my suspicions for the S.P. But here in California, they are the power. Ruthless and cunning in their control of politics and enterprise."

He's a man of about Axe's age, Patrick, although somewhat taller and bearded, and dressed much like a Canadian lumberjack. And the more he talks, the friendlier becomes his tone, as if the flood of his words is his pleasure—never mind the seriousness of the topic.

"How fortunate for Ohio not to suffer the slings and arrows of outrageous Southern Pacific."

Although Katie and Axe are familiar with a bulging roster of Ohio outrages, they choose not to mention.

"Why, their paths of lies and corruption," continues Patrick. "I could recite endlessly."

This he does—up to the point of a pervasive harangue. Yet it seems that the unbridled zeal of Henry Patrick may have a pause. While he trails up a particularly steep grade, the Lanes find a bit of level ground.

"Might I ask, Mr. Patrick," inquires Katie. "What do you do for a living?"

The reply takes a moment for Patrick to reach the Lanes. "I'm a mining engineer. Between contracts. Born, raised and educated in the state of California." Patrick's assertion comes as if he's a rare bird.

"Oh? An engineer?" mentions Axe.

"Thorp College of Technology," responds Patrick.

"Ohio State, myself."

"Ohio Wesleyan."

The trek is resumed and, shortly thereafter, reaches the roadster.

"A fairly impressive rockslide, I would say," assesses Patrick. "Not so much in mass, but placement." But then he spots another element of the landscape. "Nice automobile, you have."

It's a shrugging moment for the Lanes, who decline to hawk the virtues of the Speed Six.

"Yes, I see what you mean," notes Patrick, when he returns to the rockslide. "These boulders." He approaches said pieces, and in silence gives each one a close scrutiny.

Meanwhile, the Lanes watch with curiosity.

Several times Patrick nods vigorously, as he eyes and caresses the boulders from different angles. And then he steps back, still gazing upon the three obstacles and removing his hat to scratch his head.

"Hmm?" considers Patrick. He looks to the Lanes and offers a smile. "I believe I can do it."

"I beg your pardon?

"Wait right here." And without explanation, Patrick rushes back to his camp.

For the next twenty minutes, the Lanes are left to ponder their fix, only to be stopped by approaching brays.

"Katie. Look. He's returning with his packed mule. And he's carrying a knapsack."

"Just what does our Goo-goo have in mind?"

Soon, after tying the mule's lead to a wheel of the roadster and producing a spade and pickax, Patrick approaches the rockslide. He selects the largest boulder, drops to his knees and begins a sharp excavation. And happy Patrick seems to be in his work, like any honest engineer tackling a conundrum of physical laws.

As for the Lanes, they stand in awe—and confusion—watching insignificant tools vie against objects of impressively dead weight.

"What does he have in mind?" whispers Katie.

"Who can say?"

Yet when Patrick is done with two, opposing digs for each boulder, he doesn't stand back to admire his handiwork. Instead, he rummages through his knapsack, locating several elongated cylinders.

"Dynamite?" recognizes Axe of a trade tool.

With the tedium of a tatter, Patrick binds a bundle, while he revives his anti-railroad sentiments: rate-fixing schemes, warehouse monopolies, government subsidies, etc. Before long, however, he's pieced together three neat clusters of dynamite sticks and is ready to proceed to the next, crucial step.

"...And what sections of the waterfront they don't control have been freed by sheer force..."

Patrick reaches into a coat pocket and pulls out a loop of fuse cord. And from another he produces three elongated blasting caps, along with a smoking pipe and tobacco pouch. But then Patrick turns toward the Lanes with his sage expression.

"Perhaps you might take your roadster and my mule to a safe distance."The mining engineer continues to search his pockets. "Where did I put my crimp?"

Realizing the impending gravity of the situation, Axe grasps Katie's hand and moves toward the roadster. In no time he has the engine started and she has the Speed Six backing away from the rockslide. As for the mule, because it must have witnessed past explosive preparations, it gives Axe no trouble.

With the roadster at the safe side of the outcropping, Katie kills the engine. "Where do you think you're going?" she asks, when Axe retraces his steps.

"To see if Patrick needs any help. Stay here."

"You be careful, Axe," warns Katie. "I mean it."

Returning to the scene of the boulders, Axe finds a still busy Patrick. Apparently, he hasn't located his crimp and is using the wedged surfaces of his teeth to fasten fuse to blasting cap. To say the least, the act of compressing fulminate of mercury within its copper tube brings a cringe to Axe's knowledge of unstable compounds. But then Patrick eases his bite and appears satisfied, thus erasing visions of a maimed mouth.

"We sure appreciate this. How disastrous to have searched for a new route."

"Think nothing of it," responds Patrick. "My pleasure."

Already, two of the charges have been squeezed and packed beneath their boulders, with their exposed fuses ready to be lit. It's into this third bundle of dynamite which Patrick inserts his blasting cap.

Soon, the last bundle meets its burrow, to which Patrick celebrates by stuffing and lighting his pipe.

"Will it work?" wonders Axe.

Patrick takes a long draft. "Oh, it should stir the boulders" he spews. "As for the damage to the road?"

Meanwhile, Katie sits and fidgets, and stares at the curving road ahead.

"Fire in the hole!" echoes an unseen warning.

A jolt is sent through Katie, this heightened when she spies her frantic husband racing around the bend. But then there follows Patrick, who although walks briskly, walks nonetheless.

"Cover your ears," shouts the mining engineer, as he makes the gesture.

To which Katie complies, as does Axe, when he joins her side.

Boom! accompanied by a nearly simultaneous boom! This trailed quickly by a third boom! Patrick's timing is almost flawless.

The Lanes shutter, only to be dazzled by the resonant claps bouncing off the mountain slopes and the secondary sounds of falling and frolicking rubble. Then there arrives the creeping cloud of Sierra dust.

"Well now, that sounds successful," remarks Patrick, clinching his teeth around his pipe and clad with his knapsack arsenal. "Let's see the damage."

Unmindful of the blinding dust, Patrick rushes into it, eager to assess his artistry.

And so proceed Axe and Katie, although with more caution and with their goggles and handkerchiefs in place. Yet to their amazement, they discover that the particles of granite and road residue are settling quickly. Dropping curtain aside, what has become of the boulders?

"By God, I think I did it," blasts Patrick's announcement.

Indeed, as the Lanes come upon the stage, they can see that two of the problem boulders have been coerced unseen down their fluted channels, while the third, more stubborn rock has been nudged aside to the point where it is not a bother. Were it not for the damage to the road, the Lanes could be on their way.

"My apologies for the craters," assumes Patrick.

"Mere chuckholes," insists Axe. "We've become accustomed to repairing the Sierras' roads."

Together, the three stroll about, their heads looking down at both the damage and the handiwork. And as they do so, they kick and flick at the rocks, thus beginning the process of filling the substantial potholes. But it seems the longer they loiter, the more anxious Patrick becomes. Soon, he can tarry no more.

"My apologies. I'm afraid I must leave you to it," reveals Patrick. "I really should be off."

"Oh?" responds Katie.

"Yes. Too often, the wrong sort of people are drawn to my detonations."

"Oh dear."

"Don't be afraid, Mrs. Lane. The wrong sort for the likes of me, but not the two of you."

"We understand," acknowledges Axe. "We think."

With that, the three return to the roadster and the mule.

"Mr. Patrick. Won't you have something to eat?" invites Katie. "It's the least we can do. I can be quick."

"Oh, no. Thank you," declines Patrick, as he unties his mule. "I really must rush."

"Then how about a parting drink?" offers a prompt Axe, who locates a bottle of gin.

"Oh, no thanks." Again, Patrick declines, as he leads away his pack animal. "I never partake."

"Well, I hope you don't mind if we do." Axe pours into a couple of cups as produced by a thrifty Katie. "We'll drink to your health and future prosperity."

"Yes. Thank you, Mr. Patrick," rings Katie.

The man in question looks back and salutes with his hat. "Once again! My apologies!" To which Patrick slips away from the road to descend into trails and forests unknown.

"Yes. Strange is our Goo-goo, and yet a reasonable man," remarks Katie. "Such a contrast."

"Certainly, a contrast," agrees Axe. "When the same man who threatened us became indispensable. Just how are we to take that?"

Together, the couple shrug.

"What do you say, Old Girl? That we fill in those craters and be out of here?"

"Yes, of course. The sooner, the better."

Bit by bit, the Lanes render the road passable and so are able to meander the Speed Six through the remnants of the rockslide. Remarkably, the next dozen or more miles prove to be somewhat a cinch—free of boulders and mostly downhill. Even the engine eases its hacks and coughs, with the frame feeling a little less duress. Soon, the Lanes reach Emigrant Gap, a vast, breathtaking landmark where the traveler is assured of his victory over the Sierra Nevada. Indeed, the view is of all California and its horizons: golden hills and ranches, verdant farms and towns, rivers and bays, and perhaps an ocean or two. For the first time in what seems to be a succession of ages, Katie and Axe let out genuine sighs of relief.

Upon entering Dutch Flat, the Lanes locate the telegraph office. Yet because it is a late Sunday afternoon, the Lanes must seek the proprietor at his home and implore him to open for business. Thankfully, Mr. Sykes obliges, and delivers the message from Lisbon.

"Freddy wants us to attend a reception in Sacramento," reads Axe. "With their governor." He looks at Katie and follows the steady shakes of her adamant head. "I agree. We should skirt Sacramento. Avoid the audacities of California politics."

Her response is to alter her head to repeated nods.

Axe reads a few more of Freddy's empty pleas, all the while making farcical facial expressions for the sake of Katie's amusement. "Oh, no." He's come to the end of the telegram.

"What is it?"

"He's misplaced the key to our house. Though Jimmy has found a way through a basement window."

"Oh, dear."

"Well then? What should be our reply, Katie? Freddy is keeping touch with the Lobans."

"Well-l-l, confirm that we will be at Point Lobos. Noontime. Wednesday, the Sixth. But say no to Sacramento. And assure him we have not joined the Goo-goos, as he hints. And tell him to find that key!"

Upon paying the bill, the Lanes hurry to their roadster, which is parked in front of the post office.

"Can you imagine where we would be without Henry Patrick," comments Axe, as he grasps the crank.

"Not at Point Lobos on Wednesday," figures Katie, as she finds the driver's seat. Meanwhile, her eyes catch sight of something peculiar—or perhaps the topic at hand. "Axe, over there. The poster on the wall."

"What?" is his response to Katie's sudden fixation.

Upon liberating her ink bottle and pen, she rushes toward the wanted poster.

"Katie?" While she sketches upon the likeness of what must be a hardened character, Axe positions behind to read the accusation. "Wanted. Janwar Farquharson. For willful destruction of railroad property by means of explosives and for threats delivered upon the Los Angeles Times."

Katie's art is swift, yet full, and fairly realistic, as she applies a beard to Farquharson's face.

"Alias Justice Plateau," continues Axe. "Thetford Paine, Dick Humboldt and Jim Montrose." But then the crux of Katie's keen eyes registers, as does a Sierra of situational evidence. "Oh my God," voices Axe, while containing himself. "I believe you should add 'Henry Patrick' to that list. Can you believe it?"

"Yes, I can," answers Katie, while adding the last few whiskers. "I've learned to accept the unexpected."

"Now I know why I felt a certain kinship with Patrick?" reasons Axe. "The Times, of course. It seems we share an outright disgust for rags of that name. Hmm? Should I tear it loose for a keepsake?"

"Hmm?"

Downward continue the Lanes, this after camping near Gold Run, their night serenaded by unseen, Southern Pacific trains. And it's through the Mother Lode that now they guide the Speed Six, their backs washed by a convenient sun. But where once the western, pine slopes of the Sierra Nevada and the eastern, oak uplands of the Sacramento Valley were populated by transient Argonauts, lately the land is overwhelmed by those who seek permanency. Indeed, although the fortunes of precious metals have been scooped away, the fertility of the valley soils remain. By the time Katie and Axe reach Auburn, the distant geometries of intense agriculture are recognizable.

This is a foothills town, as the Lanes discover. But Auburn is also a place of prosperity, made plain by the architecture of its institutions and establishments.

"I believe we've stumbled upon Italy, Axe. Some centuries ago."

"So I see." With Katie behind the wheel, Axe can observe and unlock. "Where do they find the means? Blame the railroads, I suppose. The trains gather here and spread the wealth."

"Careful, Axe," warns Katie's sarcasm. "Extolling the virtues of the S.P? Alias Henry Patrick may hear."

To say the least, the conditions become vastly more favorable, with the roads guiding resolutely toward Sacramento. But when eventually the Lanes reach the dairy lands of Roseville, the moment arrives to veer south. And upon finding the strawberry fields and vineyards of Florin a couple of hours later, Axe and Katie avoid the speculated hazards of Sacramento's cadaverous governmental altogether. Indeed, the travel is sublime, the plumes of dust left behind the cruising Speed Six as opposed to choking the Ohioans.

"Look. More of Japan's people," notes Katie, as they pass through another community of busy agriculturalists and entrepreneurs. "I wonder why the Okyos didn't settle here?"

"Oh? Don't you know?" replies Axe, as he drives. "They're pioneers. Like us."

"Of course. How ridiculous of me."

The roads lead to Elk Grove and beyond. And when at last they reach the flat, maturing vineyards of Lodi, the hardships and confusions of the Sierra Nevada have eased out of view. Yet sooner or later, the Lanes will have to take a hard right turn, and thus head toward an iffy appointment with an impeached master and his agitated wife—this within the environs of a wrecked city.

By late afternoon the Lanes lumber into Stockton, stopping altogether when they find Hunter Plaza and its massively proportioned San Joaquin County courthouse.

"Are you sure we're not in Sacramento, Axe? This isn't their capitol?"

"One for the centuries," his gaze concludes. "It should last as long."

"I should hope," agrees Katie. "Just how many bushels of grapes and walnuts did they sell to build that titan?"

Onward they proceed—slowly and cautiously upon bustling Main Street.

"What is it?" poses Katie, when Axe brings the roadster to a sudden stop. "Is something wrong?"

"That store window. That dress," he insists. "Katie, I'm going to buy you that dress."

"Oh, Axe," she spies and then purrs. "Oh, Axe, it's wonderful."

Soon, a proud Axe escorts Katie out of the store, they toting under arms the boxes of her white chiffon, taffeta, jumper suit with pink floral embroidery and an accenting mushroom-shaped, street hat of Japanese braid and silk. But as well, they carry with them the directions to the Jackson Baths, an affordably elegant, mineral resort and its overnight, curative accommodations.

"Well, Katie, shall we? Mrs. Heard said the baths are only a few blocks away. We can't miss it."

"If you like," she responds, as she finds her seat. "Though I would hate to waste the daylight. Shouldn't we push ourselves closer to San Francisco? Besides, I think this dress is enough indulgence for one day."

Shortly, the Lanes find a bridge and cross the San Joaquin River just upstream from Stockton's crowded, little port. But when the road retouches solid ground, it drops a few feet in elevation and leads into yet another sharp contrast to the couple's journey.

"I didn't expect this," notes Katie after a mile or so. "Riverboats and now marshes? Dikes and ditches?" She points ahead at an embanked field of perfectly cropped grass. "And just what is happening there?"

Quite unexpectedly, Katie and Axe have ventured into the San Joaquin delta: a flat, sunken region of reclamation schemes and well-watered agriculture, and of acres of harvested rice for those natives of Japan.

"I've never seen a hayfield like that," comes Axe's reply.

Upon the westerly road, the Lanes follow the sinking sun. By the time this beacon settles upon the pedestal of a distant Mount Diablo of the Coastal Range, they've traversed the delta, their elevated path leading to the cornered community of Byron.

"It's as good a place as any," suggests Katie of a vacant lot adjacent to the post office.

And so the night of August, 4th is spent in sleepy, little Byron, where no one seems to be bothered and where only a few give notice.

The crack of dawn means a return to the road. As to the best route around

Mount Diablo, the Lanes have been told to veer northward upon Marsh Creek Road and into the hilly ranchlands of Contra Costa County.

"How far did we travel yesterday, Axe?"

"More than a hundred," he figures. "Quite an accomplishment."

"For certain. But how many miles to San Francisco?"

"Considerably less."

"Of course. But I wonder how much has been rebuilt?"

"That remains to be seen, Katie. Though they've had time to rebuild, there should still be considerable destruction. Earthquake and fire."

"So the chance of a hotel room is not likely?"

"Yes. Though we could stay in Oakland. Cross the bay Wednesday morning."

"Oh, that doesn't matter, Axe. I was only thinking of Mr. and Mrs. Loban. One can't expect them to be as handy as we. They'll need accommodations."

"Mr. Loban, especially. God only knows."

The road becomes less sure, as it picks up its namesake stream and rolling valley, both appearing to originate from Mount Diablo. Yet while Axe and Katie concentrate on sharp turns, occasionally they're afforded smoother stretches, thus allowing them to fix their attentions upon the pinnacles.

They're not the grandest, Mount Diablo and its associated peaks, as seen from the relative safety of oak savannahs. But because they arise from out of nowhere, they're a force to be circumvented, thus providing a source of fascination.

"Katie, I'm coming to the conclusion that we're circling California's pivot. It balancing the extremes of Sierra Nevadas and Pacific."

"Don't forget valley farms on one side and big cities on the other," adds Katie.

"Precisely."

"Mount Diablo? I wonder, Axe, if this is where their earthquakes are born? Hence, the name?"

"The devil you say? Makes sense to me."

The valley alters into a more rugged canyon, as the Lanes graze the outer reaches of Mount Diablo. But soon, Marsh Creek Road slips away from its stream, thus straightening its resolve. And so where once the couple motored toward Mount Diablo from due east, now they're skirting north of the summit, approaching the town of Clayton.

By first appearances, the burgh offers the feel of decline. When the roadster plies a few of its listless streets, this sense is confirmed, that Clayton is a scene of past prosperity and current readjustment.

"Empty houses? Businesses? In the middle of California?" questions Axe.

"Perhaps the earthquake is to blame?" joins Katie. But then her eyes cast a wider view. "Say, Axe. Look over there, toward the mountain. Could those structures be part of a mine?"

Axe sharpens his vision. "That they are. Though somewhat derelict."

"Then there's the explanation," figures Katie. "The mountain ran out of gold and Clayton lost its means."

"Gold, you say? Katie, remember the coal mines east of Lisbon? Doesn't that seem similar?"

"Coal? Here in California? Are you sure, Axe?"

"No. But then, what is sure about this state?"

"Who can say, I suppose?"

The loop around Mount Diablo continues, altering to a southwesterly direction when the uncomplicated road to Walnut Springs is taken. Unfortunately, not long afterward, a mechanical problem arises, the source being a Speed Six weakness.

"I can't find third," airs Axe, while he struggles with the gear pedal and shift. "Transmission."

"Can we make it, Axe?"

"We'll finish with what gears we have. Hopefully, the other two have a few more miles."

Amidst the San Ramon Valley, the Lanes reacquaint themselves with the tracks of the Southern Pacific, and at Walnut Springs they stop at the railroad's inviting station to acquire information. What they learn is that the city of Oakland and its San Francisco Bay ferries are but twenty miles away, with the Berkeley Hills situated in between. Yet even this barrier shouldn't be a problem, there being the assurances of a convenient road tunnel. Indeed, Katie and Axe need only to find Telegraph Road at the town of Lafayette, and then allow the roadster and its two gears to proceed leisurely.

"Is it wide enough?" comes a legitimate concern, when the Speed Six stops short of the tunnel.

"It should be," replies Axe. Nevertheless, he rushes from the driver's seat to the entrance and steps off the width of the burrow. "There's plenty of room!"

"But Axe! It's so dark! All I can see ahead is a dot of light!"

"I wish we had asked of its length!" Axe returns to Katie's side. "We'll have to spark the headlamps. But it should be safe. Have a little faith."

"Faith is fine. But I prefer absolute confidence," counters Katie. "What if we meet an auto, midway?"

"Hmm?" reconsiders Axe and his faith, both staring down the length of the blackened tunnel and its speck of light. "Katie, take the wheel, while I grab a lantern. I can inspect the tunnel to the opposite end and stop any approaching auto."

"Are you sure, Axe? What if one comes through while you're in the tunnel?"

"Then I suppose I should dash." Axe suppresses any trepidations. "It looks to be under a mile, don't you think? When I get to the other side, I'll shoot the pistol twice. It'll be the safe signal."

"Well-l-l, if you say so, Axe. But only if you run through the tunnel. That will be my faith."

Luckily, and with all caution, the Lanes manage the tunnel situation—minus, two spent cartridges. Profoundly, the going is downhill. Although their views are barred by the landscape, the feeling shared by Axe and Katie is that the perils of crossing the country are done.

And then it happens, when a parting of obstructions offers a fleeting glimpse of Oakland.

"The bay! Axe, I saw the bay! Can you smell it!"

"Mmm." Indeed, Axe can sniff the salt of San Francisco Bay, as carried to the heights above Oakland.

Certainly, a thriving city harbors diversions aplenty. But like iron to magnet, soon, the Lanes are drawn to the Oakland Pier, ignoring the downtown activities and surrounding neighborhoods.

Thus the Speed Six finds itself parked in the middle of a long file of automobiles, teamed wagons and private buggies. Yet in no way is the Lanes' wait for a ferry interminable, especially since they're willing participants to the commerce of a busy port.

"My goodness. I don't think the Hudson had this much hum," observes Katie of the waterway between Oakland and Alameda.

Because this side of San Francisco Bay felt only a token's worth of the '06 earthquake, and suffered none of the succeeding conflagration, it remains open as an exporter of valley goods and a conduit for its sister city's resurrection. Of course, the foremost features of Oakland's waterfront are merchant ships, tugs and barges, and bay sloops, all fed by a confusion of Southern Pacific tracks. But then there are the activities of the go-betweens: teamsters and teams, stevedores, fishermen and nets, storefront tradesmen and sidewalk peddlers, and at least one lunafied Londonite.

"Can you see the bay?" asks Katie, while Axe stands upon his seat. "I wonder how large is our ferry?"

"Sizable, if it's to carry this traffic. And yes. I can see the bay. Portions."

Katie can't resist, and so rises to join Axe. "Where? Where?"

"There. Look. The harbor's other side. Between that steamship and clipper. Beyond Alameda."

"Point my head!" requests Katie.

Calmly, Axe takes the matter in hand. "See? That patch of green?"

"Oh-h-h."

"But look," swivels a gentle Axe. "Down the channel. More green."

"Oh-h-h."

"And there," repositions Axe. "More of the bay."

"Oh-h-h. Oh? Huh? 'ORGANIZE, BROTHERS'?"

It seems that Axe's marksmanship may be off a tad, that he's aimed his wife's sights at precisely the wrong target. And therein lies the problem, this being of eye contact.

"Have you organized, brother and sister!" comes the approaching placard-upon-a-stick and its wild-eyed wielder, by all appearances a novice eager to fill a quota.

Someone needs to be quick with their wits, that is to say Katie and Axe—either or both.

"Organize? Have you ever seen a more orderly line of vehicles in your life?" questions Axe.

"Our Central Direction Authority has done a marvelous chore. Wouldn't you say?" joins Katie.

"Uh-h? You misunderstand," responds the placardist. "What I mean..."

"Yes, we, who fairly represent the masses, take pride in our organizational talents," interrupts Axe, he adopting the wild-eyed pose. "The result being of linear perfection. An inspiration to the masses!"

"Amen, brother!" agrees Katie.

The placardist's weapon of words droops at his side. "Excuse me, but I don't think..."

"We, too, have a placard," asserts Katie, as she points toward the rear of the roadster.

Curiosity has its pull, for the placardist cannot resist. "LOBAN MOTOR

OF OHIO? Coast to Coast?" he reads, appearing to become even more confused.

"Won't you come join us, brother?" invites a forceful Axe. "At the back of the line. Over there."

"Well. I-I-I. I must, uh-h," excuses the placardist, as he sidles away to a side street.

Thus relieved of an unsolicited burden, the Lanes can enjoy anew. Soon, they have an early dinner, as conveniently served by pushcart vendors of preserved meats, buns, fresh fruits and quenching beverages. And the couple amuse themselves further by contributing two bits to the local numbers racket. Indeed, the atmosphere proves festive, especially when some of the fares leave their vehicles to mingle.

But just when things become downright convivial, a few of the participants make hasty returns to their "linear perfection", only to be joined by the rest when a certain vessel's smokestack approaches.

"The ferry! Axe, can you see it! What a striking vessel!"

Wasting little time, the Golden Coast docks, releasing its consignments to take on the new. But while this process may be a matter of routine to the other fares, for the Lanes it's a stirring moment. Cautiously, Axe follows the directions of the deckhands and parks the roadster.

"Axe. Look," alerts Katie. "Some of the people are taking those stairs."

Thus follow the Lanes—when on the Golden Coast, do as the Golden Coasters—and after taking the final step, they find themselves upon the upper deck and its grandiose views.

Toot! Toot! Toot! Thus the ferry announces its intentions.

The Lanes flinch, their proximity to the whistle coming as a start. Yet they recover, while the Golden Coast slips its berth and steers toward mid-channel. Even before the ferry picks up steam, Katie and Axe feel the wind and salt air—head on. Yet the sensation is not one of sublime intoxication or even stunted perceptions. Rather, the briskness of the moment serves to enhance the surroundings.

"My goodness, Axe. Those gulls," alerts Katie of a raucous flock gathering at the Golden Coast's agitated stern. "So demanding." She pauses, to watch passengers toss morsels of food. "Look how they beg."

On the other hand, her husband's interests gather elsewhere, toward those individual pelicans of a brown persuasion. "Look at them dive, Katie. Such expertise and precision."

"Where!" she reacts. "Point my head!"

The efforts of the marine avifauna continue, as do the commands of the Golden Coast's captain. Before the Lanes can realize, the ferry rounds the point of Alameda Island and enters San Francisco Bay proper. A curtain rises, thus revealing an unobscured stage of white-cap waters and churning traffic, enveloping hills and peaks, harbors and municipalities, and at least one developing intrusion of distant fog. Indeed, there's enough scenery to occupy the Lanes for hours on end. But then the Golden Coast straightens its course, as it heads toward an undeniable beacon or, rather, its scheduled destination.

"Look Axe. Behind that island." Her knees weakening, Katie clutches Axe. "San Francisco!"

"Yes," he gazes, a tingling spine being his affliction. "And the Pacific beyond." He breathes deeply. "We've done it."

Such a declaration to behold, its truth doing Katie's wobbly joints little good.

"We could push our roadster to the Pacific, if need be," figures Axe. "We're that close."

"Yes, we are, Axe."

Meanwhile, the ferry bears down upon its guide. Thus the stair-stepped city of San Francisco looms—in all its past as California's principal city and into its current status of rapid rebirth. The bay crossing plods along, allowing the Lanes to gawk quietly, trying to separate destruction from reconstruction and that which has survived intact the maelstrom of two years prior.

"Look there, Katie. The tower on the waterfront. Like some Spanish cathedral, don't you think?"

"Yes," agrees a spellbound Katie. "Undamaged. What a wonderful organ it must possess." She sharpens her eyes further. "Axe, I believe we're moving toward that cathedral."

Katie's acute observation stirs in Axe a tidbit of information overheard at the Oakland Pier. "Cathedral? Katie, don't you suppose that tower is the Ferry Building? It is the waterfront, after all."

"Yes. Of course, Axe. San Francisco's Statue of Liberty. But from Seville, and not Paris."

"Precisely."

Even after a two-year duration, the foul odors of inferno permeate the western edges of San Francisco Bay. Suddenly, from the top of the Ferry Building, a bell knolls loudly, perhaps to announce a restoration or at least the arrival of the latest vessel.

"Are you sure that's not a cathedral, Axe?"

He shrugs a doubt. Yet there can be no denying of the ferry landing, to which the Golden Coast approaches in determined order.

"Katie," urges Axe. "We should go below and start the roadster."

As expertly as the Lanes were directed upon the ferry, now they're discharged. Never before has pavement felt so firm, in spite of resting upon unsure, quaked ground.

"Where to now?" questions Axe, as he tails the roadster behind a lumber-laden wagon.

"Market Street," reminds Katie. "We have to find the street with the metal slots."

As it happens, the couple need only to follow the disembarking traffic. Slowly but effortlessly, they're led to the city's widest boulevard, this being a diagonal path into a scene of unimaginable destruction. And all the while, those stenches of inferno intensify, thus dulling the senses and aiding to confusion's cause.

Keeping a safe stretch behind the sluggish wagon, the Lanes attempt to absorb the unnerving setting. The clamor is constant, the activities of human hand and human invention dominating the thick atmosphere. But as well, there persists the human voice, especially a particular surge erupting from a few blocks further down the ruins of Market Street. The dawdling traffic halts altogether, as if complying to the wishes of the commotion. In response, Axe applies the handbrake, only to leave his seat for a better view.

"What is it, Axe?"

He stares into the heart of San Francisco. "By the looks of it, this boulevard is just another Sierra road. Where is that Henry Patrick? We could use his talents."

It seems that Market Street's width has been narrowed by an indifferent pile of debris, no doubt created by an untimely collapse of the earthquake's remnants. There's but one option, that of finding an alternate route.

As it happens, upon reclaiming the steering wheel, Axe sees that for at least a block or two the street to the immediate right runs clear and free.

"Why don't you take that street, Axe," points Katie, the able navigator.

Unknown to the Lanes, they've turned onto California Street and are entering the middle of stark cataclysm. As much as the hills allow, the couple see little more than empty, swept blocks and great piles of rubble, or stubborn remains awaiting demolition. Indeed, a grand city has been humbled by geologic extremes and the fiery aftermath.

"My God," mutters an awed Axe. "What a war the earth has made. A Charleston and New Madrid. With Chicago, Moscow and Rome thrown in for good measure."

"No, Axe," disagrees Katie. "Much worse than all that."

Yet what the Lanes had discovered at the ferry landing and are witnessing further is that San Francisco is not a graveyard, if only because it swarms with citizens and their ideas of normalcy. Without a doubt, the business of the city is one of rebirth, as confirmed when the Lanes spy a block occupied by neat stacks of building material as opposed to heaps of building remains.

The roadster passes more intersections, thus allowing some much needed diversity. Sure to form, portions of California Street appear to be returning to pre-earthquake status, with the masterful assemblage of brick and mortar, lumber and quarried stone rising from the charred, fissured terrain.

"Those must be townhouses," notes Katie of a nearly-completed block. "Look. A French restaurant? Heavens. What do you suppose occupies the second floor?"

"Over there. A hotel," eyes Axe. "It seems to be open for business."

"Yes," agrees Katie. "I wonder? Could this be where the Lobans are staying?"

Axe's response is to tap the throttle and sputter up the engine.

Further construction is encountered, though of a more modest nature, as the Lanes enter an altogether different district. And it's all too obvious that the buildings' configurations are meant for shops below and tenements above—in other words, cramped spaces for the masses.

"What could they be doing?" ponders Katie of a curbside gathering. "Look, Axe. How peculiar those people seem? Are they men or women?"

As it happens, any confusion is not the fault of Katie, if only because the subjects in question sport lengthy pigtails, while wearing slippers. On the other hand, each crown is topped by a black slouch hat—with the exception of one pointed skullcap—and all are dressed in loose trousers and blouses of a thin, raven fabric.

"They must be men," perceives Axe of the tight circle. And then it hits him, when he catches sight of rattling dice and exchanging coinage. "This has to be Chinatown."

"Chinatown, you say? How different to the Japanese towns we've seen," replies Katie. "I suppose they really are distinct peoples. Like the Czechs from the Patonaians. Springfielders from Wamsutterites."

"Exactly. Opposites, in that we could sell our autos to the Japanese, but wouldn't stand a chance here in Chinatown. Hmm? Perhaps we should return to Market Street."

"Then turn left, Axe. There," directs Katie. "It should do just fine."

Soon, the Lanes are back on Market Street and its southwesterly direction.

And sure to form, the city's story remains much of the same: of a quaked earth and unfolded combustion, and of two years of busy recovery. Yet there comes into play an entirely different chapter, this standing apart from the tragic narration.

"Look at that building, Axe. It doesn't appear to be recent. A survivor, don't you think?"

"Absolutely," concurs Axe, who then squints to read the message upon the frieze. "Ah, yes. The U.S. Mint. Seems to have come through the catastrophe unscathed. Remarkable."

"Sound and solid engineering, Axe. It must have been defendable against the inferno."

"Its blueprints would be fascinating. Hmm? Seems Greek to me."

Sound design principles aside, there does loom a contrast to constancy. This coming into view after passing the beautifully Beaux Arts and intact Post Office Building.

"Did you see that?" alerts Katie. "What a hazard!"

In clear view, she's spied a structure which all along has been trying to impose its preeminence. Yet how feeble is the attempt, if only because the forces of earthquake have exposed a weak, slipshod construction.

"My God," reacts Axe, upon catching a glimpse.

It can't be helped, when his right arm overwhelms the left, veering the roadster to the strange and severe starkness of a signature edifice.

"My God."

Although in their travels the Lanes have encountered several majestic domes of governmental license, San Francisco's city hall may be the most noteworthy of all—if only for the wrong reasons. To be sure, there does thrive that innate fascination with the grim and gruesome—the cause behind the right turn in the first place. And since the streets surrounding City Hall are clear of rubble, the Lanes can commence their customary, low throttle circumnavigation. Thus begins their examination of a bizarre, ongoing razing.

"How can it still be standing?" gasps Katie. "Goodness, Axe. Tread carefully."

Indeed, City Hall is a precipice unto itself, as if awaiting for a mild tremor to finish the job—or any sudden noise, for that matter. But because the dome and its statuary seem to be intact, the lasting shock comes from the lofty tower beneath, this having been stripped of its ornamental brickwork to a skinless, steel skeleton. The only vision missing are the throbs of blood, which apparently drained away two years prior.

And the carnage continues down to the main floors of the structure, where the comings and goings of municipality no longer hold sway.

"Have we stumbled upon the Forum?" compares Axe of two stubborn Corinthian columns and a section of cornice to that of ancient ruin. "Are those pilasters?"

Already, it's become apparent to the Lanes that most of San Francisco's destruction resulted via conflagration. Yet fire is not the woe of City Hall, its bared innards revealing a truer story to Axe and Katie, as they round a fourth corner and begin to retrace the block.

"Look there, Katie. Corrugated metal and cinder blocks? I wonder if the bricks were even tied to the support steel. No doubt, they used cheap mortar?"

"You couldn't say the same for the Ferry Building. Or the Mint or the Post Office," reasons Katie. "Nothing poor about those buildings."

"Apparently not," agrees Axe.

"Tsk, tsk," continues Katie. "Why didn't they find the means?"

"Perhaps they did," deduces Axe. "And squandered it away on poor materials and weak engineering."

"The telltale signs of corruption, Axe. I would say this building deserved to fail."

Thus ends the couple's investigation into San Francisco politics, and thus resumes that domineering urge for a westerly course. But as it follows, a reward for the Lanes' devotion occurs almost instantaneously, this span of two city blocks leading into a distinct boundary.

"Do those townhomes seem new?" questions Axe, upon entering an entirely detached district.

"I don't think so, Axe. Those are damaged. Unrepaired, but unburned."

It seems that San Francisco's incineration has a margin, that the relentless forces of man and weather combined to stop short tragedy's totality. Indeed, as the Lanes proceed further, they find their present setting to be a pleasant and sharp contrast to what lies behind.

"Reminds me of home," notes Katie of those signature aspects of Italianate architecture, though some of the buildings in question remain cracked and off-kilter.

Soon, the couple round the wooded knob known as Buena Vista Park, with the surrounding neighborhood consisting of three-story townhomes in their various degrees of damage and restoration.

"I tell you, Axe. Not so different from Delaware."

Yet it all comes to an abrupt end when Hanes Street leads into a solid expanse of eucalyptus, Monterey cypress and Monterey pine. The Speed Six presses onward, as do the impressions of its patrons.

"Such a paradise. But where are we?"

By adhering to their compass, the Lanes have exited a stark, urban setting of too many variations and too few contrasts. Now, they seem to be slipping into a lengthy repose of winding lanes, tranquil glades and tastefully-composed woodlands.

"This must be their Central Park, Katie. Remember Manhattan?"

"Yes. But more expansive. Even rural. Look at that row of cabins."

Obviously, a number of San Franciscans have set up residence—however temporary—their actions providing an inspiration of sorts.

"We could spend the night here, and tomorrow drive to Point Lobos," reasons Axe. "Discover the Pacific with an audience to cheer us on."

Katie ponders the offer, one containing all the logic of the moment. But then she feels her heart and those sounder deductions of accumulated miles.

"Should we, Axe?" she questions. "Haven't we earned the privilege to discover the Pacific on our own?"

"Yes." Quickly, Axe reconsiders. "Greet the ocean within our own privacy, and then make a cozy nest."

"Oh, Axe. How delightful. A perfect finish to our enterprise. Tomorrow we can restart our approach and meet Point Lobos like we did for our Lisbon reception."

"We can concoct a look of surprise," concurs Axe. "That should be simple enough."

The roadster continues to push forward on its second gear, into what is an elongated, sylvan locale—miles and miles of it. But eventually, there does come an end by the guide of a dependable, waning sun, this augmented with the developing glimpse of an incongruous vision.

"The windmill," exclaims Katie with her conclusion. "Like was mentioned on the ferry."

Of all things, it's the replica of a Dutch windmill marking the end of the Golden Gate Park, thus signaling a completion to a monumental achievement. Katie has every reason to sputter through her breath and Axe to fixed his gaze upon the revolutions of fluttering vanes. Yet almost by miracle, the roadster keeps to the middle of their particular lane, itself having narrowed to little more than a pathway.

Already, the vegetation at this edge of the park has become denser, losing in the process any lofty aspirations. And as is made plain by the strictly ornamental windmill, the reason for the change in landscape comes from the constant blows of a constant ocean. Although the clangs of Dutch invention are noisy enough, it's the sounds of natural origins, the winds of the Pacific, which seem louder.

Certainly, it is of oaken taxonomy, the overgrown scrub forest encroached by the Lanes. Yet how smooth is the foliage, as if pruned carefully to abstract topiary configurations—along with a framework of eerily twisted, rheumatic limbs. What an impenetrable barrier it seems, though vulnerable when considering the Speed Six's powers to blast through the likes of the Sierra, the Rockies, the deserts and the Springfields.

"Axe. Do you hear that?" asks Katie of a looming rumble.

Gradually, the zephyrs and the windmill's cadence have become minor nuisances to the steady poundings of the world's greatest body. Indeed, even the roadster's engine cannot overwhelm the sounds.

"I wonder how far it could be?"

The answer is short in coming, when the roadster is all but flung free from the tangle of oaks. Indeed, there is sand under tread.

Yet there's also sand to the fore, dunes of enough size to block a clear view of a frolicking ocean. The immediate response from Axe is not to follow the snaking path, but rather to bring the roadster to a stop and then stand upon his seat.

Katie gazes up at her husband and his look of amazement. But soon she accepts his hand and is hoisted to his side, only to match his expression when her eyes crest the level of the dunes.

"Oh, Axe," sputters a stunned, clinging Katie.

Arm in arm, the Lanes pose, propping each other in silent awe of what is being witnessed and what has been accomplished. And there can be no mistaking a Pacific for a Great Salt Lake, the water before them being nothing if not un-encompassed.

"What should we do next, Katie?" ponders Axe after a few moments.

Her spell thus broken, she springs with her instincts. Without a word, Katie returns to her seat and in quick succession doffs her laced shoes and stockings.

Instantly, Axe reads his wife's intent and so eagerly follows her lead. Before long, both are barefooted, racing through the dunes and passing the last of the pink and fragrant sand verbenas and wild strawberries. Quickly, the couple is upon the flat, California beach, itself. Yet there's no hesitancy with the Lanes, not even when their toes leave the feel of dry sand in exchange for the wet. The waves break and then crawl upon the beach, this motion's source being from the far side of the world. Within seconds, a reflexive Katie hikes up her skirt to above her knees, as her limbs greet the surprisingly chill Pacific Ocean.

Fortunately, the Lanes halt at a safe depth, and so are able to absorb the true brunt of their current setting—never mind the shivers to their extremities. With Axe's arms wrapping Katie and her free one clasping him, the Lanes stretch the interlude, their serenity cadenced by what must be the ultimate of clocks.

"Oh, Axe," gasps Katie, as she gazes upon a descending sun. "Our world is truly round."

"And now we can see its far end," dreams aloud Axe of the horizon's impending touch.

The day has minutes to play—if that. But even as the sun's glow diminishes it also serves to highlight, not only of the stage in front of the Lanes, but of those other venues. For a flicker of a moment, Axe glances off to his right and notices in the distance a hilly mass projecting ever so slightly into the Pacific.

"Point Lobos," he whispers, while the ocean begins to dowse the sun.

"What was that, Axe?"

"Oh. Nothing," he replies, returning to the focus at hand.

18
APPOINTMENT WITH POINT LOBOS

Morning comes with a subdued wind and a clear, nippy sky. And although the night was restless, it takes only a glint of eastern dawn to rouse the Lanes, this miracle of light coming likely from the same setting sun of the previous evening. To be sure, the dunes do make a comfortable bivouac, as well as a suitable park for the Speed Six.

Within the campfire a few embers breathe yet, making it a cinch to bring up a flame. Thus the Lanes are able to brew the last of the coffee, and concoct a stew from their diminished larder. Soon, every drop of water from their containerized reservoir is heated for a luxurious spit bath.

Fully fed, warmed and appropriately groomed, the Lanes can afford themselves the chance to sit back upon their roadster and take a deep breath. Or let out sighs, if so desired.

"What are you thinking about, Axe?"

"Oh, of how we should mark our success. Apart from the reception."

"Hmm?" responds Katie. Yet with the background of an ocean's drone, there's no chance for a quandary. "A message. Axe, we should write a message and toss it into the Pacific."

"Yes. In a bottle," agrees Axe. "But what should we say?"

Thus arrives the quandary, this being the ingredients for a potentially perpetual dispatch. Yet the pause has a short duration, for the Lanes' experiences have groomed them to the virtues of quick decision-making.

Without leaving her passenger seat, Katie locates pen and ink and stationery, and is at the ready to inscribe. "We should write some sort of sentiment, Axe?"

"Yes. Perhaps advice. From our hard-won inventory."

"Precisely," grants Katie. "Such a-a-s-s?"

"Achem. 'To whom may find this message. Follow your dreams and be guided by your own devices.' What do you think?"

"Perfect." Eagerly, Katie pens Axe's words. But inspired as such, she sees fit to add a few of her own. "'So that God may save you from the fools.'"

"'And steer you free from false prophets.'" Axe, too, is inspired. "Amen."

"Amen, Axe," concurs Katie, as she crosses and dots. Satisfied with the sentiments, she ends the message. "'Best wishes from Mr. and Mrs. Axelrod Lane of Lisbon, Ohio, but lately of a country crossed.'" After which, she scrolls the paper. "Axe, find a bottle."

Fortunately, there happens a suitable receptacle, able to float for miles—if not years—on end. Promptly, Axe locates the last gin bottle, it containing just enough ounces to evince a sobering thought. Yet it's too early in the morning, leaving him no choice but to spill the liquid upon the sand.

"How's this?"

The scrolled message fits perfectly into the bottle and, after reapplying the cork, the couple leap from their seats and race to the beach. By the time they reach the edge of the surf, Axe has the glass vessel by its neck and is ready to fling.

"As far as you can!" urges Katie. "Give it your best!"

He takes a few steps backwards to get a running start. Rest assured, Axe is well-versed with the laws of momentum and energy, and knows a thing or two about human mechanics. Thus, as he rushes toward the Pacific, he stiffens and unwinds his right arm in mock catapult fashion.

"Uh-h-h!" releases Axe at the precise apex.

The bottle finds a perfect arc, ascending before bowing to the forces of gravity. And all the while it accepts the gifts of the morning sun, glaring as a spinning beacon before taking its plunge and ensuing tour.

Katie's eyes follow every foot of the message's path, stirred not only by Axe's strengths and resolve, but of hers as well. Then comes the expected splash and a detectable bob to the surface.

"I believe the tide may carry it out," deduces Axe, as he rejoins Katie. "It stands a chance."

"Much like we did, when first leaving Lisbon," she replies. "Look at us now."

"Then I suppose our message might travel the world. And someday wash upon the shores of Manhattan?"

"It is possible," concludes Katie. "After all, had we not done the same?"

The couple finds little reason to loiter and so returns to the dunes. And because each is garbed for the approaching occasion—Katie with her new dress and Axe in his slightly soiled, blue serge coat and mended khaki trousers—they need only to pack the Speed Six for the short road ahead.

While Katie secures the cooking utensils, Axe tucks away the tarpaulin, afterwards standing back to ponder over the roadster.

"We could give it a wash," he comments. "It's been a while."

"Do you think it's necessary, Axe? Should we deny our gallant roadster its campaign ribbons?"

"Of course not," consents Axe, as he continues his gaze upon the Speed Six. But then his scrutiny compels him to double over and peek at the frame. "Can you imagine, Katie," marvels Axe upon straightening himself. "We didn't need the spare drive shaft."

"Then I suppose Mr. Loban had it right all along. Wouldn't you say, Axe?"

"Well-l-l." Axe grudges his reply. "Occasionally the percentages favor the pigheaded. I'll give him that."

"But couldn't the same be said of that original drive shaft failure?" responds Katie's immediate logic. "Occasional percentages?"

A gentle silence ensues, as a sapient point is absorbed.

"I do understand your turmoil over Mr. Loban," resumes Katie. "I have some too. But might you lay them aside? Axe, be nice to Percy Loban. Mrs. Loban seems to have forgiven him. So it's no longer your place to carry spite." Katie waits a few seconds for Axe to nod in agreement. "Percy Loban has his visions. He is a visionary of sorts. You have to agree." And then she speaks from the side of her mouth. "Though one with a long list of shortcomings."

With that, Axe's nods reinvigorate.

"So must continue your immediate future, Axe. Guiding Mr. Loban through the auto business. Being patient and accounting for his limitations. If only because he cannot."

"Like I've been doing all along, Katie. From the day Mr. Loban hired me. But I wonder?"

"Wonder what, Axe?"

"Should I remove the spare driveshaft and erect it here as a monument to our achievement?"

"Oh, why bother, Axe? Leave it as is. It'll be our secret. A secret under Mr. Loban's very nose."

"Like we've been doing all along, Old Girl."

There's time to kill—the result of an uncomplicated morning. But because the Lanes' feel an anxious mood, they cannot sit idly for any more than a few minutes. On the other hand, the desire to return to the city for another tour doesn't strike, especially when considering that the roadster may have too few miles to spare. Better that they retrace their route into the Golden Gate Park, find a suitable space for the Speed Six and stroll away their nerves until noon's approach. Then Axe and Katie can find the street leading to Point Lobos and, in front of an enthusiastic and congratulatory crowd, "discover" the Pacific.

"What time is it?" inquires Katie, while she and Axe walk beneath a stand of eucalyptus.

"Five minutes later from when you last asked."

"Are you sure? That seems like an eternity ago."

"My apologies, Katie. Closer to six."

But eventually, the hands of the clock near the appointed hour, thus forcing the Lanes to start the roadster and abandon the park by way of a northerly route.

"Turn left at the next street," guides Katie in defiance to her angsts. "That should lead us to Point Lobos."

To his credit, Axe takes her advice, forcing aside his inclination for the hard right.

The roadster straightens its course, and together the couple take a deep breath. To be sure, there's no turning back, no option but to follow the path toward rediscovery and see what future it reveals.

There's little use for a third gear, a slow, steady pace being the preferred speed, regardless. Yet from the Lanes' perspective, their surroundings are taken at a blur, so concentrated is their regard for the road ahead.

In due time, however, their senses detect that to which they've been acquainted. The breezes blow with more constancy, the result being of slanted, woody vegetation. But then there arrives the subtly of salt air and what may be the ceaseless sounds of a breaking ocean.

"Do you think this street may be rising ahead?" observes Katie of a further clue to Point Lobos' unveiling.

"Yes," replies an unsurprised Axe. "We are there." He stops the roadster, and pulls out his watch. "Three minutes 'til. I'm certain Mr. and Mrs. Loban are present. Shall we be prompt or should we let them wait?"

"Well-l-l?" considers Katie. "It is our whim, is it not?"

Immediately, Axe nods. But then he ceases, as a glowing notion takes hold.

"It's your whim, Katherine Marie Lane." Axe takes her hand, and then turns to step upon the road. And with his gentle reach, he urges his wife to the driver's seat. "If you please."

"Why, I accept, Axelrod William Lane," answers Katie. "Like I always have and always will."

Axe rushes around to the passenger's side and his rightful place.

"If you don't mind, Axe," she announces, when both have settled. "I think we should continue as before. Whether they must wait or not, my whim doesn't care."

For at least the moment, the tension eases a bit. But when their route empties onto the beach immediately adjacent to Point Lobos, the Lanes feel a rise, the sure accumulation of so many miles revealing itself.

"I can see people," alerts Katie, as she steers northward, all but ignoring the ocean. "Perhaps a crowd."

Indeed, it just may be. Yet as far as Axe is concerned, the gathering harbors but a single face.

"Do you see him, Katie? Is he there?" With a sharp look, Axe culls the crowd for Mr. Loban's presence.

Honk! Honk! greets Katie via the windbag. "Wave, Axe. Wave to those nice people."

Easily, they number a hundred, the assembled, who applaud at the Lanes' approach. And they stand upon that slight promontory known as Point Lobos, itself drawing as the tip of San Francisco's Pacific hills.

Honk! Honk!

The roadster begins its brief ascent. Meanwhile, Axe's arms stretch their enthusiasm, as his piercing eyes search for a familiar face, ignoring the assortment of parked vehicles. And although the brims of fedoras and bowlers do mask, he spies a singular figure, one housed in an identifiable grey shadow check, double coat.

"Mr. Loban," mutters Axe to himself.

"I see Mrs. Loban," announces Katie. "Why, I would recognize that red velvet, picture hat anywhere."

Upon a wooden podium they await, the Lobans, along with what must be a sampling of local dignitaries. And in front of this, a couple of uniformed policemen shoo away enough of the crowd to make a parting.

The hint is taken by Katie, who guides the roadster into this empty space.

On the other hand, Axe's own immediate course is more complicated. Indeed, should he establish eye contact—firm and consistent—or should he allow events to control the moment and, thus, the future? Or could it be that Axe has little choice, but to follow his own instincts and let come what may?

Unfortunately, it seems that Mr. Loban may not be cooperative. As the

Speed Six comes to a stop in the midst of the celebratory clamor, his concerns are fixed upon the roadster and not his assistant engineer.

Axe, too, is able to ignore the proceedings, to the point where he can read lips or at least surmise what their mouth is saying. And so he detects a vague phrase, accompanied by a facial expression: "Look at my poor roadster," or "Could it be the same roadster?" or even "How dare they abuse my roadster?"

Yet before Axe's indignation rises to the occasion, it's placated by the scene of Mrs. Loban's elbow making its point, followed by the stern language of her own facial expression.

With that, Axe all but leaps from the passenger seat and rushes around to assist Katie. Arm in arm the couple waltz, urged to the podium by the beats of bravos and Pacific winds. And it's midway that Axe gains his eye contact, it mattering little that it comes with the better half.

"Mrs. Loban," rushes Axe with a cheek-to-cheek kiss. "We're so happy you're here."

"Congratulations, Axelrod. Katie," returns Mrs. Loban with her heartfelt sentiment. "Such an achievement. Such a monumental, glorious achievement."

"Thank you, Mrs. Loban."

"And you both look so well. So well after your hardships. What a remarkable journey."

"Thank you, Mrs. Loban." Katie, too, delivers a kiss.

"We're so proud. All of Lisbon. All of Ohio."

But then there arrives an intrusion to the reunion, one which has been forced to bide its patience.

"Achem."

"Mr. Loban," perks Katie, whose reluctance to embrace, nonetheless, emerges. "How delightful to see you." Thus she extends her hand.

"And delighted I am," shakes Mr. Loban, whose irrepressible habits seem somewhat quelled.

To be sure, that moment of truth has arrived, with its confused, unresolved conflicts funneling into this instant. But although this fleeting span could draw out into an awkward moment, its duration succumbs to Axe's firm control.

"Thank God, you made it, Mr. Loban," he expresses, while grasping his employer's hand. "Katie and I were worried. Worried that you and Mrs. Loban would have a safe journey and find suitable lodgings."

To say the least, Mr. Loban seems taken aback, especially since his left hand must steady his fedora in response to Axe's vigorous greeting.

"Thank you, Axelrod. Our thanks to both of you," acknowledges Mr.

Loban, as his arm is allowed to dangle free. "Mrs. Loban and I have had a splendid trip. But we're more interested in you, Axelrod. Of the journey you and Katie have accomplished. Accomplished with aplomb."

With that, Axe allows himself a smile, and with that, Katie lets out a sigh and clasps her husband, perching her proud head upon his shoulder.

Regardless, that there might not follow an immediate discussion should come as little surprise. The enveloping applause subsides, as if in response to a command from on high. There reigns, after all, the never-ending cravings of San Francisco's political finest.

"Thank you, my fellow citizens," come the piercing words—not so much by a shout, but with a captivating, sonorous voice.

And as if by magic, the crowd calms altogether.

"Who is he, Mr. Loban?" whispers Axe of the obvious.

"Eugene Schmitz," comes the reply. "The mayor."

"Impressive." But before Axe can fall in line, he feels a tug.

"Axe," alerts Katie, as her apprised lips touch his ear. "Mrs. Loban says he's the mayor. Schmitz. Remember. Mayor Schmitz."

Bearded and handsome, the mayor stands courtly, with arms stretched skyward as if to accent his wishes. And then there are his apparent attendants: three ladies immediately behind, each of whom is just as handsome and courtly, but most definitely beardless.

"Thank you, my fellow citizens." Thus satisfied, Schmitz gestures to his immediate right. "Mr. and Mrs. Lane. On behalf of the City of San Francisco, welcome to the Pacific Ocean."

Wasting no time, Mayor Schmitz steps to Katie and takes her hand, unashamedly applying a kiss. But then he loosens his delicate grip, and offers a handshake to her husband.

"A pleasure to meet you, Mayor Schmitz," clasps Axe.

"Yes," replies the mayor, returning his attentions to the crowd, while he poses with the Lanes.

And almost like clockwork, a camera captures the moment.

"Impressive," mutters Axe.

Meanwhile, Katie smiles as best she can, for she, too, is "impressed."

"My friends," resumes Mayor Schmitz, after taking a step forward. "As I spoke moments before, it is an esteemed honor for our city to play host for this momentous occasion. Once again, thank you, Mr. Loban, of Loban Motor of Ohio, for choosing San Francisco as the conclusion to your company's remarkable feat. The first man and wife autoists to have crossed the country…"

This is news to the Lanes, that they are a groundbreaking couple. As the mayor speaks on, Katie and Axe glance at one another, and then peek toward their nearest Loban Motor benefactor.

Mr. Loban's response to his engineer is a slight smirk, which could be taken as a demonstrative shrug. As for Mrs. Loban, she offers the genuine look of surprise and a nod of approval for that wife in question.

"…So that by keen observation, Mr. and Mrs. Lane and Loban Motor's timely arrival, having kept its precise schedule, is a herald of kind providence's approval. Approval of our resilient city's renewal in keeping to our precise schedules. Dare I say…"

"Mrs. Loban?" Discreetly, Katie asks of news from home. "Where are the boys?"

"Oh, they remain in Columbus," murmurs Mrs. Loban. "With my brother. Having a splendid summer."

"How nice."

As for Axe, he feels a mumble at his right, unoccupied ear.

"Achem. So Axelrod, did the windscreen shatter along the way?"

"No, Mr. Loban," replies Axe from the side of his mouth. "It lacked my confidence. We left it in Delaware."

"Hmm? I was afraid of that. We'll have to do better."

For Axe, there's a bit of shock from Mr. Loban's reply, in that it lacks an admonishment and comes replete with a sound judgement.

Mayor Schmitz' speech pauses for the crowd's reaction, compelling the Ohioans to clap in compliance.

"But I'm always moved by how smart the fairer sex of our city has kept up their…"

"That mayor can blow more wind than I," resumes Mr. Loban in his low voice. "We may be in for a trial."

Axe's words exactly, which cause him to smile. Once again, he makes eye contact with Katie, and ever-so-subtly motions his head back toward Mr. Loban. But then Axe delivers a few faint nods, a resounding confirmation that all is well.

"…And in conclusion, we do have that matter of…"

Axe leans to his employer. "How is production?"

"As ably as can be expected. But with orders coming in, we need your vim." Mr. Loban stops to join an applause. "I plan to make permanent that trio of new engineers and put them under your charge. You'll have Lepper's title and he'll become senior engineer."

"Wonderful, Mr. Loban."

"They're college boys. But you'll whip them into shape for me."

"I will," agrees Axe, who then is able to capture a Katie glimpse and give it a wink.

"...Though I am reminded on that terrible day when..."

"Oh, Katie, you should know," whispers Mrs. Loban. "Freddy wired that your house key was found. So I took it upon myself to have him move the Kimball into your parlor."

The revelation renders Katie speechless, which is just as well.

"...But our architects have assured me that the new city hall will..."

Axe listens briefly, only to resume his muted discussion with Mr. Loban.

"Sir, have there been other changes? I know of additional machinists. But are there more staff hires?"

"Yes. I've given Clapsaddle a junior draftsman. From Pittsburgh."

"Good. Willis has been overwhelmed."

But then an unashamed Axe can't contain himself, when concerning those affairs of familial fidelity and marital pledges. Confidently, he knows that Mr. Loban remains ignorant of his engineer's encounter on that late night in early June.

"You added another secretary, I discovered. To aid Miss Charnwood."

"Achem," reacts Mr. Loban. "Yes. Mrs. Irish. Miss Charnwood had to return to Youngstown, so I convinced Robert's mother to come work for us."

Certainly, Axe could extend his employer's squirm, so rich are the resources. But, surprisingly, he feels an absence of pleasure and, thus, lacks the resolve.

"You'll be happy to know, Mr. Loban, that the people we encountered were genuinely impressed with the Speed Six. Impressed to say the least."

"A wonderful bit of news, Axelrod."

The mayor's speech drags on, thus giving Axe the opportunity to ponder further.

"By the way, Mr. Loban. You do remember the Kimball? Katie will insist."

"The Kimball?" Mr. Loban offers a sly grin. "Hmm, I do recall something. We'll have to look into it."

Mercifully, Mayor Schmitz' wind does have limitations. Indeed, the moment to relinquish the moment can be delayed no longer.

"Thank you, my friends!" The mayor takes a step back and clasps the hands of his guests. "I give you Mr. and Mrs. Lane of Ohio! Who together have motored across our great country! A deed to be celebrated in history!" And then Mayor Schmitz makes a request. "Might you offer us a few words, Mr. and Mrs. Lane?"

To say the least, Katie is caught unaware, her thoughts being devoted to her piano deliverance.

As for Axe, not only is he unprepared, he's not of the mood to concoct a spontaneous oration.

"Speech! Speech!" comes a sprinkling of petitions from the crowd.

Axe nods to the assembled, and even takes a step forward. With little consideration, he bellows forth.

"Good citizens of San Francisco! On behalf of my wife and Loban Motor, I thank you! And as a token of our gratitude, Mayor Schmitz has asked me to invite you to his table of refreshments! Shall we dine!"

But as an enthused Axe's looks toward Mayor Schmitz, he's met by an expression of consternation. It seems that things are done differently in San Francisco than in Lisbon, and that no table has been set. So reads the message on Mayor Schmitz' fazed face.

"Uh-h-h?" is the mayor's unrehearsed reply.

Fortunately, there's not an autoist in the land who's as fleet as Axelrod Lane. "Good citizens! Pardon my error! The feast is scheduled for tomorrow! In the city! In the meantime, what we have in mind is a brief recital.!" Axe turns to Katie. "As performed by Mrs. Lane and her talented violin!"

Katie beams and nods her acceptance, and then rushes off the podium—soon to become a stage. She's quick to return, taking her place beside Axe and the Lobans while she tunes her instrument. But when Katie wields her anxious bow, a glancing eye spies an unexpected, even peculiar, sight. It seems that Mayor Schmitz, himself, has been handed a violin, with the obvious intention of forming a duet. As to what degree of talent this man possesses, Katie hasn't a clue.

The mayor rejoins the Ohioans. Yet instead of asking for an invitation, he beseeches by striking his bow.

The first note reaching Katie's ears comes with the air of competence. But then it's joined by several others, which to her surprise flow fluidly into the construction of a Viennese waltz. She's seized in wonder, of how a member of the low political caste could possess such a high, artistic gift. Perhaps her assessment of San Francisco's officialdom has missed its mark.

"Mercy," Katie mutters.

Indeed, who is she to suppose that her abilities could match a duet? Katie turns to Axe, with a bit of panic scored upon her face.

"By all means, join in," he encourages upon quick assessment. "Enjoy yourself."

She looks at the mayor, who bows politely. Then Katie glances at the crowd, who bend and sway in preparation for a rousing frolic. To be sure, the inspirations are aplenty, while the cadence is a cinch to find. Adroitly, Katie mimics the movements.

"Do you know Strauss, Mrs. Lane?" asks Mayor Schmitz, his agile violin not missing a beat.

"Please, lead on." Conveniently, Katie's reply comes with her perfect pitch.

As for Axe, he's seen it all before, of his wife making a little music to the delight of others. While she and the mayor continue the waltz, with many in the crowd having paired up, he abandons the Lobans and the podium, stepping aside in order to relish from a wider perspective.

The impromptu dance progresses through a few selections of Mayor Schmitz's waltz repertoire. And it should go without saying that Katie is up to the challenge, even to the point where her violin harmonizes instead of mimics and dares to conjure a counter melody or two.

Yet, soon enough, the mayor tires of Vienna, as he signals to Katie the finale of the current waltz.

The applause from the crowd is immediate.

"Thank you, my friends! Thank you!" addresses the mayor. "And thank you, Mrs. Lane!"

In return, Katie smiles her gratitude.

"Shall we take this to another direction, Mrs. Lane?"

"Certainly, Mayor Schmitz. What do you have in mind?"

"Hmm? Now let me see." The mayor chins his violin, strumming at its strings as he considers his choice. "I think I have something." With that, Mayor Schmitz strikes his bow and lets the music flee.

Katie's head jolts a bit, as well it should, what with the music altering from a steady waltz time to the speeded cut. Yet her instincts are to make the adjustments, her inclinations to nimble her fingers and flail her bow. One thing is certain, reckons a cavorting Katie, this being that Mayor Schmitz has an Irish mother.

As for those who have assembled? They seem to take it all in stride, as if they're used to having a jig follow a waltz, or perhaps have heard other successions of disparate pieces of music.

Once again, the duet melds, and once again the twin violins capture the crowd.

"How fortunate for your city to have such a mayor," confesses Katie.

"You're too kind. Too kind."

The crowd gambols along, some of its members swinging with a partner, some tapping lightly upon the ground, while most are happy to bounce in place.

Ah, but then there's Axe, who migrates toward the Speed Six. What an ideal position to observe the proceedings, to let it all sink. Certainly, it is a joy to watch his jubilant Katie rub a musical elbow with San Francisco's elite. Has any person from Lisbon, Ohio ever come so far? Yet even Mr. Loban seems to have traveled a long way, especially with Mrs. Loban holding the loop of his arm. Indeed, as Axe leans against a fender, he could say much of the same about the roadster. Now it's coming to a culmination, made official by the presence of the Pacific Coast's movers and shakers.

Axe gives the fender a few pats and then looks over the rest of the roadster, proud of what it has accomplished on his behalf.

"Don't worry, Old Girl," he mutters. "I'll take you home on a flat car. Take you home and mend you good as new."

Yet it should come as no surprise when the question arises from within, of how many miles the Speed Six has left. And so Axe begins to wonder, that, were he to find a suitable garage and the appropriate replacement parts, a repaired roadster could make a return whirl to Lisbon? Indeed, should he attain Katie's immediate consent so that he and she might head east by the guide of their own devices? What a wonderful journey that could be, dreams Axe, though what wonderful journeys they have become—each and every.

"Congratulations, Mr. Lane," approaches an open hand. It seems that at least one person other than Axe is taking a break from the reception. "Bob Robertson, of the Socialist Voice."

"Please to meet you." Axe isn't perturbed by the interruption. In fact, he takes it all in stride. "Socialist Voice, you say?" Well, have I an automobile for your readers. And quite a story behind it. It all beginning in Lisbon, Ohio and at Loban Motor. Where the workers have a say in production, and where no defenseless woman or children are exploited."

"Interesting," replies Robertson.

Thus continues Axe, relating things' technical and matters' social, while dropping those names brushed in Reno and Nebraska. And then he tells of that Springfield incident, doing so with an undeniable pride.

"Interesting," notes Robertson. "I must say, Mr. Lane, you come across as a socially enlightened man."

"'Enlightened'?" responds Axe. "Hmm? 'Enlightened'? A compliment, and yet a slap. Such a double-edged word."

Robertson seems confused by Axe's comment. Nevertheless, he's able to return to the matter at hand.

"Mrs. Lane certainly can play. Did she really do a portion of the driving?"

"Not just driving, but also maintenance and repair," insists a swollen Axe. "Yes. Resourceful and gifted, with never a whimper."

As he gazes toward the podium, the reporter is rendered silent, as if he's stunned to hear such genuine respect bestowed upon a woman.

"Speaking of talent." Axe breaks the momentary lull. "That mayor of yours is flowing. A professional, no doubt. Good God, I've never come across a politician with so much feeling. San Francisco is lucky to have such a man for its mayor."

"Excuse me?" reacts Robertson. "Mayor?"

"Yes. Mayor Schmitz."

"I believe you're mistaken, Mr. Lane."

"Beg your pardon?"

"Schmitz. He's not our mayor."

"He's not?" Now it's Axe's turn to be baffled. He stares at the man in question, who happens to be orchestrating Katie through the Jack Tar March.

"Schmitz is our former mayor," explains Robertson. "Former because he was convicted of corruption."

"Convicted? Corruption?" For Axe, the revelation comes as a true shock. "But he's so cultured. So genuine. Look at these people. They adore him."

"So they do," shrugs Robertson. "Adore a man who was released from jail only this January."

"The devil you say. I'll be damned."

"We do try to educate the people. We at the Voice. A frustrating challenge it seems."

"So echo the floors at Loban Motor. Believe me, brother," agrees Axe—to an extent. "Then again, perhaps to 'educate' is the wrong approach? Who am I, after all?"

The two might well wax their philosophies, that is were it not for an overpowering urge.

"Say, Mr. Lane. You wouldn't by chance have any spirits on hand? I forgot my flask."

"Sorry," answers Axe. "We tossed our bottle this morning. But let me see. There may be a stray beer."

Axe throws himself into the search, and after a few moments discovers a couple of items. Adroitly and precisely, the seasoned engineer uses the shaft of the hand brake to free a crown top from its bottle.

"Here you are, Mr. Robertson."

"Much obliged, brother." The reporter downs a good measure and then returns the bottle.

Axe takes a couple of swallows himself. But then he delivers that other item, which happens to be the last of the Anti-Saloon League pamphlets.

"Imbibe this," suggests Axe. "There are many opinions floating about. And they have their arguments."

"Oh? Hmm?" ponders Robertson. "The devil you say?"

"As so often he does," concludes Axe. "Which is why I try to keep an alert ear. When crossing a country or crossing a street. It is all the same, after all. Whatever I must cross next."

READERS GUIDE

1. What could be the reason behind the author's choice for the initial setting of Lisbon, Ohio?

2. As far as the year 1908 is concerned, this holds a significance in automotive history. Why is this so?

3. Curious in that Katie's maiden name is so similar to that of her husband's surname. Why do you suppose the author chose this coincidence?

4. Is it too much of a surprise that six-cylinder engines existed as early as 1908?

5. Percy Loban is described as a Progressive Republican. Do you agree?

6. Okay, let's not mince words. Do not Axe and Katie come across as the perfect couple? Seriously, should we not consider the odds that they would have crossed paths in the first place—of a talented musician and a passionate engineer?

7. Argue this if you may: are the Lanes more the 21st century as opposed to that of the early 20th? Or could it be that they share their own common language?

8. How about that Hugh Flugan, or, for that matter, the other characters who work for Loban Motor?

9. Is it plausible to think that Axe's opinion of Mr. Loban could withstand a sudden downturn? On the other hand, is it ridiculous to think that he could adjust to the realities?

10. What are the perspectives to be drawn from 1908 New York City?

11. Have you ever known a Jimmy Swift? And does he have a chance to become a successful adult?

12. At what point during their journey do things get a bit crazy for the Lanes?

13. Contrast if you may, of Axe and Katie's upbringing.

14. And what about her uncle? And just how could the author concoct such an episode?

15. Does it seem that "Southern Hospitality" has projected itself into the Midwest? And is this an assumption from the author's own upbringing, that he is off the mark?

16. And does it appear that the further west the Lanes travel, the stranger become their encounters? By the way, when the author wrote the Iowa gumbo road segment, he was influence by Antonin Dvorak's 8th Symphony, 4th movement. Do yourself the favor.

17. Who would not love Nebraska, in spite of its certain elements? But then there arrives Wyoming, as advanced and progressive a state as there was.

18. Yet what stands in contrast: Salt Lake City and its red-light district?

19. Moving along, so much for the reputation of Nevada's most notorious road, the Lane's determination flaying such.

20. Ouch! in that the author persists in his satirical insults toward the print—all the way to Reno. Be aware, in that he does frame himself as being a clever you-know-what.

21. And so it's on to California, the Lanes breeching the Sierra Nevada massif—this with some assistance, though with much too much menace. Yikes!

22. Does it seem that the width of California is rather thin? Thank God that the Lanes choose to avoid the state's lengths.

23. And how about San Francisco and its 1908 mess, brought on by an earthquake of two-years prior? Does there persist previous and current ineptitudes, as well as persistent corruptions?

24. Once again, the maestro Dvorak persists within the author's head, this being the very last of his Slavonic Dances to end tale.

25. Regardless, just how gifted is MFG, he being able to presage historical circumstances and having no shame in doing so?

26. And to this, there are a sprinkling of genuine, historical figures. Who can they be?

27. In the end, the fate of Loban Motor of Ohio is questionable, if not bleak. So what's to become of Axe and Katie Lane? What is their future to pursue as one, of course?

As is the original intent, the author hopes that the readers will enjoy this work. Indeed, that each and every one of you will grasp or concoct a profound thought or two would tickle him to no end!

Thank you for indulging this man of words, who is forever grateful to those who surrender their time.

21. And so we come to California, the Lamps traversing the Sierra Nevada mountains with some assistance, though with much too much hurried. Yikes!

22. Does it seem that the width of California is rather thin? Thank God the Lamps chose to avoid the state's length.

23. And how about San Francisco and its 1906 mess, through an earthquake of great magnitude? Does the tragedy's descriptions and subsequent happenings, as well as persistence [illegible]?

24. Once again, the narrator, Dybeck, persists within the author's head, this being the very last of the [illegible] Dances and tale.

25. Reynolds's last love gifted a MFE, he being able to possess hindsight or circumstances and having the chance of doing so.

26. And to this there are a sprinkling of genuine historical figures. Who are they?

27. In the end, the fate of Ethan Hoton of Ohio is questionable, if not bleak. So what's to become of Sue and Karlo Lane? What are their plans to pursue as one, of course?

As is always good in many, the author hopes that the reader will enjoy this work. Indeed, that each and every one of you in a group of readers a profound thought or two would tackle this book [illegible].

Thank you for indulging this man of words, whose journey [illegible] to those who sat within their times.

www.ingramcontent.com/pod-product-compliance
Lightning Source LLC
Chambersburg PA
CBHW010747310726
48980CB00004B/394

9781632937292